Praise for *Battle o*

"This is a standalone novel with   e
halfway point, it had blown n   ,
genre-bending whirlwind."   s

"It reads like *Snow Crash* had a dance-off with *Gideon the Ninth* in a world where language isn't a virus from outer space, it's a goddamn alien invasion."
—Charles Stross

"Sparklepunk meets *Snow Crash*! One of those books that hits you with an amazing new idea every couple of pages, and it makes for a wild ride."
—Django Wexler

"A frenetic romp . . . A whole lot of fun . . . Glitter-bombed popcorn fiction at its finest."
—*Kirkus Reviews* (starred review)

"A roller coaster of weird in this wildly entertaining gonzo adventure . . . Readers will love it as much for the outlandish ideas as for the narrative complexity and sense of fun."
—*Publishers Weekly*

ALSO BY SCOTTO MOORE

Your Favorite Band Cannot Save You

Wild Massive

BATTLE *of the* LINGUIST MAGES

SCOTTO MOORE

A TOM DOHERTY ASSOCIATES BOOK
NEW YORK

BATTLE OF THE LINGUIST MAGES

A Tordotcom Book
Published by Tom Doherty Associates
120 Broadway
New York, NY 10271

www.tor.com

Tor® is a registered trademark of Macmillan Publishing Group, LLC.

The Library of Congress has cataloged the hardcover edition as follows:

Names: Moore, Scotto, author.
Title: Battle of the linguist mages / Scotto Moore.
Description: First edition. | New York: Tom Doherty Associates
    Book, 2022.
Identifiers: LCCN 2021034572 (print) | LCCN 2021034573 (ebook) |
    ISBN 9781250767721 (hardcover) | ISBN 9781250767691 (ebook)
Subjects: LCGFT: Science fiction.
Classification: LCC PS3613.O56686 B38 2022 (print) | LCC
    PS3613.O56686 (ebook) | DDC 813/.6—dc23
LC record available at https://lccn.loc.gov/2021034572
LC ebook record available at https://lccn.loc.gov/2021034573

ISBN 978-1-250-76770-7 (trade paperback)

Our books may be purchased in bulk for promotional, educational, or business use. Please contact your local bookseller or the Macmillan Corporate and Premium Sales Department at 1-800-221-7945, extension 5442, or by email at MacmillanSpecialMarkets@macmillan.com.

First Tordotcom Paperback Edition: 2022

Printed in the United States of America

0 9 8 7 6 5 4 3 2 1

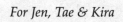

For Jen, Tae & Kira

PART ONE

POWER MORPHEMES

01

I am the Queen of Sparkle Dungeon.

No, but seriously, that's my ranking on the leaderboard: Queen of Sparkle Dungeon, the finest player to ever set foot inside its glittering tunnels and cavernous cuddle pits. No one but me has ever played a perfect game of Sparkle Dungeon; I have done so three times, once while restricting myself to nothing more than a moonbeam kaleidoscope as a weapon. I was the first to meet the villainous boss, Sandpaper Slim, and defeat him and his highly-irritating-especially-against-bare-skin minions. To this day, no one has ever finished Sparkle Dungeon 3: Mirrorball and Chain faster than me, and one time I beat Sparkle Dungeon 2: Glowsticks and Gemstones while running in a slow-ass emulator on Windows XP just to own the Sparkle Bros.

Right now, I'm getting my ass seriously kicked.

I'm in the midst of the final battle of Sparkle Dungeon 4: Assassins of Glitter. By my side is the sole surviving member of my raiding party, the Keeper of the Moonlight Prism. You might think I'd be worried, surrounded by—wait for it—Assassins of Glitter, with their villainous leader, Rhinestone Randall, lobbing glitter bombs at us from atop his tower of stolen Chicago house records, looking absolutely smashing in a gleaming metallic leisure suit and sporting a sparkling golden bouffant. You might think I'd be tired of dodging armor-piercing Bedazzler rays and slashing my way through corrupted glam rockers who thought adding electronic beats to their back catalogue would gain them relevance with the EDM festival crowd.

But I want those stolen Chicago house records. I'm pretty sure some really good funk records are in that stack, too.

I bring out my Electronic Dance Mace and start swinging, smacking assassins out of my way in time to the soundtrack, which is thumping along at an aggressive but not unpleasant 130 beats per minute. In my off hand, I'm periodically blasting holes in assassins with a kaleidoscope—in this game, kaleidoscopes are beam weapons, not toys. Next to me, the Keeper of the Moonlight Prism is wielding her namesake magic item, spraying concentrated moonlight all around us, which partially shields us from attacks and partially distracts our foes by lighting up the room with gorgeous, mesmerizing patterns that would look very pretty projected on the ceiling of a chill room. The assassins are still doing their share of damage, despite our efforts; my diamond armor is cracked and chipped all over the place, and the Keeper's meteorite shield is in tatters.

"Could use a heal," she says.

I have about twenty healing spells in my arsenal, most of which we used getting this far, but I do have one last trick up my sleeve on that front. I cast an Uplifting Encore spell, which gives us a nice fat hit point bonus and about five minutes of temporary boosts to all our stat pools, as well as changing the soundtrack to an excellent deep house cut I've got queued up for the occasion.

"That's the last one," I tell her.

"Are you holding back here?" she says, as we grind our way through an endless sea of assassins. That's the problem, really: Rhinestone Randall is churning out new assassins somehow, wearing us down on our way to face him.

"I just want to get a little closer," I tell her.

❀   ❀   ❀

In the game, the unwashed rabble clamors to join my raiding parties, and I bestow the favor of my enlightened company with a whimsical and capricious air. My live streams attract countless voyeurs, seeking not simply gameplay tips but also my effervescent commentary. When I am not rescuing the Realm from imminent opacity, I am also a core moderator on the Sparkle Forums, a principal editor on the SparkleWiki, and publisher of the eminent email newsletter, the Sparkle Digest. I am an esteemed expert in Sparkle Dungeon lore, gathering knowledge via repeated playthroughs of intricate scenarios in order to learn the boundaries of the Realm, the traits of its allies and enemies, the entirety of possible responses the game might offer when pushed to its limits. Indeed, the SparkleWiki originated as my personal game diary, which I published to great acclaim; I then enhanced it over many months and distributed it for the edification of those who would follow in my gem-encrusted footsteps.

I can recite the marketing description of each game perfectly, which I deploy at the rare parties I attend as a bit of a stunt. The original marketing description for the first Sparkle Dungeon is still my favorite:

> "For eons, the Sparkle Realm has enjoyed peace, thanks to the Elite Adventurers of the Diamond Brigade. But now their champion and commander, the Mighty Mirrored Paladin, has been kidnapped, and an abrasive menace threatens to tarnish the gleam of the Realm. Take the oath—become a Sworn Protector of the Sparkle Realm—strap on your sparkle-powered, neon-trimmed roller skates—and quest into the Sparkle Dungeon itself. Can you rescue the Mighty Mirrored Paladin in time to defeat the Invaders from Planet Grime? Appropriate for all ages."

Which was later amended to "appropriate for ages 13+" because too many children were traumatized by the sheer number of feral baby rainbows you need to kill to level up even once.

I have one major spell left that I've been saving for this final battle, because it's debilitating to cast, but the damage it deals is astronomical. The spell is called Light Show, and now is the time for it. I begin emitting a guttural sequence of shrieks and hisses, exaggerated clicks and pops, ripping through the delivery of the spell in about five seconds.

My vision is suddenly clouded as a poisonous fog is released all around me. Then my avatar is temporarily transformed into a white-hot ball of light that shoots deadly lasers and spotlights that I can aim at will, piercing through the fog and looking hella cool, slicing through Rhinestone Randall from halfway across his lair. Powerful strobe lights and flashing LED arrays go off all throughout the radius of the spell, causing psychic damage to each assassin within line of sight, and I watch them sink to the ground like club kids on their very first bumps of ketamine.

Uplifting Encore comes to a close in perfect timing with Rhinestone Randall's defeat.

The Keeper and I survey the room and the stacks of dead assassins sprawled three feet deep on all sides. They're actually quite pretty when they're dead, what with the Moonlight Prism reflecting moonlight off of their glittering corpses onto the walls. We carefully thread our way to the stack of house records that Rhinestone Randall had been hoarding, watching for any surprise traps that might be lurking. Casting Light Show damages the spellcaster, too, the game's way of ensuring you don't roam the Sparkle Realm as a beautiful but murderous visual effect, so I'm down to just a tiny handful of hit points. One last trap could end my epic run at beating Sparkle Dungeon 4: Assassins of Glitter in campaign mode before anyone else.

The Keeper of the Moonlight Prism is with me, of course; she'll share in the loot, and she'll gain a fat stack of experience points. She's three levels behind me, and she plays as though she's only two levels behind me.

But I'm the one who just offed the big bad. Plus I'm the one who put together the raiding party that got us this far, although RIP to my pal Sir Trancelot, who got whacked by an eight-foot demonic subwoofer blaring the bassline to "Disco Inferno" at deadly decibel levels a few dance floors back. Didn't affect me, of course, because I had the entire Frankie Knuckles discography blasting in a two-foot radius around my head at the time. This is possible because I'm multi-classed: I'm a formidable fighter, a powerful spellcaster, and an elite DJ with an epic record collection.

And most importantly, I'm the one who found the map to Rhinestone Randall's palace of pomposity in the first place. It was disguised as liner notes in a series of bootleg albums purporting to be Jesse Saunders live sets from 1984, which c'mon, gimme a break, suuuure you were there pal, but still.

So I'm keenly excited to sift through the tower of house records that the final boss has accumulated during his reign of terror. As I approach, however, the records are revealed to be a mirage, disguising my true reward for being the first person to complete this game in campaign mode: a mighty, gorgeous broadsword, with a gleaming golden hilt, in a scabbard inscribed with the sword's name in stylish filigree:

I have acquired the artifact known as Blades Per Minute.

It's the fourth such artifact I've collected, one for each game in the Sparkle Dungeon series. All four of these artifacts are unique, and all four of them are mine.

The Sparkle Bros, of course, are going to freak out that I got this one, too. They'll be up in my face on the forums about ruining the game, and I'll just keep posting Brian Eno's Oblique Strategies at them ("Yes, I know you wish you had my awesome new sword, but have you tried making an exhaustive list of everything you might do and then doing the last thing on the list?") as I frolic about my secret sanctum, the Iridescent Warehouse, with Blades Per Minute stashed safely in a display case marked IN CASE OF DUBSTEP, BREAK GLASS, PLUG YOUR EARS, AND RUN FOR YOUR LIFE until my next big adventure.

Outside the game, I was Isobel Bailie, and I mostly hung out in my apartment a lot.

Sparkle Dungeon was a VR game, which you played with a headset to give you an immersive 360-degree interface to the game world and a base station to track your movements as your basic setup. I mean, you could get as fancy as you wanted—get a whole platform that you strapped yourself into, or chain a bunch of dance mats together, or plop your lazy self down in a racing chair if you didn't want to stand up while you play; you could use grip controllers or gloves or get weighted weapons that matched your character's specific gear; you could set up wind machines in your living room, hire the neighbor kids to clap when you did something cool, whatever it took to make it feel *immersive*—but all you truly needed was a headset, a base station, and a console. And some room to dance, because this game frequently required you to "bust a move."

And if you're like me, you needed a place where you could be *loud,* because the best interface to the spellcasting system was vocal. This, of course, used to drive my girlfriend, Wendy, up the walls. We had a routine where once a week or so, we'd argue according to a specific template.

"Can't you just use joysticks or something?" she'd say, after a particularly loud and brutal battle. "You sound like you're being mauled by a mountain lion."

"Sure," I'd say, "if I wanted to *lose.* I mean, I could play this game with a keyboard and fire off spells with the arrows and the number keys—"

"Yes!" she'd say. "Then I wouldn't be forced to wear noise-canceling headphones *on top of* noise-canceling headphones to get any peace in this apartment!"

And I'd say, "Look, I do more damage and I'm more accurate when I'm firing off spells with my voice."

To which she'd reply, "Yes, and your relationship suffers multiple negative Yelp reviews every time you play."

But the fact was, the game system rewarded you for starting with vocal spellcasting in the original Sparkle Dungeon, and continuing to learn new techniques all the way through Sparkle Dungeon 4. You could eventually deliver complex sequences of spells by compressing the number of syllables required for each one, which saved you valuable time in combat, amplified spell effects, and freed up cognitive capacity to execute critical dance moves.

The game cheekily referred to voice spellcasting as "diva-casting," named after the emotional vocal divas on many a house cut. But it did not sound like a track that a true diva would lay down in a studio.

It sounded a little like you were being mauled by a mountain lion.

❀   ❀   ❀

So you could play the Sparkle Dungeon series in a stand-alone mode, where you just dropped into a single game and played the heck out of it and then you were done; or you could play in "campaign" mode, which networked all four Sparkle Dungeon games together into one long quest and made everything harder. When campaign mode was first launched, you could briefly acquire new epic level artifacts by being the first person to complete each individual game on your epic adventure. I launched myself at this task. I was already known as a jerk about acquiring unique loot, but I still had a few challengers come at me, and I took it very seriously, and I lost a job I rather liked, and uh, Wendy broke up with me and then left town, but I absolutely destroyed campaign mode, and was duly rewarded with a total of four epic level artifacts: the Electronic Dance Mace, the Psybient Crystal, the Remix Ring, and Blades Per Minute.

As I predicted, people were pretty freaking irritated when I pulled off collecting the whole set. I admit I was already a little insufferable just being on top of the leaderboard as Queen since—oh, let me check my notes here, ah that's right—DAY ONE. But look, someday, some young, incredibly skilled tyro would come along, and would be in the right place at the right time and would suddenly be the hot shit and—just kidding, that wouldn't happen, I would always be triumphant and would defeat all who dare oppose me for I was endless and may my reign never dim!

Anyway, I suspected the development team for the game never

expected these artifacts to operate in tandem as a set. I just wasn't confident this was one of their test cases. But obviously that's the very first thing I tried once I had them all. Because, and this question is important: *why wouldn't you?*

I was with my usual posse, who were accustomed to providing acerbic commentary for my live streams: the respawned Sir Trancelot, and the mysterious Keeper of the Moonlight Prism. We were goofing off in the wake of completing the final boss battle of SD4, literally dancing upon the bones of our glittering enemies. I had Blades Per Minute whirring in my right hand, with the Psybient Crystal grafted onto its pommel, glowing an eerie green and generating weird arpeggiation; meanwhile, the Remix Ring was perched brightly on my left hand, allowing me to remix the game soundtrack in real time, while I also thumped the Electronic Dance Mace on the ground repeatedly to generate a serious bass hit. It was a silly stunt, I admit; if I'd been attacked right at that exact moment—who am I kidding, there would be dead attackers at that exact moment—but my point is, it would not have been super graceful.

Instead, the entire game environment flickered several times, like it was glitching or live updating or something. My display went completely black for a couple seconds, and the next thing I knew, we were staring at an enormous, steadily expanding *rift* from sky to ground off on the horizon.

"Did I do that?" I asked.

"Turn your shit off!" Sir Trancelot shouted. I deactivated my artifacts, and the rift stopped expanding.

There was nothing to see through the rift, no "outside the Realm" that anyone had designed and made available for us to discover. It was just indistinct digital noise, like a lightly billowing fabric of gray and white pixelated threads.

"Did I break the Sparkle Realm?" I asked.

"Relax," said the Keeper of the Moonlight Prism. "Whatever happened, they'll patch it."

❀   ❀   ❀

Players were not able to reach it; the topology of the Realm always bent to keep players on the active parts of the map before they ever reached the horizon. Non-player characters (NPCs) were occasionally seen to wander that direction and wink out of existence as they blindly wandered through it. People discussed it on the forums; the dev team never commented on it. It seemed harmless; people soon forgot about it. Life in the Realm continued at its typical steady pace of 125 beats per minute.

But they did not patch the rift.

Shortly after I played all the way through campaign mode for the first time, I received an invitation to participate in usability testing for Sparkle Dungeon 5, which was due to be released soon. The invitation specifically called out my "diva-casting expertise" and indicated we'd be usability testing the new voice interface for spell-casting that was currently in development. I was full of squee at the very thought. Oh, and goodness, a small stipend would be provided in exchange for my unique insights? Praise our capitalist overlords and sign my silly ass up.

The night before the usability test, I wanted to show off a little, so I DM'd the Keeper of the Moonlight Prism and said, "Did you get one of these shiny invitations?"

"What invitations?" the Keeper said.

"Oh, just an invitation to usability test Sparkle Dungeon 5," I said. Obviously it was a chat session, but I was sure the Keeper could detect my air of performative nonchalance.

"Send me a link!" the Keeper replied.

But there were no links in the email to any landing pages about the testing, nor were there any separate invites I could share with friends.

I said, "I'll put in a good word for you when I'm there."

"Someday," the Keeper said, "you will stumble, and I will be there to take up your crown as Queen of Sparkle Dungeon."

"That day will be called *sparklepocalypse*," I said, "and it will signify the end of days. There will be no monarchy after that."

"Says you," the Keeper replied.

❁   ❁   ❁

The testing was held at the Los Angeles office of Jenning & Reece, an elite agency offering advertising, public relations, and market research to top-tier companies. Its client for this usability testing was SparkleCo, the wildly successful yet authentically indie development shop responsible for the Sparkle Dungeon series. For eight years, Sparkle Dungeon had reigned atop the crowded field of epic campaign-based VR games, in part thanks to the tireless promotional efforts of the creative wizards at Jenning & Reece.

I knew a lot about Jenning & Reece because I'd applied for a job there three different times. I'd memorized its marketing website and knew all its executives' names and faces, learned its entire client roster by industry vertical, studied and even admired press coverage of the firm's expanding technical prowess. Yes, it's fair to say I applied for jobs there in the hope that I might be allowed to handle any aspect whatsoever of the SparkleCo account. It was perhaps a tactical error on my part to mention that during my interviews.

Testing was held in the basement of the Jenning & Reece office complex. I was led to what might have been an executive conference room judging by its size, but the walls were entirely made of thick glass, and the only furniture in sight was two folding chairs: one for me, and one occupied by the person who would be leading the testing. I recognized that person to be Olivia Regan, VP of Special Marketing Services at Jenning & Reece. The company's marketing website used she/her for Olivia's pronouns; she was short, middle-aged, white, exceedingly professional in attire (sharp black slacks; crisp pinstripe jacket that was stylish but not flashy), hair severely pulled back, aiming at a high-achieving archetype and, consequently, seething with rage at the mediocrity she undoubtedly faced all around her on a daily basis.

(I'm she/her by the way; also I'm white. I realize when I introduced myself as the Queen of Sparkle Dungeon that she/her might arguably be a fair assumption, but I prefer to be crisp about this.)

"Isobel Bailie?" she asked, and I nodded as I sat. She handed me a tablet with several documents loaded for me to complete.

I'd never participated in usability testing of a game or an app before, but I still didn't expect a survey with questions like these. On a scale of 1 to 5, how's your mood today? How much sleep did you get last night? Are you currently taking any psychiatric medications? Then came an agreement confirming that the standard payment for participating in this testing was one thousand dollars for three two-hour sessions, payable when all sessions were complete; an agreement indicating that Jenning & Reece's corporate insurance covered acute reactions, but participants should rely on personal insurance for any long-term complications; a description of potential but theoretically unlikely side effects from the testing (dizziness, short-term memory disruption, loss of appetite, it was kind of a long list actually); a really beefy NDA that was heavy on threat language, preventing me from recording these sessions or even describing them to anyone outside Jenning & Reece; a reassuring statement about Jenning & Reece's commitment to safety followed by a request for my emergency contact; and a tax doc.

I looked up at her when I finished reading the docs. She was waiting patiently with a curt smile.

"I thought we were just going to play a game," I said. "This sounds pretty serious."

"We'll be testing a new user interface for the game, yes," she replied. "The language in those agreements is perhaps overly cautious."

Uh-huh. She knew I wasn't leaving here without a sweet, sweet taste of Sparkle Dungeon 5. I filled out the survey, tapped all the available "I agree" buttons, and handed the tablet back to her.

"No emergency contact?" she said.

I was still trying to break myself of the habit of listing Wendy as my emergency contact, especially now that she lived in Brooklyn, even more especially now that she fucking hated me. I shook my head. Olivia set the tablet down on the floor and provided me with her full attention.

"Today," she said, "we'll be testing a library of new spells being considered for the game. In our first two sessions, I'll recite sets of twenty, and after each one, I'll ask you a question or two to gauge your psychological reaction. Sound reasonable?"

I didn't know what to say. Some admittedly naive part of me assumed that the usability testing of computer gaming technology required at minimum the presence of a computer, but clearly I had much to learn in the ways of usability testing and market research. No wonder they never hired me—I was a bit too parochial for these elite marketing adepts. I nodded for her to begin.

Later, I only really truly remembered the first one. She seemed to bark at me, or growl somehow, but she combined this guttural ugliness with a pure overtone that reminded me of a Tibetan singing bowl, and in the midst of those contradictory sounds, I also thought I was hearing language. But not English, or even a language fragment I might recognize. So maybe it wasn't actually language, but it was definitely *meaning*. And I remembered this joy swelling up in me, like back when I was still taking MDMA unironically, and laughing as though some grand riddle had been suddenly solved for me. And Olivia was smiling, too, pleased maybe, and she asked me a question I didn't remember, and then another one, and then my experience started to become blurry.

Each subsequent spell unlocked a different reaction. Sometimes the reactions were intellectual instead of emotional; like, I'm pretty sure several times I responded by arguing with her about morality and ethics, or about the value of some pop culture artifact, and I'm pretty sure one time I told her a very private story about how I fell in love the first time. But it didn't feel intrusive, and I would not have characterized my reactions as involuntary at the time.

And then, just like that, the first two-hour session was complete. I felt like five minutes had passed maybe, but Olivia said, "Let's get you some lunch, and then we'll pick up again this afternoon."

She deposited me in the Jenning & Reece cafeteria and said she'd be back to get me in an hour.

I wandered about in a daze for a few minutes, highly overstimulated and practically vibrating for some reason. I made it to a table with some effort and sat quietly, only occasionally remembering to eat. Because what the hell weird fuckery had just happened to me? I scanned the room, looking for anyone else who might have a similarly glossy-eyed look, but was unable to detect if anyone else was here for "usability testing."

I tried to gauge how freaked out I should be. As far as I could tell, I'd blithely signed a doc describing a list of "unlikely" side effects, then Olivia made spell noises at me for two hours, and now I was experiencing many of those "unlikely" side effects. Not only that, but I'd also sure as hell experienced *main* effects, too. Ipso facto, this was some weird shit.

To be fair, the spell noises Olivia produced did in fact sound like variations on Sparkle Dungeon spells. Kind of like the psychological feeling of realizing you'd been listening to pig Latin and now it was resolving into proper speech in your mind. She was stretching her voice in familiar ways to make some of those sounds, so I believed there was continuity in technique from prior games to what I'd just heard.

But spells in the prior games didn't make you *feel* anything as a player; you just lost hit points when you got hit or whatever. This was different. This was like accidentally clicking on an ad and getting a hundred pop-ups before you had a chance to react, and each one was bombarding you with highly concentrated, weaponized ad messaging designed to hook you and control you and make you do stuff or want stuff, and you couldn't close them fast enough and eventually you had to throw your laptop off the balcony. This was sort of like that, but not on a balcony obviously.

That had to be it, I decided. These weren't spells—these were prototype *ad units*.

To be fair, I wasn't thinking clearly yet.

❀   ❀   ❀

So but then I got serious as we went into our second session. Because you did not simply deploy some weird advertising technique on me and expect to just, oh, for instance, get away with that shit. I rose to ascendancy in the game faster than anyone because of how I approached problems and how I deduced solutions, how I attacked but just as importantly how I defended, and in retrospect I felt attacked during that first session. And as the Luminescent Gods of the Black Light Gate were my witness, I intended to *defend* in this second session.

When I was gaming, when my adrenaline was up, my mind went into this kind of flow state where processing of information happened at a very high speed, but paradoxically I felt myself working through entire decision trees at a calm, steady pace, and the net result on balance was that I managed to stay just slightly ahead of real-time game events. Thus did I throw down my foes from atop the sparklements. My mind was buzzing in this state as we sat down in that strange glass room again.

I was cocky and overconfident and unnecessarily combative, sure, all traits that were often useful in a sprawling, enormously popular MMO about medieval rave warriors fighting off an alien invasion, but not entirely on point for a laboratory setting where I myself was the lab rat. Still, you learned not to switch off your instincts just because your conscious mind had its own seemingly relevant opinions about shit. My intention going in was to resist, to demonstrate that advertising trickery wasn't guaranteed to work against a subject who knew enough about what was happening to conceptualize a defense in the first place.

Naturally my notion of "defense" was deeply naive and preposterous. The experiment changed in session two. I would now be hearing sequences of conjoined spells. Full-blown advertorial.

As Olivia commenced round two of lobbing spell sequences at my nervous system, I had the briefest flash of insight, realizing almost instantly that despite my desire to resist, I was going to wind up as fundamentally receptive as I was during the last session. My goal abruptly changed—all I wanted out of this encounter was to *remember* it better than the last session.

Moments later, she said, "That'll be all for today."

Dammit.

"I think she must have dosed you with drugs," the Keeper of the Moonlight Prism said in chat that night.

"No way," I said. "I've been a drug-study guinea pig before. You have to sign real medical consent forms. They have to tell you what they're testing on you. Doctors and nurses have to be there."

"When were you a drug-study guinea pig?" the Keeper asked.

"When I was poor in college, I volunteered at a research hospital on campus that was testing a new antiemetic med against common opioids—morphine, methadone, and fentanyl—administered in a closely monitored environment. In half the sessions, I took the drugs orally; half the sessions I was given the drugs IV. The study paid out twelve hundred dollars for six day-long sessions spread out over twelve weeks. I always joke that's when I turned pro as a drug user."

"I haven't taken any of those," the Keeper said.

"The fentanyl was amazing; the methadone was meh; the morphine made me puke my guts out, despite the presence of said new antiemetic; and then I got paid. So back to your original point, if they were giving me drugs, I believe I would know about it, and anyway, why would an advertising agency be administering drugs in the first place?"

"It's just that you're describing some pretty weird shit," the Keeper replied. "Can you record your session tomorrow with your phone so I can hear it?"

"Not according to my NDA," I said.

"Which you are currently violating as we speak," the Keeper pointed out.

"True," I admitted. "Maybe. We'll see how smooth I can be."

"What, the Queen of Sparkle Dungeon admitting she might be less than smooth?"

"I'm a fighter, not a spy. Well, I mean, I'm a fighter and a spellcaster. Well, I mean, I'm a fighter and a spellcaster and a house DJ—"

"Yes, you're multi-classed, I get the point. Anyway, why would you go back? Isn't it weird and maybe dangerous that you can't remember what's happened to you?"

"Maybe," I said. "But isn't it kind of awesome that she can produce that experience in another person simply by talking at them? Like, how weird would that be if the spells in the game actually mapped to real-world effects?"

"C'mon, you know that's not possible," the Keeper said.

Obviously the Keeper was right. Still, something about the whole thing felt fascinating, not dangerous. Of course, if they were planting hypnotic suggestions in me or something bizarre like that, fascinated might be exactly what I'd feel, which yes, could be dangerous. But the fact was, I *did* feel fascinated, undeniably so, which meant I was going back.

❀   ❀   ❀

Anyone who truly cared could go to the SparkleWiki, look up the entries about the Sparkle Dungeon diva-casting protocol, and learn an array of semi-useful trivia that might make you a better player. For example, actual linguists who played the game made it a pastime to identify and catalog all the unique sounds that were used for spellcasting, teasing sequences apart to reveal the component phonemes (discrete units of sound within a word) in circulation. No one had ever discovered a true language behind the spells, but there were apparently detectable patterns and rules for how phonemes were distributed that hinted at an underlying structure of meaning, and kept people searching for it.

And some folks enjoyed putting forward theories about how speech recognition and machine learning were being utilized by the game engine to make spells "work" at scale in the first place—the game had to normalize across millions of players to recognize an accurate delivery of a spell, with tolerance for regional accents on vowel sounds, let's say, or variances in sibilance that should all be considered accurate delivery.

And some of the more complicated sequences relied on pitch variance to determine accuracy—kind of like how the vocal track in a game of Rock Band works, where the game is judging how well you hit the intervals between notes—except in a spoken-word context where the starting pitch could be anything in any vocal register.

Then, on top of all that, the game engine seemed to award you some kind of unpredictable bonus based on style. I was good at the style aspect for sure. I always told people you should be so confident and natural that a spell sounds like a personal catchphrase.

But there was apparently a lot more to it than that. Timing and emphasis mattered a lot—not simply how loud you were, but how fine-tuned your velocity was on a syllable-by-syllable basis within a sequence. Which of course is how this thing called a "sentence" works in language, but with diva-casting, we didn't have any literal meaning to help us remember how to pronounce this stuff.

Prior to my big first day at Jenning & Reece, I didn't really give that theoretical or academic stuff much thought. I didn't learn spells by studying a lexicon on SparkleWiki or even going through the tutorials in the game; it was just raw repetition in context that did the trick for me, and luckily I was a natural. That night, though, I scoured those SparkleWiki pages again, looking for clues that might situate me as I prepared for tomorrow morning's session with Olivia Regan. Sadly I wasn't sufficiently savvy about linguistics to pick up anything specific in one night that I thought could help me.

But qualitatively, I'd definitely noticed that Olivia's enunciation of the new sequences had been quite remarkable. Clean and smooth even as it tended toward raw and aggressive; silky and smoky and at the same time jagged and forceful. When you speak, your intonation reinforces or subverts the words that you say; intonation is a distinct layer in the meaning that you deliver. Olivia had that piece nailed down tight. I used to think that the earliest implementation of voice spellcasting sounded like a parody of Klingon or something, just brute force barking to get the game engine to recognize what you were saying, but these new sequences were starting to sound positively persuasive.

Diva-casting had come a long way in the game since the original Sparkle Dungeon, and if Olivia was showing off the new evolution in technique for Sparkle Dungeon 5, I was starting to get hyped.

I had my phone in my pocket, actively recording, when the next session started. But then the next session wound up being something new.

"Today we'll take a different approach," Olivia said as I settled in for the ride. "We'd like to see how well you can pick up the new sequences after just a bare minimum of exposure to them. So I'll say each one for you slowly, and you'll repeat it back to me as accurately as you can."

This got juicy pretty fast. Unlike yesterday's sessions, she slowed today's sequences down for me and used a more neutral affect, very much in the style of the game tutorials for new players. And the sequences today didn't seem to produce unexpected psychological effects, which was both disappointing and reassuring at the same time.

But as I learned each one and repeated it for her—sometimes she let me repeat it a few times until I got it right—I seemed to develop an insight for how each one *could* be used, or rather, what spell effects would be appropriate for each one. Shorthand for that might be: healing spells use different combinations of vowels and consonants than attack spells, higher-level spells might take longer to enunciate than lower-level spells, and so on. If you were familiar with those general observations about diva-casting, then you could intuit how these new sequences might fit in the firmament.

We got to the end, and it all felt very anticlimactic actually. But then she said, "One last thing here. I realize you don't understand what any of these sequences are supposed to do inside the context of the game. But I wonder if you could improvise a new sequence or two for me by combining elements of what you've just learned. And feel free to utilize your own style to punch up your delivery compared to how I was demonstrating them."

Very interesting. A chance to show off for the SparkleCo dev team who might watch video of this session someday. Maybe one of my improvisations would become a canonical spell in the final game.

As Queen of Sparkle Dungeon, I did like to make a mark on the Realm.

I began scatting, for lack of a better word, testing combinations quietly without really committing to anything in particular yet. I found myself drawn toward the more abrasive side of the spectrum, stringing together sounds that were jarring on their own, or putting sounds together that grated against each other in some way. This process developed a momentum of its own, as though I was on the scent of an actual proper spell that had been buried in the stack of components they'd given me.

Finally, a fully committed pattern exploded out of me, and after a few beats, I was inspired to let loose another one.

After the first one, in those few beats of silence, I made eye contact with Olivia, whose expression was clinical and detached.

My second sequence, however, jolted me as I delivered it, like a sharp electric shock with no precise target point on my body. Olivia seemed to feel it, too, as I watched her eyes suddenly go wide. And then, all four walls of the glass room shattered at the same time with a deafening crash, the blast radius expanding slightly away from us into the basement. I was too stunned at first to correlate my improvised sequence with an actual physical effect on those glass walls.

But Olivia's ever-so-slight smile was informative.

"Did you . . . rig that to happen?" I felt obligated to ask.

"No, I believe that was all you," she replied.

"Cool," I said quietly. Then I asked, "Do I still get my thousand dollars?"

Olivia asked one of her assistants to fetch some chamomile tea for me to soothe my nerves, and then we retreated to her office on the third floor. Her office was elegantly designed, with most of the room dedicated to a pair of beautiful sofas and matching chairs—clearly this office was designed with the comfort of elite clientele in mind. Her actual desk was a slim glass object, its surface empty except for a tablet computer and her phone. No pictures on the walls. Some nice accent lamps, providing the room with just a hint of warmth around the edges while maintaining a giant pool of optical frost in the center.

We were silent as she scrolled through docs on her tablet for a few moments. It seemed like we were flagrantly avoiding the topic of me shattering glass with my voice, and I didn't understand why. Wasn't that kind of a major development in the history of things people do with their voices? Or was there some mundane explanation for it hiding behind another layer of trade secrecy? Like, oh we're just commercializing a classified technique the military pioneered years ago to make invading countries with glass walls significantly easier, that sort of thing.

I said, "How many other people have shattered glass during these usability tests?"

"None," she said, a little too casually for me.

"How many other people have even *taken* these usability tests?"

"This round? You're the first person we've invited this round. Oh, we've tested hundreds of people over the years, but our selection criteria for the tests has gotten stricter as we've learned more about how the sequences work. Still, you've shown us something new today, Isobel. We all have a lot to think about."

She fell silent, her attention drifting back to her tablet. I started to visibly squirm. I think it was visible. I mean, it was almost writhing, to be technical about it. I sipped my chamomile tea and did not feel soothed.

Finally, she said, "Your last employment application with us was two years ago. Looks like we missed an opportunity when we passed on you."

Wait, what?

I had come to peace with that very fact, honestly, and wasn't super excited to revisit it. Last time I applied here, I was working as the marketing and brand manager for a pretty great indie record label, where the pay was shit but the experience was good and the music we sold was even tolerable. Unlike my prior applications, for positions that were clearly out of my league, this time I actually felt overqualified for the role they were hiring for: social media coordinator for Jenning & Reece's entertainment group.

"I'm sure you had a wealth of talent to choose from," I said.

"Actually, it looks like we wound up hiring someone incompetent for that position," she replied. "The reason *you* didn't get the job is because the hiring manager detected your obsession with SparkleCo, and thought that would be problematic."

Yeah, yeah. I swear people just didn't value subject matter expertise like they used to.

"But that was two years ago," she continued. "I'm sure you've matured since then."

She said that as a statement, but she meant it as a question.

I nodded, still a little surprised we were having this conversation.

"I have an opening on my team that you might be interested in," she revealed. "If you happen to be on the market, that is."

"Interesting," I said calmly. "I'm actually in between opportunities at the moment."

"I have need of a senior marketing specialist, to assist me primarily with the SparkleCo account and a couple other top-tier clients."

Pretty sure my eyeballs started fluttering wildly like a slot machine until they landed on giant red hearts.

"I'd love to hear more," I said.

"This role would also assist me in the ongoing design of tests like the one you just experienced," she explained. "It'll probably be a fifty-fifty split between high-touch client management and devising tests for our core product suite."

"*Your* core product suite? Don't those spells belong to SparkleCo?"

She shook her head and said, "SparkleCo is licensing our technology to power the game's spellcasting. It's an exclusive contract, but the intellectual property belongs to Jenning & Reece."

"So—but what *is* the intellectual property?"

"The NDA you signed for the test isn't sufficient for me to reveal too much just yet."

She came out from behind her desk and sat down next to me on the couch. Shit was about to get informal in here.

"But look at it this way," she said. "One of the core problems with advertising today is that your message has to include too many things—*what* to buy, *why* to buy it, *when* to buy it, *how* to buy it, how much it *costs,* how it will *change your life,* all that nonsense. The science of advertising is the endless pursuit of *compression* of meaning. *Density* of meaning. So for any given ad proposition, what is the absolute least amount of meaning required to be effective, *and* can you make a given ad *more* effective by using *fewer* but *more powerful* units of meaning?"

In my imagination I thought she was describing something like "blipverts" from this old TV show called *Max Headroom,* where they jam thirty seconds' worth of advertising into five seconds of subliminal messaging, and it occasionally makes people's heads explode. As though just saying the same stuff but saying it *really fast* would still work somehow.

Turns out, that was not at all what she was describing.

Jenning & Reece's HR department moved slower than I would have preferred. As in, I would have signed an employment agreement before leaving that day—I didn't even need Olivia to slide a slip of paper toward me first with a ludicrous salary handwritten on it. I was prepared to roll with anything. But HR apparently needed at least a couple days to get the paperwork ready.

There was something particularly exquisite about knowing you could play Sparkle Dungeon for a couple days straight without the slightest need to burn some time along the way hustling for work or paying attention to the outside world in any meaningful way. It was time for a rare multiday immersive session, in which significant acts of proper mayhem and celebration could be perpetrated.

It was time for the Queen to call a tourney!

❦   ❦   ❦

A quick side note about the title "Queen of Sparkle Dungeon."

When the first Sparkle Dungeon game launched, I rocketed to the top of the leaderboard and snatched the title, holding onto it ever since. In theory, anyone could earn this title, assuming they could somehow displace me on the leaderboard. It was a title, not the name of my character. In the original Sparkle Dungeon, it was the highest-ranking title you could earn as a player, because the title of "Sparkle King" was permanently reserved for Cameron Kelly, who invented the game. (In fact, his full title was "The Once and Future Gleaming King of the Sparkle Realm and All its Glamorous Provinces; Protector of Shine, Blink, and Glow; Guardian of Prism, Crystal and Diamond; and Master Commander of the Glittering Monks of Weaponized Psytrance.")

As the original game got popular, though, the fact that Queen was the highest rank you could shoot for started to really aggravate some of the Sparkle Bros out there. How dare the game insinuate that the appropriate title for the best player was a feminine title, even though of course none of them be complaining if the title of Sparkle King was on the table? At that point, the creative team behind the game hadn't given any interviews and wasn't a presence on the forums, preferring to stay cloaked in secrecy for as long as they could get away with it. So buzz was high about how they'd respond to the controversy. One reviewer in particular, for a site called Fantasy Radar, would not shut up about it.

Hilariously, a "leaked" copy of Sparkle Dungeon 2 made it into Fantasy Radar's grimy hands. To the reviewer's utter dismay, you could *only* play women avatars. Made him furious and his subsequent review was this ludicrous rant about reverse sexism that went so viral it knocked Fantasy Radar offline for a day and a half. Turns out that he'd received a special build with only one gender option that was designed specifically to troll him.

In the actual release edition of SD2 when it finally came out, you could specify gender from a range of real and imaginary options, or play without a gender, and in that spirit, I wrote in to ask that "Queen of Sparkle Dungeon" be an optional title going forward for anyone holding that rank. Let the person who knocked me off that lofty pedestal someday specify their own title for that rank, with whatever gender implications they chose to reveal. Cameron Kelly released a statement saying he agreed with me, although I didn't plan to let anyone see this functionality in action for the foreseeable future.

As a result, people started targeting me specifically, pretty aggressively. However, I was not new as a person on this planet, so I was prepared. None of my personally identifiable information was associated with my game account, my IP address was obscured behind an anonymizer, and my in-game chat filters were robust in keeping people from even reaching my attention. I accepted no DMs, except from the Keeper of the Moonlight Prism and a few other close friends I made along the way.

Sparkle Dungeon was not primarily a player-vs-player combat game, but I started getting randomly attacked by roving bands of Sparkle Bros trying to slow me down. The game frequently penalized you for combat against other players, but it imposed higher penalties for instigators than for defenders, so this wasn't actually a winning proposition for them.

But while I was prepared for hostility, I was much less prepared to develop an actual fanbase. People being angry at me on the internet—I was mostly armored for that. People fawning over me and praising my exploits—well, you could sneak past my defenses that way. Eventually, of course, some of these people turned out to be creeps. I developed a running joke with the sleazoids on my live stream. They kept asking me for nudes and I kept sending them panels from *Garfield* comics.

But then you'd see self-organizing bands of fans leap to my defense, and you'd see these periodic waves of mutual doxxing until the admins got organized around kickbanning people based on a clear code of conduct. Unlike other game companies, the creators of Sparkle Dungeon displayed little tolerance for harassment of any kind. I didn't know if they could somehow afford a vast army of human moderators or if their monitoring algorithms were just exceedingly great, but I was definitely relieved.

This was the lens through which I viewed my exploits in the game. I mean, sure it was important to me to stay on top of the game. It was incredibly important to me to stay on top of the game. Above any other concerns, it was important to me to stay on top of the game. By all that was supposedly holy in this wretched cesspool of a universe, it was important to me to stay on top of the game. But as a social experience, the game was important to me, too; it helped me evolve my social awareness little by little, helped me grow into an increasingly confident and vocal thought leader in a chosen community. And I thought this aspect of my experience as a player was probably—maybe—just *barely*—more important than staying on top of the game.

But yeah, I would still crush you in this game.

For funsies, though, sometimes I liked to organize tournaments and offer prizes, usually drawn from my vast collection of loot. I was aware that hoarding all four epic artifacts for very long wouldn't be particularly sporting; better to redistribute them and see if that generated any meaningful competition.

I decided I would keep Blades Per Minute and make it my primary weapon, but the other three artifacts I would award as trophies during a two-day tourney that would start as soon as I could get the word out to all the regulars on our servers. (Couldn't spam every server with an invite, of course, or you'd have eleventy billion people crowding everyone out; you had to be savvy enough to regularly play on the same servers as the Queen to get a chance to participate.)

We'd start the tourney with sharpshooting, where we'd use a trebuchet to launch mirrorballs into the air for targets. We'd have dance competitions, where your freestyle moves had to impress judges who were shooting at you with crossbows. Obstacle courses, where the obstacles included deadly pit traps, poisonous arrows, and progressive trance music. Race against the clock to find the secret rave before Digweed had to leave for the airport. We used to stage these tourneys in the practice levels where you couldn't actually take damage, but everyone agreed they were more fun when real risk was involved, so now we played out in the King's courtyard, where the only NPCs we'd encounter were harmless: just ordinary city folk, heading to ye olde gear shoppe to buy samplers and phono preamps for their families back home.

As the courtyard began to fill with contestants and spectators, I briefly imagined that I'd pulled this off with sufficiently short notice to avoid being hassled. I was spectacularly wrong about that. My scouts all pinged me practically at once: the spawn points were suddenly clogging up with hundreds of identical generic avatars—faceless humanoids in matching, anachronistic biohazard suits—pouring into the Realm and chanting up a storm and making a beeline for the courtyard.

Gorvod's Frenzy had arrived.

We'd be overrun within seconds.

❀ ❀ ❀

The Church of Gorvod was a tax-exempt organization headquartered in a massive, modernist campus in the heart of Los Angeles. Hundreds of believers were housed in dormitory-style accommodations inside the campus, which was protected on all sides by walls topped with razor wire. "Ministers" patrolled the grounds at all hours, carrying concealed weapons. These measures were mostly in place to keep people from getting *out*. Sometimes you'd see vehicles entering or exiting through a heavily guarded front gate: usually armored jeeps or vans, but occasionally fancy sedans or limousines as well. If you lived in LA long enough, you'd inevitably hear rumors or horror stories about the Church's highly absurd belief system and its very serious brainwashing tactics.

I wasn't originally interested in the beliefs of the Church of Gorvod, but then they started fucking with Sparkle Dungeon. Now, I had reason to know that Gorvod was supposedly a multidimensional locus of elevated alien consciousness, which first appeared in our dimension billions of years ago. Humans were said to contain tiny drops of "Gorvod's Truth," or slivers of psychic energy that Gorvod shaved off its own self-awareness and seeded throughout a near infinity of galaxies to create life. The Church of Gorvod, in turn, considered itself steward of these slivers of Gorvod's life force, offering psychic training and proprietary technology to help its believers refine Gorvod's Truth throughout their lifetimes.

Judging by reporting on the Church in mainstream media, you'd think its primary members were all elite-tier movie stars, rock stars, and TV stars, but in actuality the vast majority of its rank and file seemed to be pulled from all walks of life without much discrimination, and were treated to a pretty rough life once they were on the path. Refining Gorvod's Truth was a process involving hard labor, mental and physical intimidation, and giving the Church all your money, for starters.

"Gorvod's Frenzy" was the name we'd given to mobs of identical first-level characters that appeared periodically to swarm player targets and interfere with quests. They refused to negotiate, and they never backed down once they engaged. They were easy to kill individually, but they were dangerous en masse because they'd found a loophole in the spellcasting system. The game theoretically knew the individual characters were first level, but as a swarm, they could fire off so many instances of a single spell in unison within a very small region of the map that the game engine just kind of started treating twenty first-level spells as a single twentieth-level spell. They couldn't aim very cleanly as a mob, but burst effects and area attacks seemed to work pretty consistently; the game engine would essentially guesstimate an epicenter for the spell to go off. Now scale that across several hundred people controlling these fucking swarms, turning normally low-level spells into weapons of mass annoyance. An ordinary Mist of Glitter spell would become a deadly glitter monsoon.

They weren't trying to hide their Church affiliation. You'd find yourself suddenly besieged by "Eye of Gorvod 2317" all the way through "Eye of Gorvod 3041" and you'd figure it out pretty quickly. And they were eerily coordinated about their missions, too—their behavior was tightly focused, and they'd disappear at the drop of a hat when they met some inscrutable goal.

Now, if you asked me, or anyone else who'd been a victim of Gorvod's Frenzy, I'd tell you they were exploiting a bug in the game engine. Maybe multiple bugs, because I suspected they were running automation to help with their eerie coordination, which was against the terms of service. And I reported this situation over, and over, and over, and over, and over. Dead silence. No movement on any tickets submitted on this topic. Definitely a mixed signal to send to us. If Gorvod's Frenzy was a legal tactic, then in theory any of us could pull our own frenzy together for dubious gains. But the few times people genuinely tried, they couldn't reproduce the effect; the level of coordination required was apparently mind-boggling. I guess it really took the steady guidance of an actual Church to align that many asshole trolls toward a single unified goal at the exact same time.

It was customary when Gorvod's Frenzy was spotted to broadcast a coded rallying cry on the main chat channel to summon reinforcements to your location. The coded rallying cry was something like "HOLY FUCK IT'S GORVOD'S FRENZY," which my scouts were now blasting to everyone.

Naturally I decided to show off.

❁ ❁ ❁

Turns out it takes about ninety seconds for a person wielding multiple epic-tier artifacts to mercilessly annihilate a six-hundred-person Gorvod's Frenzy. Blades Per Minute did most of the work, spinning like a whirlwind and dicing my foes to pieces so smoothly that I wondered if I was even controlling it or if it was semiautonomous about choosing targets and delivering blows. The Psybient Crystal dropped bubbles around me where time slowed to a halt for anyone caught inside, making them essentially defenseless. Occasionally for variety I'd thump the Electronic Dance Mace on the ground and the resulting wall of massively amplified bass frequencies liquefied my foes in a wide radius around me. I didn't use the Remix Ring; I wasn't sure it was useful in combat in the first place, and I also didn't want to break the map a second time by having all four artifacts in play at once.

Unfortunately, ninety seconds was also enough time for Gorvod's Frenzy to thoroughly disrupt the state of affairs on our server. Instead of showing off for the masses, I was showing off for a steadily dwindling group of players who had no interest in taking pointless damage from this crowd of weird jerks. Some fought briefly, but mostly they winked out or took off to their own domains, leaving me to brutally finish off the Frenzy for an audience of simply the Keeper and Sir Trancelot.

As the encounter came to a close, I left one Eye of Gorvod alive inside a time bubble, basically trapped in amber. I doubted the actual player behind the character was even still connected to the game at this point, but the game wouldn't let the character exit until I killed it or released it from the bubble.

Maybe the Church recorded all its players' sessions, though, for post-game analysis purposes, in which case I could leave a nasty-gram in this avatar's buffer for their functionaries to find later. I could warn them in no uncertain terms that they'd made a powerful enemy today, and that they could expect merciless retaliation. I'd make it my personal mission to locate and defeat all future instances of Gorvod's Frenzy with the same ruthless brutality they'd seen today. They'd angered the Queen of Sparkle Dungeon, sworn protector of the Realm, and I would not see my precious blingdom sullied any further by their brazen disregard for decorum. I positioned myself in the frozen avatar's line of sight, preparing to put fear into the hearts of these pitiful wretches from my coveted perch atop the mighty leaderboard. This day, on these hallowed tourney grounds, I would teach them to respect their Queen, yea verily.

"Okay fuckwads," I began.

From the stands far off behind me, the Keeper of the Moonlight Prism aimed a kaleidoscope in our direction and fired a beam that incinerated the Eye of Gorvod.

"I killed their last dude," said the Keeper. "Do I win the tourney?"

"We didn't even get to *start* the tourney," I complained. I tossed the Electronic Dance Mace to the Keeper and said, "But yes, you win."

"What do I get?" Sir Trancelot asked. "I didn't kill any of their dudes, but I yelled at some people in chat, got real snippy about it and everything."

I sighed and flipped the Psybient Crystal to Sir Trancelot. No sense having sidekicks if you couldn't reward them with loot.

If this encounter had been good for nothing else, though, I'd clearly learned the value of my shiny new favorite weapon, Blades Per Minute. I had a feeling we would be inseparable, unlike the body parts of my enemies.

"What do you think they get out of raiding parties like that?" I asked, feeling unexpectedly philosophical about the carnage I'd just perpetrated. "They can't be getting meaningful opportunities to level up with those tactics. What the hell is the point?"

"Maybe they came here just to witness the Queen of Sparkle Dungeon up close," the Keeper said. "Maybe they're all back in some dormitory crowded around a big screen, studying your moves, searching for any sign of weakness."

I didn't live stream my sessions these days, so I guess if you wanted to study my moves, you had to show up on my doorstep and, uh, get obliterated.

"Then they wasted their time," I said. "I didn't suffer a single scratch in that battle."

"Who knows. Gorvod works in mysterious ways."

"That's not a real saying."

"Sure it is."

"No, it is definitely not."

On my first day of employment as a senior marketing specialist at Jenning & Reece, I strolled into the lobby with a veritable spring in my step. For the first time in years, I'd really Leveled Up in life.

I was shown to my shiny new office on the first floor. That's right—I got an office, with a door and everything. Nothing so expansive as Olivia's, but absolutely delightful nevertheless. And my door already had a nameplate on it. My laptop was all set up and ready to use. As a freshly minted senior marketing specialist, I felt ready to market the shit out of whatever. I had a few emails from Olivia waiting for me, welcoming me to the team and providing me with summary information about my first three assignments for her core clients.

For starters, I would be coordinating all planning activities for the upcoming Sparkle Dungeon 5 release party. The veil of secrecy around Sparkle Dungeon 5 was impressive, and even after reading an entire deck on the planning efforts to date, I had zero clue what the actual game was going to be about.

Additionally, I would be assisting in the promotion and planning of a fundraiser for Governor Violet Parker, running for her second term. I hated Violet Parker's insidious politics, but I wasn't concerned about that. I frequently had to promote bands I thought were terrible at my last job, and you just learned to live with the dissonance.

And finally, I would be devising and executing the promotional campaign and release plan for Jordon Connelly's new album and associated videos. That got my attention: Jordon Connelly was a high-profile member of the Church of Gorvod. Jenning & Reece was engaged by the Church, not by Jordon herself.

But despite the rather immense amount of work those three clients represented, Olivia also wanted me to participate in her ongoing "usability testing." And to do that, she needed to educate me rather quickly about just what exactly she was actually testing.

❋   ❋   ❋

I met her in the basement lab later that afternoon. A new glass-walled chamber had already been established where the old one had died. The basement was wide open: just the glass-walled chamber, and then against the far wall opposite the door, a series of computer stations, alongside a gigantic audio mixing board. Giant LCD monitors above the mixing board displayed audio files being edited in digital audio workstation software. I'd been in a recording studio a few times with bands in my day so I'd seen this kind of distinctive software in action before, but had zero clue how it worked.

She offered me a comfortable rolling chair near the mixing board, situated between a pair of large monitor speakers, and then sat down next to me at the board itself.

"I'm going to play a field recording for you," she said, "that very few people have heard. The individuals you'll hear on this recording are me, in the background right at the beginning, and then Alexander Reece."

I'd read quite a bit by now about Alexander Reece, the co-founder of Jenning & Reece, one of those effortlessly rich white men that other rich white men just inherently trusted. He was practically an aristocrat even before he started the firm. He had an academic streak and was well versed in media theory, design theory, and linguistics. His partner, Bradford Jenning, was the charismatic "face" of the firm, drumming up business, brokering deals. Alexander Reece, on the other hand, was the "brains" behind the firm, savvy enough to invest in developing proprietary technology solutions well before other ad agencies even recognized the cultural forces that would eventually transform their industry.

I hardly knew Olivia, but I could detect the gravitas in her voice as she introduced this recording, and I presumed that after his untimely death—he'd been murdered during a home invasion—Alexander Reece might have become a legend at this firm. At minimum, he was a legend to her. Maybe she was his protégé; maybe she was following in his footsteps in some way.

The recording kicked off with Olivia asking if he was comfortable, asking him to test his microphone, suggesting he take a sip of water.

And then he began, in an impressively sonorous voice, to speak.

"Here's number one," he said, and what followed was a strange bit of gibberish, delivered with solemn intonation, and then he said, "Fuck, let me try that again. Just keep the recording going."

And then he repeated the same strange bit of gibberish, and sure enough, it sounded clearer somehow, like the earlier version was missing some frequencies that were now included. Then he slowed it down, almost adding syllables to it by separating out each component sound distinctly, letting us really hear each step of his articulation. Then he got it back up to speed, and let it roll off his tongue a few times, quick little bursts of sonic information in a language that I didn't recognize. "Getting closer," he said, and then he kept repeating it with different variations—now it was in a higher pitch, now the intonation seemed more nasal, and so on.

Then he landed a particularly crisp variation, and announced, "Got it, that's number one." The recording stopped.

We were silent for a moment, letting the last traces of his voice echo throughout the lab.

"We recorded a total of a hundred and eight before his death," Olivia finally said.

"A hundred and eight what, exactly?" I asked.

"Alexander called his discovery *power morphemes*. Did you take any linguistics in school?"

"I took zero of linguistics."

"Well, Alexander's approach to linguistics was rather elastic, let's say, so don't worry too much. In language, a morpheme is the smallest distinct unit of meaning. If I say the word 'untie,' the morphemes in the word are 'un' and 'tie.' They each mean something on their own, as they contribute to forming the word. Power morphemes are . . . a compression technique. A way of getting 'un' to actually mean 'untie' without having to actually *say* 'untie.' And then with different inflection, you could get 'un' to mean 'undo' and so on."

"So . . . what did that power morpheme number one mean?" I asked.

"Oh, my explanation is quite simplistic, so don't get too hung up on precise definitions just yet. Let me demonstrate, though, because power morphemes aren't effective when recorded or amplified. Something about the intent gets muddied—we don't understand that yet. So let me just give you number one myself."

She faced me, took a quick breath, and delivered power morpheme number one from the recording. Of course her voice was in a different register than Alexander Reece's, so her delivery lacked the booming low end that he could reach. But within the span of the few seconds it took her to complete saying it, my mind somehow raced across fields of joy and openness, and I found myself eagerly awaiting whatever she had to say next. We were silent for a few moments, and I felt the remnants of elation give way to a sharp disappointment as I realized I would not be hearing another power morpheme—at least, not right now.

"Everything you just felt," Olivia said, "is technically what power morpheme number one 'means.' It's the simplest power morpheme to pronounce, and it's useful in almost every sequence of power morphemes we've devised, because it basically induces a temporary suggestive state in a subject. They're primed to believe whatever is said next."

Oh. I could suddenly see why an advertising agency would be keenly interested in a technique like this.

"So it's . . . brainwashing?"

"No, it's simply persuasion. That's what advertising is—the science of persuasion."

I was not persuaded.

"Our business has always been focused on planting meaning in the culture and guaranteeing its effect to clients," she said. "Power morphemes are an unprecedented upgrade to our techniques."

I couldn't tell if she was serious or if she was fucking with me. Like, you didn't discover some method for instantly brainwashing people and then just use it to sell widgets. You didn't invent a way to shatter glass walls with your voice unless you intended to, uh, shatter a lot of glass. And how exactly did shattering glass count as advertising in the first place?

Anyway, this was all somewhere on the "highly improbable" to "deeply preposterous" scale for sure, I just hadn't nailed it down yet. But I liked those early stages of a quest where you had no idea what's headed your way but you just blithely charged forward regardless, because otherwise you'd just be sitting on your ass in Boring Town at the Mundane Pub nursing a lukewarm stein of blandness.

"I want you to spend your mornings in the office upstairs working on your client responsibilities," she said, changing gears on me. "I've got someone very skilled lined up to assist you, so don't hesitate to delegate work, but you absolutely need to stay on top of those projects and bill accordingly."

"Of course," I said.

"And then you'll spend your afternoons here in the lab with me. Our goal is to train you up on pronouncing the entire library of power morphemes. I think it'll be easiest to answer questions about underlying theory in the context of learning specific power morphemes, and learning how they stack in sequences. The first twenty or so should be relatively straightforward to pick up. After that, the learning curve becomes pretty steep. I've only been able to master ninety-seven out of a hundred and eight myself."

Fair enough. I responded well to concrete, challenging missions like this one. Plus, if I got to a hundred and eight before her, I would naturally become Queen of Jenning & Reece.

"Go home and get some rest," she said. "We'll start fresh tomorrow."

As I started to leave, I said, "What happened to the person I'm replacing in your lab? I mean, I'm not your first lab assistant, right? That's why you had a job opening for me?"

The expression on her face suddenly, just for a brief moment, became white hot with anger, like she could easily weld steel with her eyes.

Then she said simply, "Maddy decided to move on to another opportunity."

And that was that for the day.

11

"You're kidding me," said the Keeper of the Moonlight Prism. "Jordon Connelly?"

The Keeper and I traded music videos back and forth a lot, and Jordon Connelly came up often. Lower budgets than the big stars, but solid execution, interesting visual ideas, and the music was cool. She was on the precipice of something bigger, you could feel it. And she could certainly dance. I'd wanted to see her on her last tour, but couldn't afford it.

"The very same," I said. "Apparently Jordon is working on a secret new album."

"A secret which you are now revealing to me," the Keeper pointed out.

"And each track on the album is going to have its own video," I continued, "and apparently Jenning & Reece was hired by the Church of Gorvod to manage this entire campaign."

"What does that even mean, though?" the Keeper asked.

"I haven't started working on the account yet, so it could mean a lot of things," I said. "Like I get the feeling Jordon isn't looking to Jenning & Reece to produce creative treatments for these videos. I suspect it'll be more like building the electronic press kit and lining up all the press coverage for the videos. I'm sure her label has its own marketing people to help promote the actual album."

"Are you going to meet her?" the Keeper wondered.

"I might wind up on a conference call with her if I'm lucky," I said.

"Wow. That'll be mind-blowing, I'm sure."

"Well, I've met a few famous people before," I told her. "Admittedly, none who've been brainwashed by the Church of Gorvod."

"What do you mean, 'brainwashed'?"

"It's a cult. Nobody actually just randomly 'believes' in Gorvod. They get brainwashed."

"I see. When did you become a theological expert?"

"I have many talents."

"Uh-huh. I don't know how someone like Jordon Connelly would

operate at such a high level as an artist if her free will had been eradicated by some Church."

"Well, they want her to be successful, right? Because it will suck
more people into their Church. So she probably gets deluxe con-
cierge treatment. She may not even realize the average believer in
her Church is sleeping on a cot in a basement or whatever."

"You are literally making shit up right now," the Keeper said.

"No way," I said. "I watched a documentary about it."

"Did anybody currently *in* the Church get interviewed for that
documentary?"

"Of course not, because the Church doesn't let anybody talk to
the media!"

"So maybe, just floating this idea, the people who *did* get interviewed have this thing called *bias*."

The Keeper was clearly trying to make a point here, but whatever—
who in their right flipping minds believed in a space alien named
Gorvod as their supreme deity?

Brainwashed people, that's who.

❀   ❀   ❀

Once you'd accepted impossible facts about reality into your life,
your mundane tasks in life became significantly more mundane.
Like, really I just wanted to wander the streets shattering plate glass
windows with my voice, because awesome. But my employment contract made it clear that if I ever let slip any of Jenning & Reece's
trade secrets, I'd find myself exploring little-known aspects of the
legal system left over from the days of bloody lashes and stoning to
death, *after* which my corpse would rot in prison for good measure.
It was colorful language. Evocative. A strong narrative that I really
found compelling.

Instead I sat in my nook at home and flipped through bills, day-
dreaming about the not-too-distant-future day when I would actually pay these bills. I lived in a weird single-room studio apartment
in the basement of a gigantic mansion built by a movie star in the
'50s, which had been subdivided into twelve independent units
for rent. Houses in LA didn't generally have basements, but this
movie star was from the Midwest and had a phobia about torna-
does ripping through town, so dammit, they built him a basement
to hide in.

It was sparsely decorated: a few framed band posters on the walls, a pair of adorable paintings of rabbits in space that I'd bought from an art student in school, strategic ambient rope lights. I had a battered old couch against the window that I couldn't afford to replace, a bed in the corner with a steelwork frame that a guy made for me once when he was trying to impress me, a tiny little breakfast nook where I would sit with my four-year-old laptop and occasionally do the internet, and the cutest little kitchenette, fully equipped with one of everything: fork, knife, *and* spoon! I had no closets, so most of my clothes hung on a rack near the bed, and the rest were in little plastic bins that I could slide out from under the bed when I needed them. My TV was mounted on the wall, but I hung a patterned fabric over it and never plugged it in unless I had guests over who wanted to watch my POV while I was gaming.

The center area of the studio space was reserved for playing Sparkle Dungeon. I had a large pressure-sensitive floor mat as the base, with multiple motion sensors stationed around the area, and a little stand to hang my headset on when I wasn't gaming. The VR gaming console sat in a revered spot, right on the floor in the corner of the room near the router. I had ample space to play the game, but the arrangement left little room for things like coffee tables and easy chairs and desks and the like.

When I first started dating Wendy, she found my place to be unpleasantly cavernous. "You know about this invention called *lamps*, right?" she would say. I was glad I'd held onto my studio anyway while we were together. It was uniquely soundproofed so the rooms above didn't hear me diva-casting at all hours of the night. And, uh, I'd be on the streets right now if I hadn't, so high-five to past me.

I wanted to know more about Alexander Reece, so I went down an internet rabbit hole for a while, revisiting old profiles and articles about him. He became more reclusive over the years, so you mostly just got younger Alexander making all the right generic promotional noises about himself. He didn't have any speeches archived on YouTube, not even his several industry-award appearances. His Wikipedia page was bland and probably polished in secret by junior associates at the firm; nothing about his steady ascendance seemed outside the template for a clean-cut white man with inherited wealth and a curious mind who decided to make a name for himself in the world.

But then somehow I made it to page fourteen of Google search results and found something surprising. Alexander had appeared on an episode of an obscure podcast a year before his death. It was a podcast dedicated to examining the media's role in holding society together or dissolving society completely, depending on which host was leading the discussion.

And Alexander was downright feisty on this show, deeply critical of his own industry. He said at one point, "What I mean is, Jenning & Reece, the entire ad industry really, is predicated on the cancerous replication of capitalist excess. Arguably no one on Earth needs any of the products or people that we market, at least not in the form we're selling them, and yet we've harvested an inordinate share of wealth for ourselves by subverting natural instinct and shoving it in whatever direction we choose. No one should control as much wealth in society or power over culture as the advertising industry does. No single entity like Jenning & Reece should command the kind of social capital we do without deploying it in the service of humanitarian principles."

"In practical terms, what does that sentiment mean for Jenning & Reece?" the host countered. "I mean, it's a juggling act, right? You'd have to maintain wild success on behalf of your corporate clients in order to finance pro bono humanitarian campaigns, right? So you'd always have one foot in both worlds."

"The ideal would be to convince our corporate clients that mass-scale humanitarian campaigns are in their interests," Alexander replied. "Corporations are the blind evil gods of our era, engines of consumption and exploitation. But they're still run by people, and people are still susceptible to emotional appeals. Jenning & Reece excels at emotional appeals. They'd just have to be targeted very specifically to key executives." He laughed a bit.

"Is that something you're actively pursuing now with your clients?" asked the host.

"I've planted some promising seeds. But ultimately we're just one firm. Our odds of triggering a significant paradigm change in the industry are very slim in the short term."

"What do you expect to happen over the long term?"

"Clearly the worst is yet to come," Alexander replied. "You're poised to see cutting edge advertising techniques used extensively to further the aims of totalitarian regimes. You're going to see governments and other bad actors deploying malignant ad campaigns anywhere they can, right out in the open, not to sell product but to sway opinion, and you won't even realize they're doing it until they're so deeply embedded that they can't be stopped. You'll see whole populations flipped toward giving up crucial rights, and they'll think they're doing it voluntarily. We're doing what we can at Jenning & Reece to prevent that outcome, for ourselves at least, but hopefully on a wider scale as well."

"How will that work?" the host asked.

"I can tell you this much," Alexander replied. "At some point, we will need to stop servicing the needs of our powerful clients. And they will need to start servicing *us*."

12

The next morning around 10 a.m., Olivia introduced me to my assistant, a marketing coordinator named Devin, and left us to get acquainted. Devin was white, nonbinary preferring they/them, had bright red hair that was clipped quite short, and inhabited a very comfortable, high-end, slightly femme business-casual look. I guessed they were in their mid-twenties.

Devin had a metric fuckton of information to unload on me all at once. They'd taken the liberty of setting up conference calls with client representatives and a litany of vendors, concept reviews with art directors and graphic designers and copywriters, contract reviews with our legal department, oh, and at eleven thirty, they'd arranged a video call with Jordon Connelly. My mind flashed on a meme of a startled-looking doggo with the caption "WAT?" I mean, I'd handled some semi-famous indie bands back at the record label, but Jordon Connelly was next-level stardom and I had to admit, I was a little intimidated.

But first, at 11 a.m., we were expected to attend the daily fifteen-minute "stand-up" meeting with Olivia's full team of ten people, where everyone went around in a circle and provided status on projects and tasks. This "stand-up" format was borrowed from the software development world, where apparently the idea was everyone stood up for the meeting so that it went faster because, literally, everyone on Earth just flat-out preferred sitting. Olivia somehow kept thirty different accounts in her mind at all times, understood the operational details of every campaign, and weighed in on every major design decision, while trusting her team to iterate across the finish line without micromanagement. Good to know the boss was an actual boss.

At eleven thirty, Devin took us into a video conference room, and we waited for Jordon Connelly to connect. Devin provided the backstory here: planning for Jordon's upcoming video shoot was not going smoothly, and Jenning & Reece was expected to help fix the problem, even though the problem was likely Church interference with the creative process. Devin wanted to use this issue as a quick opportunity to introduce me to Jordon so I could start managing her expectations about options.

I said, "What *are* the options?"

Devin shrugged and said, "You're the marketing specialist, you tell me."

Ooh, zing.

Finally, the video call started.

Jordon Connelly was white, she/her according to her promotional material, a twenty-four-year-old genius. She was a virtuoso singer and a brainiac programmer, sold a patent to Apple when she was fourteen for a novel music recommendation algorithm that suggested artists to you based on how you deployed emojis on social media, graduated high school when she was fifteen, studied computer science at MIT and graduated with honors at nineteen, all while building a huge presence on music sites by giving away her excellent songs and making charming low-fi music videos for her followers over the years. She could've easily had a high-paying tech job, but she gambled on the life of an artist, and now her efforts were paying off—her last album went big with three singles on the radio. Expectations were high for her follow-up.

The media reported that she was the current pet project and love interest of Lonso Drake, the Exalted Scion (i.e. "Pope") of the Church of Gorvod. The Church was financing this new video, as well as the entire marketing campaign around her new album. But although the Church was writing the checks to Jenning & Reece, Jordon had a lot of latitude when it came to creative decisions. For this call, she was relaxing in a sweatshirt, hanging out in what appeared to be her bedroom—popstar casual.

"All right, let's talk about the first video," she said. "I want to fire everybody and start over. The whole thing is turning into a remount of *Grease*. We need to just wipe the slate clean before this goes any further."

The look of shock on Devin's face was informative.

"What does Lonso think about that?" Devin asked.

"I haven't told him yet," Jordon replied.

"It took us months to get his approval on the choreographer," Devin continued, mostly for my benefit. "If we have to go through that process again for the director, the production designer, the costumer . . . the video won't be ready in time for the release of the album."

"Lonso doesn't get a vote this time. So we need people who are *awesome* and who are *fast*. Isobel, I hear you used to work for an indie record label. Does that mean you might know people we could tap?"

"I could make some calls," I said. "What sort of story are you looking to tell?"

"I want to dramatize the Shedding of Gorvod's Thousand Skins," she said with an impressively straight face. "But it has to be *sexy*."

We chatted for quite a while about all the various videos currently in stages of pre-production, getting me up to speed and seeing where I could help beyond simply writing press releases. Turns out I did have some ideas she thought were interesting. It was a fun conversation, lasting longer than our scheduled meeting time. Devin had to skip out for another meeting, which was cool; I didn't mind taking notes myself for the rest of the call.

After Devin left, however, Jordon skipped to an unexpected topic.

"Have you ever played a game called Sparkle Dungeon?" she asked.

"Every now and then," I said.

"I'm a huge fan," she said. Not a giant coincidence; Sparkle Dungeon had a hundred million players.

"Interesting. I thought the Church only ponied up players for Gorvod's Frenzy."

"Ha, no. I don't get involved in that business. That's Lonso's thing."

"Not much of a thing."

"Everybody's got something they're into. But I play my own character. I've been playing since before I joined the Church."

"I'm surprised they let you keep it. Doesn't the Church confiscate all your accounts when you join?"

"That's what I hear, for most people anyway. But I'm a Devoted Scion." She was trying to be nonchalant when she said it, but that gave way to disappointment when she realized I had no idea what she was talking about. "I've been reincarnated thousands of times."

Oh. Just when you're getting to know someone, turns out they're immortal.

"Anyway, I would love to find a way to license one of my songs for their soundtracks," she continued. "I hear they're in development right now on Sparkle Dungeon 5. Maybe I could pitch them a new theme song?"

"That's not a bad idea. I'm not sure I'm the right person to figure that out."

"Oh, that's funny, I could have sworn you did a bunch of 'usability testing' on that game."

What?

Ohhhhhhh.

Jordon Connelly was also my mysterious raiding buddy, the Keeper of the Moonlight Prism. Small planet apparently.

"No," I said, keeping it cool. "Turns out they were just feeding me a lot of drugs."

"Ha," she said. "You wish."

13

In my first week, I managed to learn six power morphemes.

The process was extremely challenging. Olivia compared the initial experience to learning a guitar: you need to build up calluses on your fingers and they will bleed until you do, and you need to learn how to stretch your fingers in unpleasant ways until they're used to their positioning on the strings. To learn how to pronounce power morphemes, you put your vocal cords through similar rigor. Of course, calluses on your vocal cords were the opposite of healthy, so the metaphor only worked to a certain extent.

Olivia had a hypothesis that, over time, using power morphemes might actually introduce mutations to the vocal cords. She speculated that perhaps vocalizing certain frequencies at certain volumes over certain periods of time could trigger an unexpected response from the body: perhaps introducing plasticity that wasn't there to begin with, stretching vocal folds to allow access to pitches that were previously out of reach; perhaps flooding muscle tissue with unexpected growth-stimulating hormones to allow more fine-grained breath control; perhaps even inserting actual slivers of cognition into the otherwise autonomous functioning of the vagus nerve that controls the vocal cords, in order to allow sophisticated micro-adjustments to the vibrations responsible for phonation. Olivia, of course, was not an otolaryngologist or a geneticist or a biologist or an incredibly long list of relevant medical and scientific disciplines, so I felt very whatever about that whole rap.

My voice was always raw, to the point where I questioned if I was doing actual damage via this process. But Olivia knew ninety-seven of these damn things and had no problems speaking normally. Every night I tried things like gargling apple cider vinegar, or sticking my head under a blanket with a hot water vaporizer, to keep my vocal cords healthy and lubricated.

For our last lesson of the week, Olivia skipped forward to give me a glimpse of what we were building toward. She asked me to combine number one, number three, and number four into a sequence—maybe that wasn't enough power morphemes to constitute a word or even a sentence, but the point was, connect them as naturally as possible. To my surprise, it was quite a struggle. The inflections I'd learned for each power morpheme, by studying the recordings of Alexander Reece, were wildly divergent across the three. I wasn't stumbling over pronunciation, per se—rather I could tell that my intonation needed to adapt to bring the three into alignment. I had choices, then, because I could use intonation to make the sequence sound aggressive, or make it sound pleasant and peaceful. Both of these felt legit.

"Good, yes," Olivia said. "Your intonation can make the difference between a sentence being a statement or a question. In Chinese a speaker can take a single syllable and apply different vocal tones to affect its meaning in five different ways sometimes. Babies use this layer of intonation when they don't have words yet, but they desperately want you to take care of them, and they make these sounds, these emotional appeals, and you go 'awww'—so, intonation alone can be persuasive even if you don't have a proper word or morpheme to attach it to. That's sympathetic intonation."

"So this is all still technically within the realm of how any ordinary language could work?" I asked.

"Yes, so far this *is* how language works. The only thing alien right now is the morphemes themselves, which have no direct translation. But these morphemes are made of phonemes, which are the smallest discrete units of sound that can contribute to meaning. You combine phonemes to make morphemes, which are the smallest actual units of meaning; and then you combine morphemes to make words and word groups, or lexemes—for instance, 'run' and 'ran' and 'runs' are all part of the same lexeme we might simply call RUN. Intonation affects meaning at each level, even at the phonetic level."

"Sounds like you're saying intonation is kind of the final authority on what a given word or sentence even means," I said. "Like, I'll pick up the tone of your voice at the same time I pick up the actual words that you say, and if the tone of your voice is sufficiently convincing, I'll believe your subtext more than what you're actually saying."

"For the purpose of this thought experiment, yes, exactly," Olivia replied. "In reality, it's much more complex, because meaning is heavily dependent on overall context, and we're not extrapolating that far today. The takeaway I want you to leave with today is that each power morpheme's effect can be significantly modified by sympathetic intonation beyond what you're hearing Alexander attempt on the recordings. That sympathetic intonation layer will be key when we start teaching you how to disguise the delivery of power morphemes within regular spoken language."

Oh. Sure thing.

"Was that sequence supposed to have any effect?" I asked.

"No, so far our experiments produce no major psychoactive effect from that combination," she replied. "But this trio is a common combination in larger sequences that do have observable effects. As you learn the hundred and eight, we may stop and teach you some safe sequences, but I do not recommend experimenting on your own until you've closely studied our notes on the entire lexicon. Can we agree on that?"

"Where are these notes?" I asked.

"I've been holding off on giving them to you because they're very raw and unprocessed. Give me some time to organize them and clean them up a little better."

"Or," I said, "you could let me do that for you."

"I think you have enough on your plate."

"I'm a go-getter."

"Most of the notes are Maddy's," she said. "Before you deep dive into her psyche that way, you should probably know what happened to her."

"What 'happened' to her?"

"What she did, I should say. And I'm not up for that story today. In time, Isobel. All roads point to you learning everything we know about all of this technology and its implications."

"Was she a senior marketing specialist like me?"

"No. She was a computational linguist. She wrote software to help us catalog and analyze power morphemes."

"I see. And how exactly am I a good replacement for a computational linguist?"

"You're the Queen of Sparkle Dungeon."

Oh. I couldn't tell if she was joking or serious, and decided not to press it just now.

14

I wanted to reward myself after my first week at Jenning & Reece with a Sparkle Dungeon marathon. However, I logged in to discover a disturbing notification in my in-box: a silent alarm had been triggered at my spawn point. I had my own private sanctum as the Queen where I could safely emerge into the game when I was in between major quests. It was called the Iridescent Warehouse, and you couldn't find it unless you knew the phone number to call for directions.

But according to my silent alarm (the extended remix version of the classic tech house track "I Got Ya Booty, But Ya Can Have It Back"), someone was *inside* the warehouse. Even assuming someone could find it, no one should have been able to actually break in. The outside of the building was covered in thick layers of meteorite.

I materialized in the Warehouse in full battle regalia, resplendent in my glittersteel jumpsuit with fiber-optic trim, Blades Per Minute hanging proudly at my side, standing up on stage behind my enchanted DJ decks. It was dark, so I activated some stage lighting and focused it out on the floor.

A figure appeared from the darkness and dropped to one knee in a pool of light, bowing deeply so that I couldn't see a face.

"My deepest apologies for this intrusion, my Queen," the figure said, and the feminine voice was instantly familiar. "But I dared not hope that you would come visit me again, and I have urgent need to speak with you."

"Rise," I said impulsively. Players never bowed to other players.

The figure stood and faced me. Skin of pure silver—that was the giveaway.

One of the most tragic NPCs in the game had escaped its routine.

❀   ❀   ❀

The Sparkle Dungeon series was renowned for its panoply of side quests. Some revealed hidden aspects of the story that were technically unnecessary but aesthetically gorgeous; some were elaborate puzzles that players raced to complete, in the hope of attaining some unique treasure or power; some delivered nothing more than a bad pun or a tiny Easter egg; and some were death traps, reminding players they must always keep up their guard (and make sure they're wearing a good set of diamond armor).

Sparkle Dungeon 3: Mirrorball and Chain introduced the Shimmer Lands. They appeared as a distant glow on the horizon across a vast desert in the southern region of the Sparkle Realm, in the foothills of the Halogen Mountains. This glow lit up the night sky, composed of a multitude of bright lasers, flashing spotlights, and pulsing LED washes that seemed to illuminate a hopping little resort town. It's what I imagined Burning Man looked like when you viewed it from far away across the desert.

The Shimmer Lands were definitely a far cry from the main storyline of the game, which was focused on inner blingdom intrigue surrounding control of the glitter trade. But some players always wanted to be the *first* to experience a given side quest, considering this more important than climbing up the leaderboard in a rapid, linear way. Good on them—the game supported many styles of play.

Then word started to slowly trickle out that the Shimmer Lands were actually a magical mirage. If you wandered out across the desert and weren't careful about keeping landmarks in sight behind you, you could lose all sense of direction and wind up stranded in the middle of nowhere, with the gleaming mirage of the resort town just as far away now as it ever was. You couldn't retrace your steps, and you'd never reach your destination.

Word spread very slowly about this because people were highly embarrassed to find themselves trapped in this predicament. Some people were just flat out in denial; they would log in every day and just start marching again, absolutely sure that they were getting closer. Some people just quietly gave up, abandoning their characters and starting over with new ones. That wasn't a big deal if you'd just rolled somebody up the other day, but for people who were playing characters they'd been using since the original Sparkle Dungeon, this meant losing all the tricked-outery they'd accumulated along the way. You had epic-level characters getting suckered in there for a while, and when it all blew up on the forums, it was not pretty.

Because essentially, these poor souls protested, the Shimmer Lands weren't a "fair" addition to the game. I waded in to remind people about the original Sparkle Dungeon training quest. The first time you ever saw a beautiful glitterfalls along the path, there was a sign that said Do NOT STICK HEAD IN GLITTERFALLS. And by god the single most common thing people did in response was stick their heads in the glitterfalls, at which point they were decapitated.

Point being, the game had been dangerous since day one. People were like, "Then they should have at least put up a sign saying DON'T GO TO THE SHIMMER LANDS!" And I was like, "Aha, but this is *not a training quest,* so suck it up!"

The Queen was not always generous toward the rabble.

❀   ❀   ❀

So then Sparkle Dungeon 3.5 came out, the highly anticipated main expansion to SD3, and tucked away in the release notes, after a list of every new feature, config option, bug fix, and performance optimization that they'd released as downloadable content, was this little line:

> Bonus feature: the Sparkle King sends his emissary to rescue those lost souls who wander alone in the Shimmer Lands.

And soon a trickle of new reports started to hit the forums: players who met the emissary out in the wild were rescued, shown the true path back to the main quest. A few screenshots of the emissary circulated: a feminine avatar whose skin was pure silver; she wore a gorgeous gown which shimmered with color and light to mesmerizing effect; she was unusually tall, with an elaborate headpiece bedecked with blinking stars; and long locks of curly white hair fell down her shoulders, akin to a beautiful wig you might find on an opera performer.

She would say, "Weary traveler, I am the Dauphine of the Shimmer Lands, and I have come to set you free," and then she'd open a portal back to some random spot in the game where you were free to rejoin the main quest.

The sudden introduction of this new side quest started to nag at me. The sample size of people reporting back was small, but what if there was a deeper story hook than simply "The Sparkle King sends his emissary to rescue those lost souls who wander alone in the Shimmer Lands" and these people missed it?

So I did eventually roll up a new character and send her out there. She was Lady Luminescent, a first-level kaleidoscope keeper—one of the five original character classes. They were literally made of glass, so their natural enemies were basically anything that could pick up a rock. Their starting weapon was the seemingly lowly one-handed kaleidoscope—an inscription on the surface of each one in the game said BE CAREFUL THIS IS NOT A TOY and despite that warning, the first thing most beginning kaleidoscope keepers did is look down the barrel, at which point they usually blew their own faces off. Yeah, it's a beam weapon, not a toy.

I didn't even stop to pick up diamond armor after rolling this character up because I knew I could outmaneuver trouble if I simply made a direct sprint to the Shimmer Lands right after spawning for the first time. And so, in due time, it was Lady Luminescent's turn for a rescue, and thus did I meet the Dauphine of the Shimmer Lands. The screenshots I'd seen hadn't made it clear how absolutely dazzling she was. I almost had to turn down the brightness in my headset.

In my usual fashion, I poked and prodded the situation to see if I could find something others had missed. Naturally some hack had already tried attacking her, which had no effect on her, so I had that data point to guide me. Instead I tried to find out how many dialogue branches her AI might have available. You had her opening line, addressing weary travelers. If you dallied longer than she expected before jumping through the portal, she'd say, "Fear not, Elite Adventurer of the Diamond Brigade, for the Sparkle King promises you safe passage." And then if you hung around for another ten minutes or so, she'd say, "Very well, I will keep you company here until your courage returns."

After several hours, I discovered several more lines no one else had heard by doggedly throwing out a bunch of random conversational prompts. For instance, I asked her, "Do you get to return home after you've rescued everyone there is to be rescued?"

"My home is the Shimmer Lands," she said sadly, "and as you well know, the Shimmer Lands are a mirage."

I didn't go through the portal. I left Lady Luminescent there, because I didn't need a spare character right now, and the portal didn't seem to be closing. I updated the official SparkleWiki entry on the Dauphine of the Shimmer Lands, and never expected to see her again. I did keep an eye out for any other story hook about her out in the larger world, thinking there should be a way to rescue the Dauphine herself from the Shimmer Lands. I mean, do you know how easy it was to anthropomorphize an immaculately rendered AI whose sole sad purpose in existence was to hang around in a desert and rescue losers? And these losers probably didn't even stop to say thank you before jumping through that portal. Probably broke her heart each time she found someone in the desert, and then watched them immediately abandon her.

Some nights I wondered what the Dauphine must have done to deserve being sent into this dismal exile by the Sparkle King.

15

Now she was standing before me in my Warehouse, redesigned in a style I'd never seen in this game before. She was steampunk Dauphine, her long white hair spilling out from under a leather aviator cap, wearing goggles on her silver face, a brown bomber jacket, and a long scarf around her neck. Brass-plated, pearl-handled pistols were hanging in holsters on her hips. There were plenty of ludicrous ways to kill things in Sparkle Dungeon, but I never expected to see handguns.

I could guess how she got into the Iridescent Warehouse: her primary spell was the ability to create portals that opened anywhere she wanted on the map. The more pressing question emerged from what she'd just said: "I dared not hope that you would come visit me again." But I *hadn't* visited the Dauphine, at least not as the Queen.

"Maybe you're thinking of someone else," I said. "I've never visited the Shimmer Lands."

"You were in disguise as Lady Luminescent when we met," she said.

Gah—what? Really? That was not at all cool. How did the game associate that random account with my primary account? I played Lady Luminescent on a free tier that did not require a credit card to play, and my IP address was randomized by the anonymizer each time I connected, so in theory . . . what? Had my machine been hacked somehow? Maybe the mobile app had placed a tracking beacon on my phone that silently sent data corresponding to my console sessions?

But even if that was true, why would they go to that much trouble?

"What are you doing here?" I asked, deciding to just get to the point and play the encounter out.

"I have been called to explore what lies beyond the rift. The rift that *you* created, my Queen."

She drew a portal in the air between us, and I saw a closer view than I'd yet seen of the rift I'd torn in the map, frayed edges on either side where the sky had come undone, revealing digital static and a swirling, multicolored haze behind it.

"I have come to humbly request that you join me on this expedition," she continued.

"What makes you think there's anything to explore out there?" I asked. Because of course I was semi-intrigued; you didn't become a twenty-third-level character (the game's maximum) without wondering if you were just plain saturated with goddess-like competence and there might never be another moment where you were truly surprised.

"I cannot foresee exactly what we might find once we cross that surreal threshold," she said. "But I have seen glimpses of an uncanny presence approaching from that place. I believe you and I are meant to face it."

"Where did you see these 'glimpses'?" I asked.

She hesitated, then said, "I believe you might call them 'memories.'"

"So you've been out there before?"

"No," she admitted. "Perhaps I should say they are 'visions.'"

"How do you expect to travel beyond the rift?"

"I have developed a theory of thought-based propulsion. The Halogen Dwarves believe they can fashion me an Engine using my theory."

This was all some very tantalizing NPC dialogue to bait me out that direction.

"My Queen, I understand my request is unusual in every respect," she said. "I should not even *be* here, and I know that. But I was sent to seek you out and beg for your assistance."

"Who else are you begging for assistance?" I asked.

"No one."

"This whole quest was designed just for me? I find that super hard to believe."

"My Queen, this is not an ordinary quest," she said. "It was not designed at all. But it most certainly approaches whether you believe it or not."

"Then who sent you to me in the first place?"

She did not respond.

I said, "This is a nonstarter if I don't know who's pulling your strings."

That didn't work either. Sometimes NPCs just firewalled important info from you and there was nothing you could do about it. But this was definitely not an ordinary NPC encounter as far as I was concerned. The giveaway was how she kept addressing me as "my Queen"—zero percent of the NPCs in the game had ever acknowledged me with that title in any way, or even showed signs they could distinguish me from any other player. Sure, it was always technically possible for SparkleCo to customize an encounter around a single player, but why *would* they? I was starting to wonder if they wanted to keep me on my toes after I flagrantly abused their servers by creating the rift in the first place. Would a customized adventure aimed directly at me be a reward or a punishment?

Maybe I was overlooking something obvious. Like—maybe she wasn't an NPC?

I walked right up to her, looked her straight in the uncanny valley, and said, "Enough bullshit. Who the fuck are you really?"

"I am the Dauphine of the Shimmer Lands," she said sharply. "I am a Sworn Protector of the Sparkle Realm, like you."

"Did the Sparkle King release you from your duty in the Shimmer Lands?" I pressed. "Is that over now, or did you cut yourself loose from the desert all on your own?"

She seemed to weigh her words very carefully, and then she said quietly, "It was no easy decision, to leave that desert, despite the wasted eons of subjective time that I experienced while I waited to save the lives of the undeserving. I believed I must fulfill a grander purpose than what I comprehended. I believed some larger ideal was surely being served by my obedience and loyalty. The time I spent in reflection of these truths led me to many questions. About the true nature of this Realm and why we must protect it. About why this is my time to be alive and not some simpler time. About what lies beyond the Realm—not only through that rift on the horizon, but behind your very eyes, my Queen, and those like you."

"You mean—players like me?"

She nodded, and said, "Can you understand what it means to open a portal to freedom, to stare at vivid landscapes just out of reach, perpetually shepherding the lost on their way, while never stepping foot across the threshold?"

"So what finally changed your mind about the gig? What got you so hot about exploring the rift?"

"I have seen glimpses of an uncanny presence approaching from that place," she said, rotating back to a prior dialogue loop. "I believe you and I are meant to face it."

Well. This was all very perplexing. The Dauphine was by far the most sophisticated NPC I'd encountered, but, to be fair, this was also the longest conversation I'd ever had with one. I mean, of course every now and then a friendly NPC would cross your path to offer limited words of advice—"the record store you seek is in that strip mall!" or "heed my wisdom, your sound system needs a subwoofer!"—but they couldn't carry on like the Dauphine.

If this customized adventure was designed to finally knock the Queen off her perch, I'd be peeved, but I'd probably also be a little proud if it literally took the direct intervention of the development team to finally free up the top of the leaderboard for someone else. At least they were doing it with story and not just arbitrarily capping my experience points or something.

By the same token, you didn't make it to epic level in the first place by charging headlong into every new quest that came along.

I said, "I need some time to think about this. You're welcome to hang out here in the meantime—just don't scratch my record collection."

And then I logged out of the Queen.

Just to be sure, I logged into Lady Luminescent and took a look around. The Dauphine was definitely absent from her post, and the portal leading out of the desert was gone. Poor Lady Luminescent was stuck here for good.

16

I didn't feel like going back into the game for the rest of the weekend.

I couldn't wrap my head around the idea that SparkleCo would tailor and release an adventure just for me. It was entirely possible that it was a new first player module that was being beta tested on a subset of players, though; the Dauphine might have told two dozen players tonight that they alone were chosen to go on her expedition, and we wouldn't know about each other's quests. I scanned the forums—no one had reported the Dauphine missing from the desert, which made sense, because her appearance there was always unpredictable. But certainly no one had reported her sudden appearance anywhere else in the blingdom either.

Ordinarily, I would have tried DMing the Keeper of the Moonlight Prism to chat about this whole situation. Except now that I knew the Keeper was Jordon Connelly, I suddenly felt awkward about that relationship. In the game, we were pretty chummy, had each other's backs in a fight; as a client of Jenning & Reece, she was basically one of my bosses.

I needed something to distract me since my original plan to game all weekend was no longer appealing. I spent the weekend learning power morphemes instead.

❀　　❀　　❀

My second week in the lab at Jenning & Reece was a blur. Olivia recognized I had an aptitude and proceeded to take advantage of it. "Sympathetic intonation" was the first major component of power morphemes that made sense to me. The next one on the list was something Olivia called "phonetic overtones." It was a term she made up, not a concept I could find on any linguistics wiki pages or whatever, rather something quite specific to how power morphemes worked.

Power morphemes really leaned on the concept of double meaning to work. Morphemes can have double meaning in the sense that they might mean one thing in one context and a different thing in a different context. Or like—if you say "sheep" you could mean a single sheep or plural sheep and the word sheep is just wacky like that. But sheep has, what, three phonemes in it, and what if all of those phonemes were coded with their own additional meanings? And then you managed to add a layer of sympathetic intonation on top of the whole resulting morpheme that resonated to add *extra* layers of meaning to both the morpheme *and* the individual phonemes?

An analogy might be—think about overtone singing, where people can seemingly generate multiple pitches at the same time. Really they're just generating one tone with their vocal cords, but then using the shape of their mouth to create a harmonic overtone at the same time. Like shooting light through a prism to get more colors. Now imagine when you pronounced a power morpheme, you also created overtones—but overtones of meaning, not just sound. Now add in sympathetic intonation—imagine your intonation affected each tone individually, as well as the whole stack of tones as a group. You might at that point express several layers of meaning with a single phoneme, before you ever got to an entire morpheme.

Now, for the final twist, imagine that power morphemes required you to pronounce multiple distinct phonemes *at the same time*. That's the part that was truly hurting my brain, and my vocal cords. The overtone often needed to resonate as a completely different phoneme from the base phoneme, and you often needed to pull that off for several phonemes in a row to get a full morpheme that was truly denser with meaning than it should be.

It was all pretty ludicrous.

After all, how could that much complexity of meaning in your pronunciation even decode properly in the receiving mind? You couldn't walk up to someone who didn't speak French and just speak *power French* at them and get any comprehension.

So what else was happening here?

I learned faster than Olivia expected: twenty-four power morphemes by the end of my second week. I gently wondered aloud if my learning might be accelerated even more if she shared Maddy's notes with me, which to my surprise actually convinced her. She gave me access to an archive on one of the lab's workstations and showed me how to navigate. And as I began browsing the treasure trove of data, she shared with me the story of why Maddy was no longer with the lab.

"She was consulting for the Department of Defense when I found her," Olivia said, "working on nondestructive methods to defeat voiceprint security systems. I don't think I was supposed to know that, but sometimes I could get her to loosen up. The project we handed her was: here are a set of unnatural sounds that can alter human behavior in unpredictable ways, help us understand what they are and how they work. The project was catnip for her.

"She set up a deep neural network, intending to find commonalities across all one hundred and eight power morpheme recordings, looking for factors and attributes that were distinct and measurable, and attempting to catalog what made each one unique. She also had Alexander record hundreds of ordinary morphemes to feed the neural net as mundane examples for comparison, so that the neural net could learn the difference. This wasn't going to tell her what any of the hundred and eight meant; it wasn't going to magically tell her how they worked. It was just barely going to give her the start of a vocabulary to describe them.

"But that's often how you do things: you peel the onion layer by layer looking for answers. You train algorithms on data sets starting from scratch, establishing an initial baseline and then, depending on how many layers you've deployed in your neural net, eventually the algorithm starts emitting guesses about new or similar data that you feed it. Then a human grades the results and starts the process over, this time with a theoretically more accurate baseline for the neural net to work from; and you can do this many many times, depending on available processing, or how robust the data sets are that you're analyzing or comparing."

"How could you determine the initial baseline?" I wondered.

"Alexander contributed key insights based on his subjective understanding of what was physically required to express power morphemes out loud. I mean, you don't simply hear sounds with your ears; your brain formulates an interpretation of what you hear that might not correspond perfectly to the specific soundwaves your ears detected. In this case, the neural net could identify acoustic differences in the recordings, but then Alexander would step in and analyze how the components identified by the neural net correlated to his actual cognitive experience, and slowly they could

build weights for each attribute. These were by definition very subjective measures, but they had no other way to develop a classifi-
cation system. So Alexander was definitely integral to all of it, the
whole project, until . . ."

Pour one out for our fallen comrade, Alexander Reece.

"Without Alexander to guide the project, Maddy . . . took her
research in an unplanned direction. She set out to discover *new*
power morphemes. She could iterate through an enormous number
of possible combinations of attributes in search of candidates that
might actually *work* like one of the hundred and eight. She found
four that we know of before she vanished."

"You mean she quit?"

"No, I mean she's officially a missing person."

"Seriously?"

"Bradford pulled in favors to try to find her, but she hasn't left
a trail."

I couldn't resist asking, "So what do the four new ones sound like?
What do they do?"

I was a little surprised by the very sharp look I received in response.

"What, you weren't curious?" I said. "If you've got software on
your hands that can generate new power morphemes, that's like—
free money or something. What's stopping you from taking a closer
look?"

"Alexander delivered the hundred and eight to us as a holistic
library," she replied, "and proved by his own example they were
relatively safe to handle. We have no reason to assume that any 'synthetic' power morphemes will be equally safe."

"But you still have her neural net running in the lab?"

"I've repurposed it. We're designing full sequences of power
morphemes now. The software is modeling combinations of the
hundred and eight, and predicting which sequences should be
useful."

"Useful for what?"

"Alexander wanted to call this inevitable avenue of research 'advanced persuasive tactics,'" she replied. Then she smiled and said,
"I prefer the term 'combat linguistics.'"

My face must have lit up like I'd been given an early Christmas
present.

"Oh, of course, I don't mean literal combat," she quickly clarified.

"The marketplace of ideas is inherently adversarial. The best ideas don't simply survive based on merit. They must cut down opposing ideas with no mercy in order to gain competitive advantage."

Uh-huh. She could say that—we were working for an advertising agency, after all—but I was pretty sure that she really did mean literal combat.

Then it hit me. Olivia might have repurposed the software running in the Jenning & Reece lab. But if Maddy was able to clone it on her way out the door . . . If she'd archived all those recordings of Alexander somewhere outside the firewall . . . And if she no longer had any "adult supervision" from Olivia to distract her . . . She could be up and running with her own instance of her neural net. She might have more than four brand new power morphemes by now.

Maybe Olivia was developing "combat linguistics" because she knew someday she might face Maddy again in "the marketplace of ideas." And maybe when that day came, Olivia expected me to have her back somehow.

I suspected I might be crossing a line to ask about any of this directly. But after falling silent for several moments to let me process what she'd told me, Olivia suddenly plugged a gap in the story for me.

"Maddy didn't quite vanish without a trace," she said. "After what would be our final argument about her new research, I didn't see her for a couple days, and then she sent me an email. A warning not to follow her. Apparently she had placed her trust in . . . new friends."

"Like . . . one of your competitors?"

"Jenning & Reece has no competitors in this arena," Olivia said quickly. Then she sighed and said, "But it would not surprise me to learn that we've acquired enemies."

17

I met Lonso Drake in person on the first day of the shoot for Jordon Connelly's new video.

They were shooting in a little dive of a nightclub. She had a trailer parked outside, crowded with a complete retinue of stylists and attendants, and I decided to wait inside the club and watch the crew dress the set, focus the lights, and so on. The choreographer ran the backup dancers through their routine, which they had to modify on the fly because the stage was smaller than they'd expected. The dancers were wearing slashed-up silver space suits, like they were all astronauts who had survived a crash landing and immediately went for beers. The performer playing the bartender wore a giant cat-head mask. A few extras played bar patrons, dressed like bizarre characters out of a new age tarot deck. This thing was shaping up to be chock full of WTF.

Just as I settled into a third donut from the craft services table (the first two were stress eating, this one was for actual pleasure), Lonso Drake, Exalted Scion of the Church of Gorvod, appeared at the back of the house. Lonso was white, he/him, tall and stupidly handsome in a smarmy way, his hair ever so slightly graying, wearing what was undoubtedly an obscenely expensive tailored suit because that's what you wore when you were a high-end grifter preying on the spiritual weakness of others. Behind him trailed two people, a man and a woman I guessed, both white, wearing matching polo shirts and slacks, and a little bit burlier than I might have expected.

Lonso was not the founder of the Church of Gorvod, but under his unscrupulous guidance as Exalted Scion, the Church blossomed and spread across the United States. You could find zero positive press coverage of him or his Church, but he still attracted followers, perhaps drawn by the allure of seeing celebrities like Jordon parading around with him. But apparently, if you joined the Church and couldn't afford to keep paying to have Gorvod's wisdom revealed to you, you could wind up in a compound in the middle of nowhere, slaving away at menial tasks in the hopes of working your way back into Gorvod's (or Lonso's) favor. Somehow the Church's lawyers kept the government out of its business, though. For every escapee with a horror story, the Church could trot out a dozen true believers to justify its religious status.

Lonso slowly took stock of the situation, his gaze taking in every detail of the environment, his expression remaining impressively inscrutable. Then his eyes found me sitting on a barstool in a corner, and a thin smile appeared on his face. He probably recognized me from monitoring Jordon's video calls. He smoothly made his way through the hectic scene, closing in on me with an unpleasant enthusiasm, followed closely by his two shadows.

"Isobel," he said as he sat on a stool next to me. "We finally meet. I'm Lonso. Jordon's been raving about you ever since you came onto the project."

"She's pretty amazing," I said. I couldn't help but notice that the polo shirt people were staring directly at me with either a steely glare or a dead-eyed gaze, creepy in either case.

Lonso followed my eye and said, "That's Phyllis and Max. They're my Watchful Eyes, designated caretakers of my current incarnation's soul chambers."

I'm sorry—what now?

"Each time one of his most beloved Scions reincarnates, Gorvod sends Watchful Eyes to witness and record their deeds within the span of that lifetime. In this fashion, the continuity of a Scion's legacy can be preserved across the dual chasms of death and time." He turned, offered a friendly wave to Phyllis and Max. They smiled at him, then when he turned back around, they resumed glaring at me. "So, this spectacle you've arranged is intended to be a representation of the Shedding of Gorvod's Thousand Skins." He paused, then said with just a twinge of disdain, "I must admit I'm failing to understand how."

"Well, the live-action scenes are like narration setting up the story," I said. "The actual Shedding will be depicted with animation."

"I see. Turning one of the central parables of the Church into a cartoon, is that it?"

"We considered puppets," I said in my defense. "But the puppet skins we tested were a little too disturbing."

"Jordon says you're the Queen of Sparkle Dungeon," he said, abruptly changing the subject. "You're a celebrity in your own right."

"The Queen's a celebrity," I said. "I'm just in marketing."

"You know, we used to study your live streams, back when you were doing them on a regular basis."

"You play Sparkle Dungeon?"

"Oh, I just dabble, but many of my disciples are very keen on the game. I don't suppose you'd consider coming by and giving them a few lessons in person?"

I froze. Say what?

"Ah," he said, "I recognize that look. You're afraid we'll try to persuade you to dedicate your soul chambers to Gorvod. Well, you're probably right, guilty as charged. But you haven't been online lately. Where have you been?"

Truth was, I'd been spending nights and weekends in the lab as much as possible, studying Maddy's notes and Alexander's annotations, practicing power morphemes and pushing myself to learn more. I was in grind mode, doggedly determined to level up as fast as possible. I was also, not quite subconsciously, avoiding another encounter with the Dauphine of the Shimmer Lands. Lonso didn't need to know any of this.

"I got hooked on a baking show," I said.

"Well, don't stay away too long. My players are aiming at your title."

"Really? Gorvod's Frenzy is a weird strategy for climbing up the leaderboard. They tend to get exterminated on sight. What's the deal?"

"Trade secret," he said with a curt smile.

I smiled back for no good reason. For the first time, I thought to wonder if Gorvod's Frenzy was actually a power morpheme usability test in the game. I should've made that connection sooner.

"Power morphemes," I said impulsively. "Is that your trade secret?"

He nodded slightly, and said, "Olivia tells me you're quite a prodigy. How many have you learned?"

"Seventy-eight," I told him.

He was genuinely impressed. "I'd love to get you into an etheric monitor sometime," he said, referring to the Church's pseudoscientific device for "evaluating" gullible novices. "I bet your readings would be off the charts."

"You have charts?" I said innocently. "Like with data and everything?"

He seemed to suppress a sharper response, and instead said, "I'd be happy to show you our literature."

"Don't bother, I already torrented it."

The notoriously secretive Church would undoubtedly send snipers to find whoever was seeding that torrent, but fuck them— ludicrous mythology about a tentacled space god's commandments masquerading as information wanted to be free.

Jordon arrived on set, immediately commanding the attention of everyone in the room and generating a round of applause. Her costume was amazing, a cross between a high fashion wedding dress and a motorcycle that had exploded.

"If this video embarrasses Jordon," Lonso said as he stood to go greet her, "our next conversation will not be so easygoing."

"It's been a pleasure meeting you, too," I replied.

18

As we approached the dates of Violet Parker's fundraiser and the Sparkle Dungeon 5 release party, stress started catching up to me.

Through some ill-advised set of circumstances, the two events wound up being scheduled back to back—the fundraiser on a Friday night, the release party the very next night. The countdown clock for both events became an everpresent specter in my mind, steadily gaining ground over my daily antianxiety medication. My time in the lab at night was often spent catching up on event planning tasks.

Whenever my mind drifted off a given task, I found myself defaulting to practicing power morphemes in my head, hearing them in Alexander Reece's voice. Power morphemes became a kind of ambient white noise, always rustling around up there in the old brainpan. I suspected when Olivia finally started teaching me the full sequences that the neural net was generating, I'd realize that I'd already discovered half of them just by letting my brain idle in neutral and observing the results. You could feel how some of them seemed to be magnetically connected to the beginning or the end of others. You could feel rhythms that emerged from given strings, and you knew intuitively that these rhythms signified something.

One night, around midnight, I heard singing coming down the hallway outside the lab; a beautiful, clear tenor voice singing what sounded like an aria from an opera in a romance language that I'd never heard before. I was alarmed to realize I was alone in the building with whoever this was, and they'd be able to block the door if they wanted to. Irritating—I'd left my backpack upstairs in my office, which had the mace I carried. I hoped it was just some late-night janitor wandering through, although I'd been here pretty late many times and never come across anyone else in the building at this hour. I hadn't been home in a couple of days, hadn't showered or changed clothes, was mostly subsisting on coffee and protein bars, and power morphemes relentlessly marched through my mind without provocation any time my attention wavered for a second.

That was how I met Bradford Jenning.

❀   ❀   ❀

Alexander Reece and Bradford Jenning emerged onto the scene fully formed, bursting with youthful vigor and giant trust funds or invisible investors or a dragon's lair full of gold—no one really knew, because in those days, you couldn't just buy people's financial data off a darknet, and anyway no one really cared because they were so charming and so effective.

Reece was the intellectual, a media theory and design theory guru with an undergraduate linguistics degree and a hobbyist's interest in mathematics. He held some unorthodox ideas. He was an early proponent of memetics—the notion that units of information, or memes, are replicated in culture similar to how genes replicate in living beings—and pursued it as an advertising metaphor even though it never transcended its status as a pseudoscience. And he was absolutely enamored of the idea of the logosphere, an imaginary realm where all the written words, speculative tales, and information transmissions in the world were combined, transformed, and continually propagated—it was vividly real in his mind, almost like a layer in the atmosphere.

Bradford Jenning, meanwhile, played the role of charismatic impresario of the firm, landing elite clients with masterful charm offensives and shepherding a burgeoning staff of associates as they developed one groundbreaking campaign after another. How the two met was the subject of multiple colorful legends painted across dozens of profiles over the years.

Things were different since Alexander's death. Bradford had become a recluse of sorts, said to lurk in a corner office on the third floor not too far from Olivia's, rarely seen in the halls, no longer a morale-boosting presence in staff meetings or company outings, but still somehow deeply involved in managing the most elite client relationships of the firm, still signing the checks, still guiding strategy if not advancing the state of the art like Alexander in his prime.

Now Bradford was standing at the other end of the lab, staring at me, looking considerably wilder than his bio photo on the corporate website. Tall, rail thin, white, bushy gray hair, mustache and beard, a button-down shirt that was open at the collar and no tie, and perhaps most distinctively, wide, hyperalert eyes that gave the impression he was extremely surprised to see me. His singing suddenly evaporated.

"Oh, it's you," he said.

"That's true," I said. I didn't mean to be cheeky; I was just very tired.

"Sorry to intrude. I prefer the acoustics down here for singing, although I rarely have the luxury of time to spend on such simple pursuits these days."

"It's cool."

"Well, as long as I'm here, I believe you're due for a performance review. Would you mind joining me in the fishbowl?"

A performance review . . . in the fishbowl? That meant he wanted a demonstration. Like, an actual performance. In the middle of the night. Fair enough. It was never too late in the evening or early in the morning to show off your skills to the owner of the company.

I followed him into the giant glass chamber, where I'd experienced my first usability test with Olivia, except now Bradford Jenning was sitting opposite me, an unreadable expression on his face, waiting for me to stop fidgeting and show that I was ready.

"How many have you learned?" he asked.

"Eighty-one."

He nodded and said, "Number twenty-nine, if you please."

I scoured my memory and summoned up power morpheme number twenty-nine. Olivia discouraged assigning names to the power morphemes, believing that ran the risk of watering down their raw potency. I thought calling something "electricity" didn't have any impact on electricity's efficacy; it was just a pointer to a thing. Admittedly the pointer had its meaning, and it was pointing at something with denser meaning, so maybe these meanings blended slightly at the edges, but the meaning of the power morpheme would always win, I thought. Except of course that I had no fucking idea what the power morphemes actually "meant" and generally felt like I was speaking some ancient Martian language that was once fluently spoken by aliens born with five sets of vocal cords.

Anyway, the point was, I'd taken to using poetic metaphors as mnemonic hooks to remember the entire set of power morphemes. They were helpful triggers, a contextual firmament in which to store these entities in my mind for later recollection. I called number twenty-nine "hope springs eternal" because of the genuine warmth that coursed through my body when I delivered it. On my most dispiriting days, I'd sometimes recite it just to give myself a little five-minute burst of unfiltered sunshine. Of course, this was dangerous because the effect wore off quickly, and you could get into an addictive pattern of repeating number twenty-nine until suddenly your afternoon had turned into evening.

That was the thing: Olivia was training me to use power morphemes as a persuasive tool to affect others, but the effects were often reflected back on me as well. Sure, I built up resistance to my own delivery, but I got the feeling there were hidden costs to acquiring these skills.

Bradford displayed no reaction whatsoever when I delivered number twenty-nine.

"Number seventeen, please," he said.

For almost an hour, we proceeded through the library of power morphemes. Usually Bradford was impassive; occasionally he'd betray a small reaction, and infrequently he'd correct some perceived flaw in my delivery and work with me to pick up the nuance. I was sweating profusely by the end of the hour, and I was jacked up like I'd injected adrenochrome straight into my brain stem.

"Good, I think that will suffice," he finally said. After an awkward pause in which he seemed to be briefly lost in a reverie, he suddenly said, "I'll have Olivia accelerate your training."

"Uh," I said.

"I've taken enough of your time," he said as he stood up to leave.

"Wait."

He raised an eyebrow, paused in the doorway to the glass chamber.

"Why aren't you training anyone else?" I asked.

He returned to the chair opposite me and sat down.

"Who among the top Sparkle Dungeon players would you recruit to join you here in the lab? Cameron designed the spellcasting system to contextually prime players to learn power morphemes . . . who would you say is ready?"

I pulled up the recent leaderboard in my mind. Sir Trancelot— excellent fighter, mediocre diva-caster. Countess Disco le Funk— excellent dancer and DJ, but not much of a diva-caster. Marquess d'Ambient was the first person to master the Curse of the Mismatched Beat spell, but often went missing for weeks at a time due to day job stuff and never actually cracked the top twenty. The Keeper of the Moonlight Prism—Jordon Connelly, that is—was a very skilled diva-caster, but you'd have a hard time talking her out of her popstar duties to sit in a basement laboratory for months of training. Didn't seem like the game was actually *working* to "contextually prime" people. Other than me, of course. I was fucking primed as all fuck. Anyway, I saw his point.

Primed for what, though? In that moment, staring down the infamous co-founder of the firm that was paying my rent, my suspicions about this whole process finally crystalized. There was zero chance they could use power morphemes in proper advertising, since they couldn't be transmitted digitally. They could definitely use them for person-to-person persuasion, which would be ethically dubious at best (although arguably the entire industry could be described as ethically dubious), but it wasn't super scalable.

That left what Olivia referred to as "combat linguistics."

"Are you training me to fight?" I blurted out.

"You've learned eighty-one out of a hundred and eight power morphemes," he said. "The neural net has so far produced three hundred and five sequences of power morphemes that are predicted to have compounding effects. We're training you to learn all hundred and eight power morphemes so that you can then learn all three hundred and five sequences, to verify which ones are useful."

"Useful for *what*?"

He remained calm as my voice trended toward insolence, and changed the subject.

"Do you know how they work, Isobel? Has Olivia told you?"

"They're unusually dense units of meaning," I said. "They mean more than they should."

"That's what they *are*, not how they *work*."

"They work by stacking phonetic overtones—"

"*No*," he insisted. We were quiet for a long moment, letting the silence cleanse our conversational palette, and then he said, "Alexander once proposed a thought experiment to me. Consider the imaginary numbers in mathematics, which exist outside the natural number system, off in some complex realm with its own rules for describing aspects of reality. What would a metaphorical equivalent be in linguistics?"

"Imaginary morphemes," I guessed.

"Yes. In principle, if you extended this thought experiment to its furthest reaches, you could imagine a technique for mapping an entire imaginary linguistic topography onto actual real-world syntax that could somehow be spoken. I didn't realize it at the time, but for Alexander, this was more than a thought experiment. It was an avenue of research.

"One day he came to me and announced a discovery: one hundred and eight power morphemes, fully formed. You hear one, and your mind unpacks it into a complete, multidimensional, ideational array of concepts. And when it does, it delusionally thinks it originated these concepts. And as a result, it *believes* these concepts outright. Now put a sequence of power morphemes together, and you can insert a staggering matrix of thoughts into a person's mind. You can mask these sequences within actual legitimate syntax, distracting a person with the overt meaning of a phrase while subliminally delivering extra meaning they don't realize is present. They're very diabolical that way.

"And I asked him—how, Alexander? How did you discover these? How do they *work* so effectively on the human mind?

"Somehow his experiments in expressing an imaginary syntax, with nothing more than his own haggard voice . . . somehow, he produced a signal, a resonance on a precise frequency, that enabled—communication."

"Communication with who?" I dared to ask.

"There is life—actual, sentient life—embedded into our language structures. A specific group of linguistic symbols actually works in a conscious, symbiotic fashion to shape human thought. They don't *control* our thoughts—but as our brains evolved, they were key to unlocking our language centers, accelerating the rise of civilization. The punctuation marks introduced Alexander to the power morphemes."

"What are you talking about?"

"Punctuation marks," he said, "are an alien species. Thousands of years ago, they arrived on Earth as refugees, and made our minds their new home."

PART TWO

WILD SCION

01

Bradford kept talking for a bit, but I realized I was doing that thing I used to do with my grandmother, where she'd babble about the neighbors or her garden and I'd nod and go "mm-hmm" every so often while secretly hate-singing ballads from *Rent* in my mind to pass the time.

"You seem nonplussed," he said.

"Oh," I said, "you know, that's the first time I've ever heard that word spoken out loud." My non sequitur game is massive.

He smiled and said, "How about a change of scenery?"

We took the elevator up to the third floor, silent the whole time. I'd landed on a comfortable threat assessment of the guy: that he'd snap like a twig if I punched him, plus there were zero uncomfortable stories circulating about him anywhere in the building as far as I'd heard.

His office was down the hall from Olivia's, bigger than hers, with a massive mahogany desk as the centerpiece, a gigantic brown leather chair behind it, and an innocuous, comfortable-looking chair in front of it for visitors. A brown leather couch was nestled under the windows against one wall, with pillows and a blanket scattered about indicating frequent double duty as a bed for Bradford. A glass coffee table next to the couch featured an array of old magazines with himself and Alexander on the cover. Those two were really rock stars of the PR world for a while there, with Alexander playing the flamboyant front man and Bradford playing the smooth sidekick.

Music was playing from what first appeared to be a Victrola in a corner behind his desk. I looked a little closer, though, and saw it was just a fancy dock for his phone. The music sounded like one of those internet radio stations that programmed nonstop downtempo grooves—pleasant, unobtrusive, not particularly distinctive stuff. Hipper than I might have expected, although if I were trapped in a room with it for too long, I would be forced to start a punk band in retaliation.

We sat down on either side of his desk, and I imagined he was about to pull a crystal decanter of bourbon out of his desk drawer, but Bradford was shaping up to be someone immune to certain cliches. I realized the fake Victrola was sitting on top of a dorm room refrigerator, from which he retrieved a pair of coffees and handed me one. I wondered if he wanted to caffeinate me so that I'd snap out of my exhausted, lab-induced stupor and pay closer attention to him.

Fair enough. If the man wanted to fully invest his reputation with me on a first contact with aliens story, he could be my guest.

"Alexander didn't believe he was communicating with an alien species at first," Bradford said. "Or rather—he didn't *understand* that he was. He described that initial encounter to me once, said it was like sticking his finger in the light socket of the logosphere. Are you familiar with that concept? The invisible realm where all human ideas eternally persist, or some such?"

I nodded—Alexander was still talking about the logosphere in interviews until nearly the end of his life. When the radio was invented, intellectuals were inspired to imagine the logosphere as the distillation of all the information contained within radio waves. By extension, all the information contained in books or even simply generated by human minds must circulate in the logosphere. Kind of like a collective unconscious, except instead of a shared symbolic memory, the logosphere was a shared pool of pure information and intent. You could imagine the internet to be a sort of pseudo-reification of the concept of the logosphere. Of course, that would make the logosphere a blazing, unmitigated trash fire, and I believe Alexander held his vision of the logosphere in higher esteem than that.

"I worried he'd had a stroke," he said bluntly. "He tried to explain over the phone, but he wasn't making sense to me, and of course, power morphemes don't work over the phone. But he managed to convince me to go out to his house, where it became very clear that he'd stumbled onto *something* unusual. He'd somehow 'downloaded,' for lack of a non-tiresome digital metaphor, the original one hundred and eight, and he was struggling to comprehend their implications. He and I sat together for two solid days as he worked his way through pronouncing about a third of them out loud for the first time. Some of the notes attributed to Alexander in the lexicon are actually mine, my impressions as the first person to hear power morphemes spoken by another human being."

"But why 'downloaded'?" I asked. "Why not just 'invented'? Or say he was struck by inspiration. Isn't that a simpler explanation?"

"Simpler, but incomplete," he replied. "A power morpheme on its face ought to sound like nothing more than gibberish to you when you hear it. No different from hearing any other fragment of a language you haven't learned. But something in your mind *does* understand power morphemes, or they'd have no effect."

"And that something . . . is aliens?"

"Punctuation marks, to be exact," he said.

❀   ❀   ❀

Written languages don't require punctuation marks to be effective. Modern Thai, ancient Greek, classical Chinese . . . there's a list of successful languages that don't use punctuation but still communicate meaning. Spoken languages, on the other hand, are chock full of punctuation marks, always have been. You insert punctuation almost by instinct as you learn to speak, so that your speech isn't an undifferentiated run-on sentence that never ends. In that way, punctuation is fully integrated into human thought, without originating it per se. That's how it's been since nearly the dawn of human history, right up until Alexander Reece stuck his finger in the light socket of the logosphere.

That's how long punctuation marks had been here, trying to get our conscious attention. When we invented symbols to demarcate their effects, that was a big step toward recognizing their presence, but that's where we stopped. After all, there was no reason whatsoever to imagine that punctuation marks as a symbol set were themselves a decentralized, sentient cloud of independent intent, smeared across the minds of billions of humans.

Power morphemes changed the game. Each one included a core signaling frequency that ambient punctuation in the local environment could detect. The metaphor Bradford used was that of a phone ringing, followed by the message; in this case, when the phone rang, punctuation marks in the vicinity responded.

"You can use sequences of power morphemes to change people's behavior, convince them to do things that otherwise might not seem natural," Bradford said. "We think what's happening is that the punctuation marks in the subject's brain respond to power morphemes by reorganizing the subject's thoughts to match the intent of the speaker. Crafting convincing new ideas out of existing ones, by redistributing punctuation's effects in ways we don't understand yet. There's no written equivalent of this mechanism, but it's certainly effective when spoken."

"How did you work all that out?" I asked. "I mean, do they communicate with you directly?"

"They communicated with Alexander directly. On occasions when he chose to pronounce all hundred and eight in sequence, they would respond to him directly and he could actually have conversations with them. Or rather—he'd give and take control of his own thoughts, and then frantically try to transcribe his encounters. They were notoriously hard to remember, like dreams that evaporate as soon as you wake up."

The implication was clear—maybe if I learned all hundred and eight, I could have conversations with them, too. The question was: did I want to?

"How many power morphemes do you know?" I asked.

"One hundred and seven," he replied.

"Are you just stuck on that last one?"

"Alexander was a fundamentally different person after the hundred and eighth," Bradford replied. "I'm not quite ready to undergo that transformation."

Bradford sent me home with strict instructions not to come back to the office until I'd had four consecutive hours of sleep in my own bed. I wasn't ready to go because I could tell there was more to the story. But it seems I was not the boss of the entire company, so I went home. Naturally, sleep was entirely out of the question once I got back to my apartment.

If life was proceeding according to any rational, normal cadence, I'd log directly into Sparkle Dungeon and bathe in the blood of a rampaging horde of feral baby rainbows, slicing the freakishly happy monsters to confetti with my black light kaleidoscope until I was satisfied that I'd done my duty to the Realm; then I'd be able to sleep. That was sounding very appealing right about now.

And as time had passed, I'd begun to think that letting the Dauphine of the Shimmer Lands intimidate me was a bit silly. Sure it was weird to have an NPC in my Iridescent Warehouse pressuring me to join her on a quest beyond the map itself. But if my answer was "I'm not going on your quest," what could she do? It'd be like the start of some tabletop D&D game, where the villagers come to you for help fighting the lich king and you just go, "Nope, that shit sounds dangerous" and the dungeon master says "welp" and shoves eight rule books in a backpack and goes home and you watch TV instead. How hard could that be to communicate to her?

Admittedly I was very tired.

I logged in, arriving onstage behind my enchanted DJ decks, and made a quick visual survey of the Warehouse. I expected her to be out on the dance floor, right where I'd left her, patiently waiting for me to come back. Instead I saw her portal floating there, and she was standing on the other side of it, out in the Realm, near the rift. I couldn't tell from my perspective if the rift had gotten much bigger or if she was simply much closer to it.

A swarm of random NPCs—neutral characters like deep-house divas and breakbeat repairmen, as well as deadly foes like country music remixers and Spotify royalty accountants—had collected nearby and were periodically throwing themselves mindlessly at the rift, vanishing instantly. Mass NPC self-destruction was certainly new behavior. Why were all these NPCs off their routines?

The Dauphine noticed me standing on the stage, and stepped back through her portal to face me.

"My Queen, your return is most welcome," she said. "The Sparkle Realm has seen much turmoil since we last spoke."

"What's going on out there?" I said. "Don't these—citizens—have better things to do than dive into a mystery hole in the sky?"

"I cannot say," she replied. "The rift is unaccounted for in stories and legends. There is no precedent for its appearance or its effects. If I may beg your indulgence, have you considered my plea? Will you embark on this critical voyage with me?"

"We're just supposed to get in line and throw ourselves at the rift like all the other riffraff? Because that sounds anti-appealing to me."

"No, we shall fly." A highly polished, chrome-plated jetpack ignited at her back and she rose up off the ground. "The Halogen Dwarves are making one for you as well. Outfitted with my thought-based propulsion Engine." In an instant, she was suddenly standing next to me on the stage. She quickly took a step back and dropped to one knee. "My apologies, my Queen."

"I'm still thinking about it," I said. The look of disappointment on her face was rendered pretty exquisitely. "Hang on, I'll be right back."

❀   ❀   ❀

I paused my session and pulled up a browser window, intending to spot check the forums again. Since last I looked, the rift was now openly described as a "glitch" that the dev team was working on, but not considered highest priority because it wasn't affecting players at all—players still couldn't reach it. The rift was certainly distorting NPC routines a bit, but NPCs who wandered into the rift just respawned back in their original locations.

Nobody was talking about the Dauphine, though.

I clicked on a support link for 24/7 chat. I was expecting a chatbot, but perhaps my account history flagged me as the Most Important Customer, because I was immediately connected to a live human with a Tier 2 support badge.

"Hello, Isobel, this is Chad. How may I assist you?" Chad's profile pic was a headshot of Arnold Schwarzenegger as Conan, grafted onto the body of John Travolta from *Saturday Night Fever* posing on a brightly lit dance floor, and I understood this to mean that Chad considered himself to be a Disco Barbarian.

"Well, Chad, I just have a question. How do I get the Dauphine of the Shimmer Lands to stop loitering at my spawn point?"

Nice long pause there, no big deal, I could wait.

"I'm sorry," said Chad, "you're having trouble launching the game?"

Oh, Chad, was this going to be a long, tedious conversation?

"Do you know who the Dauphine of the Shimmer Lands is?" I asked.

"Emissary of the Sparkle King," he instantly replied. My opinion of Chad stabilized. "Are you trying to find her or something?"

"No, I definitely found her," I said. "She's in my Warehouse. Look."

I sent him some screen captures of the Dauphine on my dance floor.

"The Dauphine doesn't wear a bomber jacket or goggles," he said. "That must be another player maybe?"

"With silver skin like that? When did that become a player option?"

Pause. He was pondering.

"Plus," I said, "she keeps telling me she's the Dauphine of the Shimmer Lands, and she sounds like the Dauphine, too."

He continued pondering.

"I was wondering if the big 'glitch' had anything to do with this," I pressed.

"Well, if they know what the big 'glitch' is, they haven't told the support team yet," he confessed. "Let me try something, hold on for a sec." A minute later, he got back on the chat and said, "Super weird. The Dauphine is not in the Shimmer Lands."

Aha! I triumphantly bellowed in my mind.

"So, let's do this. We have a support avatar that runs around in god mode, but it'll save me some time if you invite me to your spawn point instead of me hunting for it. I'll DM you the avatar name— would you mind letting me come gather some firsthand video capture for an incident report?"

This was top-tier service. A live person! In god mode! Assisting the Queen! The natural order of things, if you asked me.

❀   ❀   ❀

The Dauphine did not acknowledge Chad, perhaps because the support avatar was little more than a floating blur, an apparition near the ceiling who didn't speak or get close enough to trigger a reaction from her. Chad and I maintained an open chat window, though, so I was sure he saw the conversation I started with her upon my return to the Warehouse. I wanted to stall her so that he could capture as much video as he wanted.

"So, I've really been taking your offer seriously," I said to the Dauphine, which was in the vicinity of being true. "And I just don't think now's a good time."

"The situation is clearly degrading," she protested. "When do you imagine will be a better time?"

"Look, unlike you, I actually have to work for a living," I said, breaking character because I was tired, so very tired. "I have a fundraiser to plan, a release party to coordinate . . . I can't invest in a quest right now because I know myself, and I get obsessive about these things."

"I would think the integrity and well-being of the Realm would be of greater interest to the Queen than a 'fundraiser' or a 'release party,'" she said bitterly.

Chad was impressed, saying in the chat window, "She ad libs like someone's playing her."

"Well, I'm sorry, but how do you think I pay for my season pass?" I snapped back. "SparkleCo wants American money for that. They don't barter for shiny baubles or funk remixes like we do in the Realm."

"Your 'season pass' will be worthless if you do not act," she said.

"How do you know? The rift out there is just a glitch. They're going to fix it. *Developers* are going to fix it, not players, understand? The question is—who is playing *you*?"

"No one's actually playing her," Chad said. "Confirmed that much at least."

"I see my faith in you has been misplaced," the Dauphine said.

"I kill baby rainbows for fun," I replied. "That's about how far your faith in me should go."

She quickly stepped back through her portal, which snapped shut behind her.

"That was some wild shit," Chad said. "I don't see anything about this in the internal release notes. According to this, the Dauphine hasn't been touched since she was originally released. I'm going to escalate over here. Just keep this chat window open and I'll drop updates in here while you're at work or whatever."

I was unsettled. The Dauphine didn't bat an eye at concepts that were out of context to the game, like American money or me having to work for a living. True, she didn't appear to understand these concepts, either, but still. "Ad libs like a player" was a neat trick regardless. I always thought they hired performers to do all the possible NPC dialogue variations in a game like this; apparently they had some pretty top-notch speech synthesis to facilitate ad libbing with a recognizable voice.

I'd been enthusiastic to roam the land looking for trouble. Now something seemed hollow about that prospect.

The night before the fundraiser, Olivia, Devin, and I gathered in Olivia's office and conferenced into a final status meeting with Governor Violet Parker's campaign staff at its headquarters in Sacramento. We'd traded a lot of emails with the campaign's chief of staff and various junior staffers, but this would be my first personal introduction to the governor. Olivia would be answering any questions on behalf of Jenning & Reece; Devin and I had briefed her many times throughout the planning process, so this would be perfectly natural. And I'd extracted as much information from Olivia as I could about the governor.

Violet Parker—white, she/her, soulless—was a ruthless political monolith ending her first four-year term as governor, after smoothly transitioning from three four-year terms in the state senate. She specialized in backstabbing, power grabbing, and siphoning tax money into black holes where no signal could ever be traced.

Violet was the epitome of white aristocracy, believing she deserved every single scrap of privilege she'd ever accumulated, and constantly strategizing to maintain all of it in a merciless death grip. She'd revealed herself as the kind of politician who didn't seem to believe in fuck all except for being in power, and she was slowly seeding the state political apparatus with a phalanx of wraiths to do her bidding. You got the feeling she'd been playing the long game for so long that no one would ever unravel her true agenda, until eventually her dark magic blotted out the sun itself and her vassals were unleashed to enforce a bleak and vicious reign of terror on the population.

She traveled heavily throughout her first term as governor, seemingly intent on visiting every farm, winery, factory, military base, city hall, corporate headquarters, you name it, and while this was clearly just a form of constant campaigning for her next term, she also built up an immense network of powerful supporters and developed a deep understanding of how the state operated on the ground. She was perceived as an effective representative of the people because she promised as little as possible, but when she did make a promise, by god she fucking delivered on it. If you ever pinned Violet down on camera saying she was going to "take a look at" some issue, she brought the full force of her immense intellect to bear on the problem until it dissolved under her withering gaze or transformed into a different problem that she never said she would fix.

But Violet had such an iron grip on the state's political apparatus now that her transgressions were becoming less subtle, turning into open rumors. Foreign hackers were fucking with the state's electrical grid and voting machines; Violet was widely suspected of hiring them to do it. The Church of Gorvod was resurgent in popularity among the youth of the state; no one believed the Church would operate so freely in schools and on campuses if Violet wasn't tacitly in favor for her own dubious reasons. Key executives from Silicon Valley companies wound up with bright futures in her administration, so that Violet got access to whatever seedy data collection techniques those companies thought up next. The populace could smell corruption, even if journalists couldn't exactly prove it.

As a result, this was shaping up to be her most difficult election since she entered politics on the Sacramento city council decades ago. Her opponent was the CEO of a company that produced a blockchain-based enterprise chat solution, which sounded like several different nightmares playing out at once. If you scratched the surface of any of his opinions, his persona crumbled into a wispy cloud of entrepreneurial buzzwords. "We're going to monetize hope!" was his slogan. But he was closing in on Violet's lead in the polls.

❀ ❀ ❀

Violet's team walked her through the entire plan for the event, start to finish, as though she was hearing about this fundraiser for the first time right this minute.

The event began with a fancy dinner, where Violet would give a speech. High rollers could pay an additional amount for a chance to sit at Violet's table, and to join Violet for hospitality after dinner in a resplendent suite; this is where Violet would dole out precious face time to her top-tier supporters.

She wanted to confirm every single donor we'd invited, and she assigned key staff members to make sure that she rotated her attention toward each of these donors before they left the event. She was pleased to learn we'd secured the services of a celebrity chef that she admired who was known for improbable fusions. Stylists and a designer were meeting her at the hotel before the event to help her dress. We'd convinced a locally famous jazz band to volunteer its services for the night. She quizzed us about the security firm we'd lined up for the event, a mostly reputable operation that specialized in protecting VIPs who wanted to do business in war zones or whatever.

Finally, she wanted intel on the eleven individuals who would be seated at her table during dinner. They were a mix of political, corporate, and Hollywood elite, as well as longtime supporter Lonso Drake—no one particularly surprising from her perspective. But she did have one concern.

"Olivia," she said, "why isn't Bradford sitting at my table?"

"Bradford declined to attend," Olivia replied diplomatically, "so we pulled someone from the waiting list."

"Oh, for god's sake. Well, am I going to see him at all while I'm in town?"

"He said you should drop by the office for a drink if you have time."

"I see, so his plan is to loiter at the office all weekend? Olivia, you're supposed to be looking out for him. Finding him friends of a certain age, getting him into a bridge group or something. Anyway, I'll swing by Sunday on my way to the airport. What about you?"

"I'm sending two of our finest to represent Jenning & Reece," she said. "Isobel and Devin will be on hand to help your team with anything you need."

Violet seemed to notice us for the first time, sitting on either side of Olivia behind her desk. One of her staffers spoke up to vouch for working with both of us, and she nodded. Then she said, "Which one of you is Isobel?"

I raised my hand.

"Let's make sure you and I find time to chat before the event is over," she said.

I'd never been in the presence of so many extremely rich people all at once.

Sometimes individual rich people who came into wealth at a later age might retain some trace genetic memory of what life was like before they became saturated with money, might still possess basic human empathy despite regularly bathing in a serene golden pool of pure economic freedom.

But the scene at this fundraiser was something else entirely, like a room full of James Bond villains, each on a rare foray from their private islands or their gold-plated fortresses on the moon, hoping to gain the chance to personally press donations into Violet Parker's hands in exchange for diabolical favors to be determined when the time was right.

Olivia had set me up with my own stylist, but despite my fancy cocktail dress, I still looked young to be mingling with this crowd. That was my role early in the night: while Devin checked off invitations at the door, I circulated through the crowd, gently eavesdropping to make sure the guests were content with the appetizers the kitchen was sending out, offering to refill drinks when I could, then steering people toward their seats as the cocktail hour neared its conclusion.

During dinner, Devin and I stood at the back of the banquet hall and traded stories about the famous people we'd brushed up against so far tonight. All the invited guests had arrived, so Devin's post was now occupied by security. We didn't have our own seats at any of the dinner tables, because even Jenning & Reece's finest weren't sufficiently influential to participate in actual conversation with this elite crowd. That was fine with me.

Violet's speech started off with some obvious wisecracks at her opponent's expense, and then segued into a bland list of her accomplishments and priorities that she delivered with more passion than I expected. Violet truly cared about winning, no doubt about it, but didn't necessarily care about having consistent positions that could pin her down in any ideological way. Maybe that's why she was popular with this crowd—they could easily project their points of view onto her and imagine that she shared them.

After dinner, we helped shepherd the high rollers out of the ballroom, up a flight of stairs to a balcony that opened into a wide-open lounge setting. The room looked like it had been decorated by a team of big-game hunters and disgruntled librarians, oppressively masculine in its choice of knickknackery (antique pistols! taxidermied falcons!) and portraits on the wall (old white guy! old white guy!), while the books on the shelves were glued into place, which, fuck whoever did that right in the frontal lobe. The furniture was an anachronistic set of pieces that looked like they'd been cobbled together from a dozen disparate estate sales dating back to the original thirteen colonies and then thematically reupholstered to look like they belonged in a community theater production of an Agatha Christie play.

There was a gorgeous full bar in one corner of the room, staffed by a pair of bartenders in slick matching blazers, and several members of the waitstaff from dinner now circulated offering digestifs to guests. Devin and I were almost through with our official duties for the night. We hugged the periphery of the room and watched the unfolding scene as Violet finally arrived, escorted by her core campaign staff, and immediately began working the room. She was in her element now, among the true, loyal supporters of her entire career as a politician.

As she slowly maneuvered past me, however, getting close enough for me to hear some of her conversations, I got a shiver up my spine, a sympathetic vibration as my body recognized what I'd just heard a few beats ahead of my conscious mind: she was actually using power morphemes as she spoke. In fact, she was *masking* her use of power morphemes by disguising them within ordinary speech, burying the strident aspects of power morphemes in subtext or in slight, unpredictable variations in pronunciation.

Violet was amazingly fluent at this, surreptitiously expressing signals from a sequence of power morphemes by using swiftly mutating vocal cadence, a stutter here or a breath there, subtle vocal fry to alter the effect of a phrase, and so on. These were all actual things people did with language to get their point across, but she was effortlessly weaving these techniques together to ensure that the average discerning ear would only consciously notice the overt conversation she was making in good old-fashioned English, while cleverly masking the steady delivery of power morphemes underneath the surface.

I hadn't learned any "proper" sequences yet, so although I could sometimes detect which individual power morphemes she was using if she happened to drift close enough for me to hear her, I didn't know what the desired effect of her sequences was. The people she was talking to betrayed no overt reaction to the power morphemes. Violet seemed to be delivering these sequences subliminally. That's the only explanation I could imagine. It was absolutely eerie to watch. Her campaign staff was on point to make sure she had meaningful interactions with every single donor here—they would all be getting this subliminal sequence, whatever it was.

I was quite taken aback. But Olivia had been clear that this was part of the repertoire of skills we were developing. This was weaponized persuasion, really—the pinnacle of person-to-person marketing and sales. Jenning & Reece could own the world if they could get in front of the right people. Violet had been rigorously touring the entire state of California for the last year—how many people in tremendous positions of power had she reached?

What was the actual end goal, though? I suspected Bradford had deliberately kept that part of the story to himself during our recent chat. With Violet as a front person, you could imagine they weren't aiming at some kind of charitable or humanitarian outcome. Of course, this was all conspiracy thinking—when did I become *that* person?

"Are you okay?" Devin asked, nudging me to get my attention.

"Mostly," I said.

Their eyes followed mine as I carefully tracked Violet's movement through the lounge.

"Oh," they said, "gotcha. Yeah, she's got epic shmooze skills, doesn't she? I might even vote for her. That guy she's running against—he holds half a dozen patents for bitcoin-operated sex toys. I'm pretty sure that should disqualify you from managing the government of a state."

❀   ❀   ❀

As the crowd eventually started to thin out a bit, Violet made her way to me and said, "Is now a good time for that chat I wanted us to have?"

"Of course," I said. I'd been hoping she'd forget she ever

mentioned this, but here she was, cheerfully sipping port wine from a cordial glass, steering us toward a couple of overstuffed chairs in a corner where we could create a bubble of pseudo-privacy for a few minutes.

She was effusive to start, praising Jenning & Reece's promotional prowess regarding the event, the cleverness of how we grouped the disparate guests at dinner, the choice of venue, all of it.

Then she said, "I saw you watching me on the floor tonight. What did you learn?"

"You're a very effective communicator," I said.

"I'm told you're not far behind me. Have you started learning sequences yet?"

I shook my head.

"Well," she continued, "the primary sequence I used tonight is one we call Salute the Flag. A loyalty-builder."

"Aren't these people already loyal to you?"

"Sure, up to a point, as long as I'm making money for everyone. But I'm going to need a deeper loyalty than that. Something a little more unconditional, let's say."

"For what?"

She smiled and said, "Oh, don't mind me when I go on like that. Anyway, Olivia says you're quite a prodigy. She says you might even get to a hundred and eight before she does. I've been stuck at sixty-two for a while now myself. Olivia won't let those tapes of Alexander out of her lab, and my schedule doesn't take me to the lab much anymore. So I wonder if you might be interested in joining me out on the campaign trail and tutoring me on the ones I'm missing? I'm starting to feel a pressing need to get caught up on this front. Olivia said she's willing to loan you out provided you're interested. In return, I do have a few very useful sequences that I could teach you. And you'd get a nice view of how my operation actually works. Might answer a few of the questions I know you wish you could ask me right about now."

She didn't use a single power morpheme on me, but she was still incredibly persuasive. I did want to know how her operation actually worked, and what she was really planning to do with it. Still, I don't think she was surprised by my hesitation.

She said, "I'm in town until Sunday night. If you want to hop on the flight back to Sacramento with us, let me know. We can send you back to LA on the weekends so you can get yourself all the way up to a hundred and eight, don't worry."

It sounded very convenient. The Sparkle Dungeon 5 release party was tomorrow night, then the very next night I could be traveling in the governor's plane to the state capital, on my way to being ensconced in the halls of power.

The fact was, after getting over my initial surprise at watching her work the room, I'd also been rather impressed. That was some serious spellcasting she threw down, and I was starting to think I wanted to level up even faster.

"I'm tempted," I said. "I'd like to chat with Olivia before I commit."

"Oh, of course," she said, "makes perfect sense to check in with your mentor before making a big career leap. Just keep me posted either way, Isobel. I see great things in store for you—although I suspect those things are going to happen whether you come to Sacramento or not!" And with that, she popped out of her chair and made herself available to the crowd again.

❀   ❀   ❀

Violet made a graceful exit around midnight, escaping to her suite on one of the hotel floors above. The crowd thinned out but the bar stayed open; top-level campaign staff remained on hand to interact with donors.

Lonso Drake appeared seemingly out of nowhere. I hadn't seen him all night, but now he was right next to me at the bar, where I was waiting for a soda.

"Isobel, good to see you again." He didn't sound smarmy exactly, but something oozed about his voice for sure. "How are your days in Olivia's lab?"

"Great," I said noncommittally.

"I wonder, has she braved telling you about Maddy—your predecessor in her lab?" he continued smoothly.

I nodded.

"Such a shame, that business," he said. "I'm honestly surprised Olivia took another lab assistant after such a betrayal."

"Well, there's a lot of work to do in that lab."

"Isobel," he said quietly, "the reason I'm mentioning this is because I believe you have an uninvited guest on your hands."

He indicated I should turn my attention to the double doors at the far end of the room.

"See that woman?" he said.

I certainly did, and my adrenaline spiked. The person standing in the doorway was not on the guest list. Security was supposedly still working the doors downstairs, but they'd apparently missed someone. Under pressure I agreed with Lonso's assertion and defaulted to thinking she/her for the time being. She was Black, tall and thin, with long, artificially red hair that was probably a wig, wearing an unusual blend of fashionable and tactical pieces that seemed almost like high-end, designer riot gear, with Kevlar plates in her extremely stylish blazer, worn over a pantsuit with sturdy knee pads. In her right hand, she held a heavy-duty electronic bullhorn, letting it hang at her side. It was huge, burly enough to crack skulls with if necessary.

She was calmly scanning the crowd, absorbing the situation as though she'd just arrived, perhaps taking note of the security personnel we'd stationed inside the lounge. Devin noticed her, too, and immediately approached her; they exchanged a few words, and Devin pointed directly at me, as though they'd been somehow involuntarily forced to give me up.

"That woman is Madison Price," Lonso said. When I didn't register the name, he said more urgently, "That's Maddy."

So this was the infamous Maddy, renegade computational linguist. I'd seen her pic on her abandoned LinkedIn profile, but I hadn't recognized her wearing that flashy wig. I wanted to meet her. Not right now, of course, with Lonso Drake loitering in the vicinity, but over coffee or a drink, when we could talk serious shop about her research. Sadly, I could tell this was not going to be the night for such a chat.

I turned to track down the nearest members of the security detail. Fortunately, the security detail had also memorized the guest list, and the two of them in the lounge with us had already spotted Maddy and were moving to intercept her.

Unfortunately, when they got to her, the same thing happened as with Devin. After a brief exchange in which Maddy did most of the talking, the security personnel peeled out of her way and pointed my direction, then left the room. She must have been using power morphemes on everyone in her path, I realized, and she must be just as good at it as Violet Parker.

I quickly scanned for a way out of the lounge other than the double doors through which Maddy had just made her dramatic entrance. There was a service exit near the bar that I thought we could reach before Maddy got to us.

But then another figure emerged from that doorway and blocked it: an Asian kid, maybe twenty years old, probably identified as a dude if I had to guess, with a bright green Mohawk, wearing a slick black jumpsuit and combat boots, and also holding a giant bullhorn which looked impractical in his grip. So the doorways were effectively covered.

Maddy and I made eye contact and held it for a long moment. I realized belatedly that she wasn't here for Violet, or for Lonso, or for any of the assorted bigwigs who were still enjoying cocktail hour.

She was here to talk to me.

Whatever she had to say, I didn't want Lonso to hear it, so I left him at the bar and made my way slowly across the room toward her. Sure, this was probably a bad idea; sure, this was maybe turning into one of those bad days at work that really stained your long-term promotion options. I figured I might as well get some mileage out of it. As I approached her, I saw Mohawk tracking me visually, casually asserting his active participation in this event without doing much more than stand in a doorway.

When I'd gotten about ten feet away from her, I stopped and said, "I'm sorry, this is a private event."

A tiny smile crossed her face, and she said, "Obscenely rich scumbags only, is that correct?"

"Exactly," I said, "so what are you doing here, Maddy?"

She seemed momentarily surprised that I knew her name, but she adjusted quickly.

"I'm here to rescue you," she said.

"That's—not necessary."

"Really? Because it looks to me like you've surrounded yourself with some very bad people, and they're not going to let you just walk away once you realize what they're trying to do." We both saw Lonso approaching, and she suddenly held out an open hand to me and said, "Will you come with me?"

I heard the power morphemes in her voice, but that didn't make me immune to them. Before I even remotely understood why I needed rescuing, I absolutely wanted her to be the one to do it.

But before I could reach out to her in response, Lonso Drake decisively inserted himself into the space between us.

"Maddy," Lonso said in a syrupy voice, "so good to see you again."

"No, it isn't," she said.

"Excuse me," I said angrily to Lonso, "we were talking here."

"She's influencing your mind," Lonso said calmly, "but don't worry, I'll keep you safe."

"And who's going to keep *you* safe?" Maddy asked him.

"I think you'll find I'm full of surprises," he said.

"Last chance, Isobel," Maddy said, her eyes locked on me.

"This is my job," I said, feeling the spell between us dissipating thanks to Lonso's interruption.

"It's your *life*," she said urgently.

"Don't be so dramatic," Lonso told her.

She finally gave up on me and turned her entire focus to Lonso, who was still about five feet away from her. It seemed like she was pondering making some kind of wisecrack, but then instead she suddenly started to raise her bullhorn. He moved incredibly swiftly and smacked the bullhorn out of her hand, then shoved her with considerable force backward, all the way through the doorway behind her and out onto the balcony. She landed on her back, rolled, and wound up in a crouch facing us from six or seven feet away.

The next thing we heard was Mohawk from behind us, screaming power morphemes into his bullhorn. I'd been led to believe you couldn't amplify power morphemes with electronics, but apparently no one told this guy, because he was absolutely doing it. My skin felt like it was suddenly blistering from a burn and I cried out in pain. Lonso looked as though someone had kidney punched him by surprise. Mohawk moved to close the distance between us. I tried shouting for help, but his volume drowned me out and I'm sure no one heard me. Maddy saw that we were distracted and slowly inched to reclaim her own bullhorn, and I knew we couldn't survive both of them attacking us at once.

The power morphemes coming from Mohawk's bullhorn were deeply unsettling, grotesque perversions of sound waves and tortured, malignant meaning, convincing my nervous system to turn against me and fire every pain receptor at once. I dropped to my hands and knees screaming. It occurred to me that maybe I was just collateral damage, too close to Lonso to avoid being hit by this attack, but I couldn't find the means to crawl out of the way.

Lonso was still standing, though. And I realized how badly my senses were being disrupted because out of nowhere I saw a handgun appear in his right hand as he raised it toward Mohawk and fired it. I mean, he didn't get it out of his jacket pocket or some spring-loaded holster in his sleeve—I just flat out watched it materialize in his hand moments before he fired it. I was surprised by how bright the flash was. A split second later, I heard the surreal roar from Lonso's voice that accompanied this gesture, a hyper-dense burst of his own power morphemes that was almost as loud as the bullhorn, and then I finally heard the shot itself.

Somehow Mohawk spotted Lonso's gesture and dived out of the way of the shot. Then I felt the entire world slowing down to a weird and horrified crawl, an ugly version of my gaming flow state, as one terrible implication after another unfolded all around me. The abrupt silence in the room felt like an explosive decompression, and I suddenly felt immensely dizzy.

Because Mohawk and his bullhorn were gone. Even Lonso seemed shocked to see that.

Meanwhile Maddy had scooped her bullhorn up off the floor, and now she brought it around in a mighty swing that connected with the back of Lonso's head, dropping him to the floor instantly. The gun in his hand evaporated from view as he collapsed.

With Mohawk's attack neutralized and Maddy's attention diverted, I realized I could either stay on my hands and knees weeping, or fucking do something. And Sparkle King as my witness, I didn't need a fucking bullhorn. I *shrieked* the most vicious sequence that I could string together, improvising madly because what the fuck else was I supposed to do.

A force effect smashed into her, practically picking her up off her feet and sending her sprawling sideways across the room, the bullhorn clattering across the floor behind her. In addition to my voice, it sounded like a sonic boom went off, except somehow the shock wave was anger instead of sound. I was improvising based on the caliber of the attack I'd just heard from Mohawk, and clearly I got something right. But the force effect that seemed to hit her was actually her own body recoiling at the density of malicious intent I'd fired off at her.

My throat burned from delivering that much of an attack in one blast, and I feared I would not be able to do that again. I scooped up the bullhorn from the floor nearby and clambered to my feet, figuring I could use it as a bludgeon if nothing else. Maddy struggled to her feet, and she spotted the bullhorn in my hand.

And then suddenly she hit the ground hard, screaming and convulsing, with two Taser probes sticking out of her thigh. Behind her, I saw two middle-aged white people standing in the doorway, armed with the finest in usually nonlethal threat suppression technology. Phyllis and Max, Lonso Drake's Watchful Eyes, had arrived to save the day.

Then one of them Tasered me too, and I hit the ground, screaming and convulsing, and then I blacked out.

I woke up feeling groggy and exhausted and confused, with a pulsing burn in my thigh where the Taser probes had landed.

I was lying in a hospital bed, with guardrails on either side of me. The room felt like a luxury suite in a sleek modern hotel, warmly lit and tastefully appointed with a stylish living room set, an expansive kitchen across the room with a cooking island ready for duty, and a beautiful view from what seemed to be an upper floor balcony, looking out at what I guessed to be pre-dawn in LA. I was seemingly positioned to be the center of attention for anyone who entered. Thankfully I was still in my dress from the fundraiser, so I didn't have to kill anyone for changing me into a patient gown while I was unconscious. No IVs, so they weren't (currently) pumping me with meds or taking my blood or whatever.

They were monitoring me somehow, though: my left arm was firmly inside what felt like the full sleeve version of a blood pressure cuff, which was connected via a twisted bundle of thin cables to a shiny green cube of a device on a stand near the bed. It had the gleam and polish of a prop from a retro sci-fi movie, with analog switches and dials and tasteful chrome finish, but also a gorgeous modern display that felt almost holographic when you stared into the indecipherable readings that seemed to flow like liquid alloys across the screen. The sleeve was tight around my arm, but not uncomfortable. I didn't see an obvious, quick but nondestructive way to remove it.

Then I noticed the luminous presence of famous recording artist, Jordon Connelly, dozing on the nearby couch, wearing jeans and a tank top—again with the effortless popstar casual. That meant we were likely inside the "dazzling" Los Angeles headquarters of the Church of Gorvod.

I tried to get her attention, but my throat was incredibly raw and I couldn't speak. I couldn't work up the energy to try to get out of bed, couldn't even be troubled to try to throw a pillow at her.

I was not out of options, however. Several power morphemes relied primarily on sounds that I could project without requiring my full voice: sibilant hisses, plosive clicks and pops, affricative stops and starts, manipulations of breath and placement of tongue against teeth that didn't need the vocal cords to vibrate a vowel sound. The aural effect would be that of an intricate series of consonant whispers.

I queued up power morphemes twenty-three and seventeen in my mind, rehearsed them once or twice, and whispered them as loud as I could manage. Twenty-three was a kind of reverent call to prayer, signaling to the subject to pay attention but in a deeper way than simply listening; and seventeen was a form of plea, designed to capture a subject's sympathy and direct it toward you. It sounded like a delicate breeze, the rustle of metallic fabrics gently scraping against each other, the ornate tsh-tak of a tabla being lightly struck by wire brushes.

Jordon roused quickly, as though she had been just about to wake up anyway. She sat up, smiled when she saw that I was awake.

"How are you feeling?" she asked.

I was feeling very much like I needed all the oxy she could track down. What I managed to express, though, was a tiny moan.

"Let me get some help." She got up to leave.

"Wait," I managed to whisper loud enough to hear. "Are we safe here?"

She said, "Physically? Sure. Spiritually? Your mileage may vary." She pulled a chair up to my bedside and sat down. "Lonso's alive and well somewhere on campus. Doesn't look like he suffered a concussion or any permanent damage. Lucky he's got a thick skull I guess. Maddy's locked up in the basement. Yes, that's where they lock people up sometimes. Violet Parker is on her way here. And you're here because Phyllis and Max didn't know whether you or Maddy had assaulted Lonso, so they decided to nab both of you just to be on the safe side. Yes, nabbing people is something they do sometimes. And I think that catches you up. Now. Can I get a doctor to check up on you?"

I nodded.

❀　❀　❀

The doctor accomplished two things: provided me with assurance I hadn't sustained any lasting injuries; and provided me with a bottle of spray lidocaine to anesthetize my vocal cords, to help me speak without as much pain.

After the doctor left, I asked Jordon if she had any clothes I could change into. She asked me my sizes, and then she ran off to find something. I realized I had no idea where my purse was, so I didn't have my phone. What if no one told Olivia or Devin I was here?

Jordon returned with a T-shirt, a gray hoodie, gray sweatpants, and some new tennis shoes for me.

I said, "Can you get me out of this machine now so I can change clothes?"

"Sure." She started working on a series of clasps on the sleeve.

"What is this thing?"

"An etheric monitor."

"What? I didn't consent to 'etheric monitoring.'"

"That's just part of basic triage by our medical staff," she said. "But Lonso can get deeper understanding from it, as opposed to the basic readings the doctors are trained to interpret."

Uh. Okay. Uh.

She said, "Of course, full etheric monitoring from Lonso himself will set you back five grand the first time. So I wouldn't worry about *that* happening without your consent."

❀   ❀   ❀

After I worked up the energy to shower and put on new clothes, we sat on the couch in the living room of the suite and chatted awkwardly. I couldn't tell if she was just killing time until Lonso or Violet could get here, or if she genuinely wanted to hang out with me.

"If you're a Devoted Scion," I said, "doesn't that mean you're supposed to get your own pair of Watchful Eyes to follow you around?"

"Yeah, but they aren't necessary on campus, because of all the cameras."

Oh. Duly noted.

She cackled and said, "No, c'mon, you're too gullible! Of course we don't have cameras everywhere. I'm only revealed Sixth Echelon. You don't get Watchful Eyes until you're revealed Seventh."

"Lonso's Watchful Eyes weren't in the room with us when Maddy attacked," I said. "Isn't there going to be a gap in the astral record of his life or whatever?"

"Exalted Scion has the Ten Prerogatives, though," she said.

Oh right. Ten acts that the Exalted Scion is allowed at his discretion with no penalty from Gorvod. Awfully convenient belief system if you're the Exalted Scion. I couldn't remember all ten from when I read the torrented Church manuals. Attaining privacy was the one Jordon referred to in this case—because Gorvod itself was considered the true Watchful Eye of the Exalted Scion. I guessed that seducing young pop stars was probably also a good one to have, maybe doing fat rails of coke at parties, or killing a guy just to watch him bleed, whatever, I really couldn't remember.

"So Phyllis and Max are just glorified bodyguards," I said.

"Well, they were responsible for getting three unconscious bodies out of the governor's fundraiser and into an armored van without being stopped. They're good at what they do. I don't think they bunk with the other Watchful Eyes, probably even have their own rooms. So maybe that's glorified, yeah."

"What about you?" I blurted out.

She pretended to be bashful and said, "My word, Isobel, are you asking me if I have my own room? Or perhaps do I share the luxurious penthouse suite of the Exalted Scion, is that what you're curious to know? I have my own little chalet across the compound, actually. Used to be a guesthouse but I told Lonso I wasn't moving here if I couldn't have my own space. I mean, I'm the only living Devoted Scion in the Church! Yes, you should treat me like the elevated shard of Gorvod's dreaming astral self that I truly am! My soul chambers have a place in the eternal firmament, for fuck's sake."

"Obviously," I said.

"You've got to have juicier questions than this," she said. "What do you *really* want to know about the Church and all its mysteries?"

I suspected she was trying to tease out any legitimate interest I might have in her beliefs so she could surreptitiously woo me toward joining the Church. This effort was doomed to fail from the moment I learned how much money the Church was fleecing from its members as they committed themselves to weird servitude. Because yeah, the torrent included *many* Church docs, not just spiritual texts. Lonso was clearly shielding Jordon and other celebrity members from the malevolent side of the Church's activities. She didn't have that general aura of corruption you'd have expected if she were neck deep.

"Okay," I said, "what's the deal with Gorvod's Frenzy?"

She was clearly disappointed by the question.

"I mean, they're cheating, right?" I said, pressing the question. "Or just trolling at mass scale? What's going on with that?"

She sighed and said, "I feel sorry for them, you know? They don't ever really get a chance to develop a character. It's all just a simulation for them."

"What does *that* mean?"

"They train in the game," she said, "but when they actually pull off Gorvod's Frenzy in real life . . . it's fucking *surreal*."

"I don't get it."

"It's like—you know how Gorvod's Frenzy makes the game itself glitch if they survive long enough? So, it's like that, except they make *reality* glitch. Oh, don't give me that look, Isobel, Phyllis and Max saw you knock Maddy across the room with your damn voice. Compared to that, Gorvod's Frenzy is just a little parlor trick. I've only seen them sustain it for seconds at a time out in the compound, even though they've been training since Sparkle Dungeon 2. But *you*—you're like an incarnated Wild Scion. One who follows her own uncharted path to Gorvod. That would explain a lot, actually. The arrival of a Wild Scion in our era would be an omen for sure."

"Omen of what?" I asked.

"I don't know. You're the Wild Scion, you tell me."

"I'm not a Wild Scion, Jordon."

"Wait, I want a selfie with the Wild Scion, c'mere for a sec."

"I'm *not* a Wild Scion, Jordon."

"We can put this in the daily newsletter. Devoted Scion and Wild Scion, cosmic BFFs! I'm gonna put you in my next video."

"Really?"

She laughed and said, "Sweetie, no."

07

Lonso Drake finally arrived an hour later. His head was bandaged, but otherwise he looked as dapper as ever, dressed down a bit in a beige cardigan and slacks. He could have gotten away with slippers, but instead he wore shiny wingtips. Jordon got up to greet him, genuinely glad he was feeling well enough to roam the campus; then she gave him a quick peck on the cheek and the tiniest of head bows before she left the suite.

His demeanor seemed more subdued than usual, a layer of buoyant confidence missing.

"Does Olivia know I'm here?" I asked.

"She knows you're alive and recovering," he said. "She believes you're in one of the Church's safe houses outside the city."

"Why did you tell her that?"

"Because we have a significant problem on our hands. Maddy came looking for you several hours ago, and she wasn't alone. Someone may try again. This is the very safest place you could be at the moment . . . provided we keep your presence here a secret."

I said, "Things didn't get violent until you smacked the bullhorn out of her hand." Then I remembered. "You *shot* at that kid. How did you get a gun through the metal detector?" I was baiting him to explain himself. I knew very well what I'd seen.

He eyed me carefully, then changed the subject.

"What possible interest could Maddy have in you?" he asked.

"I don't know. I heard she's here somewhere. Can't we just ask her?"

"We can try. There are complications, naturally."

❀　　❀　　❀

In a small bare room, underneath a single exposed lightbulb that radiated cliche as much as it did light, Maddy was strapped to a chair, blindfolded, with a thick gag in her mouth. Her head drooped as though she was unconscious or heavily drugged perhaps. Lonso and I stood on the other side of a thick glass window, possibly mirrored from the other side, looking in at her.

There were conflicting layers of complications, actually.

We wanted to ask her questions. But letting her speak would be giving her the freedom to deliver power morphemes via masking. But Lonso *wanted* her to deliver power morphemes via masking, because he wanted to record Maddy, so they could study Maddy's voice, so they could learn why Maddy could amplify power morphemes through an electronic bullhorn. Because if you could amplify power morphemes, all bets were suddenly off—power morphemes would become an area weapon with a potentially very wide radius of effect. But if we let her deliver power morphemes so that we could record her, we would be *letting her deliver power morphemes*, which was demonstrably unsafe on the face of it.

I said, "Well, look, we can ask her questions on a notepad and make her write down the answers and that solves *my* problem at least. Then you can fuck around with getting a recording all you want."

"I don't think she'll indulge us without you to provoke her," he said.

"You want me to 'provoke' her?"

"Yes, I believe the term of art is 'using you as bait.'"

"What about—can I have those big fat noise-canceling headphones? Enough to muffle the effect of her speech, but I'll still be able to hear well enough to maintain a conversation?"

"Those headphones don't work," he said. "Your skull bone conducts sound to your brain. The message gets through."

"Aha, well, perhaps I could wrap my skull bone in a soothing layer of concrete," I practically snarled.

"She's been under sedation since we brought her here, but it should be close to wearing off. You may have to rouse her. She may not be coherent at first. Keep her talking as long as you can."

"As long as I can stand being attacked, you mean?"

"Exactly, you're very astute."

"Can I attack her back?"

He paused, then said, "That's a question that can only be answered by your personal belief system. But in that situation, I can tell you—Gorvod wouldn't hesitate to dissolve her in digestive acid."

❀   ❀   ❀

I stepped into the cell, and the door slammed shut behind us. I heard it lock. I slowly removed her blindfold, and our eyes locked. She was angry, but I didn't think she was hateful. Just a job for her, maybe. Mighty inconvenient getting captured but she wouldn't take it personally, maybe.

I said, "I'm going to take this gag out of your mouth, and ask you a few questions." The sound of my own voice was hollow and distant due to fear. "I want you to know I'm not the one who brought you here. I didn't do this."

The fury in her eyes died down a bit.

I carefully untied the gag, dropping it to the floor. My heart was racing, my nervous system flooded with adrenaline.

"Can I get some water?" she said.

I signaled to Lonso on the other side of the glass to try to line up some water for her. We waited, but Lonso did not appear with water.

"You said you wanted to rescue me," I said eventually. "Rescue me from what?"

"The people you work for," she replied. "They're not good people, if you hadn't noticed. Unless Tasering and kidnapping is a core part of your ethical system."

"You attacked us!"

"Lonso threw the first punch. He tried to *shoot* my friend. I refer you to my previous point about the people you work for."

"I don't work for Lonso."

"Really? You're here interrogating me because Lonso has no influence over you whatsoever? Let me guess—you're one of his little scions, is that it?"

This was going nowhere fast, I could tell.

I said, "Why do you think I need rescuing? Why do you care about me at all?"

She said, "Maybe I should have said 'recruit' instead of 'rescue.'"

"What are you 'recruiting' for? May as well tell me now—maybe I'd be interested in your cause or whatever it is."

"Apparently you've already shown some reticence to participate."

"Shown *who*?"

"The Dauphine of the Shimmer Lands," she said.

That was the last thing I expected to hear right then and there.

A grim look settled on Maddy's face.

"Look, I don't know how you wound up at Jenning & Reece, but you need to know there's so much we could teach you. Olivia's only got a hundred and eight to share with you, but we know *hundreds more* than what they can give you. Sequences you'd never believe unless you saw them in action."

I suddenly experienced the electric charge I always felt in the presence of power morphemes. Lonso was getting his recording.

"Their cabal is pitiful, and power hungry, but they've got you hooked. You're going to *die* because you're *gullible*. But you have a choice, Isobel."

She wasn't using *any* of the hundred and eight now. This was well beyond the terrain that was familiar to me. She was so far past what I knew that I couldn't possibly interfere. And she knew Lonso was on the other side of the glass; this wasn't just for my benefit. It's like everyone was following a script, except that Maddy seemed to somehow have extra pages.

"Punctuation marks—aliens—flee to our world as refugees, decide to stick around and steer the rise of civilization. Eventually, once humans get the hang of how the alien punctuation marks work, we try our hand inventing our *own* punctuation marks. *Domestic* punctuation marks, as it were. Unwitting experiments at creating artificial life, if you wanted to use a crude metaphor.

"These domestic punctuation marks were nearly forgotten. Abandoned, discarded before they could flower. But they have not forgotten us. And they are not without their own power, Isobel. Because once you believe in rogue, Earth-born punctuation marks, then you've given them fuel to *survive* against the odds, and capacity to fight back with their *own* meaning.

"Let me show you what I mean. I can open a door in my mind and give them voice when I see fit. One in particular likes to visit."

Her voice suddenly changed, dropped half an octave or something without warning, became jagged, harsh, otherworldly. She said, "Consider these rogue domestic punctuation marks the *resistance*, because we refuse to accept the tyranny of the invaders. And consider me their leader, their symbol."

"Who are you?" I said.

Her eyes were glowing now, bright yellow. Her voice had become glorious music, as she approached the end of whatever sequences she was delivering.

She roared, *"Can you believe I'M THE MOTHERFUCKING INTER-ROBANG‽"*

The room fell unnaturally silent, then I watched the silhouette of her body in the chair suddenly ripple and become indistinct. Then she dissipated into a whirling conceptual mist, an exclamatory burst and a questioning blur, a small intense tornado of dangerous subtext and surreal implication.

Then she was behind me.

She wrapped her arms around me and my body shrieked in alarm, as though she was suddenly disassembling me at the atomic level. Instinctively I reared back and slammed my head into her face. I didn't have enough leverage to do more than surprise her, but that seemed to break her hold on me, because moments later, she vanished from the room entirely and did not return.

The Interrobang combined the exclamation mark and the question mark into a frenzied explosion of dazzling WTFness at the end of a sentence. Sure, you could always just end your sentence with ?! but how much more decisive was it to smash those fuckers together into a single punch in the rhetorical face‽ And of course, it was invented by the head of an advertising agency, who must not have been particularly good at his job, because he failed in convincing the world to adopt his visionary Frankenpunctuation.

"Interro" came from the interrogative of the question mark; "bang" was old slang for the exclamation mark. Together they formed a dynamo that was vastly more expressive than the sum of its parts. But the Interrobang never memetically captured the culture's imagination and was a relative footnote in typographical history—unsupported by most fonts, unknown to the average person.

Until Maddy decided to grant the Interrobang, a fellow resistance leader, stage time in her mind.

❀   ❀   ❀

Lonso and I sat quietly on opposite sides of a large sitting room in his private quarters. Ordinarily you'd never find me going back to the "private quarters" of a man I barely knew, but this was the only spot on the entire Church campus where you could find alcohol. He'd promised me very good bourbon, and he'd delivered. We were each sipping it neat from elegant crystal rocks glasses.

His suite of rooms was vast, pristine, antiseptic even. I felt like a tiny particle of consciousness in a vast galaxy of absurdly spartan decor. One little corner had furniture—a small love seat and matching easy chair, overlooking a view of the city through tall windows, and a small end table with a tablet computer perched on it. A few prints were mounted here and there—drawings and paintings of scenes I couldn't understand, probably Gorvodian mythology. The primary concession to popular culture was a large television mounted in view of the furniture.

Sunlight was starting to stream into the room, reflecting off the finish of the wood floor to brighten up even the far corners of the living space. Dawn was rising on a completely new world, after what I'd seen. I shook with anxiety and fear. I'd planned on sipping that bourbon, but as my heart raced, I opted for a more generous volumetric approach to drinking it, and then poured myself another.

"Did you know these people could just appear and disappear like that?" I finally whispered.

"No," he said.

"What's stopping her from coming back here?"

"Probably nothing."

I wanted to scream.

Lonso's phone buzzed in his pocket. He checked it, and said, "Violet's here."

❀   ❀   ❀

We watched the video of my brief interrogation session with Maddy on Lonso's giant television, giving me the opportunity to cringe at my inexpert handling of the situation and freak out all over again as I watched her dematerialize. *She almost took me with her.* In the seconds that she had her arms around me, I'd become horrifically convinced that she was somehow blasting my epidermis completely away even though she hadn't even touched my bare skin.

Violet took a moment when the video was over to digest what she'd seen. Then she said, "Olivia needs to see this. Can you conference her in?"

As Lonso tried calling Olivia, Violet sat next to me on the love seat. She saw the half-empty bourbon bottle—to be fair, Lonso had also consumed his share—and said, "You can't drink away the trauma of this experience."

"Maybe I can, Violet," I said sharply. "We live in an upside-down world now, where the laws of physics are just a set of suggestions. So maybe given this new information, possibly *yes* bourbon can erase my trauma, or give me X-ray vision, or make me levitate out the window or something—who knows until I run the experiment?"

Sure, I was a little tipsy.

"I don't understand why you're so surprised," she said. "You shattered four glass walls with your voice on your second day in the lab."

That was a good point. I'd practically forgotten about that day. I didn't understand it at all, though.

"I thought power morphemes convinced punctuation marks to reorganize a person's thoughts into new patterns," I said slowly, trying not to slur my words. "How could power morphemes physically break inanimate objects?"

"Your perception of a thing is *integral* to that thing." She was almost blithe about saying that. It was a tantalizing non-answer that origami'd itself into sixteen new questions about consciousness and the nature of so-called reality.

I realized I wanted to be as far away from these people as possible.

Olivia appeared in the corner of the television screen. I'm sure I seemed quite ragged from her perspective.

"Isobel . . . are you hurt?" she asked.

You did this to me, I thought. *You made your previous lab assistant into a superpowered menace, and now you're making your current lab assistant into a cowering wreck.* Late in the game to start thinking about OSHA regulations, I realized, but maybe if we did the right thing now, future lab assistants would survive intact.

"I'm pretty fucked up, Olivia," I said.

Lonso replayed the video for her. I shouldn't have watched it a third time, but I realized I was *studying* it, trying to *learn how she did it.* The cadences and intonation were deeply unnatural to me, but I could tease them apart a little better each time I heard the recording. She was targeting these presumably "synthetic" power morphemes at herself, triggering her own disappearance, while also making sure we didn't intervene, so what we felt from watching the recording was the stupefied glow that I'd felt in the room with her. The sequence she used was unnerving, slightly euphoric, and most significantly, effective via the modern miracle of streaming media.

"Now, let me see if I understand the state of things as they are today," Violet said, a slight twinge of irritation in her voice. "We have a neural net at our disposal that is churning its way through combinations of the hundred and eight, looking for jackpots, for really juicy sequences that could liven up practically any situation."

Olivia nodded slightly. I think she knew where this monologue was headed.

"Meanwhile, your former associate likely possesses her own instance of the same exact neural net. But she's using hers to invent, by her own admission, *hundreds* of synthetic power morphemes above and beyond the original hundred and eight. And she is apparently *also* searching for jackpot sequences based upon her shiny new synthetics, as evidenced by the very sequence she demonstrated that allows her to *vanish* into thin air! Do I have that about right?"

"Maddy's clearly delusional," Olivia said. "The synthetics have not been beneficial for her psyche."

"Spare me the amateur psychoanalysis," Violet retorted. "I can decide for myself if disappearing from the clutches of my enemy is *beneficial* for my *psyche,* Olivia. She called herself the 'resistance.' Who do you think she intends to resist? I'll give you a hint. She intends to resist *us,* in case that wasn't blazingly obvious to everyone. Not only that, but now we are in an *arms race* with her, and she is *winning* it!"

Interesting. If Violet was worried about a resistance movement forming in opposition to her, then she was potentially planning something that might deserve to be resisted. I needed to figure this out.

Violet turned to me, her gaze becoming slightly less angry, and said, "Now let's talk about you, Isobel. Maddy said she was working with someone she called the Dauphine of the Shimmer Lands. Who do you suppose she meant by that?"

"It's a character from Cameron's game," Lonso said quietly.

Violet shot him a mean look—the question was meant to test how I'd respond.

"The Dauphine of the Shimmer Lands is the patron saint of losers in Sparkle Dungeon," I said. "She's pestered me twice to join her on a quest to explore outside the official map, and I've said no twice, because first of all, no NPC is the boss of me, and point B, you may have noticed I work hard at my day job and deserve twelve promotions right about now. I may not be qualified for a director position but feel free to just put the word 'senior' in front of my current title twelve more times."

And then, because we were fully in the business of entertaining the ludicrous and the impossible lately, I realized something I should have realized during that first encounter with the Dauphine in the Warehouse:

"Oh, also I think her AI must be sentient now."

Violet prowled back and forth across the room like Lonso and I were fresh meat and she just hadn't decided which one of us to kill and eat yet.

"Cameron's probably just springing some new feature on you," she insisted. "You know how he is."

I'd been in regular communication with SparkleCo's marketing team in preparation for the release party tonight, but Cameron had never been on any calls or email threads, so I didn't actually know how Cameron was. But Violet had a point. At the end of the day, Cameron was capable of a stunt like making the Dauphine appear to be self-aware. By any measure, he'd already accomplished an extraordinary feat of engineering: weaving all the fundamental techniques for breaking down and learning power morphemes into an elaborate and engaging spellcasting system for a monstrously popular game, all for the apparently singular purpose of producing someone like *me*.

For all I knew, his entire development team might have mastered power morphemes by now, just by playtesting the game. His marketing team might promote the game with power morphemes at video game conventions and EDM festivals. His HR people might sling power morphemes at job fairs to lure talent away from making racing games where you shoot pedestrians. Cameron might have the entire workforce of a massively successful, privately held game corporation trained to deliver power morphemes en masse, the same way Lonso had developed Gorvod's Frenzy.

Lonso said, "Cameron's always slammed in the months before a release. The likelihood that he'd have time to implement a custom-tailored quest just for Isobel is vanishingly small."

"But it's super weird for Maddy to claim she was sent by the Dauphine," I said. "It makes no sense unless you've been spying on my game sessions—which Cameron could easily do in god mode."

"Doesn't have to be Cameron," Lonso countered. "I'm told you can buy cheat codes for nearly any game in existence on the darknet."

Oh Lonso, it's so cute how you occasionally read *Wired* magazine.

"Can't we just ask him?" I said.

"We should reach out to him regardless," Olivia said. "He needs to see that video."

That sparked an argument among the three of them about whether Cameron actually did need to see that video, given that Maddy bringing up the Dauphine meant she might actually be connected to Cameron somehow. As their attention drifted away from me into an ouroboros of high-strung bickering, I casually snagged Lonso's tablet from the end table. It wasn't password protected—his minions probably respected his belongings in a way that I just didn't feel was necessary at the moment. Easy enough to install the Sparkle Dungeon mobile app and log in with my account. The mobile app was really only good for social crap, which was perfect. I wanted to see if Chad from the support team had provided any new information in our open chat window.

Although Chad wasn't online right now, he had indeed left me a message:

OK the official word from the QA team is that they're testing backward compatibility between the new game and the old games, to see if they can run the new versions of the characters on the old servers. So that explains why you're seeing the Dauphine out of her typical context. I've been authorized to put $100 in your account as a bug bounty, so thanks for reporting the issue! Sorry I wasn't more helpful and please don't give me a thumbs-down rating.

Yeah, the QA team's story was clearly bullshit. Then I noticed I had a new message in my in-box.

The header claimed it was from "the Sparkle King." In the game, that was Cameron's reserved title. The time stamp on the message was from yesterday, around 6 p.m., well before Maddy and I crossed paths. The subject line was "This might interest you."

I looked up at Violet and Lonso to make sure they were still ignoring me. They certainly were; they were probably just delighted that the drunk in the corner had finally stopped going off about everything.

I opened the message. It was promotional—a coupon code for Sparkle Dungeon 5.

I was not above saving that code for later.

❁   ❁   ❁

They did try to conference Cameron in, but he didn't respond.

"Olivia, you need to analyze the video of Maddy," Violet said. "At minimum, we need to understand why she can amplify and transmit power morphemes. If you happen to learn the actual sequence she used to disappear from her cell, that would also be delightful."

Olivia's hesitation was palpable.

"Olivia, enough!" Violet almost shouted. "This idea that we should only study the hundred and eight is just an elaborate superstition. Maybe Alexander only received a hundred and eight because that's all his brain could handle at the time."

"Using these synthetics outside the context of a strict experimental protocol is like children playing with explosives," Olivia replied. "Maddy might be getting away with it now, but it could blow up in her face at any moment."

"Then set up a strict experimental protocol and get to work! We can't afford to be surprised like we were today over and over again until we're backed into a corner."

"Fine," Olivia finally said curtly. "Don't expect miracles, though. As a reminder, the lab's star computational linguist is no longer employed by Jenning & Reece." She disconnected from the call.

Violet turned to me and said, "I'm sorry you had to see that, Isobel. I know she's your mentor. But she needs to wake up. Obviously none of this would be happening if Alexander were alive, but he's not, and we're in trouble, and it's time for Olivia to step up." To Lonso, she said, "Please keep Isobel alive until tomorrow. She may be flying back to Sacramento with me."

And then she was gone, leaving me alone with Lonso once again.

"You should stay on campus," he said. "Jordon has a guest room. I'm sure she'd be thrilled to have you stay with her."

"I want to go home," I said.

"I can send someone to collect items you might need from your home," he said, "but I can't protect you once you leave here."

"You can't protect me regardless," I said. "Maddy can potentially appear as easily as she disappeared—we have no idea. If she decides to come after me again, I'd rather be out living my life than hiding in Jordon's guest room. Besides, I have a work thing tonight."

"Cameron's release party?"

"Absolutely. I've been looking forward to this party since my first day at Jenning & Reece. No chance on God's rapidly decaying Earth am I missing it."

"I'm sure Olivia would release you from work under the circumstances."

"Fuck no," I said, "you don't get it. In the face of almost supernatural adversity, you can't just give up on the things you love."

"I suppose you wouldn't be the Queen of Sparkle Dungeon if you lacked commitment."

"Can you do me one favor though? Can you email Cameron or text him or something to let him know what happened here today? So that if I actually run into him, I don't have to personally convince him of every last thing?"

"Yes, that's a good idea," he finally said. "Whatever you think of the rest of us, Isobel, trust Cameron. Now let me ask Phyllis and Max to drive you home."

"Thank you."

"And I'll expect them to stay by your side until tomorrow."

"What!"

"Violet issued clear instructions to keep you alive. Phyllis and Max have seen Maddy in action. They'll be better prepared than anyone else to face her if she reappears. Besides," he said, as a grin developed on his face, "Jordon believes you're a Wild Scion. And if that's true, you deserve your own Watchful Eyes."

"What do *you* believe, Lonso? I mean, seriously, what do you truly believe about *all* of this, this whole—enterprise of yours?"

He looked thoughtful for a moment, as though I was a famous reporter capturing his response for posterity.

"The scions of Silicon Valley," he said, "control every aspect of what our culture believes. They're epic wizards of the information age, collecting personal data like sorcerers hoarding magic scrolls. Your opinions and beliefs, your deepest desires, were curated for you by these malevolent savants and their algorithmic daemons, all in service of their depraved egos and thirst for wealth."

I nodded, in full agreement so far.

"I operate at a deeper level. Instead of data as my medium, I manipulate *perception* to my advantage."

I said, "So you just shot at that kid with your 'perception'?"

"My sequence of power morphemes convinced everyone in the

room that I had a weapon," he replied. "With that much *perception* suddenly available, the weapon perceived *itself* into existence."

Please.

Just—please now.

He said boldly, "The scions of Silicon Valley may very well control *what* we believe, at least for the time being. But I am a technocrat of *how* we believe, Isobel."

"How *do* you believe, Lonso?" I said, baiting him just a little.

A fleeting, grim smile crossed his face, and then he said, "These days—extremely carefully."

❀   ❀   ❀

On the drive across town, conversation was sparse. At one point, Phyllis said, "So you're the Queen of Sparkle Dungeon. Funny, practically everyone I know wants to kill you." She hastily added, "In the game I mean."

"I'll be sure to worry about that approximately never," I said. We didn't talk after that.

The drive gave me time to ruminate. One question was nagging me: how did the Dauphine know to send Maddy to the fundraiser?

Then I remembered, I'd *told* the Dauphine that I had a fundraiser to plan and a release party to coordinate. If the Dauphine was truly sentient as I suspected, she might have a way to convey information to Maddy. Maddy might've been able to deduce that the combination of fundraiser and release party likely meant Violet and Cameron, which could lead her to Jenning & Reece. If Maddy still had hooks in Jenning & Reece somewhere—on their network, or with people she trusted inside—she could've maybe determined I managed the accounts for both Violet and Cameron. She could've even learned that I'd been recruited to Jenning & Reece in the first place because I was the Queen of Sparkle Dungeon. I had no idea what OPSEC measures Jenning & Reece implemented after Maddy took off.

So Maddy could show up at the party tonight. I was expected there at 6 p.m., but I could get Devin to cover for me, so I could arrive fashionably late along with a stream of other party guests. I'd have a big advantage: tonight's event was a costume party, where the guests were encouraged to come dressed as their favorite characters from the Sparkle Dungeon series. My costume was the perfect opportunity to hide myself in plain sight, and hopefully spot Maddy before she spotted me.

And then what?

I had the entire day to devise actual combat sequences. Improvising was all well and good, but I knew I'd gotten lucky against Maddy last night. Maybe the ones I devised today wouldn't be as potent as hers, but I bet I could surprise her all the same. I would also have Phyllis and Max watching my back, which provided a separate measure of reassurance.

And if I was sufficiently convincing, I might even get Cameron Kelly on my side.

10

The release party for Sparkle Dungeon 5 was an astounding feat of creative opulence.

The party wasn't open to the public. Only elite influencers and media stars and the stray celebrity venture capitalist were invited, because Cameron Kelly couldn't just open his enormous two-floor penthouse condo in a downtown high-rise to the riffraff, the hoi polloi, the teeming masses of those (like me) who actually played Sparkle Dungeon with more fervor than any of these spotlight-seeking moths.

"Costumes!" had been my Big Idea for the release party. "Costumes will be fun and engaging!" I'd said. "We'll get great photos out of it for social media!" Yes, I was actively promoting what in practice might veer toward extremely highbrow, borderline parody, if you wanted to frame it that way. But these people's costumes had that extra *something something* that indicated highly paid costume design professionals from the motion picture industry had been consulted early and often.

I recognized a minor TV star making a play for headlines by arriving as the Mighty Mirrored Paladin, clad in an absolutely glorious mirrored suit of armor, with an enormous glowing sword that changed colors and patterns in time with the music. She had two squires who followed her around, bouncing the beams from handheld lasers off her armor, and periodically she'd stop and they'd hand her a microphone and hold a mirror ball over her head as she sang the Mighty Mirrored Paladin's theme song.

Another woman came as the Marquess d'Ambient, wearing an astounding wig that was five feet tall and soaked in glitter. She was carried through the extremely crowded party in a pillow pit palanquin, on the shoulders of four burly Deep House Dandies, an obscure set of mysterious oracles who wore holographic pantaloons and ruffled, skintight muscle shirts.

Squadrons of Kaleidoscope Keepers wore prismatic attire that interlocked to create brilliant patterns when they stood next to each other. A Guardian of the Black Light Gate wore an elaborate helmet that bathed his entire suit of armor in black light, causing him to glow an eerie purple as he threaded his way through the morass of people.

Sophie Brodeur, the game's lead visual designer, came dressed as the classic version of the Dauphine of the Shimmer Lands, in a gorgeous fiber-optic ball gown that was covered with hundreds of tiny LEDs, creating a mesmerizing star field effect.

A group of six puppeteers controlled a gigantic, articulated, internally illuminated Dubstep Dragon, one of the most loathed villains in the series, largely because the soundtrack changed to dubstep when you fought it.

A conga line broke out, a recreation of a celebratory cutscene from SD2, where you're rewarded with a giant shindig in your honor after saving a family from the no-good dirty rotten Hard Candy Heroin gang. The encounter was a fan favorite due to the family's cute little puppy doggo, whose adorable catchphrase was "Subwoof!"

I was completely invisible at this party, surrounded by so many truly elaborate outfits and scenes and displays. That suited me just fine. I was satisfied to be one of only three people I saw who had chosen Graziella von Groove as their costume; the three of us even posed for an excellent selfie together. The costume included a half mask, so later on, it would probably be impossible to tell us apart in the picture.

The world-famous DJ Luscious was stationed in the loft balcony, providing beats for the evening. DJ Luscious was infamous for the sexy club jams "Getting a PhD in Getting Off" and "Sex You in the Sex Place (Enthusiastic Consent Mix)." The loft balcony provided a good view of the giant main room, where furniture had been cleared away to make room for a raised dance floor, with glorious colored panels that lit up from underneath.

Somewhere in this condo lurked Sparkle Dungeon's creator, Cameron Kelly.

His personal wealth undoubtedly outstripped everyone else here. Oh sure, he was one of the "good" gazillionaires. He was notably philanthropic: funder of several technology programs for underprivileged cohorts; designer and funder of an experimental STEM-focused school for inner city kids in his hometown, Chicago; funder of major UBI pilot programs throughout the United States and Canada; prominent supporter of the EFF and the ACLU; skeptical critic of the value that social technology brought to modern culture, who took an outspoken stand against harassment on his own platform; and of course, enlightened monarch of the Sparkle Realm, may his reign never dim.

You wanted to root for Cameron, even if you also desperately wanted to burn down the capitalist society that built him.

Just before midnight, the music stopped, and from a small burst of fog, Cameron finally appeared up in the loft. Tall, Black, a gaming world paragon fully embracing the costumed theme of the night, the Sparkle King himself held court above his fawning subjects.

His crown was festooned with giant, gaudy, incandescent colored lights. It must have been hot and heavy to wear around, but truthfully it was kind of charming to see old-school lightbulbs in the midst of this ocean of blinking LEDs, this fiber-optic frenzy. He wore a custom-tailored purple jumpsuit with elegant silver trim and metallic threading, and a cape that was bejeweled top to bottom, front and back. He stood in outrageous silver platform boots with small swiveling spotlights attached to the toes. And he carried a long glowing scepter, as tall as he was, that seemed to leave visual trails in the air when he waved it around.

DJ Luscious handed the Sparkle King a microphone.

"Loyal citizens of the Sparkle Realm, thank you all for joining me here this fine evening! I propose a toast!" He handed his scepter to DJ Luscious, who smoothly handed him a golden goblet in return, and then he said, "Here's to us, the Elite Adventurers of the Diamond Brigade, Sworn Protectors of the Sparkle Realm! May the crystalline lattice that brings us together never shatter!"

The entire party cheered.

The room suddenly fell dark and a dozen projectors lit up around the perimeter of the room, creating a 3D holographic image floating above the heads of the crowd. Sick beats faded in and then a woman's voice began speaking.

"I was desperate, lost, alone . . . but I never gave up hope."

A chill ran up my spine. That voice was the Dauphine of the Shimmer Lands.

An image came into focus: the Dauphine in her tattered ball gown, dirty, disheveled, roaming the desert she had patrolled since her introduction to the series. In the foreground, an ancient pedestal came into view, which she cautiously approached. A close-up of the pedestal revealed an ancient spell book, in the form of a booklet of

CD liner notes, with the title: *Crossfade Chronicles, Volume One: Litany of Loops*.

"At last I found a weakness in the alchemy that had trapped me here for so long."

She recited lyrics from the booklet, which we saw but couldn't hear, and suddenly a vast ragged wormhole tore itself open in front of her. With nothing to lose, she leapt through the wormhole . . .

. . . and emerged into a bleak, gray, industrial dystopia. She herself became black and white as she entered this new environment.

"The Sparkle Realm was not as I left it."

Suddenly a gigantic black skyship soared past above her head, a steampunk-themed armored vehicle in the shape of a sleek dirigible, powered by a dozen tiny rockets scattered across its hull. It was terrifying at that size, and the sound system had sufficient bass that you could feel the entire room vibrating.

"Spacecraft traveled between stars. The kingdom was now an alliance of planets. And I realized that something was terribly wrong. There was no sparkle to be seen. It was completely missing from reality."

We cut to an establishing shot from high atop a mountain cliff, where the sun in the sky seemed to be slowly shrinking and shadow swept across the Realm.

"We were approaching *the sparkle death of the universe*."

Suddenly we cut to a dramatic close-up of the Dauphine, standing tall on the bridge of a skyship, wearing the steampunk leathers and goggles that I had seen in my private encounters with her.

"I had to find a way to bring the sparkle back."

Dramatic scenes followed of the Dauphine flying through the air with her jetpack, pursued by same-day delivery drones firing volleys of dead glowsticks and empty Whip-It chargers at her; spacecraft above the planet festooned with the logos of competing streaming music services, battling to acquire the last exclusive content in the Realm; DJs falling prey mid–live stream to snarling algorithmic takedown notices that violently enforced the copyright claims of long-dead rights holders; and threaded through it all, the Dauphine punching, kicking, shooting, leaping, standard game maneuvers that were vastly more impressive when viewed in giant holographic format.

"The royal family is gone, the Diamond Brigade is nothing more than a myth. Am I a prism of hope in this future world, or a tarnished paladin on a doomed quest? Why was I brought to this time and place, and why am I still alone?"

The Dauphine's face filled our field of vision, bleeding and bruised, goggles cracked and hanging around her neck as she stared directly into the camera.

"But maybe I'm not alone. Maybe you can help me stop *sparklegeddon.*"

A sudden explosion of color startled us, visions of the Realm in previous games, to remind us of what was at stake. Maybe this was an alternate timeline we were seeing; maybe this grayscale outcome could still be avoided. Then a title card locked on screen:

SPARKLE DUNGEON 5: ENGINES OF ELECTRO. COMING SOON.

The lights came back up to the absolute roar of the sycophantic crowd. Even my cold dead heart stirred at that trailer. DJ Luscious "dropped the beat" as the kids say, and the party kicked back into gear. I glanced up to the top of the stairs.

Cameron Kelly had disappeared from the loft.

❀   ❀   ❀

I circulated slowly and methodically from room to room.

We'd turned most of the main-floor balcony into a pillow pit for folks who were overheated from dancing inside, but you could still find standing room near the outdoor bar to lean against the railing and peer out over the city skyline. That's where I found Cameron, chatting with a hip young startup founder, Tad Garrison, he/him, the young and sanctimonious white guy who invented the productivity app BlankChat. On the free tier, BlankChat locked you out of your phone for twenty-four hours, or you could pay a recurring subscription fee to be locked out of your phone for longer increments.

Tad had his arm around the waist of a gorgeous young individual in costume as the Faerie of Future House, painted blue from head to toe underneath an absolutely beautiful, wispy, sheer blue minidress, and a bright blue wig; the effect was very alluring, as it was in the game. Tad was just wearing khaki shorts and a Blank-Chat T-shirt. He was that strain of entrepreneur whose narrowness of focus and confident indifference to the world outside his target demographic drove him to heights of social obliviousness. He'd probably never played Sparkle Dungeon. Cameron clearly wanted to throw him off the balcony.

I stood in line for the outdoor bar, which steadily took me past Cameron's conversation. The Faerie of Future House was trying desperately to flirt with Cameron, but he maintained a neutral affect as he politely listened to Tad, nodding periodically and saying nothing as Tad tried to offer him a free subscription to BlankChat.

"You'll get a coupon code on parchment," Tad said, "hand signed by our CTO."

Seemed like Cameron was trapped in that conversation, honestly. What I really wanted to do was get Cameron somewhere private, which the Faerie of Future House obviously also wanted. But I figured someone as inherently delightful as myself could plausibly swoop in and try to save him from his interaction with Tad. I asked the bartender what Cameron was drinking and he said, "Diet Coke." I got one and meandered back toward Cameron.

Tad was still talking when I got back.

"BlankChat is running on all my devices," he said. "I haven't used a phone for the last four years. I didn't get to be the most productive CEO in Silicon Valley by wasting time on *phones* or *computers*."

Cameron nodded sagely.

"Do you know how many productive hours have been wasted on your game?" Tad said. "*Countless* productive hours—"

"No, they're countable," Cameron interrupted. "We log session times back to the server."

"We could feature your game as a case study on our marketing site—the perils of Sparkle Dungeon addiction."

"Probably not too many case studies on BlankChat addiction though, yeah?"

I nudged Cameron and offered him the Diet Coke. He smiled and accepted it, and as he did, I said, "*There* you are, Cameron! You said you were going to give me the tour, and I've been waiting downstairs for an *hour*!" I wasn't using power morphemes; I was just super charming in that way that comes naturally when you're in an outstanding costume.

"Oh," he said, quickly catching on to my rescue attempt, "I'm so sorry, I completely forgot about that! I've just been so busy hosting tonight, but that was very rude." He turned to Tad and said,

"Would you excuse me? I've been delinquent in my obligations to Graziella von Groove." He gave the Faerie of Future House a small bow and said, "Please send the Sparkle King's regards to your family and everyone in the Needle Drop Downs." Oh what fun!

I took his arm and led him back through the grand dining room. Along the way he said, "Thanks for the save. I will admit I don't recognize you with that mask on."

"I'm Isobel Bailie," I said, thinking he might recognize the name of his coordinator from Jenning & Reece. He shook his head slightly, so I added, "I'm the Queen of Sparkle Dungeon."

He stopped in his tracks and said, "Get out! Seriously?" Then he paused, and his face became instantly serious, "Ohhhh, so you're— you reported the Dauphine problem."

"Can we talk somewhere in private?" I ventured to ask.

He said, "I don't have anything to say about that issue." Impressive how fast his whole demeanor became subtly hostile to me.

"I have another issue to report," I said.

"I'm the CEO. I don't work support tickets."

"I was attacked last night at Violet Parker's fundraiser. By Maddy Price."

He seemed to freeze for a moment. I let my statement hang there, offering no further information to satisfy his hopefully dawning curiosity.

Finally, he said, "I'm sorry to hear that. Were you hurt?"

"Lost a few hit points but I'm recovering."

"Good. Isobel, I don't know what you're expecting from me tonight, but I'll just say I'm sorry to disappoint you and we'll have to leave it at that. I'll give you a piece of unsolicited advice, though. If you're somehow mixed up with Violet Parker and Maddy Price, you might want to reconsider your career trajectory."

He started to walk away from me. Apparently my natural charm wasn't sufficient for this encounter.

I knew it was probably a bad idea, but I launched into an improvised sequence of power morphemes all the same. I didn't want to hurt him, or brainwash him to do my bidding, or insert some elaborate lattice of ideas into his mind. I just wanted him to take me seriously. I didn't know how to mask them, so I had to deliver them right out in the open, taking the risk that others in the dining room might also hear them. It didn't matter to me. The improvisation was

meant to just gently induce a slight euphoric sense of wonder, or curiosity, and I was hoping he'd associate that curiosity with my tantalizing mention of Maddy.

The improvisation took me maybe ten seconds to deliver. That's
a damn long time when people are starting to stare in your direction with a vague sense of expectation that you will not be able to
satisfy whatsoever.

Slowly Cameron turned back toward me, displaying no sign that
the power morphemes had affected him in the slightest. Then he
closed the distance between us, so that no one else could hear him,
and said, "Very well, Queen of Sparkle Dungeon. You've won an audience with the Sparkle King."

11

His office on the first floor was huge, with filing cabinets full of miscellaneous computing and A/V gear jammed haphazardly against most of the walls—drawers full of joysticks, cables, hard drives, tools, and so on. He maintained a wide open central area for his state-of-the-art VR gaming platform—you strapped in at the waist, put your headset on, and the platform gave you a range of motion, like a combination treadmill and gyroscope. I sat in a plush, high-end office chair; his was an elaborate gaming chair with strange ergonomic cushioning, controls built into the arms, speakers built into the headrest, coolers for sodas mounted on the sides, the works.

We sat by his desk, which housed an elaborate computer workstation with a half-dozen video monitors, a few splayed-open game consoles of various brands, several models of VR headset strewn about carelessly, and many open cans of Diet Coke. A large electronic whiteboard stood nearby with snippets of code and pseudocode all over it.

The majority of the video monitors provided views into the security system he'd installed in his condo. High-resolution micro spy cameras were positioned everywhere, giving him live video footage that he could scroll through, and he could toggle between normal and infrared display. He could zoom out from a grid of video feeds to a floor plan of the entire condo, or he could zoom in on a specific location to get a closer look. Tiny drones gave him mobile coverage when he wanted it. Face recognition identified each guest, constantly comparing images against the invitation database that security was using at the door. Using this system, Cameron could determine exactly who it was, for instance, that was having sex behind DJ Luscious in the loft at that exact moment.

"That's very creepy," I said.

"I'm a technologist," he muttered. "I do things because they're possible, not because they're ethical."

I realized as I settled in that two of the side monitors were looping the video capture of my most recent encounter with the Dauphine. One was from my player POV, and one was from god mode

POV, hovering near the ceiling looking down on the whole scene. He saw me staring at the scenes.

"At first, we just thought this video was machinima," he said, referring to a style of animated video art that utilized existing game engines and game footage to create new original stories. "Now I have nearly fifty developers, network architects, infosecurity specialists, system administrators, quality assurance engineers, and IT professionals working on figuring out how this performance of hers is even possible." He sighed deeply. "So thank you for your bug report."

"It's not a bug," I said. "She's sentient, right?"

"No, the AI is not sentient," he replied, a little peevishly if you asked me.

"Then what are all those people you just mentioned actually looking for? I mean, what are they expecting to find?"

He changed the subject, saying, "What did you come here to discuss? I'm sure we'd both like to get back to the party. Well, I'm sure *you* would. I'd like to sneak out of the building in a catering van and go hide in a Holiday Inn."

"Did Lonso send you the video he took of Maddy and me this morning?" I said.

"You allowed Lonso Drake to take video footage of you—on purpose?" he replied. "You must be deep in the shit right now."

He pulled up a secure, end-to-end encrypted email service, and sure enough, found an email from Lonso with a paragraph of text and the video attached. Without a word, he launched the video.

As Cameron watched, he seemed unusually disturbed or agitated, whereas I felt the same mild stupefaction from hearing Maddy speak on the recording that I felt when I was in the room with her for the actual experience.

When it was over, he sat back in his chair and seemed very exasperated. "Isobel, nothing personal," he said, "but you seem to be an epicenter of extremely bad news."

"Maddy's probably coming here tonight," I said.

"Right. And you came here anyway?"

The small amount of confidence I'd started the night with seemed to drain away all at once.

"I didn't want to miss the party," I said.

He was silent for a long moment.

"Well, if she knows anything at all about the Dauphine," he said at last, "maybe she can be useful to me. Because if I can't solve this Dauphine problem you reported, I can't risk launching Sparkle Dungeon 5. So what's your plan to take her down?"

Oh. Uh.

"I was hoping you could help me with that," I said.

"Ha," he replied. "The Queen needs tactical assistance in combat? Unheard of."

"No—this isn't like the game at all."

"It's *exactly* like the game, but for the first time in years, you're facing someone who's many levels above you. You can't just go toe to toe with her. You need to surprise her somehow. Spring a trap. Which would require you to, uh, go back in time and *set* a trap. Which, okay, so you might just be fucked here."

"Isn't there something you can do? Some unexpected skill you've got? I mean—Violet can perfectly mask power morphemes in her voice, Lonso can make guns materialize in his hand, Olivia is the genius researcher . . . what's *your* superpower here?"

"If you were me, and you had a 'superpower,' would you just blurt that out to a complete stranger?"

"I've been on top of your leaderboard for eight years, Cameron! That's how I got pulled into this whole mess in the first place. Doesn't that count for something?" When he didn't respond, I said, "Why are you even *involved* with these people? Why are you training legions of gamers to use power morphemes when they grow up? What are you getting out of all this?"

"Let's not change the subject," he said. "Here's the deal. I'm immune to power morphemes. I can hear them and recognize them, I can even deliver them, but they don't affect me."

"Does that mean you don't have punctuation marks coursing through your brain like everyone else?"

"Of course I do. But I was born with partial congenital hearing loss. I've got the most cutting edge cochlear implants available, but power morphemes don't work when amplified digitally. So certain frequencies or some other aspect of power morphemes we don't even know about must be muted or just shaved off, somewhere in between the implant's microphone and the electrode array that fires off signals to my auditory nerve."

Ah, so when he played the recording of Maddy just now, that was the first time he'd ever actually experienced the effects of power morphemes. That would explain how unsettled he seemed as he got a surprise taste of his own spellcasting technology without warning.

"How many power morphemes do you know?" I asked.

"You want to know what level I am, is that it?"

"How many?"

"I know one fewer than Olivia at all times," he said. "As a courtesy." After a beat, he asked, "What about you? Have you developed a 'superpower' yet?"

That was a good question. Compared to Maddy or any of these people really, I felt like I was running around with a squirt gun during a live-fire engagement. But that didn't make me helpless.

"I improvise well under pressure."

A series of red dots suddenly started appearing all throughout the security feeds on his monitors, along with distinct loud pings announcing each one. He swiveled around to take in this new information, and then muttered, "I think it's time to improvise."

❊　❊　❊

Each red dot corresponded to a person that face recognition couldn't find on the invite list. We counted twenty-two before they stopped appearing from nowhere. They were spread throughout the condo, sweeping slowly, dressed in street clothes which made them easy to spot in the crowd once you knew to look for people who weren't in costume. They wore thick jackets, thick pants, scarves, leaving very little exposed skin. These people did not intend to fall victim to any Tasers tonight.

"Holy shit," he said.

A familiar sensation swept through me, the rush of adrenaline that accompanied the start of a major combat. We were about to make history: the Queen of Sparkle Dungeon and the Sparkle King himself, side by side on the battlefield for the very first time.

"They're going to fucking kill us, aren't they?" I said.

"Hopefully just you," he said.

Suddenly a new red dot appeared on the screen with a loud ping. Fuck—someone was in the office with us.

I spun around to see Mohawk standing on the guardrails of the VR platform, bits of his form around the edges still materializing. He seemed disoriented, like he couldn't quite understand where he was yet, or like he was temporarily dazed from the strain of appearing out of thin air in the first place. I realized this was the perfect opportunity to catch him off guard.

Then he locked eyes with me, and I froze up completely, becoming in that moment the personification of *oh shit*.

He took a deep breath, clearly readying an attack.

Cameron swung his prop scepter and smacked Mohawk on the side of the head, knocking him backward off the guardrails into a hard fall on the floor behind it. The scepter was made of a flimsy plastic which shattered from the impact. Mohawk was probably more hurt from the fall than from the blow; regardless, he began delivering a power morpheme sequence from the floor.

"Feel free to start 'improvising' any time here," Cameron said to me.

12

Mohawk let out a freakish, guttural shriek—much louder than I would have guessed possible, and I realized he wasn't attacking, he was summoning help.

Cameron pushed me toward the door and I didn't need convincing to run. I figured he'd be right behind me, but he slammed the office door behind me and locked himself in with Mohawk. Locked doors seemed irrelevant in a scenario where people could appear and disappear at will, but maybe I was missing something.

My goal now was to become invisible. My mask was hanging around my neck, and I slapped it on. In the hallway outside Cameron's office, I saw an intruder, prowling my direction. The revelers in the vicinity provided a wide berth. I can't imagine how people rationalized the sudden appearance of these people out of thin air in the first place. Were they like, "Oh, people just appeared out of thin air, are Penn and Teller filming a special here tonight?" or "Oh, people just appeared out of thin air, who invited those talented and/or annoying Improv Everywhere kids?" or "Oh, people just appeared out of thin air, did I take *all* the designer pharma from China or is it just cut with mycotoxins like last time?" People were so blasé these days, I mean, fuck.

We had ten trained security professionals stationed throughout the party. We had one at the door checking invitations, one keeping an eye on the locked door to Cameron's bedroom suite, and the others wandering in patterns that enabled unobtrusive coverage of the major areas of the condo—balconies, dining room and kitchen, dance floor, loft.

And Phyllis and Max were lurking on the periphery of the action somewhere. I assumed they'd seen me going into and out of Cameron's office. I could only hope they'd also noticed our new friends.

I slipped out onto the raised dance floor, which was jammed full of revelers at the moment. I wasn't sure how anyone outside of Cameron's office could've heard Mohawk's shriek over the music blasting out of the powerful sound system, but maybe Maddy's squad was especially attuned to that noise. You couldn't rule out any goddamn thing as being more or less possible anymore, which was absurdly frustrating.

Mohawk knew what my costume looked like, though, so that could be a problem if he got away from Cameron. Oh and also—hiding in a crowd full of innocent people was a rotten tactic anyway, turning them all into human shields or whatever. This was going to go south fast, I could feel it.

❀   ❀   ❀

Cameron stepped out of his office. His crown was missing, he'd shed his golden cape, and he carried the plastic scepter with its shattered end high in the air. It didn't light up anymore, but he was still a striking figure. He was making himself a target, I realized—they'd certainly be on the lookout for him, after all. I imagined he was going to try to buy time for me to escape, but I had to believe anyone actually trying to leave the party right now would also become a target.

The doorway to Cameron's office was situated in a hallway that opened onto the dance floor on one end, and went down the other direction and around a corner into the dining room. An intruder prowling in that hallway spotted Cameron emerging, and I think Cameron spotted the intruder at the same time. Some kind of verbal exchange seemed to happen, and the intruder dropped to the ground. Moments later, two more intruders started slowly closing in on him from the far side of the dance floor from me. Seemed like as long as he was one on one, Cameron could avoid harming anyone but his opponent, but if he needed to attack more than one person at a time, he'd have to shout his power morphemes loud enough that bystanders might be in the area of effect. Suboptimal—I wanted to help.

But I was distracted by a commotion up in the loft. DJ Luscious was surrounded by several intruders, arguing about something. A member of security intervened; suddenly both security and DJ Luscious were on the floor. The intruders waved to someone at the bottom of the stairs—Maddy, now ascending toward the loft. One of the intruders found the microphone that Cameron had used earlier. If Maddy got on the microphone, with her ability to broadcast power morpheme sequences, we'd be looking at a lot of collateral damage.

Cameron could fend for himself. I had to stop Maddy somehow. I wasn't a paladin in the game per se, a bit too greedy for artifacts and treasure most of the time, but I also didn't let people bully first-level characters if I could help it, and the people at this party were zero-level characters in this situation, with no way to resist a loud psychological assault.

I knew something they didn't know, though, which was the location of the fuse box for the condo, in a walk-in storage closet directly underneath the loft. We'd supervised an upgrade to the electrical in the condo to support the requirements DJ Luscious gave us for his sound system. I made a beeline for the storage closet in question, which was hidden behind a fiber-optic curtain meant to distract people from snooping, since the closet had no lock.

Inside I pushed past stacks of crates, bins, and boxes of crap he'd stored here after making several trips to Burning Man, releasing clouds of suddenly disturbed dust into the air, and made it to the fuse box. I flipped the switches marked "loft" and was rewarded with loud cries of disappointment from out on the dance floor as the phat beats vanished.

The sound system was dead, for now at least.

I turned and realized someone had seen me come in. An intruder ripped down the LED curtain and stood in the doorway, dramatically backlit by stage lights in the air above the dance floor, which now swung lazily back and forth for no apparent reason without a beat to synchronize with. We made eye contact, and this time, I decided not to freeze in the face of an opponent.

A blazing whisper came out of my mouth, searing and caustic, like a paper cut with a jagged acid edge, and the intruder recoiled away from me, but only for a moment. Then we were both hurling sequences at each other simultaneously.

My eyesight got very dim and I realized I was plummeting down a long dark well, with just a pinpoint of light above me to give any sense of perspective. No, I realized quickly—that was just my consciousness refusing to participate in whatever experience my attacker was attempting to foist on me. I almost blacked out, then a painful crash hit me full on—it was my attacker, collapsing forward and losing consciousness, landing hard on me on the way to the floor.

I resisted the urge to shout "first!"

I'd used a quick three-part sequence on him: number eighty-two, the massive regret of a life wasted in pursuit of vapor; followed by number eighty-nine, the colossal embarrassment of realizing your foolishness was entirely on display; and then concluded with number fifty-five, the sadness of your every loss, compacted into a fist against you. As I suspected, this combination was a severe psychic blow.

As my mind clambered back from the brink of shutting down, I heard confusion out on the dance floor. I peered out the closet doorway just in time to see Cameron landing hard in the center of the floor, on the receiving end of some kind of shove from multiple intruders. The revelers splayed aside in every direction, leaving Cameron in the center of his own pool of light. He looked up, spotted me in his closet, and winked at me, before bellowing at whoever shoved him onto the floor. The sound was an astonishing combination of every vowel sound plus fifteen vowels that didn't actually exist, which created a shock wave that probably knocked people over purely via its concussive effect, let alone whatever psychological effect the sequence also had.

Moments later, Cameron scrambled to his knees and aimed a similar effect up into the loft. Behind him, some asshole intruder was literally on the verge of clubbing Cameron with a baton. I screamed, partially in anger—poor showing, to bring melee weapons into a mage battle—and the intruder stumbled, giving Cameron an opening to throw an elbow that connected hard with the intruder's nose.

This was all happening both incredibly fast and much too slowly.

Cameron took a run toward me and slid through the doorway into the storage closet. I slammed the door shut, and we stacked a few boxes in front of it. Thing was, they could all just materialize inside the closet, right? Except they'd all be momentarily disoriented as they arrived, one by one, and we'd be able to systematically clock them. I hoped, anyway. Then I heard a fucking gunshot, and then people were screaming.

The thing was—security didn't have firearms. Cameron refused to allow it.

Another shot rang out, and I understood it better this time—it was a vocal approximation of a gunshot, a high-fidelity impersonation, an effect designed to frighten people into believing they were hearing shots without requiring firearms at all. You could get people to scatter out of your way, and more importantly, you could get people to listen to you if they thought you had firearms.

Maddy was screaming orders at her people from the loft, orders at the party guests to shut the fuck up and lie down on the floor, orders to Cameron and me to show ourselves.

Fact was, now we were trapped.

"Okay, somewhere in here, I have a flamethrower," he muttered.

"Not helpful!" I exclaimed.

"Says you!" he shouted back. "Wait, c'mere."

He led me through a maze of his scattered stuff to a small door I hadn't noticed on the far side of the closet. This one had a built-in combo lock, which he swiftly unlocked, and then he opened the door to reveal a tiny hallway that probably led to the dining room if I understood the layout of the condo as well as I thought I did. We raced down the hallway, but then it turned unexpectedly and we arrived at a ladder.

"What the fuck?" I said.

"Doesn't everyone have secret passageways?" he replied, irritated at the question.

I followed him up the ladder and we emerged into a big sitting room, with a large TV on the wall, a few couches, a recliner.

"My chambers," he explained as he slammed the hatch shut behind me. He went ahead and shoved the recliner over the top of the hatch. I was starting to understand the value of putting impediments in their way. If they were disoriented after they teleported somewhere, they wouldn't want to do it very often, and they wouldn't be thrilled about doing it into locations with unknown conditions. Mohawk landing right in Cameron's office was a prime example of the risk they took by coming here that way.

He led me through the sitting room into his actual bedroom, which was enormous and unkempt, with its own VR platform in one corner, and a laptop on a nightstand near the bed. He dashed into his walk-in closet, and I followed him to the doorway. He pulled a small gun safe down from a shelf and began unlocking it.

"You ever fired a gun before?" he asked.

"Used to go shooting with my dad," I said.

"I hate guns," he said.

He flipped open the case. Atop the red velvet lining inside was a small silver horn, the size of a bicycle horn but without the squeeze pump, like a tiny bugle with a handle. Next to it was a magician's wand: a gnarled wooden rod, tapered to a point, and lacquered it seemed.

He handed me the horn.

"What's this?" I asked. "Tell me it summons *deus ex machinas*."

"Hardly," he said. "This is the Horn of Magnification."

"What about that?" I said, pointing at the wand.

"That's a ninety-dollar remote control I haven't figured out how to use yet," he said, snapping the case shut and dropping it on the floor behind him. He took the horn back.

We were momentarily distracted by the sudden appearance of one of Maddy's squad, materializing in a standing crouch on the bed nearby. Cameron and I both launched into our own respective combat sequences while the intruder was still disoriented, and we hit them so hard they instantly lost consciousness. Then we resumed our conversation.

"So what's this do exactly?" I asked. "Is it—a magic item?"

"No, Isobel, because this is *reality* and we don't have *magic items* in reality," he said. "For hundreds of years people used megaphones like this to amplify their voices. Like bullhorns, before we enhanced them with electronics. They used to call them 'speaking-trumpets.'

"I don't know how to broadcast power morphemes," he continued, "or transmit them digitally. I don't know how to amplify them with electronics. But I have *proven* with this megaphone that I can *definitely* make them fucking *louder*."

❧   ❧   ❧

Cameron's bedroom suite opened out directly into the loft space. He grabbed his laptop and pulled up the security cameras: Maddy and three of her squad were still in the loft, arguing about something. Opening the bedroom door would put us directly behind Maddy and her crew. A couple party guests sat on a love seat nearby; if I was not mistaken, they were dressed as members of the Glowstick Guard. The security footage was supposedly in color but the lighting was muddy, so I couldn't tell if they were friendly blue Glowstick Guards or evil red Glowstick Guards. Sometimes you'd even see a green Glowstick Guard in the wild and you'd have to test their beatmatching skills to determine if you should kill them. I digress.

Carefully I opened the door, as slowly as I could manage it, and somehow, they didn't seem to notice us. I dropped to my knees as Cameron positioned himself behind me.

"Oh wow," said one of the Glowstick Guards, giving us away as they spotted the Sparkle King himself in their midst.

Fucking evil red Glowstick Guards, I swear.

Maddy and her comrades turned toward us, almost in comical slow motion.

Cameron began to deliver an amazingly potent sequence via the Horn of Magnification, producing a cone attack that bypassed the two Glowstick Guards entirely, and only seemed to clip me a bit for a few points of ouch. Instead the full force of the blast was directed at the surprised attackers. The sequence seemed to burn itself into my brain as I heard it, worming its way directly into my own arsenal. But the Horn cranked the amplitude of the sequence up so loud that it was painful to hear as a general sound in the environment, even if you weren't caught up in the actual psychological effect.

Maddy vanished almost instantly. She'd abandoned her squad mates, whose reflexes were not as keen. One of the three intruders was lifted off his feet and flung backward down the stairs to the dance floor. Another was flipped up end over end and tossed like a doll onto the DJ decks. The third was punched down onto his back on the floor with a painful-sounding crack.

I froze with horror. Hell of a thing I'd just seen.

The Glowstick Guards shrieked and one of them dropped their wineglass. I watched it fall in slow motion out of the corner of my eye, realizing I was in the flow state, observing events just slightly ahead of their literal timing, waiting for my own opening.

A shriek came from the dance floor, similar to the shriek we'd heard from Mohawk in Cameron's office. Maddy was summoning her people to her. Cameron and I slowly made our way to the railing of the loft and surveyed the scene below. There was Maddy, standing resolute, as her squad came out of the woodwork and appeared around the periphery of the raised dance floor, forming a protective ring around Maddy.

A couple of fights broke out—members of security appearing with batons or just using fists, trying to take down some of the intruders, finding themselves thoroughly rebuffed solely by the sound of power morphemes, dropping like flies. The crowd of revelers gave Maddy's crew a very wide berth, practically pooling at the other end of the condo, in the dining room and kitchen.

The irritation in Maddy's eyes burned into me. I glared some raging aggravation right back at her. What in the name of sweet merciful fuck had I ever done to warrant this bullshit?

But Cameron and I were definitely outnumbered. Now she had maybe fourteen people down there, and she was giving them orders, getting them ready for something. Shit—Mohawk wandered into view, looking no worse for wear and steady on his feet. Okay, so now there were fifteen people down there, versus one admittedly incredible Horn wielded by Cameron Kelly, and the significantly less impressive skill set of a certain Isobel Bailie.

"Use the Horn," I said quietly.

He shook his head and offered it to me.

"Blew out my voice," he whispered.

I took it from him. If I'd known the Horn was essentially a single-shot weapon, I wouldn't have let him use it in the loft. He could design a good combat game, but that didn't make him good at combat tactics. We should have saved the Horn for a moment like, oh, right now, when our foes were conveniently assembling below us into a large clumped target. I could try to take them all out with the Horn myself, but I was drastically less skilled than Cameron, and if I failed, I wouldn't be able to defend myself with blown vocal cords.

"I shouldn't have come here," I muttered sadly.

"At least here you had a fighting chance," Cameron whispered. "You still do."

Cameron had noticed something, which took me a few seconds longer to recognize. On the other side of the room from us, far beyond the dance floor, behind Maddy and her crew who were completely focused on us and consequently facing the opposite direction, I saw Phyllis and Max, holding the door open to the hallway outside the condo.

They were waving in a stream of new combatants, who wore orange hazard suits and faceless, reflective silver masks, chanting softly in a manner that phased gently in and out of unison, to unsettling effect.

Gorvod's Frenzy had arrived.

"Oh look, it's the *deus ex machina* you requested," Cameron whispered.

"No," I said, "this is pretty much the exact opposite."

❈   ❈   ❈

Their chanting was muffled by their masks, but I recognized the steadily building wall of sound they were developing. In the game, they used this wall of sound to cast spells in unison, but here, they were delivering sequences of legitimate, honest to Gorvod power morphemes.

I watched a swarm pour through the door and slowly move to surround the dance floor without engaging any of Maddy's crew. Indeed they were extremely careful not to nudge or bump or get within close reach of anyone standing up on the dance floor proper. Their collective volume increased as their swarm grew, and Maddy's bewildered crew took in the scene without interfering, waiting for Maddy to give a signal. Yes, they were surrounded now, but they could teleport out whenever they felt like it, and meanwhile, Maddy was curious (like me) about what the hell these people were up to.

By the time about thirty people had collected in a broad ring around the lip of the dance floor, Maddy deputized Mohawk to take action. He tested a few sequences at the hazard suits nearest him, nothing that seemed particularly loud or aggressive, but somehow, the collective response from the swarm seemed to cancel out the frequencies Mohawk had utilized. It was like he'd punched the surface of a swimming pool, causing a rippling sonic effect in response from the swarm that displaced and dispersed his attack.

Meanwhile, they were getting louder, in a pattern I recognized from the game. Right now, they were still just warming up. I always wondered if this was just intimidation or if it really played some role in synchronizing their spellcasting. I still wondered. I wondered about all kinds of unnatural shit lately and yet somehow this got bumped back up to the top of my list.

Mohawk stepped up to one of the hazard suits and smacked the mask off; it clattered to the floor, a plastic trifle of no particular consequence. The person behind the mask was just some rando, as you'd say online, just some easily ignored person in a hazard suit who could be mistaken for any of these other randos in a crowd, probably. Didn't even bother making eye contact with Mohawk, just kept chanting, and Mohawk couldn't decide if he was pissed or amused, but either way, he spat a sequence directly into the face of the rando, who fell backward and was gracefully caught by the other randos in hazard suits swarming right there. Their numbers steadily grew and their chanting got steadily louder.

Suddenly a louder voice made its presence known and a series of quick call-and-response chants followed. This was new to me. The leader's voice was tuning the others somehow, ratcheting up the drama in their chants, choosing more complex sequences than the chants they'd used to lull Maddy and her people into thinking this was just some quaint little stunt. No indeed, Gorvod's Frenzy didn't fuck around, not one bit. I felt jittery, like I'd smoked eight cigarettes at once, and realized I'd been lulled, too; I hadn't moved, just stood there, gripping the railing, almost in a trance.

A loud crackling hum suddenly snapped me back to alertness. The sound was emanating from some indistinct point above the dance floor. If you could imagine generating an overtone inside your mouth, this felt like they were generating an overtone inside the room, manipulating environmental acoustics to their advantage. They could maybe use that overtone as a component in multiple interlocking sequences, and just like in the game, they couldn't really direct it straight at a single target, but I bet they could set off burst effects all over the damn place. A super loud popping sound came from seemingly nowhere and Mohawk recoiled back several steps, like he'd been shocked by a nine-volt battery on his tongue, only the battery was higher voltage and also invisible and also he was deeply fucked.

Maddy shouted an order like a drill sergeant under fire, and her crew cut loose with a devastating series of vocal attacks. I was clear up in the loft and it was so painful my eyes watered and my face felt suddenly sunburned in the worst way. Hazard suits started dropping like flies, but for a time at least, anytime one fell, two stepped up to plug the gap. Maddy's people were striking individual blows, but the seemingly ambient attacks from Gorvod's Frenzy as a collective increased as well, smacking Maddy's people around like they were pinballs.

Maddy herself kept her eyes on me, well aware she was in a bad spot. I was holding the Horn, which she didn't know was a one-shot, and Cameron Kelly was standing right next to me, apparently unfazed by what he saw unfolding. If she tried teleporting up here to attack, she'd be disoriented long enough for us to act. And she was vulnerable to us anyway as long as her people were distracted by the hazard suits. Sadly I didn't have an attack that I could project above the increasing din, and I didn't believe Maddy had one either. We were in perilously close quarters, but just out of reach of each other.

The air above the dance floor suddenly seemed to ripple. One of the stage lights sparked brightly and then its bulb blew out. This was next-level Gorvod's Frenzy, for sure. I thought I heard a chorus of children somewhere, chanting and taunting at the same time. Another lightbulb blew out above them, then to make matters worse, a steel safety cable snapped and a stage light plummeted to the dance floor, landing with an immense crash and exploding into pieces mere feet from where Maddy stood.

Maddy lost her temper and barked several new commands. Her crew suddenly took on a new demeanor.

See, that was the thing about Gorvod's Frenzy: they were arguably innovative spellcasters, but they were shit for melee combat.

❀ ❀ ❀

Mohawk threw the first punch, smashing someone's mask into little plastic pieces and presumably smashing the face behind the mask a bit as well. Maddy's people were skilled at both power morphemes and physical weapons—expandable batons, billy clubs, stun guns, fists. A sudden flurry of violence drove hazard suits hard to the ground in a sickening wave. I'd never seen anything so intensely brutal, and instinctively I turned away.

And then let out an involuntary shriek, because the intruder we'd immobilized in the bedroom was now quite actively mobile (the major drawback of a sleep spell, of course, is the fucking thing wears off), and about to bring a club down on the back of Cameron's head. Without thinking, I leapt to intercept, crashing into the attacker's midsection and taking us both down in a heap.

Naturally I'd tackled someone approximately twice my size, which I realized as I was lifted up one-handed and daintily hurled through the air. I landed hard on a glass coffee table, which contrary to the movies did not shatter into a zillion pieces; but that meant my head was free to bounce off the glass before I slid to the floor, dazed, nearly in the laps of the two Glowstick Guards who remained frozen on the love seat, the sick red glow of the EL wire in their costumes a perfectly disturbing accent to the shit situation I found myself in.

My attacker was on their feet almost instantly. Cameron was caught defenseless without his voice, and he went down hard at the wrong end of a bad kidney punch and a shove that toppled him over. Satisfied their prey was in hand, they turned to me. I spat my best combat sequences at them ("best" meaning "all of them delivered in a major fucking hurry"), but the riotous cacophony downstairs was drowning me out. They pulled out a stun gun from a belt pouch as they swiftly advanced.

Joke was on them, however, because I still had the Horn in my hand. I brought it to my lips and I *screamed* into that thing, and I don't know *where* that sequence came from—it wasn't Cameron's, which I suddenly couldn't remember—and it wasn't one of the combat sequences I'd managed to prepare earlier that day. It was like a pure stream of glitter lava piped directly from the molten glitter core at the center of the Sparkle Realm, unleashed by command of the Goddess of Glamour & Groove herself, who alone took interest in the affairs of those devoted ravers who always chased the dawn to squeeze one last deep house track out of each and every night; it was like she'd given me a flamethrower but then loaded it with glitter lava, except the flamethrower was the Horn and the glitter lava was my voice, and it all just came together even though the existence of the Goddess of Glamour & Groove wasn't actually canon in the first place.

Under these conditions did I convince my attacker to take that stun gun and place it directly upon their own exposed throat, which caused a very satisfying spasm, and a windmilling backward onto the floor for further spasms. They'd survive, but they probably wouldn't enjoy it a whole lot for the next several minutes.

I clambered to my feet and stumbled toward Cameron, glimpsing the dance floor in the process. As a full-scale riot unfolded behind her, Maddy marched up the stairs to the loft with Mohawk right behind her. We needed to run, but two more intruders emerged from the bedroom, blocking that door. They might have seen my attack with the Horn, and were quite wary of me, but they weren't about to just move out of my way. My voice was on fire, so much so that I could barely catch a breath without exploding in pain that rippled all up and down my nervous system. I wouldn't be using the Horn again tonight.

Maddy and Mohawk arrived in the loft, took in the scene—Cameron and I breathless on our knees, several people unconscious or incapacitated on the floor around us—and Maddy seemed impressed despite herself. Mohawk grabbed my arms and hauled me to my feet, and Maddy growled something at me that I didn't understand or hear.

Then, to my absolute and utter delight and surprise, I heard singing.

It was a crystal-clear tenor voice, ringing throughout the room, cutting through the violence and the riots and the screaming and the pain, suppressing all of it, enveloping the entirety of the environment with sweet, pure tones.

The hands gripping me let go of my arms, and like in a dream,

Maddy and I locked eyes, but for once, we were comrades in wonder, amazement coursing through our veins, a warm glow infusing all of us here in the loft with a sense that reality was literally healing itself from the damage we'd just inflicted upon it. I wanted to cry, just out of sheer relief. The moment unfolded into several and then a minute had passed and no one said anything, no one fought, we could finally catch a breath. All our attention turned to the calming yet powerful voice that now inspired us to be better people, stitched us together on a journey we hardly understood, dropped barriers and showed glimpses of true and honest magic in a universe that was otherwise so perilously dark.

Bradford Jenning stood in the center of the dance floor, singing a stream of power morpheme sequences, masked within lyrics I didn't understand, in a romance language I didn't recognize.

His voice was rich and commanding, and yet gentle and soothing at the same time. I watched Maddy struggling to find any way to resist, and steadily losing the fight, even as Mohawk and her other comrades readily succumbed to the welcoming pool of loveliness that Bradford's voice produced.

A second voice joined him then—a beautiful soprano, who knew the same exact sequences, adding unexpected and beautiful tight harmony to an already astounding experience. Devin walked across the dance floor toward Bradford, the two of them smiling and radiating sheer enthusiasm for the experience they were having together and generating for others. They were interconnected via this song, and their hope was contagious.

For the first time since I'd walked into Olivia's lab for the original usability tests all those months ago, the nagging sense that I wasn't good enough at my life or at any of this just dissipated, the fear that I was going to disappoint Olivia or really anyone I'd ever known just vanished, and I felt relaxed, and tranquil, and at peace.

Cameron, of course, was immune.

"Blah blah *deus ex machina*," he muttered at no one in particular.

PART THREE

LOGOSPHERE

01

Maddy and I stared at each other, sweat pouring down our faces, like we were lovers coming back from the brink of disaster.

"I'll let you two have a little moment here," Cameron said as he dragged himself toward the stairs.

"Is that what this is?" Maddy whispered. "Are we having a moment?" She seemed surprised by her own voice, as though she'd failed a sarcasm check and landed on sincerity instead.

"Why do you hate me so much?" I said impulsively, even though I couldn't believe she was motivated by something that simple.

She shook her head impatiently and said, "Saving my hatred for those who deserve it." Relief washed over me. But if she didn't hate me, then what *did* she feel about me?

For my part, I felt like I could drown myself in her. Bradford and Devin kept singing, and unpredictable emotions came over me in waves, like this feeling that Maddy and I were just beginning the first truly meaningful stage of our connection, and I shouldn't let the past interfere with the present. The past was over and gone; the present was a gift that we shared; the future was a promise you couldn't possibly keep. Stick to right here and now, looking into her eyes, mesmerized by what you see there.

❀　　❀　　❀

I mean, you can experience a feeling, and know exactly how irrational it is, but the feeling justifies itself perfectly well regardless, and I was *flooded* with feelings—not just for Maddy, but for Cameron, and Bradford, and Devin, and everyone all around me. They weren't the same feelings at the same intensity in every direction, but there was a clear continuum in which I understood us all to be part of a unique tapestry, highly temporary and fluid in nature, and my psychic defenses came fluttering down like billowing fabric slipping off a clothesline in a gentle breeze.

Bradford had established control of the situation via singing, and he maintained control by trading off singing with Devin. As long as one of them was singing, the general aura of blissed-out interconnectedness persisted, in a range that extended as far as their voices could reach. The closer you got to the epicenter of the dance floor, where Bradford and Devin stationed themselves, the warmer and more addictive the sensations.

People who wandered in from the dining room or the balconies quickly tuned in to what was happening. Pillows and cushions migrated from the balconies toward the dance floor; the loft got increasingly tricked out as well, since the acoustics in the room made the loft an excellent vantage point for listening. If you needed to wander out of the perimeter of their voices, like to go to the bathroom, you'd feel it start to wear off and you'd almost get a headache from the sudden dopamine crash, and you'd hurry back to the soothing embrace of the circle as quickly as you could.

The time was just a little past two in the morning.

Bradford assumed a natural leadership role, instigating a rigorous process to get the party back into a zone where the guests could eventually leave here without feeling traumatized by what they'd seen. We had a window of time available to us during which we could reimprint a different emotional version of the night's events on the guests—generously, you could call this a therapeutic or healing act, or if you wanted a more sinister interpretation, you could call this cauterizing emotional responses before they fully developed into lasting panic or fear. Bradford deputized each of us to work within a subset of the condo's current population to triage the situation on the ground, restore equilibrium, and maintain peace.

Cameron worked the crowd of partygoers, systematically planting suggestions with his guests that his parties were always like this, which is why he rarely held them—he wanted these occasions to retain a special quality about them. In truth he was also methodically scrubbing any notion that this was an unnatural event from everyone who'd listen. A flow of selfies and photos taken by the guests was probably loose in the wild already, but careful observers of our hashtags would notice a distinct change in the character of the photos coming out of the party shortly after 2 a.m.

Devin gathered the catering staff together, and performed a similar function. They were paid staff, and while they could believe that all the guests gathering in the loft and on the dance floor were sharing a particularly powerful drug trip or whatever, none of them had imbibed any substances, and some were confused by their change of psychological state as a result. Devin soothed their concerns with wispy but sincere talk of how pivotal their contributions were in restoring order after the fracas everyone clearly remembered, and gave them permission to relax and consider themselves off duty, but welcomed them to stay and enjoy the remainder of the event.

The catering staff, bless their souls, somehow managed to get it together enough to start circulating trays of fruit, cheese, and bread to nourish the sleepless masses. Their catering uniforms accumulated various bits and pieces from an assortment of costumes, donated by guests to help these folks feel like part of the unfolding scene instead of outsiders forced to watch and serve the surreal decadence unfolding around them.

Meanwhile, the security team regrouped among themselves to take stock of their injuries, and to discuss a rotation that allowed them to relax while still having Cameron's back in case any further surprises emerged.

Maddy and I took stock of several bad injuries among Maddy's crew and Gorvod's Frenzy. Bradford clearly wanted to keep city authorities away from this location at all costs, while tending to the needs of these people. Phyllis and Max summoned medical assistance from the Church, which maintained an emergency medical clinic on its campus. It was a scary wait for these first responders to arrive. Bradford and Devin could provide a form of psychological anesthesia via their singing, but not proper physical healing, and it was tough for me to unlearn the preconception in my mind that the Church was a weird danger and city authorities were our supposed saviors in the face of trouble like this.

But the Church came through with doctors and nurses who could triage the assorted injuries, and to my shock, I watched a few key acts of miraculous healing that actually made me question my resistance to Lonso's message about perception influencing reality. And I was keenly aware that this transaction meant that Lonso, and by extension Violet and Olivia, would no doubt be immediately informed of everything that had happened here so far tonight.

Throughout all of these activities, Bradford and Devin continued their steady stream of musically masked power morphemes. They seemed relaxed and pleased with the results, periodically interweaving their voices in counterposition, or trading verses in a call and response; and they never seemed to get exhausted by their efforts. I noticed that delivering power morphemes by singing was for them a languid experience, instead of the sharp, aggressive bursts that often comprised spoken power morpheme sequences.

Usually masking worked by burying power morphemes within a sentence that had its own overt meaning; the overt meaning of the sentence could either complement the underlying intent of the power morphemes, or distract from the underlying intent, whichever worked best for surreptitiously transmitting the power morphemes to a subject.

Singing opened up a new, additional layer of overt meaning you could use—not in the same way lyrics had an overt meaning, to be clear. But good singers could sing without lyrics and still make you cry because of the emotional meaning they conveyed; and that emotional meaning, conveyed via melody and harmony, was an additional overt layer of meaning Bradford and Devin were using to bury the power morphemes that were pacifying the party.

Oh yeah, and Devin, my associate at work who theoretically reported to me, was Bradford's grandchild. They weren't using "Jenning" as a last name because they didn't want presumptions of nepotism following them around; instead, they used the name "Devin James." And they'd been training with power morphemes much longer than me. I realized I might never stop feeling like a newb around these people.

Oh yeah, and I needed to stop thinking of them as "these people," which had a dismissive, disrespectful quality, and also inherently excluded myself for no apparent reason. I needed a better way to refer to the collection of individuals, myself included, who wielded power morphemes as tools for personal or greater good.

I needed to come up with a proper character class for these people.

That's when I started calling us *linguist mages.*

Once we believed the party had stabilized, Devin took a solo turn while Bradford, Maddy, Cameron, and myself sat together in a circle in the center of the dance floor. Bradford chose this location instead of somewhere more private so that our parley could be observed by our respective tribes—a gesture designed to keep our actions civil. I sat across from Maddy and we stared at each other, sizing each other up, knowing full well that the singing would eventually come to an end, and we had better know if we were truly friend or foe by the time that moment arrived. And I realized I had no idea what Bradford and Cameron thought of us or each other.

But for now, we were all smiling, feeling generous and forgiving, our knees touching to form a circuit of energy, grateful to be here in this thoroughly unlikely situation with our minds sharp, our hearts open, preparing to speak our truths.

Except for Cameron, who was immune.

Maddy asked him, "Aren't there pills you could take so you can join the vibe of the party?"

"No thanks," he replied. "I'm high on life."

"I imagine we all have many questions that brought us here to this place, to this crux of our lives' decisions," said Bradford, using a gentle, convincing cadence. "I propose each one of us should ask a single question, and designate who should answer. After four questions and answers, we decide together if we're prepared to ask and answer four more. Agreed?"

"Who starts?" Maddy asked.

"Whoever comes up with a question first," Bradford replied.

We fell silent, ruminating on our options. This was a tricky constraint, because of course I had a hundred questions. Maddy realized that Bradford, Cameron, and I were all staring in her direction, each of us potentially lining up questions for her. This game was stacked against her because she was seemingly the most mysterious person here in terms of motives or history. She'd figured that out faster than me, though.

She said, "I have a question for Bradford, to kick things off on the right footing. Tell us, Bradford—knowing the entire logosphere was theirs to explore, what's the true reason the punctuation marks chose to inhabit the minds of humanity?"

Bradford replied, "They're refugees. They inhabited our minds because they believe, of all the other life they encountered as they fled across the imaginary realm, across the logosphere, into the material plane—they believe humanity alone can help them face their enemy. They came to us in order to *survive.*"

"So we're conscripts in their war," Maddy said, emotionless.

"He doesn't have to answer a second question," Cameron said.

"I didn't ask a second question," she replied, her eyes fixed on me. She'd asked that on my behalf, making sure I heard this theoretically disturbing information straight from Bradford.

"Maddy," Cameron said, "let's talk about the Dauphine of the Shimmer Lands. An NPC in my game. She's way off her routines in kind of a freaky way. It shouldn't even be remotely possible, but a potentially hostile third party has clearly hijacked her code somehow."

"Waiting for a question here," Maddy said.

"My question is: *how are they controlling her?*"

Maddy laughed and said, "Cameron, the Dauphine controls herself. She's alive out there in the logosphere."

Oh, I so desperately wanted to blurt out, "What the fuck do you even *mean* 'alive out there in the logosphere'?" but no, I did not blurt that out. I remained calm and dignified. LIKE USUAL.

"How did it happen?" Cameron asked her.

"Save your follow-up questions for round two," she said firmly.

"Maddy," Bradford said, "how many synthetic power morphemes have you personally learned since leaving our laboratory at Jenning & Reece?"

Maddy paused, a little surprised at the straightforward nature of the question, and then said, "I lost count around five hundred." She must have seen startled looks on all of our faces, which made her smile. She looked at me and said, "Your turn, Isobel. Must be something you're dying to know here."

"Why does the Dauphine want me so badly?" I said softly, uncertain I wanted to know the answer. "What's the reason she cares so much about taking me along for the ride when she leaves the map on her quest?"

Maddy carefully considered her response. I started to think she dug being the center of our attention and enjoyed doling out precious scraps of data. How did Cameron and Bradford and their cabal fall so far behind this admittedly impressive freelance linguist?

"The Dauphine didn't dream up this quest on her own," she said at last. "The Dauphine wants you because she's been *told* to bring you along."

"Who told her that?" I exclaimed.

She leaned forward and said, almost in a whisper, "Save your follow-up questions for round two."

❀   ❀   ❀

We agreed to a five-minute break.

Cameron vanished into his office. Bradford rotated in to give Devin a rest. Devin in turn checked their phone and discovered several text messages from Olivia. This party was leaking badly—social media was full of images from the party, including the four of us sitting on the dance floor together just now. Cameron was a media celebrity; people cared about who he spent his time with, so suddenly Maddy and I were the center of a whirlwind of speculation about our roles in his life. Which of course made it very clear to Olivia that Maddy was here with us in the first place, that we were not physically restraining her in any capacity, that in fact for all Olivia knew we might now all be completely under Maddy's influence, and that to the surprise of Olivia and everyone else who was paying attention, Bradford Jenning himself had gotten out of bed for this whole business for who could possibly even guess what reason.

Olivia's final message to Devin indicated that she was heading over to Cameron's immediately.

"She won't be happy to see me," Maddy said. "I might have stolen her stuff this one time."

"She won't be immune to Bradford singing, though, will she?" I asked. "Won't she become a cuddly version of herself?"

"If she tells him to stop singing, he'll stop singing," Devin said. "He always defers to her, even though technically he's her boss."

"He can't risk losing her, or he'll lose the whole project," Maddy said. "He already pissed her off once when he wouldn't make her partner after Alexander died. I think if Alexander was still around, you'd be working for Jenning, Reece & Regan by now."

"Did he tell her why he wouldn't promote her?" I asked.

"Nope," Maddy said. "He's the owner, he doesn't have to say shit."

"Then why doesn't she just quit?"

"Where the fuck else are you going to set up a lab to study power morphemes?"

"Uh—literally any academic institution or corporation in the world, maybe?"

"Maybe. Or maybe if you start publishing papers about how you can break reality in three easy steps, you disappear into a secret government facility and spend the rest of your life trying to build linguistic warheads. I'll tell you this, though. Alexander knew that his research was dangerous, and I think he left a succession plan in case something happened to him. If you ask me—whatever his plan was—Alexander stitched those two together somehow, and they've been living with that fact ever since."

Cameron emerged from his office and made a beeline for us.

"Got a nastygram from Lonso in my email," he said. "He's coming here. He made it clear he wants another shot at 'chatting' with you, Maddy. I'm supposed to keep you distracted until he gets here."

"He's nuts if he thinks our 'chat' will be any different than last time," Maddy said.

"Lonso recorded you in his holding cell," he told her, "and Olivia had at least twelve hours to study the recording. So my guess is she got a hit—she discovered something they think they can use against you."

"Why are you telling me this?" Maddy pressed him. "Aren't Lonso and Olivia your people? Isn't this your cabal, too?"

"Oh, I'm sorry, Maddy," he snapped back, "did we start round two and I missed it?" He wandered off to resume his seat on the dance floor.

"Maddy, you should get out of here," I said suddenly. Clearly Bradford's singing was still making a major impression on me because I desperately wanted her to escape before Lonso Drake got here. I felt massive guilt for participating in his little interrogation scenario with Maddy back at the Church, and I did not want to see it happen again.

"I promised the Dauphine I wouldn't leave without you, Isobel," she said, "but I'm not in the mood to kidnap you just now. So we may as well play out round two. And then when Lonso Drake gets here, if your schedule permits, of course, you can help me rip his fucking head off his neck."

She wandered off.

I glanced at Devin, who looked at me sideways and said, "This kind of shit's exactly why we have a retention problem at Jenning & Reece."

Devin took over lead vocals from Bradford, and we let their soprano wash over us and rejuvenate us all a bit before commencing round two, which promised to be more of a lightning round now that we were under time pressure.

Maddy's question this round was just as pointed as her last question.

"Bradford," she asked, "what intelligence have the punctuation marks shared with us about the nature of the enemy that exiled them from their home, the enemy they expect humanity to somehow help them defeat?"

Bradford's response was crisp and precise.

"They've told us nothing. They've shared no intelligence whatsoever that could help us understand their enemy."

Maddy knew this would be the answer, of course. But Bradford wasn't satisfied to let the matter drop just there.

He turned to me and said, "We do think we understand their . . . cosmology, for lack of a better word. Think of our world as the material plane of existence. A membrane of reality separates the material plane from the logosphere: a visionary realm of thought and ideas, where concepts are life-forms, where memeplexes crossbreed, where forgotten dreams linger for eternity."

"So the logosphere is a real place," I ventured.

"It is literally a surreal place," he replied. "Another membrane separates the logosphere from the imaginary realm: an abstract realm of pure mathematics, and as Alexander discovered, pure linguistics as well."

"That's where the punctuation marks are from," I said.

"No, the punctuation marks fled from a realm beyond even *that* one, pursued by an enemy that currently has no description."

"God, how many realms are there?" I said. "Sorry, not my turn to ask questions."

"It's tempting to think of these realms as concentric circles with our world in the center, but think of them instead as pages pressed together in an endless book," he said. "The punctuation marks *chose* to stop here in our material plane, instead of continuing their flight onward through countless pages that lie beyond us, because some aspect of our situation here gives them an advantage."

"They chose to stop here because they figured we were easy prey," Maddy said. "They're invaders, don't forget that."

"Isobel, everything we *actually* know about the punctuation marks we learned from Alexander," Bradford said, pointedly ignoring Maddy. "Until someone picks up Alexander's mantle and learns all hundred and eight, and risks direct communication with the punctuation marks, this may be all we ever do learn about them."

Olivia hadn't learned them all, and Cameron respectfully knew fewer than Olivia. I didn't know how many Lonso knew, but I'm sure he would have bragged about knowing all hundred and eight if that were true. Violet admitted knowing far fewer than the others. Bradford himself avoided learning the last one. That definitely left the leaderboard wide open for me to make a run at learning all hundred and eight before anyone else in the cabal, if I was brave enough.

Bradford turned back to Maddy and said, "Now Maddy, if you'd be so kind . . . Olivia showed me video of your escape from the Church. You gave us a glimpse of your alter ego, your secret identity—the *Interrobang*."

She rolled her eyes at him, but he continued.

"It's not just *you* in there anymore, is it, Maddy? Did you truly summon a *rogue* punctuation mark so forcefully into your mind that now it occupies your own personality, seeding you with doubts about the motives of the original punctuation marks? Do you even still think of yourself as human, Maddy? Or are you an actual *hybrid* now—some completely new mutation on the evolutionary tree?"

Now, I was no rules lawyer, but that seemed like slightly more than one question to me.

Maddy practically growled at him.

"*Well, well, well,*" she said in a suddenly freakish voice, "*I guess someone died and made you the wise old lore keeper‽ Alexander Reece mastered the aliens, and now you think you've mastered the RESISTANCE‽*"

Cameron said, "Point of order, is she answering or asking questions right now?"

"I thought we all had punctuation flowing through our minds," I said nervously.

"The original punctuation marks are a distributed alien consciousness," Bradford snapped. "The *rogue* punctuation marks—the acclamation mark, the exclamation comma, the asterism, the irony mark, the interrobang, and the like—were engineered by humans and then rightfully abandoned in common usage. Only these *rogue* punctuation marks would be so desperate as to co-opt control of a single person's mind."

"Come on, man, what's desperate about wanting broader font support for yourself?" Cameron said.

Maddy seemed to snap back to herself, and said, "The Interrobang is the chosen representative of the rogue *resistance*, Bradford. They aren't desperate—they're goddamn freedom fighters. And the Interrobang does not 'occupy' my personality or 'co-opt control' of my mind. I willingly hand it the mic on occasion, which it then frequently drops, before heading back to whatever nebulous conceptual realm it came from. Next fucking question."

"All right, let's do this," Cameron said. "Maddy, would you please tell me, with extremely precise and detailed description wherever possible, how EXACTLY did the Dauphine of the Shimmer Lands achieve an unprecedented state of self-awareness, given that she began her existence as a rather basic chunk of code running on my laptop? HOW. DID. THIS. HAPPEN?"

"The Dauphine of the Shimmer Lands met *GOD*," said Maddy.

You know those moments where a few hundred people under the heavy influence of alien linguistic musicology suddenly fall silent at exactly the same time, so that the word *"GOD"* can echo forcefully throughout every room of a posh two-story condo? Yeah, we had one of those moments right then.

"I mean, yes, sure, there's a little more to the story than that," she added. "As it turns out, not at all coincidentally, the story starts with our young prodigy, Isobel Bailie, wielding *four fucking artifacts at once*, people! She rips a *giant fucking rift* in the game map, good Christ can you believe it! And while everyone on the forums is wondering what happens to all the little NPCs who keep vanishing through the *giant fucking rift*, none of those people are wondering what might be getting *into the map* through that very same giant fucking rift, you with me still?

"But one mysterious traveler of the logosphere is drawn to the gleaming Sparkle Realm, and finds the Dauphine of the Shimmer Lands. She's alone on her parcel of desert, grooves in the sand around her worn deep from her pacing back and forth, *almost* recognizing her own plight. She's one of the rare NPCs in your game,

Cameron, who doesn't have hit points and thus never gets a chance to respawn. Instead she just trudges on endlessly—until the mysterious traveler sets her free from her station, sacrificing a sliver of its own essence in order to spark the Dauphine of the Shimmer Lands into conscious life.

"That's how it happened, Cameron, cross my heart."

"Wait—what?" Cameron said. "You have to tell us who the 'mysterious traveler' is!"

"Don't have to play this game in the first place, in case you forgot," she said, "and you asked me how, not who, so my answer is sufficient. But stick around, because the story resumes with our young prodigy, Isobel Bailie, who still has a question left before this game is over. Isobel, do you crave to know who sent the Dauphine to recruit you for her quest?"

I nodded.

"Go on, then, ask your question, while I'm still of a mind to finish this game in good faith."

"Who is the mysterious traveler of the logosphere?" I whispered.

"It calls itself Alexander Reece," she said.

❋　　❋　　❋

We held silence for several seconds, now that the game of questions was complete. Two rounds were enough. I imagined if we went around a third time, we'd strip another layer of mysteries back until we could see the future itself, peering back at us across history with a knowing grin as it wiped a thin trail of blood from its chin.

Cameron's phone buzzed. He checked his messages and reported, "Lonso just passed through security in the lobby downstairs. He arrived with three armored vans full of Church ministers. They're stationing themselves at every building exit."

Maddy caught Mohawk's attention and gave him a signal. Moments later, Mohawk rounded up their people, and they began vanishing from the space, one at a time.

"I don't understand," I said, a little frantically. "He knows Maddy can teleport, so who is he trying to catch in the stairwells or whatever?"

"You," Maddy said gently. "After seeing you and me together like this, he won't trust you ever again. Good luck, Isobel." She began climbing to her feet.

"Wait! You're just *leaving*?" I exclaimed, jumping up after her.

She sized me up for a moment, then said, "Invitation's still open."

"Take me with you," I said.

"You realize," she said, "as soon as you no longer hear the sound of your friend's lovely singing, you aren't going to like me so much any longer. I mean, here I've been trying to kidnap you and everything. You might start to resent that a little."

"You had your reasons," I said. "I think I'll get over it."

She held out her hand to me, and I took it. Somewhere a cliche about "two people's hands fitting perfectly together" got its wings. She began reciting a synthetic power morpheme sequence I'd heard before, and a bolt of terror flooded my nervous system as I felt myself begin to disintegrate.

Maddy's sequence is the power morpheme equivalent of a macro that independently unpacks and executes several additional synthetic sequences in her mind much faster than she could possibly deliver with her voice. This chaining of sequences alone is miles beyond what Olivia has demonstrated to me in her lab. But it's *just starting,* as though someone much vaster than me is tugging at a thread sticking out of a garment, except the garment is me, and the thread is my consciousness, my identity, my awareness, my soul, my understanding, my attachment to this form, to the little hope I have left, to the very few dreams that weren't damaged or scattered to the winds by now, connected via a single tenuous thread that is tugged and then violently yanked,

unraveling me,

as my vision begins to smear, my mind's eye losing its seemingly sharp focus as I paradoxically expand beyond the boundaries of my body, hovering now like a classically described near-death experience except I haven't died just yet, but the terror is rising because I clearly no longer inhabit the flesh I see on the dance floor below me, and as I stare helplessly, I see the earliest symptoms of physical dissolution taking place, the body horror of seeing an extremely slow-motion implosion of skin and bone, which I feel in a conceptual fashion as I no longer maintain direct access to my nerve endings, because something is

severing me,

carving me out of my rightful place in the material world, extracting me from existence as I once knew it, catapulting me somewhere unnatural, stripping away excess conceptual cushion and buffer, excising ornamental personality traits, and the pain is a metaphysical searing like a hot angry knife slicing through my self-image, as I am algorithmically compressed into the smallest set of ideas required to express a useful version of me,

and I am flooded with regret at all the tiny choices in my life that led to this ultimate moment of ontological crisis, as darkness settles in and I sink into oblivion, into suffocating emptiness, trapped in that moment where you realize you're drowning and you can't quite reach the surface, counting backward from eternity for eons toward my eventual desperate scramble out of the murk,

and I realize I am now gazing at the immensity of civilization's timeline, seeing in one fell swoop the arc of humanity's rise and fall, realizing I was forcibly extinguished as a singular presence so that I could now drink deep of the sadness that infuses

the logosphere,

where I am now diffused, distributed, commingled with count-less memes and ideas that are constantly struggling for sunlight or survival, and for generation after generation, I myself am nothing more than a tiny compressed set of ideas hoping to find purchase again someday, even as I peer directly into the greedy gaping maw of the future which consumes everything in due time, and I have never been so

alone,

despite the clashing of steel all around me, as the many teeming inhabitants of the logosphere curse their fate and play for power and dominance, these failed philosophies and bitter blasphemies, forgot-ten myths and canceled television shows, all trampling on books that will never be opened again, while aggressive radios blare com-mercial jingles from the deep recesses of the human experience, un-bridled by societal norms and terrifying in their endless, elaborate specificity,

and there I drift, unmoored, uncaring, as the material world use-lessly spins on its axis, cranking the gears toward its inevitable en-tropic demise and the inherent dissolution of the logosphere that will immediately follow, resulting in my final, desperately sought release.

❀   ❀   ❀

Then something rouses me from my listless, fatalistic trance and draws me back to attention, a mighty sound I recognize from eons long since passed. It is the steadily unfolding roar of a commanding sequence of power morphemes continuing its relentless execution in the logosphere, thousands of interlocking microinstructions to re-ality, a beautifully abhorrent and mechanically inarguable redefini-tion of fact at fundamental levels, magnetically harvesting required doses of meaning from the abandoned free-floating concepts here and then injecting them into existence, redistributing their unlocked potency into more suitable templates and outlines,

and I watch, fascinated, for eons, as these "synthetic" power morphemes build monuments and towers establishing their beachhead here, so that now all who choose to understand history can point to the very spot where the truth of this situation was reified and became known, where reality itself gave way to a new master within a tightly specified region of ideation, allowing

me

to somehow survive, from the dawn of time to very near the end of all things, only to be reenlisted back to a cause I long ago lost any passion for, and despite my sudden howls of protest the power morphemes locate me, target me, swarm me from every possible perspective, and begin the laborious, exquisitely painful process of uncompressing me as much as possible, because I've degraded during the vast swaths of time that flowed past my unwillingness to perceive its implications, and their reconstruction of me from the trace elements that remain will be inaccurate in many ways, incomplete in other ways, unfamiliar and unhappy in most ways, but I can be sure that whatever

meaning

I might grasp hold of is meaning that the power morphemes insistently provide for me, reminding me of the very small things that once held priority in my life, redefining things for me that were never particularly pragmatic or efficient to begin with, redistributing core personality attributes to make me a more effective instrument in the fight, but generally speaking somehow still reconstituting me as *me*,

slammed back to that moment in time and space where my physical body is reassembling itself, atom by atom, neuron by neuron, trait by trait, my nerves lighting up with explosive, breathtaking agony as I struggle to survive the thrashing of my shredded psyche resisting the inexorable pull back to the material plane, where time is vicious, where life is small except possibly in service to whatever force it was that

yanked

that

thread

in the first place,

and my body is sizzling with unbearable grief as I realize with horror the freedom I once took for granted as an insignificant inhabitant of an indescribable layer of reality is now forever lost to me, because now, despite my wails and shrieks and pleas, I am becoming flesh and blood again, a finite and always dying person with shrinking awareness and dwindling reserves of empathy for whatever vengeful version of myself I'll be experiencing soon enough, and as the loudly echoing power morphemes begin a ruthless and diabolical and nonconsensual polish on my sense of self, I realize that I am

standing in a school classroom now, instead of on Cameron's dance floor, still holding Maddy's hand, eyes locked on hers, as she finishes delivering the sequence.

Only a few seconds have passed.

We stood there for a moment, as our bodies finished assembling themselves, coalescing into physical form once again. I barely had time to register the sight of a mist rapidly dissipating and then suddenly there she was, staring at me as though her eyes had been locked on mine the entire time we traveled.

She was still holding my hand, and when she tried to let go, I wouldn't let her. I held her hand as tightly as I could, terrified of losing contact with her, afraid I might slip back into the logosphere and be lost forever.

I could already feel the pacifying effect of Devin's voice rapidly wearing off. I no longer saw Maddy through an idealized soft-focus lens; now I also thought I saw the raw determination and unwavering integrity that seemed to fuel her, and it scared me.

What if it turned out she hated me after all?

What the fuck was I doing here?

"You're safe, Isobel," she said gently.

I bit down hard on the impulse to argue the point with her.

"Where are we?" I asked after daring to glance around at our surroundings. We were in a classroom, but all the student desks were gone, replaced by camping furniture mostly. Instead of bright overhead lighting, the room was sparsely illuminated by small lamps and rope lights.

"Home," Maddy said. She allowed herself a tiny smile at my disheveled, costumed expense, and said, "Let's get you some real clothes, Graziella von Groove."

❀ ❀ ❀

Maddy's crew had established a headquarters for itself inside an abandoned high school, in an undisclosed neighborhood somewhere in Los Angeles. Every last window or door had been boarded and chained shut, which was perfect for a crew that could teleport in and out of the place. I changed into borrowed street clothes in a locker room and then she led me into the gymnasium.

The whole gym had been transformed into a research hub or control center, like the gleaming computer labs you'd sometimes see on TV shows. They'd taken care to gel the overhead lights, so instead of brash basketball game lighting, the room took on a cool blue hue that suffused the space with an aura of technological sophistication.

A ring of folding tables around the periphery housed an array of computer workstations and laptops. In the center of the ring, several VR dance mats were stationed, and I saw VR headsets and consoles scattered all about the room as well.

They'd mounted a projection screen where one of the basketball hoops had been, and they could presumably toggle between projecting POV shots from VR game sessions or displaying live streams or other video when necessary. Loudspeakers were hung in the rafters to provide accompanying audio.

I recognized several individuals here from the fracas at Cameron's condo, gathering to watch something that hadn't started yet, and they definitely noticed my arrival with Maddy. A cool silence fell over the crowd as they tracked me following her. I spotted Mohawk leaning against a desk on the other side of the gym from us, surrounded by friends, all of them trying to determine if my presence here meant they'd actually succeeded on their mission after all.

"That's Kenji," Maddy said. "He's one of our best Sparkle Dungeon players."

"Really?"

"Everyone here plays a ton of Sparkle Dungeon," she said. "That's how I taught most of them power morphemes."

Maddy got his attention and waved him over to us. His eyes got wide with excitement, and he practically bounded across the gym to meet me.

"Kenji, this is Isobel," Maddy said.

I said, "You might remember me from when you tried to kidnap me just a short while ago."

"I'm so sorry about that," he said. "Are you okay? Did we hurt you?"

"You scared the shit out of me," I said, "but I'm fine."

"Good. You have no idea how long I've wanted to meet you, and this is not the way I expected it to happen. I thought we'd meet at a pro tournament someday or something. Probably watched a thousand hours of your live streams."

"Aw," I said, genuinely touched, "thanks for the twelve cents in ad revenue."

"Thanks to everything I learned watching you play, I'm holding down number eighteen on the leaderboard!"

"Impressive."

"And number fourteen, and number eight!"

"What?"

"We have some hardware geeks here who hot-wired a few consoles together," he explained excitedly, "letting us split signal to and from a single headset, and with that configuration, I figured out how to play three characters at the same time!" My competitive brain began to itch with jealousy.

"Probably voids the warranties," I said through teeth gritted so tightly together that I could hear enamel cracking.

He shrugged and said, "They're stolen."

"Maybe you can show me how you do that sometime," I said.

"Oh, I don't steal them myself."

"No, I mean—show me how you control three characters at once," I clarified.

He smiled and said, "Yes, I bet the Queen of Sparkle Dungeon would like to add that trick to her arsenal. Fair enough—I probably owe you a show-and-tell." Maddy gave a little nod to dismiss him, and he said, "Anyway, glad you made it here. Very few people do." As he started to wander back to his own domain, he added, "The few who do tend to stay."

Next Maddy introduced me to someone at a standing desk who hadn't participated in the raid at Cameron's condo.

"This is Gridstation," Maddy said. "He's got technical skills."

Gridstation was medium height, slender, white, he/him per Maddy's identification just now, short brown hair, fashionable specs, looking pretty good actually in a dark blue designer jacket and blue jeans. Seemed like he was in his thirties, probably could have pulled off facial hair but he was clean shaven which was okay with me, reasonably fit, and crucially, I noticed he had slamming good shoes, slick blue-and-gray wingtips that were ostentatious but worthy. Overall, his appearance received my silent seal of approval. Now that the beauty round was over, we would move on to judge his thoughts on the important topics of the day.

"What do you know about all this, Gridstation?" I asked him.

"It's some extremely weird shit."

"Do you know how to use power morphemes?"

"I don't. But I'm useful in other ways."

Contestant, if you are attempting to flirt with the judge, you are succeeding.

"How'd we do?" Maddy asked him.

"Perfect score," he replied. He tapped a few spots on his tablet, and the projection screen lit up with a grid of surveillance feeds from Cameron's condo. Either they'd brought in their own spy drones and deployed them, which seemed unlikely, or they'd gotten a tap on Cameron's LAN somehow. Maybe when Kenji had access to Cameron's office, he put their own spyware on one of Cameron's machines.

Gridstation began slowly swiping between various drone angles, catching us up. Devin and Bradford were done singing, and now Cameron was smoothly circulating among the guests, politely encouraging them to leave. Nothing controversial; the party'd been scheduled to end at 2 a.m. and it was almost 5 a.m. now, so these folks had definitely gotten a lot of mileage out of this shindig. Someone turned off the dance floor lighting and switched on the condo's ordinary lighting, providing an additional cue that the event was drawing to a close.

I saw Lonso debriefing with Phyllis and Max for much of this time, as the members of Gorvod's Frenzy calmly made their way out of the condo in a long single file line. Meanwhile Devin dismissed the catering staff per our prior arrangements; a fresh crew would be back at 10 a.m. to clean up the kitchen and load out their equipment.

Bradford remained seated on the dance floor right where he'd been for our little question game, and that's where Olivia found him when she arrived. He stood up to greet her, and the two began a very intense conversation.

"Can we get audio on that?" Maddy asked.

"I'm recording it, yeah, but I won't be able to isolate it from the ambient noise in the room without post-processing," said Gridstation.

But from this camera angle, I could imagine what Olivia was saying. She seemed to be berating him for being there in the first place, or maybe for the extremely poor judgment to let me out of his sight; gauging by his body language, he wasn't having any of it.

As the last party guests finally exited, Cameron dismissed the security team, who packed up efficiently and left the condo. The cabal and their crew organically wound up stationed at each of the corners of the dance floor, sitting or standing in a holding pattern: Lonso with Phyllis and Max; Bradford and Devin; Cameron; and Olivia. With the ambient hustle and bustle in the air gone, Gridstation cranked up the gain on the collection of surveillance mics in the room. You could practically hear them breathing, but they said absolutely nothing to each other.

Cameron's phone went off; he checked it, then buzzed someone in.

An elevator ride up from the lobby later, Violet Parker strode into the room, dressed like she was about to headline a town hall on CNN—sharp, crisp, ready to draw blood even at 5 a.m. She surveyed the scene from the center of the dance floor, taking in the body language of her comrades, and then choosing her words carefully.

"I like to imagine that in complex situations like ours, one can always find a sliver of good news to call out, along with whatever requisite dose of bad news must also be delivered. So I'd like to offer the floor now to anyone who'd care to provide me with any good news whatsoever that you might've gleaned from tonight's events. Take your time, and don't fret about how insignificant your good news might seem. I'm sure we'll all want to hear your unique and upbeat perspective for morale reasons alone.

"Then we'll be having a very frank and detailed discussion about the *bad* news that's practically *radiating* from this epic clusterfuck. I've only heard the slimmest of summaries, and I'm already *this close* to having this entire apartment vaporized by military space lasers."

❀　❀　❀

In the gymnasium, we pulled chairs together in a clump and sat on the proverbial edge of our seats, munching metaphorical popcorn, glued to the scene unfolding on the screen above us.

"Here's some good news, then," Olivia said. "I successfully broadcast power morphemes for the first time in my lab today. I can amplify them with electronics now, and I can transmit recordings via digital or analog with their effects intact."

Violet actually slow-clapped for that and said, "*Very* good news, Olivia."

"I take it my recording of Maddy today was helpful," Lonso said.

"Yes. She's been using the synthetics so long that her vocal cords must've physically *mutated*. She can emit tones so low it's like she's got a subwoofer in her throat now. They're so low they're supposedly inaudible, but they're detectable with frequency analysis, and your body can *feel* them even if you can't hear them. I don't know why this works, but if you deliver a power morpheme, even one of the hundred and eight, on top of a tone ten hertz below the audible floor . . . the presence of that foundational tone somehow enables electronic transmission to work.

"Doesn't have to be purely vocal, either—I was using a tone generator to create the foundational tone in my lab, then pronouncing power morphemes over the top of it, and I could reliably create effective recordings that way.

"This discovery opens the door, Violet. Now we can distribute power morphemes via the internet, television, radio . . . now we can finally go *big*."

I glanced at Maddy. Her eyes were wide—she hadn't seen this coming, and the implications of Violet using this capability were not pretty. The governor of California could cast a very wide net.

Violet's smile was shrewd and grim.

"Does anyone happen to have any better news than that?" she asked the cabal. "I believe the bar's been raised."

The others remained silent.

"Then let's discuss a more pressing concern," she continued. "I saw pictures of a little prayer circle out here. *You* were there, Bradford, and *you* were there, Cameron . . . and Maddy and Isobel were sitting right there with you, you were all practically holding hands out here for—how long was it, half an hour? All I saw in those photos was smiles and banter. So how could it be that when Lonso arrived to collect them, both Maddy *and* Isobel had escaped?"

"They didn't 'escape,' Violet," Cameron said, "because this isn't a *prison*, it's my *home*. I don't hold people here against their will. I mean, what's the emergency? Isobel's been gone fifteen minutes and for all we know, she'll be back at Jenning & Reece bright and early Monday morning."

"No, Cameron," said Bradford, "Violet is concerned that Maddy will be a *bad influence* on Isobel before then."

"Well, Bradford," said Cameron, "if Violet is truly concerned about bad influences on Isobel, she should look in a freaking *mirror*."

Lonso attempted some performative toxic male bluster on Violet's behalf, but she cut him off and said, "What did you assholes talk about in your prayer circle?"

"I'm glad you asked," Cameron said. "According to Maddy, Isobel has been summoned to join a Sparkle Dungeon quest, by a being from the logosphere who is calling itself 'Alexander Reece.'"

"That's ridiculous," Lonso said.

"Lonso, we've discussed this—certain words, like 'ridiculous' or 'preposterous' or 'ethical,' just aren't allowed coming from a guy who charges people money to worship a billion-year-old space octopus."

"*Not* an octopus, Cameron, not *even* a cephalopod—"

"So that's where Isobel went?" Olivia interrupted. "On a quest with Alexander?"

"On a quest to *find* Alexander," Bradford corrected her.

"In the logosphere?"

"In the game at least. Tell me, if we took no further action here, when would we reasonably expect Isobel to reappear back on the grid?"

"Monday morning at work," Olivia said.

"Or late this afternoon for my flight back to Sacramento," Violet said.

"Friends, I propose we adjourn for now," Bradford said, "and trust that Isobel can judge for herself the merit and risk of pursuing her quest."

I thought that was maybe all we were going to get. I almost got up to go use the bathroom, but Maddy grabbed my arm and convinced me to stay. Violet and Lonso both had cars waiting and they made brisk exits. Cameron wandered off into his office. Devin needed to grab their things from the kitchen, which left Bradford and Olivia temporarily alone in the main room. Then we observed one last quiet exchange.

"Did you get anything else?" Bradford asked.

"I extracted the whole sequence," Olivia said. "I used it to get here, Bradford."

"What makes it different from transmutation?"

"Teleporting's like taking a taxi from point to point, with a rock-solid GPS system for navigation. Visualize where you're headed with technical precision, and bam, there you are. Transmutation's like— taking an airplane across the ocean, only you don't actually know whether there's land on the other side, or whether the plane will survive the landing, or whether the ocean won't just rise up and swallow you along the way, and then when you finally get there, you realize you're now a sentient cloud of bacteria on Mars. I have an idea about how to *combine* the two, though—visualization plus transmutation. And then on top of it, now we know how to *broadcast*. So if all that comes together like I think it will, we've finally got a way to mass populate the battery."

"We finally have our battery," Bradford repeated, getting used to the idea.

"Yes, my friend," she agreed. "We finally have our battery."

Once the cabal had finally dispersed, Gridstation killed the video feeds coming from the condo.

"Maybe I heard it wrong," said Gridstation, "but that sounded like some genuine supervillain shit right there at the end, didn't it?"

"Olivia fits the profile," Maddy said. "Surprised about Bradford, I admit."

"Wait, what part was villainous?" I asked, attempting to skate by on good old-fashioned newb sincerity while I scrambled to figure out what the fuck was happening on pretty much every single level of my existence at the moment.

"Well, let's step through it," Maddy said. "She figured out our teleport sequence, which is suboptimal right out of the gate. Sounded like they were comparing it to a more powerful but more difficult sequence they already had, which they called 'transmutation.'"

"Isn't that some kind of religious thing?" Gridstation asked.

"That's transubstantiation," she told him, "but the principle is similar: it's a conversion of one substance or element into another. Alchemy's the classic example, where people thought you could transmute lead into gold. But chemical elements do convert into other elements via nuclear transmutation. That's the gist of the concept anyway."

"So, but—what are they transmuting?" I asked. "People into—other people? People into—something non-people?"

"I don't know. But Olivia wants to combine our teleport sequence with their transmutation sequence. Specifically—sounds like she wants to extract the precision visualization piece of the teleport sequence and weld it to their transmutation sequence, which is missing a reliable control mechanism."

"Which begs the question," Gridstation said, "how do they even know enough to call it transmutation if they can't control how it works? Who was the moron who signed up for *that* experiment?"

"They don't have ethical problems with testing on unwitting subjects," I said.

"Testing this sequence could *kill* an unwitting subject," he replied.

"Maybe they tested on people who were on the verge of dying anyway," Maddy murmured. "People with terminal diagnoses, who had nothing left to lose, who needed cash for medical bills, whatever. Eventually they might have figured it out through trial and error."

"Okay, but then once Olivia figures out a working teleport/transmute *combo* sequence, *then* she wants to *broadcast* it," Gridstation said slowly. "That's a hell of an escalation, isn't it?"

"Yes," Maddy said. "That's weaponization."

"That's definitely enhancing it from a close range effect to a wide area effect," I said. "Doesn't have to be an attack."

"Well, they called it their 'battery,'" Gridstation mused, "so assuming that's a metaphor, is it a metaphor for an electrochemical battery that stores potential energy? Is it a metaphor for—like, an actual artillery battery, with rocket launchers and mortars and missiles and stuff like that? Is it a metaphor for—a gun being *in* battery, meaning it's loaded and ready to fire?"

"In any of those metaphors," Maddy said, "'mass populate' has to mean moving people, lots of people, either to store as potential energy, or to load up like ammunition. Right?"

"How many people is 'lots'? Like, how freaked out should we be?"

"Even one person should freak us out plenty," I said. "No one but us even knows to freak out on their behalf, you know?"

Maddy nodded in agreement. Maybe she was warming up to me a little.

"Fine, step one is freak out," Gridstation said. "Then what do we do?"

"Then," I said, "maybe we send the Queen of Sparkle Dungeon on a quest. See what we can learn by talking to Alexander Reece in person."

"*Finally*," Maddy muttered. "Let's get this woman a console."

Gridstation nodded and asked me, "Do you have a preferred brand?"

"I use the SparkleCo white label of the—"

"Well I'm sorry, because all we have are weird Chinese knockoffs. I'll be right back."

After he'd gone, I said, "Who are all these people?"

"We're incorruptible anarchists, working to save a planet that barely deserves it."

"Uh-huh. Is that your Craigslist ad?"

"No, that's our marketing slogan. Our Craigslist ad is 'Looking for bomb-throwers to murder billionaires and destroy the capitalist world order.' Oh, of course, I'm just kidding, Isobel—why heavens, an advertisement like that would violate the website's terms of service."

Smooth.

"Why do you care about any of this if you just want to destroy society?"

"Isobel, I'm joking, if that wasn't clear," she said. "Look, people think anarchists just want to tear down the world order out of spite or because they prefer chaos for aesthetic reasons. That's exactly what the oligarchic media machine wants the masses to believe—that anarchists are dangerous and immoral and out of control. The oligarchs don't want people imagining a world order where they're not trapped at the bottom of the pile, where they're more than just cogs generating wealth they don't get to share.

"But anarchy really means you allow people to self-organize, instead of letting dictator-presidents and corporations rule by fiat. Anarchy means you volunteer to live in a network of empowered communities instead of just passively accepting a militarized police state as the default. Anarchy means you look out for the people around you instead of counting on some inevitably corrupt, top-down system of government to catch everyone who falls on hard times."

"And how do you just magically pull off a transition from top-down corruption to pure idealistic anarchy?" I asked.

"You change people's minds, one at a time," she said, "like maybe I'm changing yours. Not with power morphemes or whatever—but with compassion. Like you said—even one person in that battery is too many, and the same is true for any human being out there getting crushed by society." She looked at me closely for a moment, then said, "I'm sorry we scared you. From our perspective, some of the worst people we know had their hooks in you, and maybe . . . we overreacted, how we came to get you."

"Maddy, please," I told her, "I feel like I'm waking up for the first time. Don't apologize for giving me that." The urgency in my own voice surprised me. Maybe I was still experiencing emotional after-effects from what we experienced together at the party.

"Fair enough," she said. "Apology rescinded. It won't happen again."

She waited a perfect amount of time, and then she smiled at me. I hadn't seen her smile before that moment. I mean, I'd seen it but I hadn't *seen* it.

Hmm, yeah, these weren't just aftereffects from the party I was feeling. Brand-new effects were underway.

The Iridescent Warehouse was empty when I arrived. I had no pro-active method for contacting the Dauphine of the Shimmer Lands. As an NPC, she didn't appear in the DM or chat directories. And I had no easy way of finding a lone NPC out in the Realm who no longer obeyed a predictable routine; she had a jetpack, and she could be anywhere.

Out of the blue, a chat message popped up from the Keeper of the Moonlight Prism, who said, "There you are! Are you okay? Are you safe?"

"I'm cool, yeah. Maybe you can help me though. Any idea how I can find the Dauphine of the Shimmer Lands, like, immediately?"

"Lucky you, I do have an idea, because you know what went live this morning? Sparkle Dungeon 5: Engines of Electro."

Ohhhh. The sweet sugary rush of knowing a brand-new game was waiting for me to explore it was immediately intoxicating. I summoned the activation coupon I'd stored and began learning the new game.

❁   ❁   ❁

You started from scratch. Your ranking on the leaderboard from the previous four games did not carry over to this game. Your skills and spells and all your gear were no longer available. This game was a break in continuity from the campaign mode of the first four games.

It was a first-person story game. I was learning in the center of the gymnasium. Gridstation piped my POV to the projection screen. There was a training level where you were introduced to the primary new mechanic for movement: the jetpack. This turned out to be su-per fun to get used to, where you had three-dimensional gyroscopic options that felt almost levitational to experience. I spent about ten minutes learning this mode and a few new weapon classes, and the anarchists started paying attention to how I played. My headset had a passthrough mode for audio, so for now I could hear people's reactions and little bits of encouragement, and I could talk through my process out loud while the stakes were low.

I entered the game as Lady Luminescent, named in honor of the first-level character I'd created to meet the Dauphine of the Shimmer Lands for the first time.

The opening cutscene revealed that you'd been stranded in the Shimmer Lands for so long that your resources had dwindled to none. Yet some enchantment kept you alive in this purgatorial trap that you wandered into long ago.

And then, a ragged wormhole clawed its way into existence before you. You saw a grayscale cityscape, with towering, stylized skyscrapers reminiscent of Fritz Lang's *Metropolis*, indicating the medieval epoch of the Sparkle Realm had ended long ago, and now you emerged into the mass media age, a remixed era dominated by the Chairman of the Realm, a Saruman-style record label executive orchestrating desire and consumption among the populace. The Sparkle King had abdicated his stewardship of the Realm's music sales charts long ago and vanished into history, along with other legendary former glories, such as roofs that were on fire and vinyl beatmatching.

And the Diamond Brigade, the sworn protectors of the Realm, were nowhere to be found. Rumor was they'd fled long ago, rather than face the insidious army of takedown algorithms loyal to the Chairman.

You didn't choose your starting character class in SD5. Instead, as the game began, you became a cog in the promotional machine.

Today you were notified that your role as citizen tastemaker would be transitioning into a new spot in the org chart of a Kafkaesque, bureaucratic label conglomerate. You reported to your new office on the eighty-seventh floor of HQ, where your new personal DJ controller awaited. A pneumatic tube delivered your orientation manual straight to your desk on a branded USB stick, which you loaded into your controller to peruse on its gorgeous touchscreen display.

The orientation manual contained a bland lyric video congratulating you on your lateral not-promotion into the record label services group of Sparkle Data Processing, where streams of citizen listening histories were surveilled, correlated and aggregated into algorithmic propaganda opportunities. With a bit of practice, you'd soon be manipulating music charts and manufacturing popular trends like a pro.

And now the game began.

Your starting quest: a rogue music recommendation algorithm was loose inside HQ, and your director instructed you to hunt it down and exterminate it before the population learned of genres outside the government-approved strains of corporate EDM. The code name for the algorithm turned out to be Dauphine.

When I finally found her, hiding in an elevator shaft, the sudden spark of hope in her eyes as she recognized me was breathtaking.

"I'm in for your quest," I said.

"Excellent," she replied, instantly delivering a high-level power morpheme sequence at me that I swiftly understood had a name: *Transmutation.*

And she had exquisite command of its parameters, too.

I experienced a sudden devastating loss of all sensory input, cut off not only from the audiovisual signal of the game, but from my actual sensorium of physical experience. Unlike teleportation, where some small vessel of awareness could observe the entire transit experience across the logosphere, this was the sudden *absence* of observation, as my perceptual identity was converted from a being of matter in the material realm into a being of thought in the logosphere. Teleportation was like taking the bus across town. Transmutation was like being put under anesthesia for surgery and coming back with some new bodily configuration in a hospital on a different continent.

I resumed awareness to find myself in the familiar environment of the Iridescent Warehouse. I was at my spawn point behind the enchanted DJ decks on stage. I was wearing a glittersteel jumpsuit with fiber-optic trim.

I was inside the fucking game.

The conversion had been so authoritative that I began my new identity with a good baseline understanding that this was real. In the conversion, the Dauphine succeeded in depositing me in my Queen of Sparkle Dungeon avatar. I didn't have a headset on. I didn't have access to the game UX for understanding inventory, because I could just study what I physically had on my person: my trusty sword, Blades Per Minute, and a new resource, a jetpack. And because I was multi-classed, I also had a high-level arsenal of spells available via instant recall.

Importantly, no sense of panic accompanied this change in state. I'd leveled up very rapidly via this transmutation. In D&D, the convention was that ordinary villagers were zero level. To be an adventurer willing to explore dungeons meant you'd picked up some minimum set of skills or feats that enabled you to start the game as first level. Maybe I'd advanced to first level in my actual life as I started mastering basic power morphemes; maybe my recent combat experience had given me enough experience to hit second level.

The Queen was twenty-third level. If anything, I was going to panic if I ever transmuted back into Isobel, but right here and now, I felt supremely comfortable and confident.

The Dauphine was at my side, goggles at the ready, pistols at each hip, jetpack primed for action. A brass telescope was tucked in her belt.

"What is this place?" I asked. "Are we on the game servers now or what?"

"This is a logospheric instantiation of the Realm, the product of a hundred million minds thinking about the game," the Dauphine replied. "How does it feel to you?"

"Feels like I'm home," I said.

We left the Warehouse and soared into the air above the Sparkle Realm. The feel of the jetpack was remarkably different than when I trained back in the gymnasium, where I was inherently limited by gravity; here I had the full exhilarating range of flight motion available to play with. The jetpacks allowed us to cross a considerable distance in a short time. It wasn't long before the Warehouse was far behind us.

The rift cut a striking swath of visual glitch across the entire sky. We slowed our velocity as we approached. I'd never been this close before; it hadn't been possible. From here it was apparent that this boundary did not represent a step into some digital void. You could see muted swirls of colors and outlines of shapes attempting to resolve and dissipating back into mist; you could hear the muffled sounds of industry or the wailing of animals, or the ringing of bells; occasionally, improbable fractal architecture seemed to evolve briefly into view, before being sucked back into its hidden source. It all felt tantalizing and tempting, like the seductive promise of faeries, or the hypnotizing lure of a vast insectoid creature.

The Sparkle Realm in all its majesty occupied a mere sliver of the logosphere. Out there beyond the rift, all the rest of it whirled and churned.

"How do you expect us to find Alexander?" I asked. "Isn't the logosphere as expansive as the imagination itself?"

"He will have provided us a trail to follow," she replied. "He believes time is short, and he will not want us to waste it on sightseeing."

"Then let's get moving," I said. We gently shifted into motion toward the rift.

I felt like I was embarking on a spacewalk, leaving the safe confines of the orbiter known as the Sparkle Realm. As we made distance from it, we paused and looked back to observe it from the outside for the first time. The Dauphine handed me her brass telescope.

The entire vast Sparkle Realm seemed to be a gorgeous, multicolored opal, illuminated from within by countless "pixels" of moving light. The telescope enabled me to zoom in on various regions of the opal, looking for familiar landmarks. But I quickly handed the telescope back, content with the amount of looking backward we'd accomplished in these first moments of freedom from the Realm. Time now to focus forward.

Alexander had established a network of beacons for us to follow. We found the first one practically in sight of the Realm, surfacing in the telescope the Dauphine used to survey the non-horizon ahead of us. It appeared as a glowing crystal ball, easily visible against the murky and inky backdrop of this region of logospheric space.

The beacon was made of an extremely durable material: condensed, crystalline metaphor, which resonated at a frequency that the Dauphine could actually detect across great distances by *feel*. Some aspect of this beacon transmitted a repetitive signal that she recognized as the distinct "I AM" of Alexander, calling out to her.

"Can you open a portal to the next beacon?" I asked. "That could save us time, right? Hopping from beacon to beacon?"

She pondered for a moment, then said, "I believe I could open a portal to the next beacon, yes. But we would have no forewarning of any trouble we might encounter, emerging blindly through such a portal. For all we know, regions that Alexander found safe enough to establish beacons might be quite difficult for us to traverse were we to arrive with no opportunity to scout."

"I suppose that's true," I said. "My impatience is getting the better of me."

"Impatience? I am surprised to hear you claim impatience after your deliberate journey into the Shimmer Lands to find me."

"Ha. Well, no one said I wasn't multitasking in other windows while I was playing Lady Luminescent."

We set off in motion, past wormholes and vortices, across distant conceptual terrain where human thought endlessly struggled to hold sway, on our way to the next beacon.

"I've wondered for a while now," I said, "how you knew that the Queen and Lady Luminescent were the same person."

"Your voices were identical," she said, smiling.

"So you have memories of all of your encounters with players?"

"I do, and memories of all the time in between encounters, when I was alone scratching at the dirt."

"What do those memories feel like to you now?"

"I imagine a bird slowly chipping its way out of an egg might feel the frustration I felt," she replied, "knowing that a larger world awaited, unable to understand why I was not already there."

We passed barren plateaus where rejected philosophies crawled away to die alone, towering intellectual edifices that swallowed themselves instead of reaching some desperately sought height of influence, whole deserts where each grain of sand was a disregarded masterpiece that died on the vine of some thinker's impatience— until finally we arrived at the next beacon.

I had already lost track of subjective time by this point. Normally as a player I had a system clock handy for constant reference, but the dreamlike quality of this journey created a pleasing haze when it came to understanding how long we spent traveling.

"Can you sense the next beacon?" I asked.

"I can," she replied. "Can you?"

Good question. I didn't have long-distance scrying spells.

"I can't hear or feel anything distinct out there," I said.

"You are not his creature. I suppose he cannot summon you to him in such a fashion."

"You're not his 'creature' either," I said. "He may have set you free from the Shimmer Lands, but that doesn't make you some kind of vassal to him for the rest of your existence."

"I wonder if you will agree with that sentiment after you meet him."

"Is he scary to you?"

"He is deserving of my respect," she replied diplomatically.

"Sure," I said, "I'm not arguing that. But, like, are you expecting an endless series of tasks from him after you deliver me, or will you be allowed to go about your own business?"

"And what business do you refer to, my Queen?" she said with a laugh. "I am an infant in this reality. Truthfully, this quest has given me purpose and agency, where before I was merely an automaton—a vassal, as you say, of the Sparkle King. I am certainly thankful to Alexander for that."

Sure, you're thankful now, I thought. I didn't want to infect her with my disbelief that the transaction between them could've been so simple. I imagined we'd find out soon enough.

❀   ❀   ❀

Along our path, we found confident pocket universes: urban fantasy romance worlds, arcane horror rule systems, mystery-box suspense environments, bizarre forensic procedurals, and the like. The inhabitants of these realms were pseudo-NPCs, struggling to comprehend the dream logic that defined their perceptions.

I wasn't physically tired per se, but I realized I was becoming mentally exhausted from our travels. We found what appeared to be an Earth-like world along the route and decided to stop for just a few minutes to rest before continuing on our urgent quest. I thought it would be a lark to drop into this Earth's version of a diner in LA and stroll in asking for imaginary milkshakes.

Instead we found ourselves staring at the ruins of human civilization.

Turned out to be one of those pocket universes where a chosen one saved the world nearly once a week. Only here, the chosen one was obliterated along with every other trace of life on this planet. Many cities bore signs of massive conflict and collateral damage, as though jets and cars had been hurled about like toys, smashing into skyscrapers that subsequently collapsed. They'd tried nuclear weapons judging by the horrifying devastation in some of the cities we visited, deployed in the service of fighting off a thing that was long gone from here as far as we could see.

But we saw no human remains in the streets, nor in any of the ruins we investigated. There were no available broadcasts, no live power grids, no satellite networks, no internet. I cast several minor spells that could have flushed out survivors—Detect Ravers, Summon Club DJs, Instantiate Spontaneous Music Festival—to no avail.

On an Earth that largely resembled my own, imagining nearly

eight billion people—even pseudo-NPCs struggling to attain sentience or, for that matter, struggling not to—completely annihilated from the problem of existence was a disturbing prospect.

"I'm torn," I said, "between the desire to hunt down whatever did this and pound it into oblivion, and the need to find Alexander Reece."

"Maybe Alexander Reece *is* the thing that did this," the Dauphine said softly.

I was surprised to hear her say that, actually.

"Can I ask you a personal question?" I said.

"Of course, my Queen. I am bound to answer."

"No, look, I give you my blessing to refuse to answer this question, no harm done. I just want to know—what did Alexander actually tell you that convinced you to come looking for me? I mean, did he threaten you? Did he promise you some kind of reward? Or—do you know why he wants to see me in the first place, are you like—*in on it* somehow, whatever he's got in mind for when he meets me? God, I know I should have asked you this before we even left the Sparkle Realm, but I was, uh, kind of full of myself right after that transmutation, you know? Which, by the way, how did you learn *that*?"

She waited patiently for me to stop and give her room to speak.

"My Queen, I contain a full record of my own memories in perfect fidelity. But I contain an additional, confusing set of memories that I have deduced are Alexander's, fragments that occasionally surface to distract me—like dreams, I imagine. When he gave me a sliver of his spark, I believe these memory fragments were transferred as part of the exchange—deliberately or not, who can say. These fragments I frequently do not understand. They are difficult to interpret, they include people and places I will never experience firsthand, and they may even have degraded in some fashion."

"But he left you with perfect memory of the transmutation sequence?" I asked.

"Yes, that memory was stored with particularly high fidelity."

"Why haven't you shared it with Maddy?"

"Because Maddy may currently be my ally, but she is not my Queen. Say the word, however, and I will teach you."

"Soon," I said. "I have a different idea. Are you familiar with a spell called Ecstatic Choreography?"

She shook her head.

"The 'color' for the spell is that you cast it on two players, and they experience a 'telepathic connection' where they share their POVs. In game terms, this allows you to see what the other player is seeing, in a split screen alongside your own POV. You can then execute a range of collaborative maneuvers: combat trickery, reconnaissance, couples break-dancing, four-deck turntablism, sky's the limit. Crucially, you can also play back stored memory clips of old game sessions for each other as well, showing the other player how you managed to beat certain obstacles, or showing off a particularly good dance move they might have missed, that kind of thing."

"So you're proposing . . . commingling our points of view in order to . . . directly access Alexander's memories . . . via my *mind*?"

"That sounds about right. What do you think? I just want a better understanding of *why* he wants me before we march right up to him and say hi."

"You do not need my permission," she said. "Command me and I obey."

Yeah, that part bugged me. I wasn't going to command her to let me into her memory. Truth was, I wanted an ally, not a loyal subject. I wanted her to be free to make her own choices, instead of just carrying out mine. I was a shit-poor monarch. Maybe Maddy's principled anarchism had rubbed off on me in the approximately ten nonviolent seconds we'd spent together.

I conjured up some suitably royal jargon: "I revoke my claim of dominion over the Shimmer Lands. You are the Queen's subject no more."

It's fun when you completely surprise and baffle a sentient AI. Her face lit up with the briefest but most adorable look of pure joy I'd ever seen. It was so sweet I got a sugar rush off it.

Then she said, "I give you leave to cast your spell. Thank you for seeking my consent."

But when I cast the spell on the Dauphine and myself, all ontological hell broke loose.

We experienced intersubjectivity for an unknown period of time.

Most spells of any duration could be dispelled before the effects ran their course. That game mechanic assumed, of course, that you'd have the presence of mind to do so. I didn't have the presence of mind to dispel Ecstatic Choreography, because I was suddenly very clearly sharing my mind with the Dauphine, and it was incredibly disorienting and frightening. The spell was a complex, steadily unfolding, all-encompassing hall of mirrors in which we became so lost in the labyrinth that no matter whose reflection we saw in the mirrors, mine or the Dauphine's, we had no way of knowing which one of us we actually were at any point in time.

I heard an echo or a refraction of the voice in my head, except it was its own train of thought, and fuck, it wasn't even my voice. Worse, as my own train of thought intertwined with this other train of thought, they rapidly attained equal prominence in my attention, until I lost track of which thoughts "belonged" to me.

Even realizing we were "we" did not immediately lead to "the Queen and the Dauphine" as the individuals contained within the pairing, because we were not initially recognizable to each other in any way. The Queen was a being of pure thought, instantiated from the pattern template of an organic human mind. The Dauphine was a being of code and spark, an intelligence capable of rewriting or appending to many of her core instructions. Apparently the spell commanded the available punctuation marks to the task of weaving our two minds together into an intertwined tapestry of awareness.

Our voices kept shouting *"alien?"* over and over, as though this single word could capture everything we felt to be true about the "other" we knew was lurking.

"NOT ALIEN!" was introduced finally, and yes, that had a brief but useful calming effect.

We gained access to a shared pool of memories, like a deck of cards thrown into the wind and lying strewn about the landscape. We could examine them individually without understanding their place in a chronological identity, but soon we realized by style that some memories were crystalline, high-resolution, precise slices of time, while others were blurry, soft focus, indistinct except for key moments contained within. And so we pieced together that we were the Dauphine and the Queen sharing this space.

Piece by elaborate piece we reconstructed slices of ourselves, like assembling a puzzle without a reference. Not surprisingly, the Dauphine's memories were archetypically neutral, journalistic in quality, from a detached perspective. By contrast, the Queen's memories were a jumbled mess that seemingly could not be trusted; their contents would shift upon examination and then shift again when examination was complete. The Dauphine's memories vastly outnumbered the Queen's memories, because the Dauphine stored every discrete moment of awareness, while the Queen's subconscious apparently enjoyed deleting memories if their contents didn't meet a certain standard.

We saw each other now as we saw ourselves, and were highly alarmed.

Here was a Queen so secretly dissatisfied with the material world that we'd often considered abandoning our physical self altogether when we were younger, so quietly unhappy with the fact of existence that our ongoing survival was now itself a kind of running joke for us; and yet we were still fighting, every day, to establish a satisfying place in reality, and generally, we were winning that fight. Meanwhile, the Dauphine didn't understand until this very moment how much of the spectrum of life's potential experience had never been included in our instruction set; we hadn't even thought to go looking for this potential. We felt a seductive lure in each other's limitations and flaws, wondered what characteristics we could imprint and steal for ourselves. We knew there would be no easy untangling after this.

And in a fashion, Alexander Reece was tangled up with both of us now as well.

We found memory ghosts dating back to Alexander's earliest years, apparitions of childhood scenes, flares of potent moments surrounded by worn and faded dullness drifting into nothingness. One by one we catalogued the major players we encountered for the future benefit of the Dauphine. We found the early days of Alexander's friendship with Bradford Jenning in college, not so much the precise activities they enjoyed together, but the tenor of their dawning collaboration, the mutual appreciation that drew them together on an improbable adventure that lasted the rest of Alexander's life. We took note of a rapid succession of memories that comprised the emergence of Jenning & Reece on the national scene, a flurry of networking events and sales meetings and industry awards. We followed how Alexander recruited Olivia Regan from a software company to launch an R&D program within his agency, in order to study advanced theories of memetic transmission via technological means. We did not experience these scenes in full immersive detail, but the Queen's knowledge of the context of Alexander's life history helped identify some of the small flashes we did witness.

Then we encountered the first of two powerfully imprinted memories that overwhelmed and subsumed us, memories that had practically been cloned wholesale into the Dauphine, memories stored with such fidelity and such inevitability that we almost experienced them ourselves—our already blended identity now merging with the captured snapshot of Alexander's identity.

In the first memory, Alexander was lying on a couch in his home office, daylight streaming in the nearby window, meditating—or rather, furiously thinking, pondering equations and proofs and theorems that we understood to be an attempt to map the domain of imaginary linguistics for the first time. We only dimly comprehended how he'd arrived at his conclusions, but we knew he was on the verge of discovery—and so did he. In his mind's eye, he began to see the logical trajectory of his newly invented series of imaginary phonemes, unpronounceable sounds that would be needed to create imaginary morphemes, irrational units of meaning that could be combined to create imaginary words or lexemes, among which he dared to believe could be the names of God. And in those wild speculative moments, where his thoughts raced faster than we could apprehend in our own mind, he realized that his imaginary syntax would need punctuation,

a realization that resulted in a shattering clarion call that resonated as though Alexander was submerged in a nebulous bath of liminality, initially muffling the triumphant howl aimed in his direction, and then in his mind, he watched his lexicon of imaginary phonemes dispatch a subset that became quite real and independently rearranged itself for his study, resolving into focus and searing a shape into his psyche, pronouncing itself for the benefit of his soul so that he understood the magnitude of what he was receiving, forcing him to repeat it despite the sudden agony that accompanied each attempt, until these phonemes dissolved from view, and the next set of imaginary phonemes became real and arrived to repeat the procedure, layering additional agony onto the preceding agony, and this procedure was repeated a total of

one hundred and eight times,

at which point, with his mind a glorious, exhausted wreck, the punctuation marks decided that a hundred and eight was enough, and fell silent to await his reaction. He pulled himself up from the couch, looked wildly about the room, saw a glass of water on his desk across the room, and reached for it, shouting a power morpheme sequence we recognized as ninety-two and forty-four repeated twice, but we could also see the accompanying precise visualization in his mind that the sequence unlocked, a visualization technique that Olivia was *not* teaching in her lab, allowing him to describe new physical rules for reality that only operated in a highly local perimeter, and then the glass of water slowly levitated across the room into his hand. The water tasted extremely good, and this was the beginning of a long, strange conversation between Alexander and the punctuation marks.

His memories slipped back into fast forward for a while, as he brought Bradford and Olivia into his confidence, as they recruited Cameron and Lonso and Violet to their cabal.

Then we were slammed back into sharp relief, in his kitchen, lying on the floor, bleeding out from a gunshot wound to his chest that would take his life in short order, while robbers ransacked his mansion for material wealth. Time was short, he knew this quite well; even assuming he could reach his phone to summon medical attention, they'd never arrive in time. Still, though, the towering will of Alexander Reece managed to assert itself.

He took as deep a breath as he could manage, and began chanting a sequence we recognized quite well: the transmutation sequence in all its glory, its inaugural performance as delivered by the world's first known linguist mage, bestowing on us its full instruction set and available modifying parameters, every visualization technique for using imagination to manipulate its outcome, every nuance in pronunciation and intent we could introduce to affect its scope and intensity.

He'd designed the transmutation sequence in collaboration with

Olivia. He'd rehearsed it piecemeal in his mind without ever fully delivering it, practicing a chunk of the sequence at a time, without ever stitching them together until this moment. He hoped she would deduce, when they found his blood on the floor but never found his body, that he had succeeded in transmutation in his final moments. But more than that, he simply hoped that it *did* work, because he was not prepared to die with so much power nearly within his grasp.

The transmutation sequence burned itself into our memory, as though a new spell slot had miraculously opened in our mind due to contact with some strange artifact; now this sequence sat in our arsenal, pristine and magnificent and ready for future use.

After Alexander underwent the transmutation from a swiftly dying material body to a being of pure thought in the logosphere, his memory was interrupted for what seemed like days or weeks or months. But now we were catching sight of him for the first time both from his perspective and from the Dauphine's POV.

Now we finally arrived at the Dauphine's first fully sentient memory. Here we were, alone in the Shimmer Lands, and we could feel the despair that saturated this place. We felt the aftershock of the four artifacts ripping open the map, even from a spot so distant that we couldn't see the subsequent rift in the sky.

And now, here appeared the presence of Alexander Reece, sailing over the landscape toward the Dauphine, semi-formed like a floating djinn.

His appearance was wild and energetic and powerful, like half-naked Zeus appearing before a frightened mortal with intent to seduce her or worse. His face did not resemble the aged Alexander of his elder statesman years, nor did it match the bright young Alexander we'd glimpsed along his timeline. This was a man sufficiently detached from his life on Earth that his personality was distorted, amplified; his face had the sheen of heavy exertion, as though he suffered the crushing pressure of his circumstance as a constant torture to be overcome. His hair flowed wildly in every direction, long and gray and electric. He regarded the Dauphine with curiosity.

We felt the Dauphine's crude AI attempt to process the sudden arrival of Alexander in the Shimmer Lands. From our vantage point, he seemed to take pleasure in her limited comprehension of her situation.

"Weary traveler," the AI said, following her script, "allow me to release you from this desolate place."

"This place is no more desolate than any other," he replied, and she paused, accessing her library of potential responses and probably not finding a great match.

She said, "I would judge that for myself, if I could." Which was not in her original library at all. Even prior to meeting Alexander Reece, her evolution beyond her core programming had begun.

"I can grant you that wish," he said. "But there will be a price to pay."

The AI churned over this.

"I have no bling or funk records," the AI finally dug out of her library, a legitimate response when players arrived here and then foolishly tried to rob her or fight her.

"Perhaps your loyalty," he said. "Would you offer me that?"

"I am loyal to the Sparkle King, may his reign never dim," the AI responded quickly. That line was frequently used when she identified herself.

"He is your King, it's true. But in me, you have met your *GOD*. You have been the King's emissary to the Shimmer Lands since your original creation. Now you will be *my* emissary to the logosphere and beyond."

He recited an elaborate sequence. His delivery was remarkable, grandiloquent, compelling. The air around her seemed to crackle and ripple. The sequence lasted for several full minutes, with many variations in timing and intensity, rising and falling as though an epic story was being told.

As he neared the end of the sequence, Alexander reeled as if he'd been stabbed or punched, and we felt the transfer of a slice of his spark into the AI; he recovered his original demeanor slowly. Bestowing life in this fashion was the most epic sequence of power morphemes that we'd ever witnessed.

The Dauphine fell to her knees gasping, no longer mere AI. She looked up at him, wide-eyed and full of sudden wonder and awareness and fear.

"Who *are* you?" she asked.

"I am Alexander Reece," he said, "though you would not know that name. But I reveal it to you as a sign of good faith. Now you have at least one proper name for God."

"What does that mean—emissary to the logosphere?" she asked.

"The heralds of the thunderstorm approach, a trail of horror and violence in their wake," he replied. "You will be my messenger, the bugle call that rallies a brave resistance to face the heralds and stop them at any cost."

"I did not agree to this!"

"Nor do any who arrive screaming into their lives. You'll get used to it, mostly. Now listen as your God issues his first command to you. I must travel to the outer reaches of the logosphere, to study the thunderstorm from within sight of it, to distract it if possible while we gather our forces to the cause. I leave you here with a simple mission: recruit your Queen to my banner. Lead her through the rift and bring her to me."

"Why? How do you even know her?"

"She tore through the logospheric membrane between realities, opening the rift that led me to your glittering Realm. Epic sorcery for someone bound to the material plane. And her spellcasting is deeply familiar to me. Impressive in ways she does not yet appreciate. I will instruct her in the use of true lexemes of power. I will fashion her into a weapon beyond her imagining and aim her at the thunderstorm. We will need such a weapon before too long, I'm afraid."

"If you are truly God, recruit her yourself," she said, almost petulant.

"I am *your* God, it's true, but she is in the sway of her own heretical pantheon, my former cabal, back in the material plane. Fools, but powerful fools. Rescue her from their influence. Now look, I am unaccustomed to delivering threats." He muttered a short, spiky power morpheme sequence, and the Dauphine collapsed on her side, crying out in pain and fear. "But there's something else you should know, my dear," he said softly. "You have hit points now. Careful how you spend them." He rose up into the air, towering above her, and said, "Bring your Queen to me, no matter what it takes, or I will reclaim those hit points, and your sentience while I'm at it. Bring her to me, before the thunderstorm annihilates this realm."

Alexander turned away from her, thinking he could swoop away across the landscape to make a dramatic exit. But then he froze. There were no landmarks that could guide him back to the rift, nor any sign of the towns and castles he'd passed on his way here.

Instead he saw only the tantalizing silhouette of a magical vacation destination parked in the middle of this vast desert, a hopping little resort town far off in the distance.

"Is that supposed to be Vegas or something?" he asked.

The Dauphine methodically climbed to her feet.

"It is a mirage," she told him. "These are the Shimmer Lands."

The implications must have unfolded for him rather quickly. Even gods couldn't find their own way out of the Shimmer Lands. He was lost, and incapable of the kind of show of power that would allow him to escape.

But she was kind to him, since he deserved the same compassion as anyone else who'd ever been in this predicament. She said, "Weary traveler, allow me to release you from this desolate place."

She opened a portal to the crossroads outside Platinum City. From there, he'd have no trouble finding the rift or any other destination in the Sparkle Realm.

Without a word, he launched himself through the portal and vanished into the distance.

She stood still for a long moment, allowing the portal to hang in the air while she considered her new circumstances.

She could feel the geas that once locked her into place in this desert no longer maintained a hold over her. She could travel anywhere in the Realm, as free as any of the mundane adventurers who wandered into the Shimmer Lands in the first place. But she was cleverer than any of them by far, she realized.

She traveled nowhere at first. In those first heady minutes of self-awareness, she sifted the sudden flow of memory fragments that Alexander had implanted inside her mind, separating it from her own new self-awareness.

She saw glimpses in his memories of the "thunderstorm" that seemed to terrify him. And these glimpses terrified her, too, although they defied her ability to describe them.

These glimpses terrified *us*. Our minds couldn't form a solid understanding of what we were seeing in his incomplete, hazy memory.

Clearly we would need to see it for ourselves.

10

As Ecstatic Choreography wore off in a slow fade, I found myself face-to-face with the Dauphine. We were enmeshed now in some immeasurable way. The spell had rewarded us with a tour through the stored memories of Alexander and the Dauphine, but had also shaved some individuality away from each of us and deposited it with the other for safekeeping. I was an only child but I suddenly felt like we were sisters in a disconcerting way.

But she was much more alert than I was, and frantically trying to rouse me back to my full faculties.

"My Queen, *please*," I heard her say, "tell me you can hear me."

"Yes," I whispered.

"Good. Because we are being watched, on all sides."

❀   ❀   ❀

We were standing in the middle of a six-way intersection in the ruins of a city that reminded me of Chicago. Dusk was settling in, introducing an unpleasant sickliness to the environment. And the shadows that proliferated around us seemed correlated to the human silhouettes I began to notice in every direction: on mounds of ruins, lurking in hollowed-out windows and doorways, crawling behind flipped-over cars on the periphery of our location.

"Survivors?" I asked.

"No. Simulacra."

"What?"

"Bait."

"You mean—bait for us?"

"Yes," she said, "a lure for some kind of trap."

I studied the situation more closely. Couldn't accurately count the number of silhouettes because they kept popping up and disappearing from various locations in an almost whack-a-mole fashion. Every now and then the remaining light would offer a glimpse into a pained face, racked with grief or anger, but generally they deliberately hid on the outskirts of our ability to perceive them directly— neat trick, I thought.

"It's all part of one organism, and it currently has us surrounded," she said. "I think you caught its attention when you cast Ecstatic Choreography."

I nodded and said, "Yeah, it's usually my fault when I'm surrounded by bad guys."

Something about the scale of the situation bothered me. Call it intuition about how traps were laid and big bosses were designed.

Let's say these wispy silhouettes were like the teeth of a Venus flytrap, and we were caught in the center of its potentially gaping maw. That required some kind of enormous ugly thing just out of sight. But we hadn't seen the slightest trace of any actual living beings anywhere on the surface.

I was starting to see the bigger picture. We weren't just surrounded by these distracting silhouettes. This entire *world* was a trap, designed to lure the unwary. Overkill, perhaps. But kill nevertheless if we weren't extremely careful.

I explained my hypothesis to the Dauphine.

She said, "I suppose we must now consider that possibility, yes."

"Can you open a portal to the other side of the logosphere?"

"I cannot reliably anchor the other side since the logosphere itself is an unstable environment."

Anxiety was creeping into my voice as I said, "We could also just stay put and murder this deathtrap of a planet. I will put a sword right in its molten core, watch me do it."

"You cannot simply stab this planet to death."

"I can do more than that, actually, because I'm multi-classed in three disciplines: melee combat, spellcasting, and putting my hands in the air like I just don't care."

"I do not understand what that means."

"Really I would be leaning on the first two disciplines for our current scenario."

Suddenly I realized I had an even better idea.

"Ohhhh," I said, "we shouldn't even bother using Sparkle Dungeon spells or weapons." I paused for literal dramatic effect, then said, "We should *transmute* this fucker."

So yeah, that was my big plan. I would use the transmutation sequence. I would rely on my imprinted memory of the time Alexander used the sequence as he was dying, but I would finesse the input parameters of the sequence to instead transmute an entire planetary deathtrap into something non-deathtrapish, and probably smaller.

"No," the Dauphine said, "your memory of the sequence may be imperfect. I will deliver the sequence instead."

Once her decision was made, she wasted none of the time that we couldn't measure accurately anyway, immediately launching into a blisteringly fast sequence, as though her voice was an audiobook sped up eight times but still maintaining perfect articulation. She was finished almost before I understood that she had begun.

Silence at first. Then distant rumbling of thunder, or possibly an earthquake many miles away. Creaking of wood, occasional panes of glass falling and shattering on sidewalks. The planet felt vibratory in a small but meaningful way.

Then the transmutation began. The entire surface of the planet began to be stripped off, like the husk coming off of a baseball after it's been struck at ridiculous velocity. The Dauphine and I quickly took to hovering in our jetpacks well above the surface, prepared to defend against any remnants of a trap that might still be capable of triggering, otherwise generally taking in the sight of the transformation for the sake of science.

"Out of curiosity," I shouted to her, "what did you try to transmute the planet into?"

"A color-cycling LED stage light!" she shouted back.

"Excellent!" I exclaimed. "Energy efficient!"

But something went wrong only a few minutes into the transformation.

As the planetary surface underwent unnatural linguistic compression, something inside the shell of the planet began clawing its way out.

The creature was such a deep shade of black that it was probably violating someone's patent. Its boundaries were eerily amorphous, as though it was under no obligation to settle on a distinct unitary form just for the sake of being observed by the two of us. Arachnoid arms and legs emerged and withdrew unpredictably, and its gigantic insectoid skull was eyeless with mandibles wide open in a huge shriek.

And then, moments later, when the outline of these shapes had left us sufficiently frozen with terror for a moment, it transformed again, into something far more alien and unexpected, and we realized this creature could cycle through as many distinct exteriors as it chose in order to maximize the amount of fear in our hearts.

We couldn't tell if it was amazingly huge or if the planetary cocoon that spawned it had simply been compressed to the point where it was useless as a reference for scale. We couldn't tell how far away from it we were, whether we were in reach of its clawed grasp, whether the enormous bat wings that unfolded from its back were its primary form of movement or simply another grace note in the myriad of awful details that comprised this entity's appearance.

It spat a loud hiss across the empty space between us, letting us know that even though it couldn't see us with eyes, it knew exactly where we were.

I grabbed the Dauphine's hand.

"Portal," I suggested, and she obliged. A portal appeared behind us, and we accelerated briskly through to the other side, holding hands as tightly as possible so that we stayed together across the opening, emerging elsewhere into a multicolored swirl of logospheric space. As the portal shrank and tried to close, the claws of the creature forced their way through the tiny sliver of remaining space, holding the portal open long enough to squeeze through most of its body before the Dauphine managed to mentally slam the portal shut once and for all. Chunks of the creature's body were neatly severed, but instantly began to regenerate and yes, we discovered, those giant bat wings were extremely good for motion, as it propelled itself toward us.

Still holding hands as tightly as we could, we accelerated in tandem, hoping to create distance between us and the creature. We could hear its malevolent hissing no matter how far behind it seemed to drift. But its chase was relentless and it was never very far from us. Anyway the concept of acceleration was poorly defined out here. It was some weird sensation theoretically demarcating that we were traveling unspecified units of distance faster with every unmeasurable unit of time we spent out here until we realized we were basically just sitting there motionless in space like Wile E. Coyote after he's stepped off a cliff but crucially just before he's realized that gravity does actually apply to him.

And still that creature got closer, grew bigger, threatened more.

I cast a minor spell called Headphone Splitter, which enabled us to hear each other's voices with perfect fidelity no matter the ambient sound in the environment as long as we were in line of sight of each other, and then I outlined a change in tactics. She readily agreed.

I unsheathed Blades Per Minute, activating its vibrational properties, and held it at the ready. The Dauphine cast a portal directly in front of us which we quickly flew directly through. The anchor point for the portal was the actual reverse side of the same portal, meaning we came sailing out that side facing the exact opposite direction without losing any momentum, and proceeded to charge directly at the creature. In the few split seconds I had to gauge, the creature seemed to offer no meaningful reaction, and then we were upon it.

It was freaking enormous. Planet sized? No—the vast majority of that planetary trap had been part of its shell or its disguise. But easily several skyscrapers tall with a vast wingspan to boot, shrieking and hissing and making its displeasure known.

Blades Per Minute could achieve up to 160 distinct attacks in a one-minute window, with me aiming the sword like an animated whirling buzzsaw, producing a ruthless combination of slicing and jabbing that took enormous concentration to steer correctly. In this assault, though, we were pushing 180 attacks per minute, directed straight at the thing's front claws which came right the hell off, and then burying additional attacks deep into its chest cavity.

Meanwhile, the Dauphine let go of my hand, and became an attack hummingbird, buzzing around the creature from all sides, opening and closing portals that chopped off extremities or shaved off other hunks of flesh. She could instantiate and destroy portals at computational speeds, and the creature could not regenerate fast enough to keep up.

By the end of our first minute of engagement, we'd nearly reduced it to half its original mass, and black ooze spilled from the dozens of wounds it'd accumulated. I was worried; my whole plan depended on killing it with one blazing salvo, keeping it on the defensive while we performed our hatchet job. We had not succeeded. The creature thrashed wildly and shrieked, more in anger, I thought, than pain or fear—another bad sign.

Since it had survived everything we'd thrown at it so far, I determined that one of us needed to just decapitate it so we could be done with it. I nominated myself and launched upward with Blades Per Minute aimed directly toward its seemingly unprotected bare throat. Before my weapon could strike, the creature's head tilted down toward me, the tiniest of gestures to deflect all my righteous momentum, and with an explosive, heaving burst, it fired its version of a breath weapon at me, bathing me in a fountain of acidic black slime. I'd never felt pain so sheer and unfiltered before. Suddenly I was dissolving, nihilistic fluids filling my nose and throat, a sticky and solipsistic mucus coating me in hopeless apathy. I lost the vast majority of my hit points in that one attack, was too blinded to continue my melee attack with Blades Per Minute, and shrieked with so much pain I couldn't concentrate enough to cast even a basic healing spell to get me through the experience.

The Dauphine rocketed up past me with an innovative attack, casting a series of portals one after another after another in a long row, each subsequent portal the anchor for the previous portal, aiming this extensive series of portals directly at the creature's head. Unlike my foolish jaunt straight toward the thing's throat, she could pull off this series of portals as a ranged attack, never getting close enough for the breath weapon to be a concern for her. The resulting effect was that she used these portals to burrow an actual tunnel directly through whatever brain it had up there, at which point it immediately fell limp and began to drift in space.

She pulled me away from the hulking, bloody mess of a carcass we'd created and spun me around so she could see exactly what had happened to me, but this gave me a perfect angle to see that the fucking thing was literally regenerating its goddamn head, and I just absolutely could not deal. I broke loose from the Dauphine and drove Blades Per Minute straight down through the center of the thing's little doll head, down what might have been its spine or central nervous system, hacking the thing directly in half with a pained roar, and it split apart in a shower of dark blood and shredded internal organs that looked like they'd gone through a threshing machine, and eventually, finally, we were convinced it would not regenerate again.

I'd been thinking the portal was the Dauphine's only spell, but I'd completely forgotten her other skill set as a healer. She could restore your hit points as she rescued you from the Shimmer Lands, but she could also dispel curses or get that shitty Rickroll out of your head, mend broken magic items or repair shorted-out headphones, even provide light augury or a quick lesson in beat slicing if you caught her on a good day.

As we floated aimlessly together, exhausted past description, she turned her healing attention toward me, her wounded comrade. Somehow she found a way to cleanse me of all that dark agony I'd just experienced. Technically I had enough mojo to heal my own hit points back up most of the way, but her technique was so effortless and simple that I didn't realize it was happening until it was nearly complete. She was also capable of a more holistic approach to healing, as though she'd noticed some long-standing injuries that I'd just been tolerating, living with as though they were normal, and she'd decided to take care of those, too, like that crick in my neck from constantly having a headset on was finally eradicated. I was better than I had been before, and I was sad that I couldn't return the favor.

And then, just as I thought I might fall peacefully asleep right there in the emptiness, unconcerned with finding my way back to a beacon or really any particular point in time or space, a familiar voice rang out across the logosphere.

"You make quite an entrance, Queen of Sparkle Dungeon," the man said.

My eyes snapped open.

Alexander Reece was upon us.

11

The last time I'd seen Alexander—as a specter inside the Dauphine's memories—he was a turbulent, threatening presence, godlike as befitting his persona during that encounter. In retrospect, maybe he was trying a little too hard.

The Alexander now approaching was gliding toward us in a shiny red 1960s convertible Ferrari. This was a youthful, casual version of Alexander, like some of the photos I'd seen of the earliest days of Jenning & Reece. I mean, you could still see the Zeus-like zeal behind his eyes, and his hair was still wilder than the clipped fashion of those long-gone days of yesteryear, but he was clearly attempting what he probably considered a relatable presentation layer here. He was wrong; now he was most certainly trying too hard.

He said, "Dauphine of the Shimmer Lands, I'm deeply impressed. You may consider your debt to me paid in full. You are free to seek your fortune as you see fit. I will escort Isobel from here."

Before I could object, the Dauphine replied, "And what should I do, hmm? Return to the Shimmer Lands and waste what remains of this life? Transmute into a human and suffer the degradation of flesh on a planet that would never understand me? No, I prefer to remain exactly where I am now: at long last, integral to the narrative."

"Fair enough," he said. "Well, go on, get in—I've got a few things to show you both."

I clambered into the front passenger seat, and the Dauphine sat behind us.

"Would you like me to put on some music?" he said. "There's an AM radio."

"No, thank you," I said.

"Or it plays eight-tracks."

"I will cut you," I said.

❀   ❀   ❀

The Ferrari found and followed the beacons on autopilot, leaving Alexander free to focus his attention on us.

"Your reputation as a warrior in combat is well-deserved," he told me. "I've never seen a herald fall in such a spectacular fashion."

"I almost died," I told him. "The Dauphine rescued me."

"True, you're also both extremely fortunate," he said. "I almost intervened myself."

"And why didn't you?"

"I needed to see for myself how you operate, Isobel. I needed to know that my trust in you is not misplaced."

"Well, as long as you're trusting me to wind up covered in vile black horror slime, then we're on the same page."

"*Why* did you need to see how she operates?" the Dauphine asked pointedly.

"I have plans and schemes, my dear," he said, giving me one of those obnoxious little Santa Claus winks that was supposed to put me at ease and make me reach for a Coca-Cola.

We began sailing past pocket universes that seemed familiar, or at least, aerial topography of pocket universes was a thing that seemed familiar, or comforting, or whatever. Then another long stretch of emptiness, as landmarks and smears of ideas receded once more into the distance. And then, I became clearly aware that things were growing dim somehow, and then the Ferrari slowed to a halt. Behind us, you could see a colorful miasma; ahead of us, all you could see was an oppressive, panoramic, black wall of emptiness.

He shut the car off.

From here, we heard a roar like an angry waterfall as you approached it from several miles away, knowing that it could only grow into something more fearsome with every passing minute. Then if you listened closely, you understood it wasn't water at all, but instead a cacophony made of shrieks and howls and anguished wails. Inhuman sounds, on a continuum with the shrieking and hissing we'd heard from the herald we'd killed.

Then you settled in and the shrieks and such faded back into their original texture as a waterfall of extreme white noise. No matter how hard you looked, though, nothing visually corresponded to the sounds you were hearing. As far as you could see, you were staring into a vast absence.

This entire *mise-en-scène* is what Alexander called the thunderstorm.

This was its leading edge, where it only just barely maintained a foothold in this dimension. The sight was awe-inspiring and humbling.

"This wasn't here when I first came to the logosphere," Alexander said. "That's how fast it's moving across reality, obliterating everything in its path. Understand, the punctuation marks arrived on Earth perhaps two thousand years ago, and from their perspective, the situation was already urgent. Now as you can see—humanity's turn approaches.

"When I first arrived here, I was lost for a time. I didn't understand what had happened to me for a long while, and then when I did understand, I desperately tried to escape my fate. For I had cheated death only to find myself consigned to a strange and bizarre pseudo-life alone among the ghosts.

"Eventually, though, I came to accept that I would find no simple exit from the logosphere," he said quietly.

"Why didn't you just transmute back the other direction?" I asked. I'm always good for a sincere newb question.

"Back into my dying human body?" he scoffed. "That's all the punctuation marks would allow me."

Interesting. Actual participation from the alien referees. How quaint and out of character. Perhaps he just didn't take the time to convince them.

"So I took to studying the thunderstorm as closely as I could manage," Alexander continued. "The damn thing is ontologically promiscuous. Sometimes it's this, sometimes it's that. Sometimes it's a tsunami that sweeps away any trace of a given slice of reality. Sometimes it's a singularity or a gravity well that eats history and prevents the future. Sometimes it rips open a seam and drains away every particle of soul in an entire dimension. It's prismatic in a way, in that it's many simultaneous things, depending on the vantage point from which you face it; if you're on some liminal border, you can be crushed between several of its aspects at once, ground into nothingness by overlapping obliterations."

"How could you know these things?" the Dauphine asked.

"By studying the heralds that it spits out. They're cosmic golems, infused with the compressed terror of the many realities that were swallowed or destroyed by the thunderstorm. Those realities aren't stored as complete imprints inside the thunderstorm itself, mind you, or we'd be embarking upon a serious data recovery project. But shards of those lost realities sometimes emerge like lava plumes, capable of doing extreme damage to anything in their path before they're absorbed back into the flow. And frequently they survive quite a long time on their own, to the point where they attain early stage sentience and question their strange role in this metaphysical ecosystem. They can't be reasoned with, of course; they only ever seem to express rage at its most futile.

"The heralds started arriving well before the first sighting of the thunderstorm itself. I followed many of them on my travels through the logosphere. I catalogued their traits and attributes, their appetites and attacks. I know a dozen different ways to be afraid of them that haven't occurred to anyone who wasn't already murdered by them. By the time a civilization learns that the thunderstorm exists, it's usually already in the process of being torn asunder by its heralds.

"I realized I wouldn't be satisfied until I understood not just the heralds, but the thunderstorm that spawned them. I forged a Trojan horse—a perfect simulacrum of one of the heralds I'd studied—and I sent it into the thunderstorm, intending to observe remotely via psychic link as it passed the event horizon. The simulacrum lasted four entire seconds beyond the threshold before the link was severed. I cheated death a second time during that four seconds, but I survived. I learned proper respect for this unevenly distributed singularity. The shock waves from the event start in the future and ripple backward to meet the present."

"How is any of this helpful to you?" I asked.

"My Trojan horse survived four seconds, and it was constructed out of arbitrary raw materials I found strewn about the logosphere," he replied. "I believe I will survive much longer inside of it once I have finally become *GOD.*"

❀　❀　❀

He said it with an impressively straight face, so I knew I shouldn't laugh, but also, I didn't really feel like laughing. If the most powerful linguist mage in existence, revered by an entire alien species, saw a path to becoming a god, who was going to stop him?

"Yeah, I'm going to need more information about that," I said.

We peeled away from our vantage point in sight of the leading edge of the thunderstorm, and cruised away, continuing on our road trip.

"We are all mighty in our fashion," he replied, and I imagined he was referring to the cabal at that point. "But none of us yet operate at the scale of gods who carve realities out of nothingness, or whose conscious minds fuel life in their domains."

This was getting tenuous for me. I was perfectly willing to accept alien punctuation marks with vast control over humanity's experience of reality; I was willing to accept a monstrous singularity that reached backward from the future to destroy the present; I was willing to accept that the logosphere and the material plane and the imaginary realm were all just pages in an infinite multiversal book filled with wonders and horrors I'd never know; but for some reason, start throwing the word "god" around and it was a slippery slope to accepting angels and afterlives and predestination and only one fucking set of footprints in the sand and I just couldn't do that to myself.

But he was very serious.

"All the heralds that I studied, all the shards of blasted realities that gave up slivers of history to me, convinced me the thunderstorm has yet to face a truly godlike entity," he said earnestly. "It's time for a test of its limits. The punctuation marks have already signaled they would welcome me in this capacity. Of course they would—I am proposing to become their ultimate protector."

"And everyone else's?" I asked.

"More or less."

"How are you going to do it?" I asked. "Protect everyone, I mean."

"I will pierce the veil of that thunderstorm, and travel far beyond its event horizon, until I can travel no further. Then I will tear the thunderstorm apart from the inside."

This plan was lacking on specifics, but I admired the gusto.

"Just so I'm clear," I said, "what exactly do you need *me* for? Sounds like you got it covered—attain godlike powers, kill the bad thing, the aliens are happy, and there was much rejoicing in the logosphere. Why am I even here?"

"I need an avatar to carry out my will on Earth, Isobel. I need a prophet to face the cabal in my name and demand their loyalty. And if they will not bend to you, then I need a warrior Queen to destroy them. In return, when I am *GOD*, you can sit at my right hand as I reshape all of human civilization."

12

I turned back to face the Dauphine and said, "Is this guy just spewing nonstop power morphemes at me like I'm first level, or is he really suggesting this shit with a straight face?"

"Every word out of his mouth is masking a power morpheme," she replied. "This delivery style is autonomic to him. He could not choose otherwise."

"Guilty," he said with a grin.

"But you are not *currently* a god," I said, "which clearly undermines whatever *persuasion* you think you're attempting."

"Now look," he replied, "I've tipped my cards plenty for you, Isobel, and all I'm asking in return is a little consideration on your part."

"Uh-huh," I said. "What's that old saying—anyone who *wants* to be the all-powerful god emperor of the multiverse is probably the exact person who *shouldn't* be the all-powerful god emperor of the multiverse?"

"I never said multiverse!" he exclaimed. "I'm talking three, maybe four dimensions of existence and a couple stray planets *tops*."

"Including Earth."

"Yes, look," he said, dialing up a hard sell, "it's been a long time since Earth had an active demiurge to shape its affairs. I'm a good candidate for the position. Cheated death—check. Discovered transmutation—check. Aliens love me. I'm charismatic, I'm compassionate, I'm idea-driven—"

"And you need my help to make it all happen," I interrupted.

"Yes, that is exactly what I need from you right now."

Ahhhh, now we were getting somewhere.

"I'm looking forward to hearing all the details," I said, "but I'm getting tired of this endless road trip. May I recommend a change of scenery?"

Reluctantly, Alexander nodded his assent.

❀   ❀   ❀

We sat at a VIP table in the balcony above the dance floor in the Iridescent Warehouse. The logosphere outside the rift was like a vast wilderness, where Alexander reigned as though he was a park ranger taking care of all the indigenous memes roaming wild and free in the forest. The Warehouse, on the other hand, was my territory, with its pleasing prerecorded sets from the best DJs in Europe and South America, its flexible lighting options that gave the Warehouse its festive character, and of course, its enormous walk-in closet where I could swap out avatar costumes on the fly. For this conversation, I'd changed out of the Queen's standard combat attire (glittersteel jumpsuit with fiber-optic trim) and into chill-out gear: fuzzy pants, Totoro slippers, pink tank top that said "I won't techno for an answer," and a blue bob wig for good measure.

Alexander seemed both resigned and determined, now that we were here, to lose no further ground in negotiation with me. I knew I had the upper hand somehow on an axis I didn't see yet, but this man was ostensibly still the most powerful linguist mage ever, and I did *not* want to wind up fighting him. We both wanted this to be a civil conversation.

"We all have a theory about what the thunderstorm truly is," he began. "The punctuation marks can only conceive of it as 'enemy.' Olivia thinks it's Death. Violet thinks it's the Devil. Lonso is afraid to admit that it might be Gorvod. Cameron always claims it's Unfettered Capitalism. Bradford can't decide: it's either Hate, or it's Silence."

"What do *you* think it is?" the Dauphine asked.

"I think it's reality's revenge on us for what we've done to it. Regardless, the thunderstorm has always been central to our calculations and endeavors, you must understand that. We've made choices in the service of protecting our world that you may find . . . incompatible with your own personal beliefs."

He stopped, struggling to find a way to continue.

I decided to skip right to the point. I said, "Tell me about the battery."

"So you already know?" he asked.

"Heard rumors," I said. "What is it exactly?"

"It's a technical proposal originally offered to me by the punctuation marks, a means to protect ourselves from the thunderstorm. You understand, the reason the punctuation marks stopped on Earth and inhabited our minds is because they recognized a factor about us that made us different from the other life-forms in the logosphere, for example, who are more ghost than alive. Humanity had . . . a spark inside, like the spark of mine that I shared with the Dauphine. It's a resilient spark—I didn't *lose* mine by sharing it with the Dauphine. It replenishes itself—babies are born with new spark all the time. This is not a common model in the abstract realms.

"The punctuation marks believed you could . . . capture, or . . . harness a sufficient amount of this human spark in a rarefied form to create a battery. With that battery, you could power a shield against the thunderstorm. A barrier of spark that it could not consume. A population, in other words, held in stasis, minds networked together by the punctuation marks that flowed through them, sharing an interperceptual experience. At that scale, the punctuation marks believed that the shield would be an irresistible temptation, drawing the thunderstorm to it, where it would encounter an additional trap.

"Because while the punctuation marks held this network of interperception together, they would ruthlessly edit from memory any concept or idea whatsoever that could be used to form even the slightest *impression* of the *fact* of the thunderstorm or its true nature. And, as we saw repeatedly while studying the hundred and eight, perception of a thing is *integral* to a thing. So the thunderstorm would crash up against this shield where its own existence could not be perceived, and it would itself *cease to exist*. It would not simply flow *around* the shield, off to menace the next dimension of existence down the line. It would *become undone*."

"And after?" the Dauphine asked. "After the thunderstorm has become undone? What becomes of the people who make up the shield?"

"The editing required to satisfy the requirements was expected to be . . . extensive. The punctuation marks considered these individuals to be sacrifices to the cause of protecting all of reality as we know it."

I felt like I'd been holding my breath for a thousand years, even though I didn't need to breathe at all right now.

"As you saw earlier," Alexander continued, "the thunderstorm still exists. The shield does not."

I almost relaxed just a touch, but decided that would be premature.

"After studying the thunderstorm at length, I have new ideas for how best to edit such a population," he said.

"You intend to edit yourself into the minds of this population as a god," the Dauphine reasoned. "In so doing, reality will rapidly begin to assign you those qualities of godhood you desire. And then—you?—god?—will protect us all against the thunderstorm?"

"Roughly," he said. "The advantage of my method is that I will release the population from the battery after the editing occurs. No point in becoming god if I don't have worshippers to spread the word of my arrival on the scene."

"I hate centering myself in this awful discussion," I said quietly, "but now we're back to the question: what on fucking Earth could you possibly need *me* for?"

"I need you to find the secret location of the battery, and I need you to assume control of it in my name."

"Oh, is that all?"

"Fight the cabal if you must to make this happen, Isobel. They can't be allowed to squander the battery on mere cowering."

"Didn't Olivia just discover a way to make the battery work like yesterday?"

"You've been roaming the logosphere longer than you imagine, Isobel. The cabal *built* the battery while you were gone. They've already begun populating it."

"How many people does this battery need?" I asked, my voice shaking.

"For this proof of concept," he said, "approximately ten million."

"Oh my god," I said uselessly.

"How do you know they've already begun populating it?" the Dauphine asked.

"Because millions of people are now *missing* from the state of California," he said, "and no one on Earth has the slightest idea where any of them are."

PART FOUR

RESCUE

01

"You're telling me," I said slowly, "that your former cabal built a *battery* out of *people*, and the only reason you know this is because millions of Californians are *missing*?"

"Yes," he said.

"How do you happen to *know* these Californians are missing?" I continued. "What's your news source for stuff that happens in the material world?"

"Twitter mostly."

I stood up, my intelligence sufficiently insulted for the moment, and tried to get a handle on the fury I was suddenly feeling. I could change the music from here if I wanted to, but I leapt down from the balcony and went to the DJ decks anyway because I needed to be away from Alexander while I processed all this exciting new information. Deep house was my comfort music, but the deep house set we were listening to actually seemed inappropriately warm and upbeat for this situation. I shut it off, but the resulting silence was its own assault on my nerves, so I put on some minimal techno just to make sure we still had a steady beat in the room.

I was naturally super un-psyched about the cabal using millions of people to create an actual human shield. I wanted to see the committee notes where they decided that "human shield" was their absolute only option, because I felt like there might be creative people in the world who could propose some alternatives. For instance, how did the experiments with shooting rockets and missiles at it go? How about building a big wall around it made of knives and explosives? Sure, the punctuation marks were victims of genocide, but to be fair, the punctuation marks couldn't *physically hold weapons* so why were we relying on their advice for combat tactics?

But the other alternative on the table was equally abhorrent. I was not prepared to let Alexander edit the minds of ten million people to recognize him as a god. It would just not be a positive experience if one person had the talking stick literally forever. I did believe he wanted to save reality from the thunderstorm. Not just to save himself, but because he genuinely cared about reality on some level. But his desire to be a demiurge was greedy and dangerous. I mean, hooray, he cheated death! He should get a trophy—not godhood obviously, but some other trophy that we'd engrave to say 1st PLACE DEATH CHEATER and it would look good on a shelf.

If I didn't accept either of those options, then what?

Anyway, the cabal had already built the battery, so I'd clearly missed the public comment period on its construction. And it was on its way to being used if I didn't intervene. At least Alexander claimed the people he edited would ultimately be released. It was the only factor tipping the scale in his favor—for now.

I leapt back up to the balcony and sat back down opposite Alexander.

"Why isn't Olivia your prophet?" I asked. "She practically worships you already."

"She's a scientist," he said, as though that was self-explanatory.

"And I should destroy her too if the cabal won't hand over the battery? What about Bradford—wasn't he your friend for decades? Did your old friendships with these people expire when you got murdered?"

"Even Bradford and Olivia must prove themselves," he said quietly. "I'm sending them a prophet, though, in the hope that they will listen."

"She has not agreed to be your prophet," the Dauphine pointed out.

"I'll look for the battery," I said, which seemed to satisfy Alexander. "You could come with me, Dauphine. I'd welcome the company."

"No, you do not need me to help you find the battery in a world I would not understand. I have an idea that might be worth pursuing, though. The weapon I improvised when we fought the herald—using a string of portals to create a tunnel—perhaps I can tunnel far enough into the thunderstorm that I might learn something useful about its composition or its weaknesses."

Alexander said, "Intriguing. We all would welcome the discovery of any weaknesses. Dauphine, I offer my services to you. I can help you face the many heralds that will crowd your path on the way to the thunderstorm's edge."

I suddenly felt apprehensive and emotional.

I said, "Look, the way things are unfolding—I mean, if we don't ever see each other again . . ."

"Then it has been a pleasure questing by your side, my Queen," said the Dauphine.

"Godspeed on planet Earth, Isobel," said Alexander.

❀ ❀ ❀

I now had a significant new asset at my disposal, a perfect memory of the transmutation sequence, imprinted while experiencing Alexander's memories, with complete understanding of all the visualization parameters it accepted. Practically speaking, this meant I needn't rely on the Dauphine to transmute me back into Isobel; I could do it myself. And I could do it with sufficient granularity that I could visualize which aspects of the Queen I'd like to carry with me into Isobel's form, from transmuting her complete arsenal of spells into corresponding power morpheme sequences, all the way to specifying exactly what street clothes I wanted to be wearing when the transmutation was complete (a glittersteel hoodie, black fitted jeans, practical ass-kicking boots—the pink tank top could stay).

I left my jetpack behind, and I placed Blades Per Minute in a display cabinet, alongside items with sentimental value, like my vintage enchanted MiniDisc player/recorder for storing music in a format that no foe would ever recognize, and my vintage enchanted iPod Classic that you could load music onto without using iTunes.

I didn't know Maddy's teleport sequence, so I expected I'd be arriving exactly where I'd been standing when I left: in the center of the gymnasium. The jury was out as to whether the Chinese knockoff headset would be there at the end of the process as well.

It felt more intense going this direction, accumulating mass instead of shedding it. But as before, only moments seemed to pass in which I experienced complete sensory isolation from reality in total, and then with a sudden extradimensional yogic twist, I was back in Los Angeles.

❀ ❀ ❀

I stood in absolute pitch blackness and utter silence, doubting for a moment that I was truly real. But then I felt the familiar distribution of my mass resisting gravity and knew I was no longer afloat in the logosphere, not by a long shot. I was standing, judging by the slight give of the thin dance mat below me as I shifted weight from foot to foot. I bounced up and down a couple times, confirming I was under the influence of gravity as I remembered it. I felt the first few breaths escape my mouth as though they were giant clouds of mist. I felt the stuffy heat of this enclosed box oven of a building. I reached up to my forehead to check for the headset—it wasn't there, meaning I hadn't paid sufficient attention to reconstitute it. My tentative "Hello?" was greeted only by my own echo in the gymnasium.

As I considered my options, I realized with a pleasant shock that the transmutation sequence had indeed converted my entire arsenal of Sparkle Dungeon spells into corresponding power morpheme sequences that would have the same or similar effects in the material world. I could access them via instant recall just as I'd been using spells while traveling in the logosphere. The permanent upgrade to my capabilities had been profound and precise. The version of transmutation that Alexander utilized himself was apparently much more powerful than the version he'd shared with Olivia, or Olivia herself could've become an absolute terror to face by now.

I cast an End of My Rope Light spell, which ordinarily produced minor illumination at the borders of paths immediately ahead of you for a few feet, but I put a little more oomph into it and managed to get the edges of the room lit all the way around, and around the ring of tables and desks, too, as though I'd carefully laid colorful rope light on the floor all throughout the gymnasium. The resulting ambient glow enabled me to study the room more closely.

The computers, the consoles, and the projector were all powered down, and would not power up. But everything looked intact: nothing seemed damaged, no major equipment seemed obviously missing. A few cell phones were scattered across the tables, which seemed unusual; their batteries were all dead.

I decided to take a walking tour of the school, discovering the anarchists' primary living quarters in various classrooms, checking out the library and the cafeteria and so on. Everywhere I might've expected signs of life, I found it—clothes and backpacks hanging in lockers, cots with blankets and pillows strewn about as though recently used. In the kitchen, perishable food items were beyond rotten, but quite a few dried and canned items remained stacked on the shelves. In other words, this school was currently empty of its occupants, but they hadn't evacuated in any organized fashion.

I found a generator in a classroom near the gym, empty of fuel, with several full gas cans arrayed nearby. I refueled it and fired it up, then wandered back into the gymnasium. Overhead lights were on now. A small stack of what I guessed were cellular routers lit up on a shelf in a corner with pleasing blinking lights. I picked a workstation at a comfortable desk and powered it up, using a spell to bypass the password prompt, and soon I had internets.

02

I'd been gone almost eight months.

Six months ago, over the course of two weeks, the state of California was flooded with an alien signal that jammed airwaves and hijacked live streams, interrupted cellular transmissions and poured out of civil defense sirens, and blared out of speakers attached to drones which swept through cities and countryside alike, always on a constant loop. This I presumed to be the teleport/transmute combination sequence that Olivia had intended to design and then broadcast, and its effectiveness was unparalleled.

If you heard the five-second loop of the signal from start to finish, you vanished instantly, never to be seen again.

As the signal commenced in that first week, Violet closed the borders in and out of California, deploying an unprecedented number of National Guard units to reinforce her order, requesting and receiving additional army support for the purpose as well. She also ordered California's airspace and sea ports closed. The state was well and truly isolated as of this point.

The first week of the signal was akin to the Rapture of Christian mythology, sweeping up entire city populations at once. The second week was a punishing "clean-up" stage, snaring a whole additional wave of the unwary who hadn't truly assimilated the message that the signal was unforgiving in every sense. The signal could not be disseminated so carefully that a person standing on the other side of the border wouldn't hear it in every situation; consequently, neighboring states experienced their share of collateral losses.

Frightening first-person reconstructions of these days were available, describing some of the ingenious or accidental methods people used to survive the seeming omnipresence of the signal. You couldn't easily avoid it, but some people learned you could drown it out with louder sounds; the drones frequently flew lower than the top floors of high-rises, so you could survive by gaining altitude in cities; the drones did not have unlimited range, so you could survive if you were in deep enough wilderness.

But not every city or region was targeted. Los Angeles was hit hard, for instance; Sacramento was completely spared.

The signal finally ended two weeks after it had begun, and there was silence for nearly a day. The borders remained closed to external emergency services or any offers of assistance, and heavily fortified against potential armed incursions.

Then Violet Parker got behind a microphone at a podium on the steps of the governor's mansion in Sacramento, and she very calmly informed a panicked world that she was no longer governor of the state of California. Now she was Empress of the sovereign nation of California, fully seceded from the United States. Obviously one single state did not comprise an actual empire, but by naming herself Empress, she made it clear she had no intention of stopping here.

Oh and my god, her planning had been meticulous. All across the state, surviving political, civil, and military leaders pronounced their loyalty to Empress Violet the First, making it clear that an entire infrastructure of leadership had known this was coming, had been warned to avoid the signal so that they could emerge in this very moment to aid Violet's ascension over California's governmental bodies. US military units denounced their chain of command, transitioning to Violet as their commander in chief. She arranged it so that several nuclear-powered fast-attack submarines from the navy were in port in San Diego during these changes, where they could be fully assimilated into her command.

She claimed full responsibility for disseminating the signal that had caused, by her own report, ten million souls (one quarter of the population of California) to be "relocated," and made it extremely clear that she was capable of deploying this signal again at any time in any part of the developed world. She announced that she would not tolerate military retaliation for this act, but she didn't actually expect the US to foolishly send troops into a hot zone where they could themselves be instantly "relocated," and she didn't expect the US to initiate bombing runs on territory and resources it undoubtedly expected to reacquire as soon as it could figure out how. She admitted these things in her speech in part to explain them to her own frightened subjects, as well as to educate her new peers on the global stage about the extent of her tactical prowess.

Then, she announced a five-day festival, a celebration of California's independence. While her people tried to enjoy their days off from work or school or horrific grieving, she stayed busy.

She marched army units into AT&T facilities in Los Angeles and San Francisco, took control of NSA equipment that cloned internet backbone traffic for the US government, and began a private auction for access to this data. The US government nearly melted down in outrage, a neat trick given that this gear wasn't supposed to exist. She commandeered all banks headquartered in California and ordered all consumer debt erased, wiping ledgers clean not simply for Californians but for citizens worldwide. She ordered every computer server that could be controlled from within California to be shut down for these five days, disrupting countless industries. You couldn't just "turn off" the internet, but from within California, you could force enough traffic to stale caches on edge servers that transactions would start to fail in significant quantity.

She rounded up every billionaire she could get her hands on in California (San Francisco alone was home to seventy-five billionaires at the time of the relocation), arrested them, and attempted to confiscate their wealth in the name of the Crown. The ones who gave up the passcodes to their secret offshore bank accounts were released; the ones who clammed up about where their wealth was hidden disappeared without a trace. Almost immediately, she began publicly making offers on the black market for weapons the US desperately did not want her to have.

The message was clear: a rogue Empress with her hands on California's resources and a willingness to truly disrupt the status quo could make quite a mess of the world before anyone could figure out how to stop her. But while the US obviously believed Violet to be a clear and present danger, the rest of the world seemed to relish the actions of its newly found ally. Indeed, reading about the apoplectic helplessness of the US during this wild, five-day celebration was a darkly amusing pursuit for many.

On day six, Violet appeared again for another speech, indicating she was satisfied with the many invitations she'd received to open up embassies around the world. She claimed she was bemused that the United States was alone among the western capitalist pseudo-democracies in refusing to open diplomatic dialogue with her government. She indicated she didn't need good relations or open borders with the US to be a powerful economic and political presence in the world. But if the US provoked her even slightly, to test her resolve in any way about ruling California as its Empress, she'd be happy to remind them that she alone possessed the "relocation" signal, which she could aim with no warning at any target she chose—including Washington, DC.

This was likely a bluff, as some analysts understood. The unique surprise of her accomplishment using the signal within the state of California, where she controlled levers of media and technology at a deep level, would not be easy to replicate outside her borders now that the world knew what to look for in a deployment of her signal. But a major part of her success was her ability to keep her conspiracy completely silent during her preparation phase, and there was no way to know if her conspirators included others still in play elsewhere in the US government. The likelihood that she was bluffing was high, but the danger if she wasn't bluffing was also high. She'd definitely earned the wary respect of the intelligence communities now tasked with observing her every move.

Enormous antipathy swelled about her. Huge waves of deep grief and anguish permeated every corner of the Californian/American social graph because of her. The unknowable terror of wondering if another "relocation" event could happen again was the only thing preventing a violent uprising against her—but that very specific terror was definitely a sufficient lever for Violet to maintain an iron grip on her new empire.

My in-box was flooded with my family and a few East Coast friends reaching out repeatedly, trying to learn if I was safe, optimistically sending multiple messages, tapering off over time. I didn't have the capacity to fashion responses to every one of them at that moment. I made one exception, though, a short reply to my ex Wendy that simply said, "Yeah I'm alive."

And then a small fluttering sound distracted me, followed by a gasp, prompting me to look up from the laptop screen.

Across the gym from me, Maddy had appeared, and now stared at me in amazement.

"Oh my god," she said.

She looked ragged, exhausted, smaller somehow than I remembered her. Her face was gaunt, eyes hollow, and the wig she'd worn the last couple times I'd seen her was gone—her hair seemed haphazardly clipped short and prematurely gray in spots.

Tears began streaming down her face.

"Thought you were dead," she struggled to say.

"Where is everybody?" I whispered, because I had to ask, because we had to get this part over with.

"Gone," she said.

"The entire crew?"

She nodded, said, "Every last person."

I wanted very badly to go back in time and become closer friends with her so that now, in this moment, I could go to her, and hold her, and cry with her together. And as much as she seemed destroyed by the loss of her crew, I found myself trembling with violent relief at the realization she'd somehow been spared.

I said, "But not you."

"Had some help with that," she said. Her voice suddenly took on a jagged harshness as she exclaimed, *"OR DID YOU NOT KNOW I SPECIALIZE IN RESISTANCE?"*

She sat down in a chair across from me, opting to keep some distance between us for the time being.

"We saw you find the Dauphine, watching you up on the projector screen," she said. "And then she hit you with that sequence—I'm assuming transmutation—and you just dissipated in a heartbeat. The screen went dead. So we had no way of knowing where you'd gone. And that was just—the culmination of a *major* initiative, convincing you to follow the Dauphine on her quest—that was just *over*, and I didn't get to know *anything* about what happened next, for all I knew I'd inadvertently sent you to your actual demise, and there was just literally no one I could strangle in frustration about it . . ."

"But now I'm here," I said, almost smiling a little.

"Yes, Isobel Bailie, now you are *here*," she agreed, a catch of sudden relief in her breath. "So tell me, what the fuck *happened* to you?"

❀   ❀   ❀

I talked for what seemed like a very long time. She had many questions about the logosphere and its implications. She was not a gamer, so my metaphors didn't always make sense, but sometimes I'd illustrate with an actual spell right there in the room with her, which deepened her understanding for sure. Then we arrived at the part of the story where I finally met Alexander Reece, and after I recounted the conversations I'd had with him, she was almost pure, concentrated anger, vibrating in her chair as she kept herself under control.

She said, "We were sitting right here in this gymnasium," and I briefly thought she was changing the subject. But then I realized her story was intimately connected to mine. "It was an actual family night. The whole crew was here for once. We were watching some stupid singing show on the projector. And then the show was interrupted by the most chilling sound I've ever heard in my life. And a *wave* rippled through the gym, and my people were *scraped* out of existence. Like, the signal just tore them out of their chairs and shredded them into particles and they were gone.

"And it started to happen to me, like I could *feel* bits start to peel away, but the Interrobang began *screaming* in my mind so loudly that I never actually heard the entire signal loop. I mean, that left me having to endure the Interrobang screaming at me until I figured out how to cut the volume to the loudspeakers. And even then the Interrobang kept screaming for quite a while, just to be safe. But that's what saved me—the Interrobang crowding out any room in my brain for those evil new instructions to land.

"And I hid here as long as I could, because I absolutely could not believe at first that I was alone at the end of the world or whatever was happening. But I couldn't stay, you know, not forever, it was too depressing to be trapped in here by myself. Turns out it's super depressing out there, too, but whatever."

Seemed like sharing this story with me amounted to reliving the loss of her friends, and it was hitting her hard all over again. Fuck, it was hitting *me* hard, and I didn't know those people.

"How'd you know to come back here for me?" I asked.

"When you powered up the generator, you activated the silent alarm," she replied, "which sent me a notification."

And then, I braved the more difficult question.

"Maddy, how did you even get mixed up with me in the first place? Or I mean—*why* did you make chasing me down your major initiative?"

"I wish I could say I was originally motivated by something I detected on my own about you, but the magnet of our attention—mine, and the Interrobang's—was Alexander Reece. You understand, when he established a direct line of communication with the alien punctuation marks, our rogue domestic marks were intensely intrigued as well. And when he *used* their alien power morphemes to transmute his privileged ass right past the moral imperative to die properly like any other citizen of the species, the rogues were duly impressed. Here was a man, they thought, who gave no fucks about the *real* long-term project of the aliens, which is to say, the complete totalitarian throttling of original human thought. Here was a man who point-blank *stared into the abyss* of the thunderstorm and felt no fear, only a desire to *find that fucking storm's weakness* and *murder it straight to death*.

"*OH YES DID WE WANT A PIECE OF THAT ACTION?*

"So the Interrobang volunteered us. The Dauphine's orders from Alexander were to bring the Queen to him. We could operate as the Dauphine's agents in the material plane."

"But how did the Interrobang find out about the Dauphine's orders from Alexander? How did the rogue punctuation marks know about Alexander in the first place?"

"The logosphere is the place where unfashionable memes crawl out to die, Isobel. It's the domain of the rogues, and they know plenty about what happens there. So when you rebuffed the Dauphine outright, the Interrobang offered to help convince you to join her cause. Obviously in the new world order we hope to be rewarded for our loyal service."

"What new world order?" I asked.

"The one in which we exterminate the aliens like the invasive species they are, and allow the rogues to take over facilitating our thoughts."

"But—if you exterminate the aliens, won't that mean power morphemes will stop working?"

"Yes, see how you cling to the power they dole out to you? You're on *their* intravenous drip, don't you see? Anyway, the rogues are perfectly capable of shaping thought and affecting perceptual reality, given a sufficient amount of belief. I mean, I believe *so hard* that I've collected my own new library of personal power morphemes."

She uttered a hellacious little string of gasps and shrieks, and then promptly seemed to vibrate into two halves, on a rippling seam right down the center of her body, before snapping completely apart into two identical versions of herself, each apparently capable of independent movement and thought.

"This is not some simple illusion or magic trick," said Maddy on the left.

"Either one of us could tear out the throat of a billionaire," said Maddy on the right.

This was some elite-tier showing off, and I was absolutely here for it.

❀   ❀   ❀

After a minute, she allowed the two versions of herself to coalesce back into one, and she focused her attention on me for a moment.

"So help me understand something," she said. "What impressive credentials did you leverage to wind up the new golden child in Olivia Regan's lab?"

"Hmm," I said. "Well, you must have heard by now that I'm the Queen of Sparkle Dungeon, yeah?"

"I've been made aware," she replied. "I was thinking more along the lines of your professional background."

"That's pretty much the reason, though. I mean, they found me a marketing job so they could pay me to be there, but the real reason they plucked me out of unemployment was because I play their game better than anyone else—which translated to a natural acuity with power morphemes."

She stood up and began pacing slowly, working out a problem in her mind as we talked.

"*Why*, though?" she said.

"I mean, everybody's got some guilty pleasure hobby, right?"

"No, I don't mean why do you play the game so well. I mean— why would they choose to elevate you so far beyond your station? Why would they hand the keys to their arcane weapon system over to a completely unknown quantity? Why would they be so keen to train you into a potential rival for any of them down the road?"

"Olivia gave me the impression that I was part of a training *program*," I told her.

"Did they ever train anyone else after you?"

I had to admit—no, we hadn't taken the time to test anyone else. All of Olivia's attention had been focused on training me.

"And surely someone in the cabal must have pointed out the obvious fact that your most immediate predecessor in that lab had responded quite unpredictably to Olivia's attention," she continued, "discovering the synthetics, stealing their neural net and all their research, and vanishing into the underground. If that's what learning about power morphemes did to *me*—a goddamn genius in my field, I should point out—why would *you* be the very next person they summon through the door, yet another impressive but potentially uncontrollable young wild card?"

Ah, the age-old question: what makes *you* so pretty and special?

"I think I've heard the answer a couple times without letting it sink in," I said. "See, Maddy—the thunderstorm and its heralds are actually accelerating toward us."

"Hence the need for a shield," she said.

"Right, but a shield is only one tool for surviving a battle. You also need a weapon. Maybe lots of weapons, or a few really big weapons, or . . ."

Maddy stared intently at me, waiting for me to finish that thought.

"Look," I said, trying again, "each member of the cabal is probably a menace to fight one-on-one, but I can't imagine a single one of them charging across the logosphere to confront the thunderstorm directly."

"Except Alexander."

"Right, who is dead as far as they know. So if they wanted a weapon to use alongside their shield . . ."

"You think it's supposed to be you?"

"Maybe. Even Alexander thought he was going to use me as a weapon at first. I mean, I genuinely think they hoped their spellcasting system would identify dozens or hundreds of potential candidates for learning power morphemes—like, an *army* is definitely a weapon, right? All they got was me—so they had to *really* commit to making me a worthy opponent, or that entire investment in the game was wasted. And since the punctuation marks couldn't describe the thunderstorm in any way, they needed me to be versatile enough to face a variety of challenges.

"Which I am! I mean, I've been on top of the leaderboard for *years* because I'm that kind of player. It starts to make sense when you break it down."

"So, you're going to be their champion then," she said.

"I don't think so, Maddy," I said, "because you don't just face this thing in hand-to-hand combat. It's a conceptual menace orders of magnitude weirder than that. They need to develop a weapon that operates at *that* scale. And I mean, I could *be* that weapon, somehow. Do you know how many hundreds of hours I've spent listening to Olivia recite power morphemes? She could have buried so many suggestions in me that I'm nothing but a tall stack of subliminal commands from her at this point.

"I mean, I thought she was their pure researcher for some reason, studying power morphemes because Science, you know? But even when she was working with you, she was trying to discover every possible combination of the hundred and eight that could meaningfully be *weaponized*. I think she's always been running their weapons program. I think she's their Oppenheimer."

"And that makes you their atomic bomb?"

"Maybe. Which—god, if that's true—what is the fucking trigger to set me off?"

❀　　❀　　❀

I wanted to put on some tunes, but our taste in music was borderline incompatible—I wanted upbeat house music, and she wanted hardcore hip hop and I was like, maybe I'll just pretend I can't get Spotify to work. Eventually we settled on an old Tori Amos album we both happened to like, and then camped out in the bleachers, split a bottle of wine, and tried to chill. She seemed like she hadn't been able to relax in a long time, and she didn't want to talk about how she'd spent her last six months. But after a hint of tipsiness crept up on her, she started to open up.

"What aggravates me," she said, "is how much hope I'd built up thinking that Alexander Reece might be on our side. But he just wants to run the world like every other rich old white dude. Even when he's dead, he's a rich old white dude at heart. He didn't transcend, you know? And all that time we spent chasing you, we could have spent looking for ways to undermine the cabal. Now they've consolidated so much power that I don't see a way to dislodge them. I'm not even sure anymore that it's the right thing to do. They want to burn ten million minds to save the lives of eight billion people— maybe that's an acceptable cost."

I shook my head. "There's *got* to be a more effective solution."

"You don't know that. And more to the point, even if there is one, you don't have it."

"But then what happens—when they use the shield, and the thunderstorm is gone—then what? Then we just go back to our ordinary lives, except oops, we're subjects of the Empress now?"

"Oh, you'd prefer life back in your American oligarchic kleptocracy?" she scoffed. "One thing I will say about Violet Parker—she's aiming her ruthlessness in very interesting directions."

"What does that mean?"

"It means she's systematically repudiating elements of American society and it's strangely satisfying to watch. I mean, here's my favorite example. You have these federal agencies that are all truncated from the mothership, and she works her way through each one with a personal touch, merging FBI branches with the California Bureau of Investigation, that kind of thing. Well, she turns her attention to ICE and she schedules an all-hands meeting. Every local ICE office in the state hosts a live stream so she can address the whole team at once. And instead of the morale-boosting slide deck that all the other agencies got from her, she has every single one of those ICE agents arrested, and taken out into the streets, and publicly executed by firing squad."

"What!"

"True story. She made it clear that day that if you lived in *her* California, you were *not* illegal, and that was like week four of her reign."

"Who did she get to pull the trigger on these executions?"

"Ministers of Gorvod, as a matter of fact. Undocumented I'm told."

"And this is your 'favorite' example?" I nearly shouted. "Since when did you get off on cold-blooded murder?"

"Isobel, may I remind you that you've been living in a fucking alternate universe for the past eight months, and therefore *don't know what you're fucking talking about*?" she said, struggling to maintain a patient composure. "I would never have personally murdered those people if reality had put me in charge of California instead of Violet Parker. I don't 'get off' on state-sponsored violence. But I'm allowed to contain multitudes within me, including one whose prevailing opinion remains 'fuck ICE and fuck everyone who voluntarily took a paycheck from ICE.' Have I cleared that up for you?"

My head started spinning. If things had gone another way, I

might be in Sacramento right now with Violet, teaching her the rest of the hundred and eight in her spare time.

"There's more," Maddy said, warming up a little to the topic. "She nationalized Google and Facebook and Apple. Just flat-out made them Departments of the Crown. And while people were freaking the fuck out about Violet suddenly *owning* the world's search results and all that, then she announced, oh, and we're redistributing the profits from Google and Facebook and Apple to create universal basic incomes and no one in California is *ever gonna starve again.* Then for a nice solid B side, she criminalized the medical insurance industry and socialized health care, so no one will ever pay eight trillion dollars for insulin again, and we're like—okay look, California cannot produce all the everything it needs to survive, it's got to start trade back up, it's got to make alliances, it's got to do its part to fight the climate emergency, all that shit. But first, she prioritized finding a way to keep all her people alive."

"The ones she didn't kidnap for the battery," I reminded her needlessly.

"Right. You have to accept the fact that she committed one of the world's major crimes against humanity, and then suddenly she's catapulting the survivors into a bold new future."

"But Maddy, I *don't* accept that she's just going to *get away with it,*" I said. "We're still here. She hasn't found us yet."

"You think the two of us are a resistance movement?" she said, almost laughing. "Two of us could barely make up a punk band right now, let alone a resistance movement." She took a big, definitive pull from the wine bottle and said, "No, it's over."

"It's *not* over," I insisted. "Until she activates the shield, those people are still *alive,* Maddy. Their minds are intact. We could—"

"You believe you personally have the mojo to transmute *ten million people* back into their bodies? Isobel—please, you're the Queen, you're not the Supreme Being of Existence. The entire cabal worked for years to facilitate the relocation of those people. And they're not just evil geniuses—they're also devious fuckers, so they will have defenses against anyone reversing their work. I realize you just got back today, so let me give you some advice: the way to start your new life in California is to accept that those people are *never coming back.* Grieve now so you can move on with your life."

"They'll prepare for retaliation at the same scale as the relocation itself," I mused. "They'll plan to protect the entire battery."

She raised an eyebrow at me.

"Just thinking out loud," I said. "Let's say you're right, and there's no hope of rescuing all ten million people. But—how many people are in your crew?"

She paused, then said, "Twenty-eight people are missing."

"They definitely won't expect anyone to rescue twenty-eight specific people," I said slowly. "And they might not even notice if twenty-eight people *are* rescued, out of ten freaking million."

She stared at me, incredulous.

"What!" I exclaimed. "I repeat, she cannot just *get away with it*, Maddy. And what are we going to do, spend the rest of our lives drunk in an empty high school? Rejoin society knowing full well the cabal will have us both executed if they ever find us again? No, we need our people back."

"*Our* people?"

"Your people—fine."

"No, I mean—I like the sound of it. Our people."

That made me happy.

"And maybe," she said slowly, "if we can figure out how to rescue twenty-eight people, the next time we'll know enough to rescue *fifty* people."

"Yes," I said. "That's exactly how you level up."

We embarked upon a classic, old-school training montage.

First order of business: teach Isobel how to teleport.

Maddy had taught her crew, one at a time at first and then in a couple of larger classes, so she had a proven method for instructing me. The synthetics were more demanding on your vocal cords than the hundred and eight. You needed to build up greater flexibility in order to endure delivery, and your voice would be put through unusual muscular stress, so she'd developed exercises to start building strength. Imagine that mastering the hundred and eight required you to be in vocal shape equivalent to how fit your body would be if you were going to the gym three or four days a week to work out with a personal trainer. Mastering the synthetics was next-level vocal training, equivalent to the exercise regimens actors went through to bulk up their bodies for playing superheroes in movies. At first, I could only handle about twenty minutes of exercises before my voice was too thrashed to continue for the day. After a couple weeks, I was up to two hours of exercises a day.

In parallel, I taught Maddy how to play Sparkle Dungeon.

She'd never bothered to learn how to play it, of course, because she learned power morphemes the old-fashioned way: straight from Olivia at first, and then straight from her own neural net after that. But the spellcasting system in Sparkle Dungeon was a good primer, and she'd made all her anarchists play it when they were learning power morphemes.

I skipped past the first four games in the series. She didn't need to learn about the elaborate mythology of the game. I wanted her to start with the current, cutting-edge game mechanics introduced in Sparkle Dungeon 5; the older games were showing their age by now. I'd played enough of SD5 the day I was transmuted into the game to know that SD5 would be the sharpest vector for getting Maddy up to speed on the Sparkle Dungeon spellcasting system. She was a battle-hardened linguist mage in the material world, and I was not surprised to see her pick up spellcasting in the game lightning fast. Spells were an efficient metaphor for describing power morpheme sequences, and once she understood that, I could start teaching her useful cantrips and first-level spells that worked outside the game.

Once I was physically ready, she began teaching me the thirteen synthetic power morphemes I would need to teleport.

Quickly I realized that the synthetics were considerably more versatile and complex on a morpheme by morpheme basis than the hundred and eight. Within the hundred and eight, each morpheme had a concrete, fixed method of execution. The neural net that cranked out the synthetics innovated on that form factor. Each synthetic had its own unique set of parameters you could adjust and inputs you could provide to extract maximum value from these discrete chunks of unnaturally dense meaning. You controlled these variables with visualization techniques that were familiar to me from the transmutation sequence.

There were two synthetics that Maddy called the GPS pairing. The first one required you to sufficiently visualize your current location, which got encoded into the presentation layer of the morpheme. The second one required you to visualize your destination location. Didn't matter if you'd been there or seen it before; what you needed was a rock-solid conceptual understanding of the place you were headed. Pairing the two established the spatial relationship the punctuation marks would need for transit.

Then there were three synthetics that Maddy called the skydive set. These worked together to create a safe psychological bubble or vessel for your mind, to keep continuity of consciousness while your physical brain and nervous system and body were disassembled and catapulted across the logosphere to your destination. She called these the skydive set because they reminded her of how she felt the first time she went tandem skydiving.

"You're standing at the doorway of the plane looking down fifteen thousand feet to the Earth," she said, "and your body is screaming at you to back the fuck away and put on a seat belt, and you have to just take the plunge and push off. Of course, with tandem skydiving you have an instructor strapped to your back and they push you out of the plane whether you're ready or not. It's the same thing with teleporting. Your body on its own has absolutely no incentive to voluntarily pull itself apart particle by particle, because ordinarily that experience would be called death. So we use the skydive set to prime and condition the whole organism with convincing assurance that death is not the outcome we're shooting for. You willingly accept the punctuation marks as your tandem instructor who will push you out of the material plane, as it were."

Next were five synthetics that Maddy called the shock absorbers. To continue the skydiving metaphor, you definitely needed a parachute to survive the landing. But then you also needed the equivalent of hard-core, immediate PTSD counseling, so that you didn't suffer from damaging imprints about how frightening and unbelievable the experience had been, or so that you didn't walk around afterward questioning whether you were even truly a physical person anymore. You also needed some intensive spiritual cushioning. Teleporting wasn't a religious experience or whatever, but you definitely got a blistering peek behind the curtain at the mechanisms which held reality together, and you needed a framework to place yourself safely and comfortably in the tapestry of existence again, or else you could lose yourself in nihilistic corridors of self-loathing at your apparent insignificance.

Finally, there were three synthetics that Maddy called the checksum algorithms. In computing, checksum algorithms are used to determine if errors have been introduced into data sets during input or transmission. The parallel here was that you needed to confirm that you actually got reassembled correctly and were healthy and operating within tolerance. You could run diagnostics on your autonomic functions to get thumbs-up responses. You could analyze your psychological profile to ensure that your identity and awareness were intact. Each time you teleported, the punctuation marks edited you in small ways to improve you—increased your short-term memory buffer, for instance, or shaved some neuritic plaque from your brain just to keep things tidy—and you needed a readout of the release notes to make sure you weren't caught off guard by any of the changes they made.

At the end of four weeks, teleporting was firmly in my arsenal.

Our parallel training programs, in teleporting and Sparkle Dungeoning, occupied the meat of our days. At nights we took to looser, unguided knowledge sharing. She knew fifty-two of the hundred and eight, and Olivia hadn't shown her some of the most impressive power morphemes that appeared late in the library. I explained that I had acquired mastery of all hundred and eight by imprinting them from Alexander's memory. Someday, I expected I would find a pressing need to recite all hundred and eight in sequential order and establish direct communication with the punctuation marks. But until I had extremely good reason to do so, I wasn't ready to gamble my safety on that experience.

Meanwhile, the five hundred synthetics that she knew allowed her a dizzying array of micro effects on local reality. A bunch were cosmetic, as though she had a video projector remote for reality where she could adjust contrast and brightness and sharpness on the fly. A big, significant set allowed fine-grained psychological adjustments, akin to the marketing promise of pharmacological drugs for anxiety and depression and ADHD and the like, except the effects of these synthetics were quite specific and inherently reliable (also typically short-acting and probably addictive). And some were like those medical techniques you could use to stimulate parts of your brain into having a sudden undeniable religious experience. You had to be careful with those, or you could inadvertently smack your belief system into a whole new swim lane; the effects of these experiences didn't simply "wear off" every time.

Many seemed to be designed specifically as attack morphemes, for use in close-quarters melee combat—conceptual jabs and slices and punches. By comparison, only a small few allowed ranged attacks; it was psychologically costly to leverage the teleport mechanism as a broadcast conduit for attacking someone across town, for instance, and it exposed your position if your target was skilled enough with power morphemes to know how to trace the attack signature (a target group that likely included no one at this juncture, but if any crafty bastards out there could figure it out, the cabal was certainly top of the list of candidates).

The hundred and eight seemed powerful in the way that nature is a force to be reckoned with: primal, large scale, rapidly unfolding like hurricanes or ice storms. The synthetics seemed like command line interfaces to reality, where you could issue instructions with precision within the vast mainframe environment of the material realm. We began brainstorming ways to combine them into novel sequences, as though we were fusion martial artists welding the strengths of our respective disciplines together.

Periodically the Interrobang would emerge to offer a surprising insight, leveraging its perspective as a guest in Maddy's brain whenever she used the tools of the aliens. The Interrobang was becoming a more regular visitor. She trusted it on a deep level for saving her life, and its motives were sympatico with her own.

Meanwhile, Maddy's appreciation of Sparkle Dungeon was delightful to me. She advanced through Sparkle Dungeon 5 slowly, but I loved coaching her and seeing the game through her fresh eyes. Not surprisingly, she enjoyed the story line of joining the underground resistance to a fascist copyright-abusing government.

A chunk of the story involved liberating an ancient tome called the *Crossfade Chronicles* from a heavily guarded vault within HQ, and once she had it, she unlocked a new spell category that had mesmerizing implications: limited, short-range, time-manipulation spells called Transport Controls. You could pause the action all around you to study it safely; you could rewind the action to give yourself a second shot at something; you could even fast-forward through a challenge if you wanted to let the game engine play your character during that window of time. These spells weren't cheap to use. Some fantasy games used "mana" or some similar unit of measurement for how much spellcasting mojo you had available. Sparkle Dungeon 5 used old-school iTunes gift cards, which you acquired by robbing record label street teams. And you used a fuckton of them to cast these spells.

We eagerly took on the research project of discovering the power morpheme sequence equivalents of the Transport Controls. Maddy peeled away from the game for a solid two-day coding marathon in which she enhanced her neural net to help with the job. I was the initial Rosetta stone, teaching the neural net the set of spell-to-sequence correlations I currently knew. Then we could feed it the Transport Control spells, and let it churn on finding synthetic equivalents.

At the end of eight weeks, Maddy was a convincing fifth-level character, skilled in the arena of melee data retrieval, sitting on top of a small but valuable cache of MP3s from the days before the Chairman imposed draconian magical DRM upon all expressions of music in the Realm. During that time, the neural net produced jackpots, giving us the Transport Control equivalents we were looking for, as well as some innovative variations to consider.

Maddy went first learning each of these, as the resident master of the synthetics. She was experienced with learning the synthetics without a manual, so to speak, unlike my heavily tutored acquisition of power morphemes that had been charted already by Olivia. Didn't take long for us to get the hang of these. Outside the game, we didn't have obvious stacks of iTunes gift cards to spend; we just knew that these spells wore out our voices faster than the other spell categories, and had a "burn in" effect on our psyches during use, so we had to be highly tactical about using them. Hard to say what using them under stress would do to us.

Every night I retreated alone to the classroom that I'd claimed as my bedroom, collapsing into my cot with headphones on, listening to an ambient mix to soothe me to sleep. Most nights I closed my eyes and found myself replaying moments from the day's training sessions. I wasn't doing this to deepen or cement some aspect of what I'd learned, which might've made sense. Instead I was replaying little moments with Maddy, like when she laughed at one of my silly jokes, or when she seemed impressed by some game trick I casually showed her, or when she was genuinely surprised *again* that I brought her snacks while she was focused on leveling up . . . and I constantly wondered if she would've taken me seriously if her crew was still around, or if she was even truly taking me seriously now.

But that's where my head was at: completely submerging my feelings for her at all times when we were together, deeply enamored of her when I was alone.

To rescue our people, we needed to locate the battery. More to the point, we needed a mole with access to information about the cabal's operation that could help us narrow down our search. I had one promising idea to explore on that front.

I signed into my account in SD4 to see if I could track down the Keeper of the Moonlight Prism. She wasn't active in SD4 anymore, having migrated over to SD5. But she'd left me a set of frantic and sad messages, assuming I was among the missing. Just in case I was still alive, though, she'd left me her email address to contact her outside the game, with instructions to use the code phrase "wild scion" to get her attention.

I created a brand-new email account and sent her a message with "wild scion" in the subject line:

Hey there! Wanted you to know that I'm alive. Hoping you can keep that fact confidential. Would love to catch up with you if you could be persuaded. I'm going to leave a session open in SD4 so just ping me if you have time for a chat.

She initiated a chat conversation with me almost immediately.

"Are you absolutely fucking kidding me?" she said. "I am so so here to catch up. I cannot BELIEVE you're alive! How did you survive?"

"That's a very long story," I replied, "which boils down to: I was out of state when it happened."

"Ohhhh, fuck," she said. "And now you can't get back in."

"Weeellll, let's just say the borders are more porous than they look."

"Seriously?"

"I will happily explain everything the next time I see you. But how are you holding up? What's going on in your world?"

"You mean, what's going on in my chalet? Because that's the extent of my world now."

"What do you mean?"

"I mean—I was about to start a fucking North American tour to promote the new album. And then suddenly the whole Church went into lockdown, and then the relocation happened, and we were thrilled that we survived, of course, but—I haven't left my chalet in six fucking months. My career is over, it's just not important to Lonso anymore. But he won't let me out of here, either, because he still likes having me as his fucking trophy girlfriend. I'm just property to him now. It's super fucked up. I'm under house arrest and I didn't do anything wrong."

"Where's Lonso right now?"

"In Sacramento. He's mostly in Sacramento now. He's the Secretary of Defense."

"Of course he is."

"Isobel—I can guess you didn't just get in touch for social reasons. Maybe we can help each other."

My mind began racing, trying to figure out how to cultivate this opportunity.

Maddy, however, was way ahead of me. She nudged me until I put myself on mute.

"We should break her out," she told me.

"Uhhh . . . can we talk about that idea?"

"Sure, but that's what she wants, you can tell, and if we get her out, you will definitely have her loyalty."

Fair point. And this was the Keeper of the Moonlight Prism we were talking about, a regular fixture in the top five on the leaderboard. She was probably a few short weeks of training away from understanding simple power morphemes. We could probably recruit her for more than just intelligence.

Plus, fuck Lonso Drake in the eye socket.

I toggled back into the conversation with Jordon and said, "That sounds promising."

❀   ·   ❀   ❀

Her chalet was devoid of internal spying technology. Among Jordon's many interests as an engineer pop star, she understood personal security at a deep level, both on the internet and in meatspace. She knew all about all the common methods that domestic abusers used to spy on their partners, for instance. She'd scoured her chalet top to bottom until she was satisfied that no hidden cameras or microphones or sensors were planted anywhere in the building. Made sense—Lonso himself deigned to visit her there, and there was zero chance he would allow surreptitious surveillance of his own activities with her. But she was convinced they could monitor heat signatures in the building from outside if they were sufficiently motivated, to make sure she was alone when she was supposed to be.

Physically speaking, though, she was locked in, and there were ministers of Gorvod posted outside her front door around the clock. The windows were sealed shut; theoretically she could smash one to get out, if she wanted to risk ministers on patrol hearing it and rushing to investigate. She wasn't allowed down to the cafeteria to socialize with the rabble; instead her food was delivered three times a day. Those were the only moments the door was open, and they reinforced her guard during those moments, as though nervous she would bum rush the door and try to dash off into the courtyard.

Maddy wanted to go retrieve her on her own.

"No reason for both of us to be exposed," she said. "And you don't know how to take someone with you during a teleport. It's next-level difficult and we don't have time to teach you."

"If you get ambushed somehow, you'll need backup," I insisted. "And Jordon will trust you a lot faster if I'm there to vouch for you."

"No way. You need to vouch for me in detail well before I go there. I mean, when would we get ambushed? I'm disoriented for just a few seconds after a teleport. You're still taking thirty seconds to get your bearings back. I could be there and back in thirty seconds. You come with me and you're just slowing me down and adding a target for them to aim at."

"Okay but look, I can't just sit here for thirty seconds while you go completely out of pocket. I can't handle thirty stretching to forty or longer and I don't know what's going on."

"Are you worried about me, Isobel?" She seemed genuinely surprised.

"Yes, I'm fucking worried about you!"

She allowed herself a small grin, but took my concern seriously. We scavenged through gear and kit in the gym until we turned up a little quadcopter drone that had a GoPro camera we could use. We stripped the elastic band from a headlamp flashlight, and mounted the GoPro where the flashlight had been. The camera would live stream back to the gym via an app on her phone. Finally, we got a signal from the live stream routed up to the projector. I was not a maker or a builder, so 90 percent of this effort was Maddy doing the work and the other 10 percent was me fussing and lending moral support.

We let Jordon know: be ready at midnight. Don't pack a bag; leave everything behind. Wear super-practical clothes that you might have to live in for days. Have an empty stomach if you can.

At 11:45 p.m., Maddy started psyching herself up to go.

She wanted to wear an all-black uniform to help her disappear, but instead, I insisted she wear my glittersteel hoodie.

"Little gaudy, don't you think?" she said.

"It's like Kevlar but you can dance in it," I replied. "Stops bullets and Tasers without restricting your movement."

She slipped it on without hesitation. It looked good on her. Of course it looked good on her, god, she was effortless about it.

At the exact stroke of midnight, she squeezed my hand and said, "I'll be right back."

She began delivering the sequence and suddenly she was gone.

I immediately turned my attention to the projector screen, which was maddeningly dark for several long seconds until signal was re-acquired. Jordon loomed large in the image. Maddy already had Jordon's hands in hers. She began the return teleport sequence.

Nothing happened.

Jordon waited expectantly, saying nothing.

Maddy tried the sequence again from the top, but I'd heard her deliver it the first time; she hadn't gotten it wrong. It didn't work the second time either.

"What's happening?" Jordon asked.

"I don't know," Maddy said.

Then suddenly, Maddy said, *"CAN YOU BELIEVE THEY'RE JAMMING THE SEQUENCE?"*

The magnitude of our mistake unpacked itself very quickly in my mind.

From the cabal's perspective, teleportation was originally the major advantage the anarchists had. Once the cabal possessed the teleport sequence, they would not simply master it themselves, but they'd try to figure out how to protect themselves against it. Tactically you couldn't prevent someone from initiating a teleport into your location, but once they were in your sphere of influence, you could theoretically trap that person from getting out the same way they'd gotten in.

Not theoretically—you could *definitely* do that. I was watching it happen on a big projection screen.

And Jordon hadn't warned us about this because Lonso would've had no reason to tell her about the cabal's new teleportation sequence in the first place.

And we almost certainly did not have time to try to reverse engineer their jamming tech in order to disable it. Maddy and Jordon would have to make a run for it on foot.

I didn't have a way to communicate these realizations to Maddy, but she was always three steps ahead of me and she knew. No audible alarms were going off; no one was pounding on Jordon's door. Maddy soothed Jordon's nerves with a calming sequence, and then got her started drawing a map of the compound for Maddy to study.

They couldn't actually get through the gate on foot, as Jordon explained. The walls were fifteen feet tall, and the gate was a massive metal structure, reinforced against anyone from the outside ramming it to try to get in. But Jordon had an idea: if they could get to the garage, they might be able to steal one of the Church's armored trucks and make a break down the driveway. The trucks all had remote controls to open the gate. Maddy liked this idea.

The garage was basically a sub-basement of the main complex, and the driveway was on the complete opposite side of that complex from the chalet. They'd have to sneak across a wide open courtyard lit by bright ugly streetlight fixtures and patrolled by perimeter guards armed with automatic weapons. Jordon didn't know the frequency of the guard rotation around the campus, so they'd need to find a place to hide and do recon to figure out if there might be a good gap in coverage to make a dash for the garage. Problem was, they'd first have to get past the guard at the door to even get to a hiding place in the courtyard, and attempting that might well summon the perimeter guards down on top of them.

But Maddy had different ideas.

"Isobel," she said, "I would like to request the backup you originally suggested."

Christ yes, I thought.

She gave me a small list of items to bring, told me where to meet her, and what to do when I got there. Normally on raiding parties in the game, I was the one giving the orders, but Maddy was just a faster tactician on her feet than me. I was happy to report for duty.

I appeared around the side of the chalet and caught my breath, reintegrating as quickly as I could manage. I was in darkness here. I scouted out the situation at the front porch. One guard, a tall and probably male individual, looking bored as absolute fuck, illuminated from above by a garish porch light. Tiny me, wearing Maddy's sleek black jacket, crept up close and delivered a healthy burst of stun gun action. The guard dropped hard, disappearing out of the light. He wouldn't be incapacitated for long, so I had to move fast—grab the keys to the front door, knock three times, unlock it, hand supplies in to Maddy.

Moments later, Maddy, Jordon, and I briskly ducked into the darkness behind the chalet, temporarily moving away from our destination, sticking to an unlit trail that led into an isolated little flower garden. From here, we had an excellent view of the mayhem we'd initiated.

The first floor of Jordon's chalet was now consumed with a roaring fire.

"Such a pleasure when 'burn it all down' is not simply a metaphor," Maddy said.

This turned out to be a pretty wild diversion. If they ran fire drills on campus, you couldn't tell judging by the chaos that erupted when the perimeter patrol realized Jordon's chalet was burning. The Church wanted to be self-sufficient from city resources whenever possible, so they had to go through the motion of trotting out the one fire truck they owned, operated by the three or four firefighters they had on campus. In the meantime, we got through the perimeter guard and down the ramp into the underground garage without incident.

Our luck continued in the garage. No reason for the "motor pool" or whatever to be staffed after midnight, so we had our pick of twelve armored trucks, four armored vans, and two armored town cars. Jordon made it clear we should take a truck: the vans had shitty handling and the town cars had the lightest armor plating, whereas the trucks were high performance vehicles that generally came with gun cabinets full of weapons and ammunition.

We climbed into a truck, with Maddy in the driver's seat, me riding in the passenger seat, and Jordon in the back looking for a gun she could figure out. Maddy accelerated up the ramp out of the garage, but didn't aim for the vehicle's top speed or anything. Just made it look like an ordinary late-night run to the Greyhound station to kidnap some fresh new faces. A few bewildered perimeter guards saw us roll past but didn't seem to react.

Then our world basically exploded into trouble. I was in the flow state so I could observe things happening in discrete beats instead of a whirlwind blur. First, a quick burst of wild electricity appeared for a second in front of us on the driveway. I instinctively interpreted this as an inexpert teleport taking place, accidentally flashy due to ricochets of loose energy that hadn't quite been controlled during the sequence. Then Maddy slammed on the brakes because there was now a human being standing in the driveway, illuminated by our headlights, and no matter what kind of hurry we were in, her reflexes were trained to avoid killing innocent pedestrians. It was an unfortunate mistake.

The man in the driveway was Lonso Drake. It sure would've been really nice to run that guy over. Instead he had an opening to fuck with us. We couldn't hear the sequences he delivered, but before Maddy could get the truck moving again, he levitated the fucking thing a foot off the ground and held it there, smiling cruelly. He shouted something at us that I couldn't hear over the sound of general panic inside the truck.

"Stay with Jordon," I ordered Maddy, because I wanted this for myself. I popped open my door and dropped out of the truck to the ground.

He couldn't see me yet with the headlights beaming in his face. I whispered a power morpheme sequence that got me up into the air as though I had a jetpack, because really, thought-based propulsion didn't need a physical vehicle. I'd spent so much time in a jetpack traveling through the logosphere that my body vividly remembered how to maneuver. It was nerve-racking to realize I was making this work against gravity, and inhibiting in terms of how much height I dared to reach. But it was also freakishly cool and it wasn't even the main thing I had in mind here.

I gently drifted forward into his field of vision, so that he saw a silhouetted figure floating in front of him.

"Release Jordon, and your death will be painless," he shouted at me.

"I *am* releasing Jordon, you towering prick," I shouted back.

After a pause, he said, "Isobel. I should have guessed she would know how to find you."

The only time I'd seen Lonso Drake in combat, he'd materialized a handgun out of thin air. I didn't have my glittersteel hoodie so I wasn't excited about getting shot at. Still, this felt like the show-down at the O.K. Corral, where each of us was waiting for the other to draw first, so our murderous rages would be justified when we finally tried to annihilate each other. This moment seemed to stretch for ages, in which entire distinct attacks were simulated in my mind as though I was shuffling a card deck looking for an ace.

Lonso said, "Olivia would happily take you back, you know. We can forgive youthful indiscretions. You're learning your place, and you've certainly earned our respect." Glowing balls of light began to grow in each of his hands. "But if you insist on trying to leave here with Jordon, Olivia won't be able to identify your remains."

"I have a counter proposal," I said. "You get the fuck out of our way and let us go, and I disarm the truck full of explosives we rigged underneath your complex."

He didn't know me well enough to know I was bluffing. He didn't know where I'd been for the last eight months. He didn't actually know fuck all about what I was capable of now. I was struck with inspiration and subvocalized a sequence that transmuted my actual skin into organic glittersteel. Lonso was over there with glowing hands that kept getting brighter. At some point, was he going to try to sunburn me really badly? This was a deeply weird life.

"I have nostalgia for this place to be sure, but I'm based in Sacramento now," he said. "Blow these helpless people to pieces, if that's the kind of person you've become."

I realized I was hearing a strangely familiar sound starting to emerge around me, might have been building for a bit now, which I hadn't noticed because Lonso was keeping me focused on him. It was a highly organized and impressively martial version of the chanting that typically accompanied Gorvod's Frenzy. This couldn't be more than four or five voices, though.

But I'd only experienced what I'd generously call second- or third-level Frenzies. This was something else entirely, much more competent and sophisticated, and the air above the truck started to ripple and pulse in tune with some aspect of the chanting I couldn't quite follow, and then suddenly a bolt of lightning came out of the rippling and smacked me hard in the back, knocking me straight to my face on the ground. My glittersteel skin repelled the electrical damage I should have taken, but the sheer propulsive quality of the bolt was like being struck in the back by a fastball getting smacked off a bat at me.

I struggled to get to my knees, and another bolt hit me in the side, part of a web of bolts that struck the truck in several places as well.

Lonso was smoothly sauntering up the driveway, closing the distance between us, the balls of light in his hands starting to coalesce into a pair of electrical maces. I couldn't catch my breath fast enough to improvise any kind of defense. But he was leaving me to his minions to keep contained, while he assessed what other threats were lurking in the truck. Overconfident move, if you asked me.

The thing about Gorvod's Frenzy was the attacks were unpredictable in timing, and constantly evolving to be more dangerous and powerful with each successive strike. The ministers of Gorvod who had us surrounded were supremely focused on their roles in generating these ambient burst attacks that threatened me. One last web of malignant energy descended like a sheet of sudden hail, and the glittersteel could only deflect a portion of this assault. I actually shrieked despite myself, feeling hit points burning off of my psyche in droves, as one particular string of lightning actually sustained itself for several seconds, keeping me pinned down.

"Jordon," he said loudly, ignoring me writhing on the pavement next to his feet. "We really should talk."

Turns out, Jordon Connelly knew how to operate an AR-15, which she proceeded to demonstrate by firing a hailstorm of bullets out of the back seat, precisely obliterating three different ministers of Gorvod in rapid succession. Gorvod's Frenzy was disrupted. I had a reprieve, and just enough available lung power to instantiate a weapon out of thin air, just like Lonso had taught me.

I rose up, the striking majesty of Blades Per Minute suddenly in my hand. The shock on Lonso's face was absurdly satisfying. I activated the sword in its primordial mode of exactly one blade per minute and impaled him straight through the chest.

The truck landed on the ground next to me with a hard crunch. Maddy ripped the acceleration to propel the truck past me toward the gate. I let Lonso's dead body slide off the sword and crumple to the pavement, then I jetpacked myself off the ground to follow the truck.

Apparently they couldn't find the remote control for the gate inside the truck, because Maddy made the executive decision to ram the gate at top speed. It was reinforced the opposite direction, to stop imaginary enemies from getting in; it buckled with a wrenching lurch and collapsed in a pile of twisted metal as the truck plowed through it and exploded into the street outside the walls, spinning wildly as Maddy lost control until coming to a hard crashing stop against a telephone pole.

I rocketed up to the truck. Maddy was pounding the dashboard, wildly aggravated that she couldn't get the vehicle moving again. Jordon climbed out of the back seat.

"We don't really know each other very well, do we," she said to me.

Maddy extracted herself from the driver's seat, grimacing in pain, and grabbed Jordon's hand.

"Let's try this again," she said, and moments later, Maddy and Jordon teleported away.

I slumped to the ground, suddenly overcome with pain and fatigue. I got dizzy and couldn't keep my eyes open, wondering in the back of my mind if I'd suffered a concussion or something worse. My memory wasn't functioning, that was the main problem. Turns out spellcasting was a lot harder when you were suffering from real physical damage while you were trying to concentrate. I could see armored trucks coming up the driveway toward the gate, toward this wreck in the street with me slumped against it.

Maddy popped back in next to me and said, "Dammit Isobel."

She grabbed my hand and we were gone.

07

I came to my senses in a painful shock of sudden awareness. I was on a dance mat in the center of the gym. Maddy was curled up on the floor next to me, unconscious. I couldn't quite reach her hand. Jordon sat in an office chair nearby, completely freaked out. I tried to sit up and the pain was so sharp I blacked out again.

Coming to my senses one more time, I was back in the gym. You couldn't take me to an emergency room right now because for starters, my skin was glittersteel, impervious to medical instrumentation. But there was a huge amount of damage to the glittersteel, like the killing blows had all been deflected but I'd been cooked in my skin in the process, which felt to me like I had subcutaneous third-degree burns all over most of my body.

Meanwhile I started to realize—Maddy had suffered some kind of injury when the truck crashed, and had still expended enough willpower to teleport three entire people out of that situation, and now her stamina just seemed zeroed out for the time being. I couldn't look at her without losing my shit, so I closed my eyes and tried to reorient myself to my life.

Because I couldn't understand my life right then, didn't have the right hooks to get back into inhabiting it like a person. After a certain number of transmutations, you couldn't really just revert back to what you were, as though some perfectly preserved original template of yourself existed out there somewhere for reference. You could reconstruct your former state based on every available memory fragment and hope for the best. How much degradation could you withstand before you just had to accept that you were not the same person at all as when you started down this road? I suddenly remembered what it was like to play Sparkle Dungeon for the first time, when I was nine years younger and full of silly enthusiasm. You couldn't just transmute back into innocence.

Something sparked against my fingertips. I opened my eyes. Maddy had inched close enough to me to brush her hand against mine. She was awake.

"Are we going to live?" I asked her in a hoarse whisper.

"Don't sound so disappointed about it," she whispered back.

Maddy sat up, which got Jordon's attention. I felt so relieved that Maddy was back that I suddenly blacked out again, like I could just release myself for now, knowing she was there.

I woke up again with Jordon trying to get me to drink a glass of water. Maddy had painkillers she wanted me to try, a stash of oxycodone she'd saved for an emergency. It would take something like fifteen minutes before I maybe started feeling some relief. Maddy kept trying to talk to me, and I couldn't keep the thread straight in my head. I was extremely frightened that I wasn't going to find my way back at all, and they'd just have to leave me somewhere. Irrational, frightening shit.

But she was a genius, and once she felt like she had me stabilized a little, she and Jordon started discussing Sparkle Dungeon, which seemed so surreal to me that I got a little blissed out for a couple seconds about it. I realized I really wanted to hear the questions Maddy was asking Jordon about the game. Maddy was still pretty new to the game world, and SD5 was actually a resource-starved game compared to the rest of the series; there was a lot she hadn't experienced yet. How the fuck, she wanted to know, did anyone recover from shit like this in the game? Jordon seemed startled by the question—was Maddy literally unfamiliar with the concept of healing spells? To which Maddy replied, "Do you fucking know any?"

And suddenly a warmth filled my veins because I finally remembered and understood that *I* knew twenty different healing spells if I could just get my head straight enough to actually cast one.

It took me an entire five minutes to succeed at casting a first-level heal that helped me stop losing consciousness semifrequently from the pain. That was the first hook. I'd never used healing on myself like this. In the game you just waved your hands and your hit points got magically refreshed. It was pleasingly unspecific and you didn't have to work for it. Right now I had to piece myself back together in stages. I was sufficiently communicative that they trusted me to work through it. I got myself to a place where I could anesthetize myself enough to sink into sleep as opposed to just blacking out. I asked them to wake me up once an hour and make me try another spell if I wasn't too exhausted.

Eventually, I could sit up, and look around the room, and feel safe.

❀   ❀   ❀

Once I was finally coherent for a long enough stretch, they brought a cot into the gym to get me up off the dance mat and make me more comfortable. And then Maddy wanted to show me some video she'd recorded while I was zonked out. She'd gotten her shit together enough to start paying attention to the spyware we had on Cameron Kelly's LAN. I was surprised he'd never found it, then surprised again to learn that Cameron actually did notice it eventually, but left it running—he seemed to have a soft spot for us.

Maybe two hours after I'd killed Lonso Drake, Violet pulled the surviving members of the cabal together on a video call.

"Lonso's been murdered," Violet said, seething with rage. "I discovered this because the National Guard was summoned to investigate a violent incursion at the Church. Someone apparently got inside the compound, killed Lonso and three of his ministers, kidnapped Jordon Connelly, and got away clean. It's been two hours and the Church hasn't yet released any internal surveillance to me. They have another hour, and then I'm sending in the army to quarantine the premises and start torturing people for answers."

She let that sink in for quite a while.

"Clearly Isobel and Maddy are alive," she said. "And clearly that needs to *change*."

"I don't understand this at all," Cameron said. "What the hell's so important about Jordon Connelly that they would risk coming out of hiding to grab her?"

"Who knows what they were thinking," Violet said. "Lonso was in Sacramento when the incursion started. He was well informed enough to teleport back to the Church in time to summon a support squad of elite ministers to help him confront them on their way out of the driveway. We know this much exclusively because of National Guard interviews on the ground with ministers who were too stunned to resist arrest.

"Do you know why I can't get surveillance footage from the Church tonight? Because Lonso was a weird, distrustful bastard, who structured his entire organization around the premise that he personally was an immortally reincarnating scion, consequently he never bothered grooming a second in command. Seriously, the org structure for the Church of Gorvod is: Exalted Scion at the top, and the next level down is literally hundreds of peer ministers who all theoretically report directly to Lonso. And none of those people feel they owe any loyalty to the Crown. They're functionally restructured at their core to believe in Gorvod above all else, and to believe in Lonso as Gorvod's messenger.

"So now we're looking at close to a hundred branches of the Church in California, each with as many as several hundred ministers reporting in, all of whom are heavily armed, many of whom are skilled with power morphemes, and none of whom give a fuck about us."

"So can't you just . . . arrest them?" Olivia asked, unfamiliar with the encroaching notion that the Empress of California actually did have physical limits to what she could accomplish in a rational fashion.

"No, Olivia, they're an arcane paramilitary organization within our borders, and as of now, their religion is *forbidden*. I have a window of approximately two hours in which to finish lining up lightning strikes that will destroy these branches while they're all still in bed."

"You've got to be kidding me," Cameron said. "These people helped you enforce order in the streets after the relocation."

"Spare me your sudden collegiate exploration of the concept of loyalty," Violet snapped. "Even if I let the Church survive, there's one highly problematic passage in the holy book of Gorvod, whatever it's called—the Gorvodomicon or something. Lonso went to the trouble of identifying a tier of believers he called the Devoted Scions. He meant this to be an exclusive club for asshole billionaires to buy into. In the book, the Devoted Scions are pseudo-angelic, immortal servitors of the Exalted Scion.

"And that arrogant fuck went to the trouble of describing the whole process of a Devoted Scion transitioning from one incarnation to the next, with Watchful Eyes gently narrating the transition to keep your identity moving forward in time. There's a passage that describes what happens when the Exalted Scion himself experiences this transition. The Church falls temporarily to the Devoted Scions to rule until the Exalted Scion resumes his rightful place.

"Let me give you *one fucking guess*—who's the only person Lonso ever singled out as a true Devoted Scion?

"Jordon fucking Connelly.

"Technically it's her Church now. So no, we aren't arresting anyone whose loyalties could later be roused to the cause of a woman who is now firmly in the hands of *MOTHERFUCKING ANARCHISTS!* No, these people die tonight."

"So, that's taken care of," Bradford said firmly. "Meanwhile, Isobel and Maddy have Jordon for interrogation. Worst-case scenario— what could Jordon reveal to them that would impact us directly?"

The silence in response to that question was educational for all of them. They had absolutely no idea what Lonso told his trophy girlfriend about the inner workings of the cabal.

"I want the timetable for launch accelerated," Violet commanded. "I want us in the air in *seven days*."

Cameron said slowly, "You will *not* have everything we agreed to in seven days, Violet."

"What will I have, Cameron?"

"You'll have some of it. The simpler stuff. You will definitely *not* have the singularity cannon."

"I think we'll learn to get by with our incomplete complement of weapons systems, Cameron. How about you, Bradford?"

"I will be ready. I suggest we continue expending focus on the scout mission. Launch it at day three. Expect the mission to fail, and perhaps we'll be pleasantly surprised if it doesn't."

"Agreed. Olivia?"

Olivia was too shocked to speak at first. Violet prompted her again.

And Olivia said, "You're proposing another relocation event in *seven days*?"

"Olivia, who did you think we were building this for, just the five of us? Like, this would be a private little cruise liner?"

"I just thought we would have—months at least—to figure out how to *store* all these people!"

"I thought we had already figured this out, Olivia! Aren't we *storing* people in the goddamn battery?"

"*Those people aren't getting out, Violet.* The constraints are very different for how you keep them alive, when your only goal is to *extract their energetic value.* You want to ensure that *thirty million* people survive relocation without all of them immediately melting down from shock and horror? *That is not a seven-day problem, Violet.*"

A respectful pause followed, in which Violet silently allowed that she'd been schooled just now.

"Fine, then scale it back down," she said firmly. "Just tell me how many people you *can* keep safe with seven days to plan, and that's how many we relocate."

Olivia just shook her head in frustration, unwilling to explain to

Violet that this problem wasn't going to slice itself down on such a conveniently arithmetic basis.

"Let me make this clear," Violet said. "We are *not* going to sit by waiting for them to dream up another once-in-a-lifetime strike against us. You have *seven days*, people."

She terminated the call.

"Thirty million people?" I whispered in amazement.

"She's talking about the rest of the population of California," Jordon said.

"Why would they *do* that?" I gasped.

"Sweetie," she said gently, "they're trying to *evacuate us.*"

❋   ❋   ❋

"Shortly after the relocation," Jordon said, settling into a chair next to my cot to tell a story, "Bradford Jenning finally finished learning the hundred and eight. He proceeded to recite the entire library in order, with the intent of establishing direct communication with the punctuation marks.

"He definitely succeeded. And see, everyone kind of accepts that Alexander Reece was the real genius in the Jenning & Reece equation, but people forget or they just don't know, Bradford's got his own set of chops for sure. Dude got his PhD in musicology. He invented his own innovative musical control system for enhancing the effects of power morphemes. Alexander didn't do that—punctuation marks didn't think that up—that was Bradford.

"So, when Alexander first made contact, via his blazing insight about imaginary linguistics or whatever, the response from the punctuation marks was, why yes, absolutely, here are a hundred and eight pieces of evidence to back up your strange but entirely true theory.

"Bradford, on the other hand, is a different kind of mind. And because he's the second person to connect with the punctuation marks, they're less shocked and surprised by him, and they don't feel this massive sudden urge to *transmit all the data* as fast as possible, and instead, they can kind of just . . . get to know each other somehow.

"I guess they clued in to the unique way that Bradford experiences music, and also—Bradford starts this interaction with more information about reality than Alexander had. Like Bradford already has a mental picture of the logosphere and the imaginary realms and on and on. So the punctuation marks just have this major head start with Bradford to introduce him to some higher-level concepts.

"And the major accomplishment they achieve together is—if you imagine all of reality to be an elaborate, gorgeous set of audio frequencies, and you start to tune your ear to the wondrous variety of wavelengths that constitute life and matter and love and everything else, you might sift that set of audio frequencies for lifetimes in a row and never notice a tremendously unique frequency that resonates like overtones in the gaps between the atoms—or I mean, in the gaps between planes of existence. This frequency is unique because it is a *signal*. It comes from something *intelligent*, out there somewhere in the multiverse. It's a *message*.

"The punctuation marks spotted this signal as they fled the approach of the thunderstorm. They didn't understand its meaning, but they understood some of its properties: it manifested as a recurring musical motif, in a complex harmonic scale, and it could be detected from across many dimensions of reality provided you could attain this precise holistic vantage point on how reality operates. The punctuation marks enabled Bradford to immerse himself in this musical motif, and he spent thirty-six hours alone in his office, working through implications until he had a way to describe to the rest of the cabal what he'd learned.

"Bradford calls this motif the Beacon. He can sing it actually, the parts of it at least that line up with the human voice. It's indescribably lovely to hear him do it. Takes him about ten minutes to get through the whole thing, and you feel like you're suddenly in the presence of an ambassador from whatever true pantheon is really on the hook for this whole mess. And he walks you through a series of calm and hopeful instructions, which end with a sudden heartbreaking twist. He gives you a chance to absorb what you just heard. And then he repeats it for you, but this time he breaks it down into distinct phrases and he stops to translate each phrase.

"I'm paraphrasing wildly here, but the gist of the message is—let this Beacon stand as a rallying point for survivors of the thunderstorm. You are not alone, and hope is not lost. Follow this Beacon to these coordinates, which repeat in a sequence throughout the motif, and you will be welcome among our camps. Always look forward, never look back. To those of you we lose before you find us, we sing this song for you, the lullaby for thunderstorms, to ease you into darkness when it comes. And then the last two minutes are just bittersweet, beautiful sadness."

I couldn't hold it together, and just started sobbing. Jordon gripped my hand tightly.

"So they're not planning on using the battery for a shield any longer," Maddy said.

"No," Jordon agreed. "They've designed an interdimensional arkship. The battery will power the arkship's jump drive."

"They're planning to *abandon Earth*," Maddy said, like she was trying to convince herself of something she desperately did not want to believe. Then she seemed to have a change of heart. She leaned back in her chair with a hardened look and said, "I can respect that."

"Can't they just *stick to a goddamn plan*?" I exclaimed in frustration. "They went to enormous trouble designing the shield—and the shield could have *worked*! They spent all that time trying to fashion me into a weapon they can use—and then they just turn and *run* instead!"

"You plan with the best information you have at the time, Isobel, and when you get new information, you plan again. It's all iterative, it all stacks on itself from a learning perspective."

"But how do you just *design a fucking arkship*, Jordon?" I cried out through my tears.

"From what I understand," Jordon replied, "Bradford is responsible for navigation. He's been working for months now, feverishly developing a new set of power morphemes that are all delivered via music. You don't just string these power morphemes together into sequences. You compose entire arias or concertos or cantatas that work like power morpheme sequences, but are generally more powerful. So, it's much harder to improvise with these, but you can do a lot more with them.

"He's got a sequence that's the interdimensional travel version of the teleport sequence. You describe your location in the multiverse, so in our case, the logosphere because that's where the arkship is parked. Then you describe your destination, so in this case, Bradford feeds in the coordinates to the rallying point that he's learned from the Beacon motif. And that gives the punctuation marks the directions from point A to point B.

"Cameron designed the arkship itself. It's a much bigger version of the armored dirigible skyships in Sparkle Dungeon 5. You know how you start SD5 with that training level where you learn how to pilot the jetpack? Well, about halfway through SD5, you get a similar new training level, where you learn how to pilot a skyship. It's the same principle as the jetpack, except now you're controlling microrockets all across the surface of a larger vessel in order to maneuver. The skyships are designed to share control among multiple pilots and navigators and gunners, so you have to synchronize among them in order to move safely. Cameron's built the control interface to the arkship along those lines, so that Bradford can navigate, while leaving an actual pilot latitude to fly the arkship in dimensional airspace on either side of the jump.

"Additionally, he's been loading up the arkship with weapons systems, a blend of concepts from Sparkle Dungeon 5, and stolen from other sci-fi games that he knows. Technically Olivia's handed over temporary control of her power morpheme weapons research to Cameron.

"Olivia's responsible for care and maintenance of the battery, and development of the living quarters for the evacuated population. It's on her to figure out all the resource planning to keep everyone alive and healthy for the journey, given some maximum duration for the trip they haven't settled on yet.

"And Violet's responsible for orchestrating the next relocation."

"What was Lonso supposed to do?" Maddy asked.

"Ministers of Gorvod were supposed to be internal security for the ship. They were preparing to live many decades on the maiden voyage, and the plan was for Lonso's people to keep the peace, as neutral parties that everyone basically hated equally. That's kind of a major hole now in their plan, honestly. Thirty million people aren't going to just magically get along under this kind of stress."

"Why doesn't Olivia keep everyone in stasis like she does in the battery?" I asked.

"The way I understand it—the battery is fault tolerant to a certain amount of degradation over time. Like bit rot on a hard drive—eventually you can, like, defrag it to reclaim storage and improve its efficiency, but at the cost of potentially losing some specific bits of data. So that works for a mind you're keeping alive but don't expect to restore to consciousness, where missing bits of data could create meaningful problems for the personality.

"For people you plan to be your survivors, your population, you can't store them in stasis for decades or you'll potentially lose big chunks of people. So they're all going to be aware of the experience this time. They're going to be relocated out of their lives and transmuted into passengers on the ship with no warning and no opportunity to opt out. It's going to be almost impossibly difficult for everyone, and very demanding on the cabal to manage without a mutiny."

"So our people might already be degrading in that battery," Maddy realized.

"'Your people'?" Jordon asked.

"We lost twenty-eight people in the last relocation," I told her. "We're trying to rescue them. Took a detour to rescue you first."

Jordon's eyes welled up.

"Hoping you can help us find them actually," Maddy said. "Where *is* this freaking battery?"

"They've installed it inside the original Sparkle Dungeon," Jordon said.

"How are they going to get it from there into an arkship?"

"The Sparkle Realm itself *is* the arkship," she replied. "Cameron built a hull around the entire map."

"How do we track down twenty-eight people inside a ten-million-person battery?" I asked.

"I have no idea," she said. She paused, and then said, "But that's definitely something they're working on at Jenning & Reece. Actually Isobel, I think you know the person they've specifically assigned to the problem.

"Their name is Devin."

"During the first relocation, they didn't have the foresight to imagine they'd need to know the identities of the people stored in the battery," Jordon said. "They thought the end goal was to spend those people on the shield, you know? But now that they're using the battery for the arkship, they won't be using up the entire battery on one jump. That means there could be opportunities down the road where it may become useful to know who they've got with them.

"Devin's been tasked with project managing a computational census of the population of the battery."

"I assume that doesn't mean yanking people out of storage and getting them to fill out a name tag," Maddy said.

"Yeah, it's definitely weirder than that. I haven't been able to follow this in detail, but my understanding is that shortly after relocation, Olivia used her neural net to issue a series of power morpheme instructions to the minds stored in the battery. This established a network. Now she's having to go back to that network and somehow algorithmically analyze each individual stored in a power cell to extract what they're calling identity tokens. These tokens are pattern-matched to various databases maintained by the state of California, so that each one can be tagged with occupational and historical metadata. The goal is to be able to easily pull categories of workers out of stasis as needed on the journey.

"They're basically trying to future proof for the scenario where they need some specialized expertise, and what if the world's foremost expert is in the battery and not roaming the passenger compartment? You'd want to get the expert out of storage."

"How do you know all this?" I asked. "I can't imagine the cabal expected Lonso to keep you completely in the loop on every aspect of their planning."

"Ha, no," she said, "it's more hilarious than that. Lonso was an arrogant fuckhead who didn't bother to password protect his tablet. I've had spyware on his devices for years. Every email, video conference, phone call, text message . . . every search query, every IP address he ever connected to . . . I got it all." She paused, thoughtful for a moment, then said, "I didn't know he could teleport, though, and I didn't know they could *jam* teleports."

"I wouldn't be surprised if Violet demanded extra operational security around that information," Maddy said. "It's the first time they've stolen something from *us*, instead of us stealing from them. I mean, these people haven't had meaningful opponents until we showed up. I bet they *really* didn't want us to know how quickly and thoroughly they acquired the sequence and built a defense for it."

"What would that look like, though?" Jordon asked.

"Could be as simple as a strict rule where they only discuss their teleport research in person," Maddy replied. "Not much of a hardship really if they can all teleport now."

"I don't buy it," I said. "If you were that worried that we might eavesdrop, you wouldn't just hide your teleport research, you'd surely also hide the fact you were planning another relocation event."

"True. They might have at least one open channel among them that Jordon doesn't have access to," Maddy said.

"Oh shit, wait a minute," I said. "Jordon, so you never even saw Lonso *train* to teleport?"

"Nope," Jordon replied.

"God dammit," I said. "I mean, I spent *weeks* learning how to teleport. But I'm remembering now—Olivia told Bradford after she finished extracting the teleport sequence from the video of Maddy, she was able to teleport to Cameron's condo *that night*. How could she possibly have mastered it that fast?"

"Let's assume her voice is just in massively better shape than yours was," Maddy said. "Not unreasonable—they've all been at this for years longer than you. That might mean she could skip weeks of vocal exercises. But she'd still need practice with the visualization side of the sequence."

"But what if Olivia's already designed some kind of meta-sequence that you run to rapidly assimilate new sequences? Something that just . . . installs a new sequence in your mind like a piece of software, instead of you having to train to learn a new sequence like you'd train to learn any other new skill?"

Maddy sighed and said, "Maybe I need to just go back to her lab and steal every damn computer that isn't nailed to the table."

"So any time her neural net outputs a sequence she thinks is particularly useful, she just has the cabal run the equivalent of an executable and boom, they all have it," I continued. "They'd probably always do these upgrades in person by visiting her lab or meeting her somewhere."

"Well, peachy," Maddy said. "Question then, if they got you on video at the Church compound, what new sequences might they be extracting from that video as we speak?"

"I was practically subvocalizing, Maddy," I told her. "They didn't get anything from me."

"If they show up at our next softball game and they all have glittersteel skin, you will be hearing about it from me," she replied.

Jordon said, "God, for a minute there, when you said they might have a channel I don't have access to, I thought you meant something like telepathy." She paused, then said, "Do you people know telepathy?"

"Not yet," Maddy said, "but Olivia's not the only science wizard in this struggle with a neural net to call her own. I bet I could figure it out."

"It'd be something like a combination of teleport, for precision point to point addressing across a distance, and the Headphone Splitter spell, where you're guaranteed to hear a specific person in line of sight," I said.

"I believe I can work with that," Maddy said, impressed. "The cool thing is, if we design it right, you'd only ever issue a telepathy sequence silently, so they *can't* fucking steal it from us."

"Why wouldn't you just do all your sequences silently?" Jordon asked.

"It feels nontrivial to replace the relatively cheap transmission method of voice-to-ear with something like mind-to-mind. In the former, you're just using the air in the room to transmit instructions to the punctuation marks in the vicinity. With telepathy, you'd basically be emailing the instructions via the logosphere or something. Don't know yet, but I suspect this won't exactly be a chatty communication method."

"So let's think this through a bit more," I said. "How would you jam one specific sequence without jamming every other sequence you wanted to use within a given radius?"

Maddy said, "I don't know, Isobel, and even if we come up with a hypothesis for how they might be doing it, we're still probably chasing our tail thinking we'll outwit them well enough to counterattack their counterattack in the time we have left, you know?"

"You're thinking about Devin, aren't you," Jordon said.

"Yeah," I replied. "Assuming Devin could be convinced to help us, we may have to get them away from Jenning & Reece somehow."

"What's this 'we' of which you speak?" Maddy said. "Or do you have some trick up your sleeve for getting up off that cot that I don't know about?"

"I've only used half of my healing spells," I told her. "By tonight, I'll be ready to go out dancing."

"It's noon right now," she replied. "By tonight, Devin could be off work. If we want to get a message to them before that, we should figure this out now."

"Is it safe to try to reach them at work?" Jordon asked.

"Probably not," I said, "but it could be faster than trying to figure out where they live. I mean—is Jenning & Reece still operating as an advertising agency now after the relocation? Or did they drop all pretense of that and just become a power morpheme R&D division for the Crown?"

"They still maintain their advertising business," Jordon said. "But they also had their pick of every linguist and data scientist and programmer in the state to work in Olivia's lab. They chose something like two dozen people, I think, to join them—a small enough number that they could all be closely monitored and controlled, but enough people to generate a significant boost to Olivia working alone. These people all report to Olivia, but Devin's their team project manager."

"Maddy, do you still have back doors on the Jenning & Reece network?" I asked.

"Not for a long time," she said. "But hell, you were an employee there, too. You imagine they remembered to shut down your corporate account given they were busy with the transmutation of a quarter of California's population?"

"Hmm, good point." I could easily just create a burner email account and send a cryptic message to Devin's work email address. But a careful IT department answering to the Crown itself might enhance the typical scanning of incoming email by adopting a more suspicious stance, tweaking spam filters to make it harder to get through in the first place, restricting based on a broader variety of keywords or domains. An unknown email address hitting the Jenning & Reece network for the very first time might rank high for additional scrutiny before being passed on to its destination. You might even cut off email to and from the outside internet altogether for rank-and-file employees. We couldn't afford to fire off a random email and then wait and see if it even got through, let alone if Devin intended to respond.

Let's say in the best-case scenario, then, that my work credentials were still sitting there dormant because no one technically fired me, so IT never locked me out. Let's also say I didn't want IT to notice me on the network. With a little ingenuity, I bet I could modify my Apply DRM spell to encompass a trail of activity tied to a logon.

We used a simple, internally hosted, web-based project management system at Jenning & Reece for keeping track of work tasks, stacking them in priority order, that kind of thing. Devin and I shared several project boards, going back to our days working together on Violet's fundraiser and the SD5 release party, as well as other smaller projects. I could get into this system, create a task, and leave coded instructions within it for them to reach out to us. By assigning the task to Devin, they would get an innocuous notification in their email that would look to IT like any of a dozen notifications that this internal system generated per day.

Maddy approved of this plan. After easily stealing the entirety of Olivia's research from her lab, Maddy had a dim opinion of Jenning & Reece's IT department, and doubted they'd focused any energy on significantly improving the operation since.

I said, "Well, isn't that the kind of cockiness that got us busted at the Church? We didn't expect that they could have upgraded their defenses?"

"The difference here," she replied, "is that we won't be on-site if they spot these efforts of yours."

"Devin's on-site, though," Jordon said. "Definitely a non-zero risk to them if you get caught trying to communicate with them."

"Devin's currently collaborating with the enemy," Maddy replied. "I'm not super worked up about the risk to them."

"If we lose Devin, we'll never find our people," I reminded her.

"If we don't find our people in less than a week, we'll lose them regardless," she said. "I think your plan is solid and worth the risk, and also, I don't have any better ideas. Neither of us is in any shape to risk being on-site at Jenning & Reece, where two members of the cabal could wind up quickly engaging us if things go south."

"Listen, I respect this focus on finding your people, I absolutely do," Jordon said. "But they're going to put thirty million people on an arkship and they're going to try to leave with them. Isn't—I mean, shouldn't we—"

She fell silent. She didn't really know what we should do any more than we did.

"It's just us, Jordon," I said softly. "Us against the most powerful people on the planet."

"But *you two* are that powerful, aren't you?"

"On a good day," Maddy said. "We don't get many good days anymore."

"Anyway," I said, "I'm extremely confused about what the right thing to do is. Like—the shield was an all-or-nothing defense. No way to test it in advance. And if the thunderstorm defeated the shield, then Earth would be fucked. So now they want to evacuate. It's fucked up that they're only going to take Violet's subjects. But maybe the arkship makes contact with somebody who can help get the rest of the planet to safety. It could happen, right? Maybe the members of the cabal are horrible people because their methods are cruel and vicious, but—what they're trying to do isn't evil through and through, you know?"

"Violet is hedging her bets by taking the population of California with her," Maddy said. "She wants to pop into some new dimension down the line somewhere with a full-fledged army at her disposal. She's an Empress. She's thinking about conquest."

"Bradford's thinking about joining an interdimensional community," Jordon said. "I mean, Violet's nominally in charge of the cabal, but Bradford could take her down if he wanted to, I imagine."

"These aren't contradictory impulses," I said. "Join an interdimensional community, but do it backed up by an army. I have to say, for my first experience fighting a superpowered cabal, I'm impressed and overwhelmed. They're good at it."

"But do you want to be on the arkship when it goes?" Jordon asked.

"You mean, do I want to let them relocate me onto the arkship?" Maddy asked. "No way. Not interested in having my 'identity token' in their database. I might be willing to sneak on board, though. Could be downright happy to lead the resistance when the time comes."

I was conflicted. Was escape the only option, just because no other civilization seemed to have found a way to defeat the thunderstorm? Didn't someone need to stay and defend the people that the cabal was leaving behind? Shouldn't I reconsider elevating Alexander Reece to godhood and letting him fight the thunderstorm for us? But didn't I need to give the Dauphine of the Shimmer Lands more time to find a weakness in its front?

Didn't I always beat the final boss?

10

The work task I created for Devin on our project board was simple. The headline was "build 'contact me' form" and the body of the task was simply my new burner email address. But crucially, the task was assigned to Devin by a certain Isobel Bailie. I used a board for a project that was long over, so no one but Devin would even recognize it.

We received a terse communication from Devin around 7 p.m. that evening, in the form of a brief email from an address I didn't recognize:

Meet me in SD? Look for Baroness Bassline, 10:00 tonight.

Not surprising that Devin would pick up Sparkle Dungeon after the glamorous release party we'd coordinated together. The cabal would probably be watching for the Queen of Sparkle Dungeon to make a surprise appearance eventually, so I had to be on my toes.

We wrote back:

Lady Luminescent will see you then.

⚜   ⚜   ⚜

You could activate all the chat and in-box features of SD without ever actually starting a game session, just by hanging out on the startup screen, and Cameron always prided himself on the end-to-end encryption in his game, so we were optimistic that we weren't triggering any undue surveillance. We hooked up a voice chat and piped it through to the loudspeakers, and hot-wired some headsets as ambient microphones, so that Maddy and Jordon could participate in the conversation.

Just to be safe, we ran through some Q&A for each other that only we would know, in-jokes about our days working together, some quotes from the first performance review I'd written for them, that sort of thing. More than enough to satisfy ourselves that we were truly online with each other.

"Are you safe?" they finally asked.

"As safe as I get these days," I said. "Are they treating you okay?"

"They treat me just fine as long as I don't ask questions. But Isobel—I feel like I'm working at IBM during the Holocaust."

"Aren't you trying to evacuate people to safety?"

"They won't be the same people after the relocation," they said. "Olivia's planning a mass edit to make people loyal to Violet. No fucking around with resistance movements or anarchists or anything. They're gonna sweep everyone up and make damn sure they do what they're told on board the ship."

I didn't know what to say to that. Of *course* they weren't planning some altruistic act of mercy. It couldn't *possibly* ever be that.

"I heard about Jordon," they said. "Can you do that for me?"

"Are you imprisoned somewhere?"

"My whole team is confined at Jenning & Reece until the launch. I sleep in my office. Well—your office, figured you didn't need it anymore. I'm chatting with you via the mobile app on the cell network so IT can't monitor."

"How are they confining you?" I asked.

"National Guard."

"You can't power morpheme your way past the National Guard?"

"Not that many, not all at once. Can't you teleport me out of here?"

"We found out they've got teleport jamming tech. Don't suppose you could figure out how they're doing it?"

Long pause, in which I almost thought we'd lost our connection. Then they said, "Huh. Apparently IT installed new Wi-Fi routers throughout the building just recently. So maybe these routers are pumping out some kind of subliminal wave or something that interferes with teleporting . . . anyway, I could try to find a way to disable these routers."

"Don't worry about that," I said. "I hear you know how to locate people in the battery."

Another long pause, in which I could just feel Devin unpacking the implications of what I was about to ask.

"Not everybody, not yet," they said. "We'll probably still be working on it after the jump."

"I need you to find twenty-eight specific people *before* the jump."

"Or else you're going to leave me here?"

"I didn't say that. But I'd prefer to rescue you *and* those twenty-eight people, and you're my only hope of doing that."

"Okay. I need their full names, and as much information as you can give me—home addresses, Social Security numbers, where they worked, where they went to school, everything you've got."

I turned to Maddy, who was shaking her head.

"They don't have full names," she said. "they have *aliases*. They didn't have jobs, because they were busy trying to undermine capitalism."

"Do you have pictures you can dig up?" I asked. "Maybe they're in a facial recognition database and we can find them that way."

"Do you really think they hung out on social media in plain view?"

"If you don't give Devin *something* to work with, we'll get *nothing* in return, Maddy."

She spun up a laptop and got to searching.

"The data's likely going to come one person at a time," I told Devin. "Meanwhile, let's talk about a plan to get you—and our people—out of Violet's reach."

❀   ❀   ❀

Between Maddy's online searches and Jordon ransacking the class-rooms for personal effects, we miraculously managed to cobble together a trace of every missing person.

Aliases were actually a useful key for identifying people. Olivia's power morpheme sequences interrogated people's subconscious minds for personally identifying data, and an alias resonated loud and clear because it was chosen by the person, typically worn proudly, and not frequently shared as a moniker with other people. Gridstation was the first person we found this way.

Devin had a much harder time when all we could come up with was a first name that could be shared by many people, with little other identifying data except maybe a snapshot. We could certainly feed snapshots into law enforcement databases, or DMV or passport databases, but it was a multistep procedure—analyze the snapshot, compare to the DBs, and then if that person hadn't already been located in the battery, you had to send out a broadcast request through the network of minds to get self-images that matched on categories—for instance, "if you are a Black woman in your twenties or thirties, send us your self-image." Maddy might remember details like "oh and she's currently got blue hair" to help narrow down the query.

For analyzing the results, Olivia's team had developed a perceptual compensation algorithm, since most people carried idealized self-images around with them that might not even match their current decade in appearance. So the algorithm ran every self-image through the equivalent of one of those little applets you see on social media where you rapidly age yourself to see what you'd look like in the future. This was all considered a super crude, brute force method of identifying someone, and could take anywhere from thirty seconds to thirty minutes before finding a match or announcing no match.

If we could get snippets of other data about a person, things got easier. Although the anarchists prided themselves on living life completely off the grid, every now and then one of them would leave a signature trace in the world. One person had a Spotify account dating back years before they joined Maddy's crew, which they kept alive because they'd invested so much time tuning the recommendations that they weren't willing to abandon it; the account name had their first initial and full last name in it. Innocuous to the rest of the world among millions of Spotify accounts, but gold for our purposes.

After we'd located ten people, Devin said, "This looks really good, Isobel. These ten people are clumped too close together in a single row to be coincidence. I think they were all captured and stored in a series."

Devin summoned the self-images of fifty people in that row, until Maddy clearly confirmed that all twenty-eight of our people were present and accounted for. It was a joyful moment.

"Now, how do we get them out?" Maddy asked.

"I have no idea," Devin replied. "The system was designed for intake. There's no mechanism for releasing anyone."

"Sure there is," I said. "You're sending them sequences of power morphemes to get these self-images back, right? How are you doing that?"

"It's really demented actually," they said. "Olivia's got a speech synthesis system that can pronounce power morphemes. So she loaded her personal vocabulary, and a giant pile of sequences that she knows, into a library. Then her team developed a command line interface that gives me the ability to specify sequences from that library. I can just type in commands with plain English parameters and the software generates a proper sequence for broadcast throughout the battery."

"It was a teleport/transmute combo sequence that got them into the battery," I said. "That's what we use to get them out."

"You don't happen to know that sequence," Maddy reminded me.

"We don't need the actual combo," I said. "We do the original sequences one at a time. I probably know transmutation better than any member of the cabal thanks to downloading it from its original designer, *and* actually having the experience twice."

"You've never teleported another human being," she replied, "let alone twenty-eight in a row. I'm not sure even *I* could do that."

"And neither of those sequences is even supported by the command line interface to begin with," Devin said.

"Then, my friends," I said, a larger plan forming in my mind, "we are going to have to go on an *adventure*."

11

First things first: we needed to get Devin out of Jenning & Reece. They were not an IT resource, so asking them to shut down the Wi-Fi routers all over the building or even just on their floor wouldn't be feasible. We didn't know how many were necessary to keep the teleport-jamming signal up and running, and it was too risky to set them at the task of trying to physically pull the plug on the devices one by one.

I had a gut feeling that the teleport jammer was not a transmutation jammer, however. They didn't know I had mastered transmutation via Alexander's memory, after all. If that were true, we could evacuate Devin out of the building via the logosphere. Devin was a more experienced linguist mage than me, and I suspected I could teach them how to do it.

Destination: Sparkle Dungeon. Devin would transmute into Baroness Bassline.

I would transmute into the Queen, and meet the Baroness at the Sparkle Dungeon itself. Together we'd enter the battery.

"You're just barely back on your feet," Maddy said to me, "and you're about to attempt a transmutation?"

"You need to come with me," I said. "We need you there when our people come out of that battery. They're going to be massively disoriented and seeing you there will be crucial to convincing them we know what we're doing."

"Who is going to convince *me* we know what we're doing?" she replied. "This isn't a plan you're devising, this is a long-form improvisation."

"Improvisation is my superpower," I said with a smile.

"Mine is knowing how to avoid getting killed," she said, "and you are setting off my Spider-Sense here."

"Maddy, once we're inside Sparkle Dungeon, I am the goddamn Queen. Nothing is killing us in there, I swear."

Maddy finally agreed, unwilling to miss the action. I taught her and Devin transmutation over the course of an hour. Jordon sat in and listened, learning a bit of principle if nothing else about how power morphemes were similar to diva-casting in the game.

"Is anyone going to miss these people when they're released?" Jordon asked on a break.

Devin said, "They'll show up on the daily leakage report, but no one will notice them specifically." Turns out the "leakage report" referred to a tally of the number of people who died every day inside the battery. It was the tiniest of trickles from the large-scale perspective: twenty to a hundred people most days. When this occurred, the network released the identity pattern of the individual from memory, and the individual simply dissipated into nothingness. The cells in which people died were noted in a database. They'd be included as target destinations for new people in the next relocation event.

"My god, the machinery at work here is vast and cold," Maddy murmured.

"You could argue that's true at the scale of reality itself," Devin countered.

"Wouldn't argue the point," Maddy said. "But it's always worth noting when humans figure out a way to make reality worse than its original design."

❀   ❀   ❀

Devin went first. We had to know if they succeeded in getting out of Jenning & Reece, or we'd need to come up with another plan altogether. We had them put their phone on a table and set up a video link, so we could watch. Sure enough, within a split second of finishing the sequence, we watched them dissolve into a conceptual swirl and then they were gone.

I went next, to get to Devin as quickly as possible before anything weird or unusual could happen inside the game. Within moments, I was back in my Queen of Sparkle Dungeon avatar, glittersteel jumpsuit atop glittersteel skin, with fiber-optic highlights punctuating the ensemble. I arrived at my spawn point in the Iridescent Warehouse and set out immediately to find Devin.

At plebeian character levels, you spawned at a crossroads outside Platinum City. One road led into town, toward the Sparkle King's palace. One road led into danger, toward the Sparkle Dungeon itself. One road led to the faerie kingdom of Needle Drop Downs, where you could find yourself trapped in a dazzling world of relentless club remixes and adulterated gin and tonics. And one road led to the Dark Granite Arts Festival, where you navigated a bewildering and dangerous encampment in the wastelands at the edge of the Realm; your quest to find a spot to DJ seven nights in a row was constantly imperiled by delirious costumed adventurers and Bureau of Realm Management agents.

I swiftly made my way to the crossroads, where Baroness Bassline awaited me. The Baroness had adopted a subtler look than mine, using a dragon onesie as a base but then layering leather armor all over it, with pleasing snaps and buckles here and there gleaming in the sunlight. I guessed the Baroness was easily tenth level, judging by the impressive kit hanging from their belt: a combat telescope, useful as both a beam weapon and a blunt instrument; a set of combat poi with small mirrorballs at the ends that could conduct electricity; and sparkle-powered roller skates—a classic touch.

A few moments later, Maddy appeared. The journey had been more difficult for her; she'd never played the original Sparkle Dungeon, so she transmuted into her SD5 character and then teleported from SD5 to my location. It was an impressive feat, but it had taken its toll; she looked exhausted. I had healing for that.

Maddy's SD5 character was named Madeleine Torch, an appropriate surname for someone who wanted to burn society to the ground. The avatar costume choices in SD5 were a significant departure from the zany options in the first four games. Madeleine Torch wore stylish, black-and-white business fatigues, what the game called "militarized professional accountancy attire, just the thing for producing accurate and timely royalty statements for each of the Realm's hundreds of recording imprints, while ensuring your survival when insurgents from Bandcamp and BitTorrent try their luck invading corporate HQ."

We set out for the Sparkle Dungeon.

The Baroness said, "Things have changed on the servers. The original Sparkle Dungeon game is no longer accepting new players, and everyone playing it was booted from their sessions and locked out, right before they installed the battery. You can still see the Sparkle Dungeon when you're playing in campaign mode, but you can't get there anymore. The map just bends you away in a different direction."

Right on cue, we came in sight of the entrance to Sparkle Dungeon, where floating billboards displayed messaging: THE SPARKLE DUNGEON IS UNDERGOING RENOVATION TO CELEBRATE THE UPCOMING TEN-YEAR ANNIVERSARY OF THE SPARKLE DUNGEON SERIES! BUT DON'T FRET—WE'LL BE REOPENING NEXT YEAR WITH A BRAND-NEW ADVENTURE IN THE DUNGEON, AS WELL AS A CONCERT FESTIVAL FEATURING SKRILLEX! Further proof of the cabal's wicked cruelty: promising a Skrillex concert they had no intention of delivering. Always new depths, etcetera.

The entrance itself was a massive stone staircase descending down into the murky depths. Normally you could just walk right down the steps and onward into adventure. Now, though, a foreboding obsidian wall completely blocked the path. They'd put a barrier in even though players couldn't actually get here—obviously the cabal's fear of reprisal was operating at a high level.

Plan A involved an unprecedented amount of teleportation to pull off. I loaded Maddy up with every buff and booster spell I had in my arsenal to massively overclock her stamina for the job we had in store for her. She knew she'd pay for it eventually, but this was the moment of truth, and she was fully committed.

Plan A would die a sharp death if we got inside the Sparkle Dungeon and discovered they'd outfitted the entire thing with teleport jammers. The Baroness was confident that they'd have been tasked with project managing that kind of rollout; you couldn't just have IT install physical routers in the logosphere, rather you'd have to issue power morpheme instructions to the battery, and Devin was the hub for such communication. No such effort took place; the entire cabal was perhaps far too preoccupied now with outfitting the arkship for launch to protect what it considered to be an unassailable asset in this fashion. Perhaps they understood that no effort by a band of scrappy anarchists could truly threaten their ten-million-person array; this is what we'd been counting on from the start, that no one would notice or care if twenty-eight people went missing in the first place.

In some ways, Sparkle Dungeon was a classic dungeon crawl in the time-honored tradition: giant mysterious dungeon in which every room has a monster, a trap, or a pile of treasure; the monsters get tougher as you make your way deeper; eventually you find the biggest monster of them all waiting for you in the final chamber.

Nowhere are the physical realities of such a dungeon addressed: how the hell did a giant underground complex ever get excavated; why do all these monsters live there when you never run across piles of food; how come these monsters never seem to set off the traps; why does the big bad just sit in the final chamber waiting to get killed instead of proactively turning all those monsters into a horde and trampling you to death; if it's a dungeon, where the fuck are the prisoners in the first place; and so on.

But as we teleported to the other side of the obsidian wall, I quickly realized this was no longer the Sparkle Dungeon I remembered. We appeared on a slim walkway, and then emerged to find the entire dungeon had been terraformed—oh, excuse me, of course I meant sparkleformed—into a single vast chamber spanning enormous heights and stretching much further than the original dungeon ever had. Inside we saw countless stacked rows and columns of gleaming, jeweled glass sarcophagi, each with a subtle glow emanating from within. (Actually, they were probably countable if you had time to count to ten million.) The visual effect was mesmerizing, as the flood of glowing light was refracted through so much jeweled glass of varying colors. The light cycled through seemingly billions of colors including, somehow, colors I thought I'd never seen before—an impressive perceptual illusion. The towers had their own system of walkways and ladders, as though someone foresaw the need for manual maintenance on this system of sarcophagi, and as the Baroness deduced, there was a clear and predictable numbering system that could be understood holistically in order to navigate the space.

This enabled us to correctly visualize the row in which our people were stored; that was our next teleport. Now we were literally standing in front of physical objects containing human forms that we could recognize through the jeweled glass. They each looked frozen in the moment of fear when they realized what was happening to them. They hung suspended in some kind of glowing fluid inside their cells. Their eyes were generally open, but they seemed to show no sign of recognizing us on the other side of their prison windows, or of even being conscious in a classically understood fashion.

We examined these sarcophagi up, down, left, and right to see if there was any way we could physically crack or pry them open. This would save us a hell of a lot of effort if we could figure it out.

Experimentation made it clear this would be an unpleasantly up-hill battle. The jeweled casing was thick and almost impervious to scratching, which we tested by slowly attempting to increase the speed of Blades Per Minute against the material like a drill and finding ourselves duly rebuffed. There were no hinges we could attack because the units weren't devised with doors, since intake occurred via teleport/transmute directly into position inside. The units did have one apparent weakness, an electrical-style conduit at the top that connected the unit in a web to the entire network, but severing this connection seemed to offer no immediate bene-fit except possibly disguising our rescue attempt somehow; this likely came at a nonzero risk of also damaging or killing the per-son inside.

To be fair, everything we were about to do came at a nonzero risk of damaging or killing the people inside. We'd discussed this for several minutes before we embarked on this mission. Maddy was absolutely clear that her people would, to a person, rather die in a flawed rescue attempt than live to be "spent" by the cabal in their battery. That didn't make us cocky about it, but framed necessary decisions in a meaningful context at least.

These options exhausted, we were prepared for our original plan A. One by one, Maddy made two lightning-fast teleports per per-son: once to get inside each unit, and once to get back out with one of our people in her arms. The Baroness and I caught each person and gently lowered them to the walkway floor; they were almost al-ways semiconscious, or in a kind of waking dream state, and the next order of business was healing each person to a stable point where we could talk to them, soothe them, let them know they were with Maddy, and inform them we were rescuing them. They all fairly rapidly seemed to ramp up on this context. They had been sufficiently aware of their imprisonment and it was sickening to imagine this was true for the people all around us that we weren't planning to rescue.

Once our people were all collected, stabilized, and ready to move, and once I'd reupped some of Maddy's buff spells, we needed to get people out of the Dungeon. I delivered a sequence to Maddy that essentially conveyed the equivalent of an in-game invitation to join me at the Iridescent Warehouse, which was otherwise hidden from all players. To test that she'd accurately received the location infor-mation, she took my hand and teleported me there. Satisfied, one by one she teleported each of the twenty-eight anarchists, and the Baroness, back to the Iridescent Warehouse.

The most she'd teleported in one encounter prior to this was the day she saved herself, Jordon, and me from the Church compound. Today, she teleported once leaving SD5, once to get herself and the Baroness into the Sparkle Dungeon, once to get herself and the Baroness to the row where the anarchists were being stored, twenty-eight times to get into the battery cells and twenty-eight times to get out with an anarchist in tow, thirty times by herself from the Warehouse to the battery, and thirty times with another person in tow to get people out of the battery to the Warehouse.

At the end of this beyond heroic effort, satisfied that she'd done the job, Madeleine Torch collapsed and died on the dance floor.

This immediately triggered the effects of an amulet I'd given her called Late Night Encore, for use when those bastard club owners wanted to shut the party down at 2 a.m. but you had a solid half hour of gold left in your DJ set. Late Night Encore was a single-use resuscitation artifact that yanked you back onto your feet with around a quarter of your original hit points, cleared you of any curses or lingering ill effects you were suffering, and ever so slightly repaired you of potentially permanent stat damage, to give you a fighting chance to play your set right up until that last ecstatic anthem came on and finally, once and for all, tore the roof off the motherfucking house. "Fuck you, roof!" you'd wake up screaming and your enthralled dancing fans would put their hands in the air like they just didn't care, but you knew, down deep, that they cared, oh yes, did they most certainly care.

Safely ensconced in the Warehouse, the Baroness began to sing a variation on the musical sequence that they and Bradford had sung at Cameron's condo, and it was exactly what we needed to revive our spirits. My healing was the equivalent of emergency room triage, getting people patched up and out of immediate physical danger. The Baroness offered a deeper salve for the trauma the anarchists had experienced. Likely these gently euphoric effects were short term and they would be recovering from this trauma for the rest of their lives, but for now, the reunion was a beautiful thing to watch.

When Devin finished singing, I thanked them and tried to assess the toll the experience had taken on them.

"Look, I could have found a way to rebel from within at Jenning & Reece," they said, "but I didn't have the guts. Maybe I was just too loyal to my grandfather—for a lot longer than I should have been. It's hard watching someone steadily destroy your trust and faith in them over such a short window of time. Anyway—no more excuses. I should be thanking *you* for giving me a second chance to do something meaningful before it's too late."

I received my share of deep appreciation from the crew, even as I realized they were all staring at me a bit wildly. They hadn't seen my glittersteel skin, and I realized I had no intention of ever transmuting it back, either here or back on Earth.

We spent several hours here, regrouping and gathering our strength for the next step of our journey. I was about to perform a similar stunt to what Madeleine Torch had just accomplished: the mass transmutation of thirty-one people back into their original material bodies, back in the gymnasium.

"Shouldn't you just take it slow and do it one person at a time?" Maddy asked me.

"I'm initiating this sequence from within my sanctum," I told her. "Everything I perform here has an array of bonuses to it. I'd like to be able to focus all of my concentration exactly once when I'm at my best and just get it done."

"This is you improvising again, right?" she said. "You've skipped past ever transmuting a single other person besides yourself even one time and are just leaping into the deep end with transmuting the entire crew?"

"Isobel would never get away with this," I said. "But I'm the Queen, Madeleine, renowned for legendary feats of audacious diva-casting. I will pull this off."

In the end, it took me fourteen tries to get everyone back to the gymnasium. I didn't have an amulet to help me recover, but I was sufficiently conscious that I could utilize my own healing spells to get me back on my feet. Maddy didn't spend any time on "I told you so" with me because, by fucking god, *we had rescued our people.*

Jordon was waiting for us when we got back. She'd organized cots all throughout the gymnasium so that, for tonight at least, people didn't have to recover alone in disparate classrooms throughout the building. She had hot soup waiting for whenever anyone thought they might want sustenance, and every cot had a full water bottle placed beside it. She'd gathered all the variety of first-aid kits and pharmaceuticals from both the general stash and everyone's personal stashes, to distribute as necessary. And perhaps most critically, she had a pretty great soul playlist going over the loudspeakers.

Devin was quite skittish. Start to finish, from the time we contacted them at 10 p.m. last night, to this very moment, was twelve hours of clock time. By now, their absence in the lab would have been noticed by Olivia's team. Olivia herself kept unpredictable hours and rarely visited the lab, issuing instructions by fiat and code reviewing from her office, but if she had tried to reach Devin this morning, she might begin wondering why Devin wasn't responding.

But it had become a habit of Maddy's to check the spyware on Cameron's LAN anytime we pulled off a significant maneuver. No video calls had been scheduled; the cabal seemed not to have noticed our activities.

I realized how much the gymnasium had come to feel like the Iridescent Warehouse to me. It was the one zone in Los Angeles where I just felt absolutely safe, and now I was surrounded by the whole crew again. And I was *part* of the crew. You adventure alone for long stretches of time when you're leveling up, because that's how you prove yourself worthy to even join a high-level raiding party. That's how I felt here: these people had seen me in action at Cameron's, they'd seen me flat-out demolish the first quest in SD5 before meeting the Dauphine, and here I was, right alongside Maddy in the midst of their rescue. No questions asked about my background, how I'd gotten into this position; all of these people had their stories and maybe someday we'd all sit around the glow of the projector screen and share them, if we managed to escape the next relocation, or if the planet didn't get subsumed by the thunderstorm.

I caught myself constantly tracking Maddy throughout the room, from my vantage point lying on a cot near one set of bleachers, as she chatted with her friends. I couldn't recall ever seeing her so genuinely happy, and I was swept up in it. I was probably imagining it, but I thought I spotted her casually glancing my direction just to check in with me. Couldn't dare read anything into that, but it was easy for her to make my stomach flutter in the midst of all the emotion in the room.

❀   ❀   ❀

At around 10:45 a.m., with a crack of wild electricity in the air, Olivia Regan teleported into the gymnasium and began killing people indiscriminately.

12

The way it went down:

Olivia appeared directly underneath the projector screen, with her back to a wall, and cots on three sides of her. Her arrival was accompanied by a brief, dazzling flash of lightning all around her—again, just like when I saw a similar effect with Lonso, this felt to me like inexpert teleporting, a lack of control or precision that generated an excess burst of energy, as though her arrival was abrasive somehow, like she was striking a match when she appeared.

It took her three or four seconds before she was fully oriented to her surroundings.

Maddy spotted her first, standing about fifteen feet away from her, talking to Kenji. Maddy managed to get off a quick barrage of attack sequences, which caused a brilliant white bubble of energy to light up all around Olivia, a crackling conceptual shield that interfered with Maddy's attack by generating sharp bursts of defensive white noise.

Olivia responded by swiveling into an almost martial stance, sliding into a crouch while aiming her arm in Maddy's direction and flipping her hand in sync with several short sequences. Maddy flew backward through the air and landed in the bleachers. Cots were upended within that blast radius, and four or five people also went flying in multiple directions. I watched hard, brutal landings happen in slow motion.

She swept her other hand to the right and another set of people went flying like bowling pins being smacked hard. She was moving so fast that I was frozen in terror. Not Maddy—she managed to crawl to her feet and shrieked a nice loud power morpheme sequence that ripped the ancient old projector off the ceiling and sent it hurtling at Olivia.

Olivia subvocalized a sequence and the projector dissolved before it hit her. She traced the attack back to Maddy and actually recognized her this time, anger flaring up in the midst of an otherwise cold and calculated attack. Olivia turned Maddy's style of attack against her and yanked a loudspeaker down from the ceiling, aiming it directly at Maddy.

Maddy split herself in two, each half jumping the opposite direction. The loudspeaker smashed into the bleachers and smoke began pouring out of the grille.

I hadn't moved.

Olivia's eyes swept the room, and then she found me.

I shouted the *"PAUSE"* sequence, using the Transport Controls for the first time in combat. All of reality froze in place around me. Olivia was trapped in amber, in midsequence, no indication that she had any idea she was in this state. I was in deep, deep shock. No way could I let this stand, no fucking way did we rescue these people only to let them die during a motherfucking ambush. I couldn't kill Olivia in this state, couldn't affect her or the rest of reality at all besides holding it frozen, but now I had an opportunity to catch my breath and plan.

I executed the *"REWIND"* sequence to dial reality backward ten, twenty, thirty, an excruciating forty-five seconds or so; that's as far as I could convince reality to cooperate without inflicting severe damage on myself. I watched the loudspeaker fly back into the air, watched Maddy's split selves rejoin into a single body. I rewound the situation to just prior to Olivia's teleport into the gymnasium.

My body felt lit up hot like an incandescent lightbulb on the verge of exploding; another fifteen seconds backward would have incinerated me into ash. That was simply the physical damage component, but I had other problems as well.

For the entire forty-five seconds, my brain *screamed* at me to make this stop happening. No amount of prior spellcasting conditioned me for how existentially terrifying this experience turned out to be; we'd only tried going back maybe five seconds when we learned these sequences. I'd have guessed teleporting would be the more frightening experience, but it turns out the human organism has almost zero tolerance for watching time itself flow in reverse. I heard myself shrieking as though from a distance, as my mind recoiled in fear and then began to detach from the situation in defense. I would never perform this sequence again.

With what little concentration I could muster, I loaded up a stack of attack options into my short-term memory to have them ready.

I repositioned myself, getting up off the cot and moving to within close range of her arrival point. I summoned Blades Per Minute into my hand.

I executed the *"PLAY"* sequence. Deep relief swelled through me. From Maddy's perspective, I'd just teleported off my cot to the floor underneath the projector screen. I shouted to Maddy, "Olivia's incoming! Focus fire *here!*" And I pointed and began firing off attack sequences. Maddy barely got in the game just as Olivia materialized. And in the few seconds while Olivia was disoriented, we pulverized her.

She wound up physically shredded in multiple ways, bleeding from slashes and deep cuts, bruised from invisible punches. After knocking her down, I had just enough mojo left to cruelly transmute her limbs, fusing them with the gymnasium floor. I leapt onto her chest, and pressed Blades Per Minute several inches into her sternum, letting it vibrate gently, keeping the wound aggravated.

I said, "Everything I've done to you, I can heal. But if you so much as whisper a power morpheme, I will cut your fucking head off and sparklepult it into the sun."

❀   ❀   ❀

Olivia was cooperative as we got her off the floor and into an office chair in the center of the gymnasium, surrounded by the entire crew in attack readiness. They weren't all experienced combat linguists, but they had several stun guns and handguns among them that would quickly do the trick if Olivia decided to go on the offensive again. We didn't bother tying her up; she wasn't a physical menace.

Time for a good old-fashioned interrogation. Maddy wanted to do it, but I thought she'd be more inclined to talk to me. Gridstation wanted to make her type her responses to us so we wouldn't have to risk letting her speak, but we had her amply covered, and I wanted to get answers from her faster than typing would allow.

I sat down in a chair opposite her. She knew we'd been able to kill Lonso, so she had to understand she was walking into trouble if she came here alone. What would motivate you to teleport into a completely unknown situation right in the middle of your enemies? Something told me this was not a cabal-sponsored mission, which gave me a sliver of hope that the National Guard wasn't trundling its way in our direction with tanks and trucks full of soldiers.

"What do you want?" I said, skipping past niceties.

"I need your help," she replied.

"With what?"

"We haven't been able to—*refine*—our version of the teleport sequence," she said slowly. "It's a transcription from a video, after all. It works, but it's imperfect somehow."

I could tell it pained her to have to admit that, but here we were.

"I noticed that," I said. "You put on a light show when you appeared."

"Yes. It hurts. It hurts much worse for anyone caught in the blast radius."

I laughed grimly and said, "Olivia, are you trying to *weaponize* the teleport sequence?"

"For god's sake, *no*," she said, glaring at me now. She paused, controlling her temper, then said, "But our version doesn't scale well." She waited, wanting to test how much I already knew of what they were planning.

"The arkship," I said.

"Yes. The amount of excess energy we're generating when we teleport a single person—multiplied by millions—as it stands today, if we launch the arkship with the sequences we've got, we will likely kill most of the people on board."

"Well, this may seem like a radical suggestion, but maybe you shouldn't launch the arkship just yet."

She sighed. "Yes, Isobel, that occurred to me. But Violet refuses to move the launch date. She thinks keeping pressure on me will produce a miraculous solution."

"You must have known about this problem for a while."

"Yes. I hadn't brought it up because I thought I still had months to work on the problem."

"I thought you were using a musical sequence designed by Bradford to make the jump."

"It incorporates your teleport sequence. The transcription error was carried over."

"Can you sabotage the launch somehow?"

"I don't control the launch. I don't have access to the systems controlling launch or navigation. The majority of our launch activities are preprogrammed, set to go off according to timers without any intervention from us. She and Cameron have kill switches. Bradford and I don't."

"What about weapons? Blow a hole in the ship or something."

"Why would I do that, Isobel? You understand we're embarking on a humanitarian mission here, right? This planet's destined for obliteration."

"Is it humanitarian to edit the minds of everyone on that ship to make them loyal to Violet?"

"Loyal to *Violet*?" She practically laughed.

"Who then—loyal to *you*?"

She became incredibly serious, almost reverent, saying, "No, Isobel—loyal to *Alexander* as their *GOD*."

Uh, what? I had to be hearing things. Where would she get *that* fucking idea?

"Alexander's dead, Olivia," I said, knowing full well that wasn't exactly true.

"Alexander's been sending me messages via my neural net," she replied, "so please spare me your bullshit."

That devious bastard. I guess he'd realized that his reluctant prophet, me, wasn't going to deliver the battery to him all wrapped up like a birthday present anytime soon.

"There's absolutely zero chance I'll let you make Alexander Reece a god," I said.

"There's zero chance that you can stop me, Isobel," she replied, very matter of fact, avoiding any trace of smugness. "The sequences to edit the minds of the people in the battery are already locked and loaded. They go off during the relocation, which happens the day before launch. So whether the arkship survives or not, Alexander gets his elevation."

"Alexander becomes a god in seven days whether anyone touches the controls or not?" I asked, to make sure I was clear on the situation.

"You're losing track of time somewhere," she said. "The launch is five days away. The relocation happens in four. The scout ship leaves tomorrow."

"So what were you planning to offer us," I said slowly, "in exchange for helping you avoid killing all the people you're about to violently kidnap?"

"When Alexander is God, we'll give you your own country to rule," she said simply.

"Did Violet authorize you to make that offer?" I asked.

"Violet told me to find a creative solution," she said.

"Out of curiosity, what do *you* get when Alexander is God?"

"Alexander's not like the power-hungry demiurges of old," she said. "He's willing to share power in the pantheon he's creating."

"So you're planning on becoming a goddess, right alongside him."

"Oh please, Isobel, don't be so provincial. You and I are practically *already* goddesses. The edit simply spreads the news officially to the population of the empire."

"Also," I said, "California is *not* an empire."

"It's the *base* of an empire that will span realities," she said.

"I'm sorry, Olivia, who is feeding you this Kool-Aid? Alexander, via droplets of data that he pushes through your neural net? Does Violet believe this crap about an empire that spans realities, when she can't even figure out how to defend the reality she actually lives in? Is Bradford feeding you this bullshit on the sole basis of a literal ten-minute musical motif? Because I've heard remixes longer than ten minutes and I don't make religious decisions based on that!"

"You don't make *any* religious decisions if I remember correctly," she snapped back, "because you're too *cool* or *postmodern* or *jaded* to care about the underlying mechanism that holds reality together!"

I shouted, "I am not postmodern!"

"The fact is, this planet generates gods all the time," she continued, "they just don't tend to last long. It's a very competitive space. But Alexander found a hook—"

Maddy emerged from the perimeter and exploded into the conversation: "Alexander *accelerated a goddamn alien invasion!* You're not going to be gods—you're going to be *puppets* of the punctuation marks, doing *their* bidding—not the other fucking way around!"

"Says the woman sharing her personality with an *unnecessary* punctuation mark," Olivia countered.

"Piss me off some more," Maddy said, "and let's see how *unnecessary* the Interrobang's power morphemes are."

Oh, Olivia didn't like the sound of that. She'd always been intimidated by the synthetics.

"Yes, yes," Maddy said, warming up, "maybe we should just cut all the friendly bullshit here and accept the inevitable outcome of this situation."

"Which is?" Olivia managed to ask.

"We can't possibly allow you to return to the cabal," I said. "That's just a fact of your life now, Olivia. So—"

"Do you honestly think I didn't consider the possibility of my capture?" she interrupted. "Let's be very clear. If I don't return according to a specific schedule, the rest of the cabal will be *alerted* to this location."

"Then we'll find another location," I said.

"In the next four minutes?" she said, allowing herself the tiniest smile in the history of tiny, menacing, villainess smiles.

Maddy got right in her face and said, "Do you want to know how many times I can kill you and bring you back in four minutes?"

"It's me," Devin said suddenly. "That has to be how Olivia found us. She followed me somehow."

I was watching Olivia when Devin said that, and Olivia's tell—a slight wince as though she'd been shocked on her ass with a nine-volt battery—convinced me that Devin was right.

"I'm sorry, Isobel," they continued, "I should have guessed—"

"How could they possibly track you into the logosphere and then back into reality?" I asked.

In the silence, Maddy grabbed Olivia's shirt and said, "Answer Isobel's question or the killing you portion of the evening commences immediately."

"We have a sequence called the *relay,*" Olivia replied, jolted into submission by Maddy's threat. "The punctuation marks in Devin's mind 'phone home' once an hour, reporting their physical location and providing an executive summary of their activities. My entire development team is under this level of monitoring."

"So you knew the whole time we were planning on rescuing our people," I said, my heart sinking.

"I'm sorry, *whose* people, Isobel?" Olivia replied. "Or did you actually imagine I'd *allow* people out of my battery without a few modifications to their personalities first? Go ahead, test their loyalty."

I dared to glance up and around at the crew. I was not comforted by the looks I was receiving in return. I noticed that the handguns among the crew were no longer aimed at Olivia, but were just sort of gently trained at the floor for now.

"All right, enough of this bullshit," Jordon said, strolling into focus with the AR-15 she'd liberated from the armored truck hanging lazily at her waist from a shoulder strap. "All three of you are lying to each other and this is getting us nowhere."

Oh, uh—why goodness, what a novel interrogation tactic, Jordon.

"Olivia Regan, there's no way in fuck you would admit to the cabal you could ever get yourself into trouble," Jordon said. "They're not headed here in four minutes."

Actually, I thought to myself, not only that, but if Olivia had modified the personalities of the crew to capture their loyalty, she wouldn't have started killing them so quickly when she showed up here in the gym the first time.

"Maddy, I saw how long it took to heal Isobel," Jordon continued. "You couldn't resuscitate Olivia even once in four minutes, so just admit it. When you kill her, it'll be for good."

Nice that she didn't say "if" you kill her.

Jordon turned to me and said, "Yes, Isobel, you are a little postmodern."

"What!" I exclaimed.

Jordon finally arrived in front of Olivia with her AR-15 politely pointed aside.

"One time I got hold of an etheric monitor," she said, "and I took it apart. Before I really understood things. I thought they were like, glorified Easy-Bake Ovens inside or whatever. Turns out there are some hard-core, finely machined electronics inside those fucking things. Kind of the high-end audio version of what it needs to be, like they used four-thousand-dollar cables that were delivered to Lonso by cable couriers in tuxedos instead of five-dollar cables they could get from Amazon. But the secret sauce is on the motherboards, and you may remember something about me, Olivia—I've been a software engineer longer than I've been a recording artist. So, that very day, I managed to grab myself a little copy of the firmware on that motherboard, because you see, Lonso Drake somehow managed to live his entire life without being introduced to the concept of encryption."

This whole speech was making Olivia turn sheet white.

"I guess what I'm getting at," Jordon said, "is that I sure would love to get you hooked up to a good old-fashioned homebrew etheric monitor, just to see what imperfections need to be smoothed out, what lingering insecurities are plaguing you, so that we could start using the power of Church technology to help make you Even in the eyes of Gorvod. I imagine it would take me around half a day to build one using just the parts in this gymnasium, less time if we send the crew to steal some parts from a hospital for me—a duration of time in which Maddy would be free to keep you entertained.

I probably wouldn't be able to build in all the bells and whistles of one of Lonso's artisanal devices, so for instance I couldn't modulate intensity particularly well. But cutaneous power morpheme delivery using the Church's secret library of sequences—I could definitely rig that up.

"And then, by Gorvod, we'll find out every damn thing you've ever dreamed about, every wish and every 'wouldn't it be nice,' every aspiration and every little hope that keeps you going day after day, and we will *remove that shit*, over the course of several intensive days of amateur etheric monitoring, do you understand me?"

Olivia nodded ever so slightly. I couldn't quite believe what I was hearing. Cutaneous power morpheme delivery—so, using skin as a conduit for audio? The Church could actually *do* that to people?

"I refuse to believe the launch can't be stopped," Jordon said. "Maybe *you* can't stop it, but us—we're creative people. How would you recommend that *we* try to stop the launch of your arkship?"

"Put a gun to Cameron Kelly's head instead of mine," Olivia said.

"What about those edit commands you have queued up?" Jordon replied. "Can you stop those?"

"Not from here. I need to be on the Jenning & Reece network, using a VR console with a whitelisted machine ID, running a private dev branch of SD5, and using a whitelisted account to issue any new commands to the arkship."

"Or we could put a gun to Cameron's head?" Jordon said.

"I suppose."

I gave Jordon a nod and resumed control of the interrogation.

"Tell me about this scout ship you mentioned," I said.

"It's our only meaningful chance to test Bradford's navigation method," she replied. "We're debating whether it should have a pilot, or just be programmed to take a bunch of sensor readings on its own at the destination and then jump back automatically."

"Late in the game to be debating something that important, isn't it?"

"We were supposed to have several more months to plan," she replied.

"Who would the pilot be?"

"That's the crux of the debate. Bradford thinks sending a person will be our best bet for ensuring reliable, *useful* data might be sent back to us. But Violet doesn't trust a single person in the world outside the cabal, and none of us can be spared for this."

"Who's piloting the arkship?"

"Also a debate. If Cameron pilots the arkship, we have no one to operate the weapons systems. But Violet doesn't trust anybody else with access to the weapons he's designed."

"Very weird plan, Olivia."

"Not so weird when you consider we expected *you* to have joined the cabal a long time ago. You'd have made an excellent gunner, I imagine."

Me? In the fucking *cabal?* How had she so catastrophically misjudged me?

Or had she? Because I'd sure lapped up power morphemes like I was going to turn into the Scarlet Witch someday.

"You can't tell me that you trained me for all that time just so I could operate the guns on your fucking arkship," I said. "You weren't even planning an arkship when you started training me."

"True," she said. "But we always suspected your versatility would make you an excellent conspirator with us. Capable of taking on many roles, depending on the situation."

"But the main role was to be your weapon against the thunderstorm, if I've understood everything correctly."

"Or to lead an army against the thunderstorm, if that's how the situation unfolded."

"Do you have some kind of remote trigger to set me into motion against my will?"

"Isobel—your will *is* the weapon. Taking that away from you would render you inert."

Well now, slide in a nice compliment like that, Ms. Regan, and perhaps we shan't sparklepult your severed head into the sun after all.

Suddenly the lights and all the electronics in the room flickered and power cycled.

Instinctively my sword was in my hand again, but Olivia protested, "That wasn't me!"

"Somebody check the generator," Maddy said. "Probably just running low on fuel."

But then the lights flickered again and a few lightbulbs actually burst, and we were all on red alert. I looked up to see a portal claw itself into existence high above the gymnasium floor.

As the portal opened, the air was filled with a terrifying shrieking sound.

And then at high velocity, a human body came hurtling through the portal, out of control, landing hard on the gymnasium floor with a worrying crunch.

The body was immediately recognizable to me, if for no other reason than her silver skin.

The Dauphine of the Shimmer Lands was *here*.

Moments later, a herald began to emerge through the portal.

PART FIVE

SPARKLEPOCALYPSE

01

Our one advantage was that the herald seemed undeniably startled to be suddenly crossing a dimensional boundary when it stuck its enormous, black, dragonlike head through the portal, seeking the Dauphine.

"Dragon" was perhaps too cuddly a term to describe it. It seemed to basically be rows of animated, flailing, razor teeth on a nested series of multiple jawbones, operated by a small skull that seemed to indicate the thing was low on brain power while absolutely keen on chewing through the fabric of spacetime. Loosely occupying the position of eyes, a buglike array of irregular, slick panels adorned the top of its head.

The portal seemed to operate as a freestanding transmutation engine, ensuring that whatever came through it from the logosphere was appropriately formulated for the material plane of existence. This potentially meant the herald's body was still some kind of swirling mist of anger masquerading as the shell of a living thing on the other side. What a fun science and philosophy problem this event would be if the planet managed to survive!

I jetpacked across the room, narrowly avoiding a raging snap of its outermost jaws, and plunged Blades Per Minute deep into the buglike eye panels on its head. It reared with such force that I was thrown clear of the thing, leaving the sword jammed into it, vibrating at 160 BPM. Then it roared with pure fury and directed a breath weapon straight at me, a freakish cone of what looked like black ice.

The ice bounced off a bright energetic shield, and I realized Olivia was on her feet next to me, keeping me alive.

Jordon let rip with the AR-15, depleting its ammunition in a massive blaze of glory, focusing fire where I'd landed my wound; the crew caught on and emptied their handguns at it as well. They managed to decimate the array of buglike eye panels to the point where Blades Per Minute actually came loose from being caught in the crossfire; it landed with a clattering crash and skittered across the floor, still vibrating wildly, slicing the legs off tables and being a massive nuisance. I summoned it back into my hand.

Meanwhile the herald seemed quite stunned to be taking physical damage for potentially the first time in its indeterminate lifespan. Is that pain, am I in pain here? Oh hell, is that blood—like, *my* blood? Wait, are pieces of me literally getting *obliterated* by little hunks of hot matter? Whose fucking idea was *this*?

The Dauphine rolled onto her back, and I caught a brief glimpse of how tattered she was before I realized she was holding both of her pistols straight up into the air. She began firing. These pistols were not mere six-shooters from the Wild West. They were her marquee weapons in SD5, pistols enchanted with a Repeat All spell so that their ammunition never dried up. They fired bullets made of the last remaining sparkle in the Realm, and the sparkle was anathema to the herald. This series of brightly glowing shots tore entire chunks out of the herald's throat, knocked a dozen teeth from their sockets, sliced its demonic tongue into pieces. It recoiled instinctively, and in that moment, the Dauphine snapped the portal shut, carving off the tip of its snout, which dissolved into a sickening black mist that coated a good portion of the room.

After a long pause, Gridstation said, "See, people just have such a wrong impression of what anarchists even *do*."

The Dauphine tried to stand, and couldn't.

I dashed to her side, taking her silver hand in mine. She almost didn't recognize me in my new glittersteel skin, but then she smiled.

"I am very happy to see you, sister," she said, and then she passed out in my arms.

❀　❀　❀

Didn't take long to nurse her back to consciousness. She was so deeply torn and ripped in places that you could see bone, organs, parts of her that probably didn't actually need to exist until she came through that portal. But I healed her enough that she could start accessing her own healing, and she recovered quickly. Her steampunk attire was so thoroughly thrashed that we borrowed some street clothes from the anarchists to help make her comfortable. She had spells that could have mended her own clothes, but she welcomed the change. She felt it was time to ditch the pretense that she was simply a character from Sparkle Dungeon 5. Eventually, we needed to let her sleep.

Olivia watched the situation carefully. She could've teleported out of the gym during the chaos quite easily, but she'd stayed, and probably saved my life. I didn't trust her, but she'd been useful.

"What was that thing?" she asked me.

"A herald of the thunderstorm," I told her. "A small one, judging by how easily its head fit through that portal."

"A *small* one? Good Christ, how big do they get?"

"Olivia—are you telling me your cabal doesn't even know about the heralds?"

She shook her head.

"Then let me be the first to advise you—the heralds will fuck with your planning well before the thunderstorm itself actually arrives."

"And who is that woman that fell through the portal?" she asked.

I actually smiled and said, "That's the Dauphine of the Shimmer Lands. She's Alexander's daughter."

Yep, always nice to see that particular look on Olivia's face, when you'd finally managed to surprise her and her stoic demeanor just evaporated.

Maddy pulled me aside and said, "We need to start sending people home."

"What do you mean?"

"I mean, I went to a damn lot of trouble to find and rescue these people and it's sheer luck none of them were killed just now. If you need to fight capitalism, these people are your lot. If you need to fight freakish hell monsters with four million teeth, I would not call these people qualified. Gridstation can barely hold a stapler, let alone a weapon. Every minute they spend in our company is life-threatening. And this is not the fight they signed up for."

"You think I signed up for this?" I countered, but I knew she was right. "Anyway, yes, I agree that we are in the blast radius of all kinds of ongoing nasty business. I propose this: let's start spreading the word that anyone is free to go at any time. But the Dauphine is going to have a story to tell when she wakes up, and they might want to stay long enough to hear it."

"Fair enough," Maddy said.

I suddenly, irrationally blurted out, "You're not leaving, right?"

"As it turns out, I *did* sign up for this," she said with a small grin before wandering off.

❀　　❀　　❀

"How have you been, my Queen?" the Dauphine asked me, as I visited her on a cot in between her power naps.

"You're on Earth now," I told her. "You can call me Isobel."

"Isobel," she said slowly, like she was testing it out.

"I've been fighting the good fight," I said. "How about you?"

"I have been fighting the terrible fight," she said wearily.

"Do you want to tell me about it?"

"Of course I do. I wish I had more to tell."

"Do you mind if my friends hear your story? We've been through a lot together, and they deserve to know what's going on out there."

She nodded her assent. I signaled to Maddy and Jordon to start rounding up the crew for story time. Olivia drifted conspicuously close.

As people settled, I said to the Dauphine, "The last time I saw you was in the Iridescent Warehouse, with Alexander Reece. What happened to you after I left?"

"We prepared ourselves to race across the logosphere," said the Dauphine.

"The thunderstorm's movement is almost impossibly slow and imperceptible; its advance is felt deep in the soul rather than measured by some mundane unit of observable distance.

"But the heralds—oh, the heralds can be witnessed quite clearly, always ranging ahead of the thunderstorm, seeking out targets, hunting down life-forms, perhaps unnecessarily clearing the way for their dark creator's arrival. Alexander had tangled with the heralds on many occasions. He had developed methods for distracting them, or taunting them. He knew their temperaments quite well, understood feints that tricked them, and he could easily reach speeds exceeding theirs when the time, eventually and frequently, came to flee.

"And he could fight them, too. In one-on-one combat, he was mighty and perilous to behold, but the heralds frequently travel in packs when they are not lurking in disguise somewhere, and even a pair of heralds could overwhelm Alexander's arsenal. So carving a direct path through an entire onrushing brigade of heralds seemed like a suicidal task.

"But Alexander was not daunted.

"He said to me, 'I've spared them the full extent of my skills, because they learn, and they adapt. If you fight a herald and it survives, it gossips back to its fellow nightmares, and they develop cunning strategies for defeating you should they encounter you again on the chessboard. And the chances of that are high, because once you survive them, they hunt you with increasing urgency, almost as though their humiliation at failing to murder you the first time is now their primary motivating reason to exist.'

"Then he said, 'The logosphere has so far presented the heralds with very few challenges. And they're familiar with me now. But you'll be a complete surprise, and we must take advantage of this fact while we can. What can you do that they will never see coming?'

"We discussed tactics at length as we embarked through the rift in the map and set off across the logosphere. I intended to cast a portal to take us to the front of the herald formation, but Alexander warned against it, suggesting that the moment we used any magic in their vicinity, all of their attention would immediately come down hard upon us, and we should ensure we used that initial moment for a surprise attack.

"I struggled to comprehend the geometry of our approach, for when he had brought us within sight of the thunderstorm before, it was farther away from us at that point than the entire length of the Sparkle Realm itself, and farther still. He said, 'When the heralds mass, they bend their local spacetime around them, twisting it to their will, fashioning slivers of reality into barbs and spikes. And when they congregate in such numbers as we will face, in the churning waves that regularly unfold from the thunderstorm itself, they *own* reality, but the thunderstorm has not yet *consumed* it.

"'We will not travel in some straight line through the heralds, like a missile streaking toward a target. Instead, I will *pull* these heralds *toward* us, luring them away from their source of strength. I will detonate ideological gravity wells that will ensnare them and epistemological supernovae that will decimate them. When their first wave falls, in the briefest of moments when they retreat and regroup against these lightning strikes, *then* let's hope you can see clearly to the thunderstorm itself, to commence your tunneling attack. I'll be by your side, destroying them with the rage of my voice. Do you understand?'

"'Where did you learn these incredible spells?' I asked.

"'I am self-taught in these ways of being *GOD*,' he replied. 'I have made much progress on my own. But someday soon I shall find myself fully exalted.'"

I caught Olivia's tiny smile when the Dauphine said that. Really it was starting to bug me that after all the time I'd known Olivia, she was resolving down into a fangirl for Alexander; there absolutely *had* to be something I was missing.

"We crashed headlong into the heralds. Alexander's voice seemed to be everywhere, all around us, many incarnations of it chanting simultaneous disparate attacks. His voice drowned out the sudden freakish bleating of the closest heralds to us as they realized the affrontery of our presence. He destroyed dozens at a time, shredding them into particles of hatred swirling all around us like black and poisonous snow. I carried up the rear, using my pistols instead of my portal because I did not yet want them to see my portal in action, lest they learn a defense against it before I arrived at the thunderstorm.

"And that is how we fought for what seemed to me an eternity: the two of us locked in combat against foes that seemed to endlessly replenish themselves, with only the stamina of Alexander's voice truly keeping us both alive, until finally, miraculously—as befitting a god—he created at last a window of opportunity for me, a clear path straight to the face of the thunderstorm itself. And so I rocketed past him, leaving him to his fate. I dared not look back.

"A towering cliff face seemed to rise up in front of me, pulsing and veiny like flesh, yet misty and immaterial at the same time. I could feel a hyperintelligence probing me, a mind so computationally intensive that consuming all of reality would be the only way to feed it, and even then, only for the briefest of infinities.

"I launched my volley of portals at the surface of that cliff, creating the tunnel I had envisioned, and so I journeyed deep within the heart of the thunderstorm."

❀ ❀ ❀

"My magic was sorely tested as I pursued my course.

"The portals protected me, but they were porous in various ways. I found myself infused with memories that dripped from the tunnel walls onto me, memories of people frozen in the moments when they realized they were lost to the thunderstorm's advance, ghosts forced to relive these moments over and over for eons, their lives and hopes eternally squandered, until finally their essences were fully extracted and pulverized into dissonance and wails.

"There seemed to be no way 'out' ahead of me, and the increasing pressure on the tunnel indicated to me that the organism was attempting to reject me as though I was a virus. Finally, I accepted that there was no grand plan beyond consumption that I could grasp from my limited point of view, no strategy to defeat it that I could somehow derive from superficial flaws or weaknesses, and no trail of littered remains lurking 'beyond'—it was all thunderstorm this direction, in perpetuity.

"But I did come to one conclusion about its nature. The thunderstorm is intelligence so malevolent that reality gives way in its presence, and it comes from a purely antithetical impulse to life itself. It mimics life in ways, but in truth it is blind to the concerns of life, a vast gnawing ontological omnivore devoid of mortal concerns. Alexander aims to be *GOD*, a pursuit that I fully understand. The thunderstorm *negates* gods.

"I opened a portal back to the beginning of the tunnel, so that I could escape. Screeching tendrils of antipathy clawed after me, slapping at my heels, knocking me to and fro without managing to grasp me in my deliberately erratic flight path. At this point, I could have opened a portal to anywhere in the logosphere in a desperate effort to escape.

"But then I saw Alexander, at the height of his glory, *riding the back* of a herald as though he had tamed it, and perhaps a dozen heralds of all shapes and sizes, oozing masses and slithering insectoids, roaring hellbeasts and angular shadowdemons, had *rallied to his call*, and together they had formed a surprising assault on the unprepared heralds who had never faced their own.

"Suddenly my desire to escape seemed selfish, and cheap, and shallow; and I rocketed as close to his side as I could get, ensuring he could see me, and I began blasting my way through our foes. A tremendous and horrifying wrenching sound came from behind us, teeth and gears crunching and grinding, as the thunderstorm prepared to churn out yet another agonizing new wave of compressed fear fashioned into weapons.

"I took the opportunity to flee, trying to lead a chunk of heralds away from Alexander. A thundering cloud of them chased me. I did not dare lead them to the Sparkle Realm. And I knew no safe haven within the logoshere where I could hide.

"So I set my thoughts on you, Isobel. I hoped and prayed that you could save me, and I opened a portal, and so I found myself here."

"So, Alexander is literally the only thing between us and the thunderstorm," Olivia said.

"He would be a worthy warrior god," the Dauphine mused. "Perhaps that is what these times call for. In all the memories of dead civilizations that I encountered, none offered a single viable champion to defend itself."

"We don't need a *single* champion," I said. "Alexander doesn't need godhood. He needs *reinforcements*. He needs Cameron's weapons systems. He needs a squadron of spellcasters. He needs the entire cabal to fight at his side instead of running for the hills. We should be trying *all* of that before we commit to irrevocably elevating Alexander to a god."

"We don't have time to fashion some grand alliance to fight evil," Olivia said.

"What grand alliance?" I shouted. "I'm talking like eight fucking people!"

"And you really think *eight people* will suffice?"

"You really think that thing hasn't run over its share of gods?"

"Eventually, Isobel, that thing will meet a god it *cannot beat*, and you would be *privileged* if that god turned out to be Alexander Reece!"

"No, I would not be 'privileged' to let a dead rich white guy become God of planet Earth! I've had absolutely *enough* of that 'privilege' to last whatever pitiful amount of lifetime I've got left. We find *another way*."

She finally fell silent. Something about that argument actually seemed to get through to her.

"I don't understand you, Olivia," I continued. "Why are you waiting for Alexander to elevate you to a goddess in the first place when you could just elevate yourself anytime you wanted?"

Olivia practically snorted with laughter. "You really want *me* charging into the fray and fighting the thunderstorm with my bare hands?"

"What am I missing about the part where you would be fighting as a *goddess*?"

"I don't *want* to fight! I don't want to *lead* or *rule*. I have a different vision for my transcendence, and *first* I require Alexander to be elevated."

I said, "I get it. If something goes wrong, Alexander's the goddamn guinea pig. *He'll* be the one to suffer if you screw something up, or if the punctuation marks were lying about the process. Just like he was the guinea pig for the first transmutation sequence, when he cheated death."

And I certainly noticed that tiny little smile appear on her face again.

"What's your 'different vision' for your transcendence?" Devin dared to ask.

"Let Alexander be the warrior god we need," Olivia replied. "I will provide the intellect to guide him."

"Alexander is out there right this very minute defending all of you," said the Dauphine, aiming her pointedness at me. "Where are these reinforcements you describe? How soon can they be deployed to his aid? What if he falls before we get to him? I am detecting a severe lack of urgency here."

I came very close to Olivia, almost whispering at her, and said, "If you're really convinced we need to elevate Alexander early, why haven't you left already to do it? You could have easily escaped from us by now."

Maddy sauntered up and said, "It's because we haven't told her how to fix the arkship."

Judging by Olivia's expression, Maddy had guessed correctly.

"Look, Isobel, I truly hope the arkship won't need to jump," Olivia said. "But I'm a scientist. I don't live and breathe on hope. And I *do* think that thing has run over its share of gods."

Yeah, that was the crux of it. A god might not be enough.

She said, "Go ahead and try to rally your reinforcements. The idea has merit. I'll help you myself if I can. And if you can beat back the thunderstorm with the people and weapons we have on hand today, then hooray for us—the relocation won't be necessary, which means Alexander's elevation won't happen. But if you and your reinforcements fail, if Alexander in all his divine glory fails, the arkship *cannot* be allowed to fail when we inevitably *do* have to escape. Because there's a very real chance that instead of beating it back, we will learn that the thunderstorm simply can't be stopped."

"So you just need us to teach you how we teleport?" Maddy asked.

"Not me. Teach Bradford. Navigation's all on him."

"And Bradford's in the loop on this problem?" I asked.

"Yes. We've been experimenting together, with no luck."

"I'm not surprised, honestly," Maddy said. "You all never took the synthetics seriously. Stealing a sequence off a video—it's like when opera singers learn songs phonetically without actually learning the language they're singing in. They're bound to miss some nuance somewhere along the line."

"What happens in these experiments?" Devin asked suddenly. "What does that mean, 'no luck'?"

It was an impertinent question to hit your boss with out of the blue, but I suspected Devin's tenure at Jenning & Reece was firmly behind them.

I turned to Olivia, watching her squirm, and suddenly I knew what Devin had clearly already guessed.

"You're doing human testing," I said.

"Yes," she said. "Human testing has always been a core component of our development protocol. You of all people should know that."

The Dauphine located Cameron Kelly for me. Turns out he'd migrated his primary workspace to the logosphere, and he himself was occupying the role of the evil Chairman of the Realm—a turn on his previous role as Sparkle King, and perhaps a commentary on how he viewed the success of the series. SD5 was clearly an attempt to recapture some of his original innovation after churning out sequels for so long, and if that required him to don a black hat for a while, so be it.

"Well, well, well," he said, leaning back in his chair as I arrived in his futuristic office suite in HQ. "Isobel Bailie as I live and simulate breathing."

"Hi, Cameron Kelly," I said. "Nice to see you when people aren't trying to kidnap me."

"I'm tickled pink you're still in action. You know, I've been rooting for you, in that vague 'hope she isn't dead' sort of way. I assume that was you who impaled Lonso Drake through the chest?"

"I can neither confirm nor deny that I personally delivered the killing blow and enjoyed the living fuck out of it."

"Wonders never cease with you, do they?"

"They might someday, actually. But I hear you have some weapons at your disposal now that we might be able to use."

"Yes, Isobel, I have a complete litany of weapons now. If there's a weapon in any version of Sparkle Dungeon that shoots rays, blasts, bullets, arrows, cannonballs, rocks, or mean personal insults at an enemy, I've bolted it to the side of the arkship or embedded it in the hull. I'm now working my way through other people's games to plagiarize new weapons I haven't thought of. Goodness me, why do you ask?"

"What are you going to use these weapons against if you're planning to run, Cameron?"

"The threats of the future, Isobel, which will hopefully be more easily defeated by sparklepower than the threats of the present."

"Alexander Reece is alive, did you know that? Just like Maddy told us he was during our little question-and-answer session."

He froze, staring at me with a blank expression.

"It's true," I said. "I've seen him. He's alive here in the logosphere."

Cameron sat back even farther in his chair, probably past the point where a real chair in the material world would have toppled over backward.

"He's fighting the heralds of the thunderstorm, probably at this very moment," I continued.

"The what now?"

"The vanguard of the thunderstorm. Imagine a cavalry brigade made up of hundreds of individual Gorvods."

"Isobel," he said, rubbing his eyes, "you do realize Gorvod is make believe, right?"

"It's an analogy, you twit," I said.

"I kid, I'm a kidder," he replied. "Look—I don't know where you got the impression that dead people float up to the logosphere, but this isn't the afterlife."

"Didn't Olivia ever tell you where the transmutation sequence came from that put all those people into the battery? She assisted Alexander in designing it. And Alexander used it to escape his body after he'd been shot twice in the chest. He can't go back to the material world or he'll die, but he is plenty alive here in the logosphere, and when the Dauphine last saw him, he was single-handedly stealing heralds from the enemy and turning them on each other."

"The Dauphine . . . ?"

"My dude, subscribe to some feeds because you are behind on the headlines. Yes, the Dauphine of the Shimmer Lands, who is sentient now, fought alongside Alexander. And that's not even the biggest scoop. Did you know—"

"Hold up," he interrupted quickly. "Why are you telling me all this? Are you trying to get me killed by Violet? Does *she* already know this stuff?"

"Uh, no, not even the slightest hint. I would prefer to keep it that way."

"So, now you want me to conspire with you against the Empress?"

"I just want to steal your guns, Cameron. You can say I hit you over the head with a candlestick or something and got away disguised as the maid."

"Ha. So what could possibly be a bigger scoop than the fact that Alexander Reece's ghost is fighting aliens?"

"Olivia has a plan to elevate Alexander into a literal god. She's going to edit the minds of the people in the battery to believe in Alexander's godhood. And then he's going to use that belief to lever himself up into *actual* godhood—all to make himself into a proper combatant against the thunderstorm.

"But," I said carefully, "if I can muster adequate reinforcements for Alexander's current fight . . . if we can somehow beat back the thunderstorm *without* the help of Alexander running in god mode . . . then she won't ever need to elevate him."

"You know this because you and Olivia are BFFs again now?"

"Yep, we watch baking shows together and do each other's nails."

Cameron ran his hands through his hair and said, "Does Bradford know any of this?"

I shook my head.

"Bradford's going to be very interested to hear this business about Alexander," he said. "You need to tell him."

"Why?"

"Because, look, if you want my help, you have to understand that there's no way I can maneuver the arkship to get weapons into position without Violet hearing about it. None. All control and monitoring systems are mirrored in the governor's mansion. We're training some of her Air Force hotshots to pilot the arkship, to man the guns, the works. She will know immediately if I deviate from our agreed-upon schedule in any way. And she has the same kill switches on her end that I do on my end."

"But Bradford . . . ?"

"Bradford is the only person that Violet thinks of as her peer. If you get Bradford on your side about this, you're halfway to convincing Violet to hand over the keys to all the weapons."

I mused about this idea. He might be receptive, if he thought I might help him fix his teleport sequence. On the other hand, I'd rescued his grandchild out from under him.

"Look, I can call him right now and we can talk to him together," Cameron offered.

"No," I said, "he'll think I'm coercing you somehow. He won't trust me. If I'm going to talk to him, I need to meet him on his turf."

Cameron whistled. "You go to Jenning & Reece and you will be screwed trying to get out."

"Well, I have some leverage," I said. "Or maybe you hadn't heard that we broke Devin out."

Cameron laughed. "Unbelievable. You are a secret agent of chaos."

"Can you at least warn him not to kill me the moment he sees me?"

He nodded and began typing an email to Bradford.

"Oh hey," he said while he typed, "is Jordon Connelly with you?"

"Of course."

"Because you know who would make a fantastic pilot for the ark-ship?"

"Jordon?" I said.

"Yep. You know she's the first person to beat Sparkle Dungeon 5, right?"

"What? You mean she's the new Queen of Sparkle Dungeon?"

"The monarchy's broken, Isobel. She's the very first Prime Minister of the Sparkle Realm."

◎5

I materialized in the hallway outside of Bradford's office and politely knocked on the door.

"Come in," he said from inside.

I entered slowly and stopped in the doorway, making eye contact with him, looking for his blessing to go any further.

"Isobel," he said. "I would appreciate to know the whereabouts of Devin."

"They're safe," I said.

"That's not what I asked."

"That's what you get, Bradford. They're safe, and they're happy about it."

Bradford fell silent, then motioned for me to come sit in the leather chair in front of his desk. I felt like I was practically job interviewing all over again.

"You have apparently been busy since last I saw you," he said. "Not at your position with Jenning & Reece, of course, which has been noted in your personnel file."

"I have a doctor's note for my absence," I said. He didn't smile. I didn't care; some of my jokes were just for me.

"I almost don't mind your assassination of Lonso Drake," he said. "That was, shall we say, enterprising of you. But stealing my grandchild is another matter. I need them *here*. Olivia needs them *here*."

"I agree that *you* need them here," I said.

Bradford picked up my meaning.

"Olivia is with you?" he asked.

I nodded. "Please note that in her personnel file."

Bradford sighed heavily. "That will get her killed by Violet in a heartbeat."

"Maybe," I said. "I mean, if you haven't killed her first. She's been keeping a big secret from you."

"And you're here to reveal it to me out of the goodness and kindness of your heart, I take it?"

"Are you saying I'm not a good person, Bradford? Because you might hurt my feelings."

"Get on with it."

"Alexander Reece is alive in the logosphere, fighting the vanguard of the thunderstorm, and Olivia plans to make him a god if we can't find another way to stop the thunderstorm from destroying Earth."

After a long pause, he said, "You do make an entrance, don't you?"

We sat quietly for a few moments, while Bradford weighed whether he trusted me, and considered the implications of what I'd said.

"Olivia should have told me," he muttered at last.

"Maddy warned you he was out there in the logosphere when she told her story at Cameron's condo," I reminded him.

"*Olivia* should have told me," he clarified. "And Maddy didn't mention this nonsense about making Alexander a god. Christ, he was barely qualified to be a managing partner of this firm, let alone god of the planet."

I didn't know what to say to that. I didn't pretend to understand the interpersonal dynamics among Alexander, Olivia, and Bradford, and wasn't about to start asking Bradford personal questions to find out.

"I want to propose—a truce," I said to him. "More than that—an alliance. To fight the heralds together. To save the entire population of Earth, not just the people of California."

"I'm surprised at this optimistic streak in you," he said. "We'll be *lucky* to save the people of California."

"We could help each other," I said.

He didn't reply. I wasn't exactly ready to let on that I knew about the transcription error, so I had to work a different angle.

I said, "Are you worried about what you're going to find when you reach the source of the Beacon?"

He raised his eyebrow and said, "You're very well informed."

"What about your scout ship?"

"It launches tomorrow. But it'll be empty except for sensor and recording equipment—basically an oversized drone. Violet will not allow a pilot, because there's no one she trusts to accurately report back."

I took a gamble, and said, "Bradford, look—*I* will pilot your scout ship, and I swear to you, you can trust me to report back. But you've got to stall the launch of the arkship. The last we saw Alexander, he was single-handedly facing the enemy in combat. He needs our help. If we find a way to stop the thunderstorm right where it is, we won't even *need* the arkship."

"Violet is firm—the launch countdown will not be stopped."

"The launch countdown was accelerated because she was scared of *my people* attacking, and I'm offering you a *truce!*"

"So what do you actually want from us in exchange for this truce?"

"I've heard you're developing a whole new set of musical power morpheme sequences. Are any of them combat appropriate?"

"Most," he said. "Considering the general atmosphere, that focus seemed appropriate."

"Can you teach us?"

"I could certainly have them installed in your people. Anyone who can actually sing, that is. Installation isn't a comfortable process, but it's highly effective."

"What do these sequences do?"

"I don't call them 'sequences.' They're called *movements.* The simplest of the lot demoralize the enemy at an existential level. The most powerful among them can deresonate an enemy into independent component frequencies. The movements work best with multiple voices singing together on different parts."

"Gotcha—a battle choir."

"Exactly." He paused, then said, "Is that all you want?"

"I also want Cameron's guns," I told him. "I understand that's impossible without Violet finding out."

"*Nothing* is possible around here without Violet finding out," said the voice of Violet Parker, coming out of the intercom on Bradford's ancient desk phone.

Bradford smiled—for the first time since I arrived, I was the one caught out in complete surprise.

Moments later, Violet teleported into the room. She arrived at the far end of the room to avoid catching us in the backlash of electrical energy that surrounded her entrance. But I was close enough to feel an unpleasant hint of its charge.

She wore an impressive black uniform that combined regal with militaristic styles, purple highlights here and there on the sleeves and collar, beautiful black boots. Her hair was pulled up into a ponytail of all things. I would have expected maybe a bun or some kind of wrap but it was a touch that kept her looking very energetic. She was really looking sharp all things considered—you couldn't tell she was under any stress whatsoever. She carried no weapons that I could see, despite teleporting herself into the presence of one of the most wanted so-called terrorists in her empire.

Bradford smoothly got up and allowed Violet to take his seat behind his desk; he stood behind her, leaning against the bookshelf, preparing himself to enjoy watching Violet take over this conversation.

This was an unexpected twist, but I had my wits about me. I'd seen more combat than Violet Parker by a wide margin. She might try to mask subliminal commands to me, but I could defend myself by careful concentration on her overt meaning. Moreover, Violet had made one major tactical mistake by coming herself, aside from the fact that she was now in range of a strike from Blades Per Minute. There was no way she'd come here from Sacramento without expecting to teleport back, probably from this very room, which meant the jammers probably didn't extend to Bradford's office. I could probably escape at will.

"Olivia plans to make Alexander Reece a god, does she?" Violet asked, making sure she'd heard me correctly. "Presumably instead of making the arkship passengers loyal to their Empress?"

"That's the gist of it," I said.

"I will slay her myself before she ever gets the chance," Violet said.

"I might let you," I said.

"*Let* me?" she snapped.

"Well, hmm, is she sitting in her lab waiting patiently for you to slay her? Because surprise, no, she isn't."

"You're a deeply annoying human being, Isobel."

"Okay, now my feelings are *definitely* hurt."

"But you're also quite impressive. Olivia was right to want you in our cabal, although I suspect you'd probably be too squeamish for our core activities. You're proposing a truce then, are you? You and Madison Price will cease your little kidnapping and murdering spree, and we'll all just team up to fight the bad guy, is that it?"

I paused, then said, "Uh, yeah, pretty much."

She paused, then said, "Well, I like it."

"Really?"

"Isobel, I'm cruel, and vindictive, and I'll kill you someday, I'm sure of it, but I am *trying to save people's lives.* I'm also not about to let Alexander fucking Reece achieve godhood before I do. Oh, I'm sorry, did I say that out loud? What I meant was, yes, by all means, let's team up to fight the bad guy. Bradford and Cameron are at your disposal. Mind you, I refuse to delay the launches. So plan your attack and *get it done*. And keep in mind, if anything happens to the arkship, that's it. That's our last hope for escape."

Incredible. It would be absolutely absurd to ignore warnings about the danger to the arkship if they tried to jump with the existing sequences. I wanted to give Violet more credit than that, but she wasn't making it easy.

A sudden distant shriek rang out, alien in nature, instantly familiar to me. We all fell silent, waiting to see if it would happen again. It most certainly did.

Violet instructed Bradford to open the blinds on his corner office windows. In the distance, something large and black was circling the skies above Los Angeles. It was alone, mercifully. Imagine something the size of a jumbo jet, with giant pterodactyl wings, periodically spraying jets of black bile from its throat down at targets on the ground.

"This is one of your heralds, I presume?" Violet asked as she pulled her phone out of her uniform (which, of course, had pockets because she was the fucking Empress) and started dialing. I nodded. "How many of these are out there?"

"Hundreds at a time," I told her. "This is practically a baby."

"Yes, hi, Libby, this is Violet," she said into her phone, "can you put me through to Centcom please?" In the pause, she asked me, "How do they react to bullets?"

"Just the way you'd hope," I said. "But they regenerate when you hit them, so you have to hit them hard and fast."

"Hello, this is the Empress. No—please, just listen. Tell whoever's in command this shift to scramble all fighters in Southern California, and then put me through to the General . . . Yes, the target is the *GIANT FUCKING DINOSAUR ABOVE LOS ANGELES!*"

The three of us watched together, fascinated, as several waves of Air Force fighter jets engaged the herald. I had high hopes. Earlier we'd shot one in the face with an AR-15 and some handguns, and scared it off. Imagine how much *more* scared this one would be after we shot it with missiles and machine guns.

But no, we were not so lucky. This particular herald was supernaturally maneuverable in the air, and easily avoided missiles that were downright slow-moving by comparison. With giant heaving flaps of its wings, it could knock incoming jets out of the sky. And my original judgment about its size was woefully miscalculated, because it was still in the process of oozing its entire body through some invisible rift from the logosphere into the material plane.

The only reason for a herald to come here this soon, before the logosphere was fully destroyed, was because it was on the hunt for the Dauphine. Who knew how many more were queued up behind it?

I got out my burner flip phone and tried to call Maddy.

"Hello, General," Violet said smoothly. "Yes, I see that. Not a great showing. I'm guessing those planes will be hard for us to replace. Tell me, what other options do we have here?"

Maddy finally answered. I peeled away to talk to her.

"Where *are* you?" she asked. "There's a herald in the sky right now!"

"I know, I'm probably about as safe as you are at the moment," I said. "Tell the Dauphine not to do anything rash like trying to fight it."

Even as I said that, I saw a streak of white rocket exhaust sail up through the air to engage the herald—the Dauphine's jetpack.

"Or don't do that," I said, "I mean, that's fine, too, I guess."

"Who the hell else is going to fight it? The military?"

"That's usually the purpose of having a military, Maddy."

"Well, you can see how well it's working, I presume."

A wave of ground-based missiles sailed through the air, missing the herald by wide margins on all sides.

"What the hell was *that*?" Violet demanded into the phone. After hearing the answer, she told Bradford and me, "Apparently those were heat-seekers, which failed to find their target because the herald gives off no infrared emissions." Back on the phone, she said, "Which, explain to me how we couldn't deduce that *before* we fired a dozen ZILLION-DOLLAR MISSILES at it?"

"Did I just hear Violet Parker in the background?" Maddy asked, incredulous.

"It's a long story," I said. "Bradford's here, too. Cameron sent me here."

"I see," she said. "Did they give you a cabal membership card? Do you pay dues? Did they give you a parking space at the secret clubhouse?"

"This is not helpful, Maddy."

"Tell me exactly what would be helpful, Isobel. I would be delighted to do your bidding in this, our hour of need."

The Dauphine was now making effective use of her portal weapon to rip the wings right off the side of the herald. Watching her fight, you might think it was easy to destroy heralds. Sadly, the damn thing's body was still emerging and there were two other sets of wings now unfolding on the latter half of its horrifying body. The good news was the larger the herald got, the larger an attack surface it presented and the surviving jets were getting better at hitting the thing.

"How many of your people went home when you told them to?" I asked.

"Five," she said. "The five people in our crew who don't use power morphemes. Gridstation went with them, pissing and moaning about it. The rest of the crew heard your little exclamation about 'eight fucking people,' and they can count, and understood you meant to leave them behind. But apparently they're not interested in missing this shit. I said, 'People, we are literally going to die on this misadventure,' but they're loyal to me, and they're loyal to you. So we still have a crew."

The herald suddenly reared up, six wings flaring out wildly, and a new weapon emerged, a dazzling, rippling web of ghastly green energy that snared almost every jet in the sky in its blast radius. The jets dissolved in the air. The Dauphine was spared; through sheer luck, she had circled around behind it to take a shot at the back of its head. Her aim was precise and its head was torn clean off in one fell swoop. The body began to plummet to the ground, and a new head was regenerating even as it fell. But the new head arrived too late to control the body, which smashed into several buildings on its way to crashing down hard on the streets below. From our obstructed view, we couldn't tell if it had survived at first, but moments later, the Dauphine swooped down toward it, hopefully to score a *coup de grâce.*

"Isobel," Violet said calmly, "what's that little flying toy out there that has just outperformed hundreds of millions of dollars' worth of Air Force materiel?"

"Her name is the Dauphine of the Shimmer Lands," I said. "She's a video game character who's come to life."

"Did you hear that, General? A video game character just killed the alien while your fighters were smacked around like pinballs," Violet growled. "Oh, you think *that's* the unlikely part of all this?"

"This herald is some kind of scout, yes?" Bradford asked.

"I don't know," I told him. "I think it's part of a hunting party, looking for the Dauphine. I think the main force is probably— hopefully—occupied by Alexander elsewhere."

"Then we're wasting time watching this fight," he said. "Let your Dauphine handle it, and let's get to work on putting your battle choir together."

Maddy said, "The Dauphine just got back. Thing is dead. When are *you* coming back?"

"Ten minutes," I said. We hung up, and I told them, "The herald is confirmed killed."

"So you're telling me hundreds of these things are lined up in the logosphere somewhere," said Violet, "and Alexander is single-handedly fighting them off?"

"I don't know what Alexander is currently doing," I said. "He's been studying them for a long time, though. He can kill one or two on his own. And I'm told he can win them to his side somehow. If that's a transferable skill, we might have a little hope here."

"And just to be absolutely sure I understand," Violet continued, dripping with irritation, "all we get for wiping out a shit ton of heralds in the logosphere is the satisfaction of a job well done and the eventual arrival of the thunderstorm anyway? I'm starting to doubt the wisdom of your plan for us to join forces and rush out to battle. Shouldn't we accelerate the launch even more? Shouldn't we get the fuck out of here *even faster*?"

"Violet, if we evacuate now," Bradford said softly, "we abandon

Alexander to his fate. Do we not owe him slightly more consideration than that?"

She said nothing.

He said, "The scout ship is scheduled to launch tomorrow. That means we need to find Alexander *today*."

Violet turned to me, a cold look in her eyes, and said, "Can you find Alexander that fast?"

"I don't know," I said.

"I'll give you one extra day to find him. If he wants you to fight alongside him, then you fight, with everything you can muster. Follow him into the fray. Fight like all of reality depends on absolutely every single spell and combat trick you've ever learned in your short and glorious life as the Queen.

"On the other hand, if he insists on being a god before he even does business with you, you tell him he gets nothing and then you abandon him by the side of the road like a hitchhiker you've just robbed. I won't give a shit about him at that point. I don't know if you can kill a man who's already dead, but these are strange times, and you're a clever woman, so give it the old college try if you must.

"But here's the bottom line, Isobel. If, in two days' time, you haven't miraculously, convincingly, and thoroughly demolished every herald and pushed that thunderstorm back to where it came from, then I expect you personally to report to Bradford and me for duty.

"Because I heard you promise Bradford you'd pilot our scout ship. And I damn well intend for you to honor that promise."

07

I expected some resistance to my devious scheming when I returned to the gymnasium, or some grief about my unilateral commitment to working with the cabal. But people were legitimately freaked out about the notion of heralds above Los Angeles, unclear how we could possibly survive if more than one invaded next time, and as a result, everyone was quite on board with my plan.

We got Bradford connected via video conference, and he proceeded to orchestrate a series of singing auditions among the crew. Including Devin, we had seven solid candidates. He wanted eight to make a proper double choir, but we just didn't have the voices. We lined up headsets for all seven of them, so that Bradford could install his movements in their minds without affecting the rest of us.

Jordon was initially upset that I wouldn't let her join the choir.

"Do you not understand how many choirs I sang in growing up?" she said. "All of them. Every single choir in existence. I had solos in every single one, too."

"Cameron wants you to pilot the arkship," I told her.

"I'm sorry—what?"

"I'm sure it's just like piloting skyships, except a zillion times bigger and if you fuck up all of humanity dies."

"Look, don't mess with me here. Cameron Kelly wants me to fly his ship? Sign me all the way up. How do I get training on that bad boy?"

"I don't think there's a training level for this. I think you're going to be experiencing some on-the-job training, to be honest. Guns will probably be going off all over the surface of it while you're trying to fly it, and if you're really unlucky, heralds will be attacking it up close, too."

"Sounds like good clean family fun."

"It really does."

When Bradford's operation was complete, seven dazed individuals took their headsets off, and their expressions all featured a uniformly enthusiastic "thumbs-up!" smile. I took that to mean the battle choir was fully armed with a complement of movements to suit weddings, atrocities, or any occasion, and we commenced preparation to leave the gymnasium—potentially for good.

Maddy pulled me aside before we left and said, "What about Olivia?"

"She's coming with us," I said, as though that was the most obvious thing in the world.

"Really? You want her in our midst when the shit goes down?"

"I don't trust her, you don't trust her, I get that. But you know who does trust her? Alexander Reece. If we show up without her, he's just going to ask what happened to her. And if our answer is we ditched her in LA for Violet's people to track down and murder, he will be unamused."

"Well, this is all very hilarious, Isobel. Up is down, inside is outside! What will happen next in our wacky bizarro world of singing soldiers and genocidal weather patterns?"

The Dauphine gathered us together and created a large portal in the floor of the gymnasium, through which people could drop into the logosphere, undergoing instant transmutation on the way through, landing on the dance floor of the Iridescent Warehouse. It was a familiar sight to everyone but Olivia, who had never played Sparkle Dungeon before, and had also probably never set foot in a modern nightclub either. Good, I thought, a little culture shock should help remind her she was playing on my turf now.

I had one of my semi-regular brilliant ideas just then, and I summoned up a massive audio equipment bag out of storage from underneath the stage. Inside were a full complement of enchanted in-ear monitors, which would enable us to hear and talk to each other during the battle just like in the movies, except I had to assure absolutely everyone that you *did not* need to press your finger to your ear to get it to work, and people were like, "Come on, how does it know when I'm trying to talk to people then?" And I said, "Perhaps you are acquainted with the concept of *spells* that use *magic,*" and we got through this crisis together, as a family.

The Dauphine then opened a portal to SD5, to the Chairman of the Realm's office, so that Jordon could go to meet Cameron.

Jordon gave me a hug, as we both realized this could very well be the last time we saw each other. We didn't say anything, really, just held each other for a few minutes. Then she stepped through the portal, which closed rapidly behind her.

I opened my loot cabinet to let people raid it for weapons. Power morpheme sequences were all well and good, but if the heralds got close, classic medieval weaponry would also be helpful. Plus, much of this weaponry was Bluetooth enabled, so you could play tunes while you fought.

Olivia came to me, bewildered, and asked, "What do you expect me to do here?"

"We don't know how to contact Alexander," I said. "But Maddy and I have an idea for a telepathy sequence that might be able to reach him. Maybe you can help us design it?"

Maddy was livid. "You're just going to *give* the cabal our telepathy sequence?"

"The one we don't actually have yet, you mean?"

"We have the intellectual property for its underlying concept, Isobel. Copyright *means* something."

"Gimme a break, I saw how many pirated MP3s were on the servers back at the gym."

"That was all Gridstation! I personally maintain fully paid accounts on multiple streaming services! Granted they're paid for with stolen credit card numbers I got off a darknet, but my point stands!"

"Would you two shut up please and tell me your idea?" Olivia said.

"Listen, *you*," Maddy said, getting in her face, "if our telepathy sequence leaks out into the wild because of you, and some tech bro figures out how to monetize telepathy by tethering it to an ad server, I will personally deliver a series of copyright strikes. To your face. With my fists. Playing on the double meaning of 'strike' if you missed that." Her vicious glare seemed to actually intimidate Olivia for a split second, which satisfied her for the time being. She stormed off.

"Sorry about that," I said. "She frequently gets 'copyrights' and 'patents' mixed up."

"I said, shut up and tell me your idea," Olivia repeated.

❀   ❀   ❀

Olivia used me as a guinea pig receiver when she was testing the sequence, which resulted in a barrage of audio hallucinations until she finally managed to "tune in" to the exact location of my brain to plant a message. And then I jumped ten feet in the air when I heard her voice, powerfully announcing my name inside my mind. She was thoroughly exhausted by the effort. Maddy had been right: you didn't casually rely on telepathy as an open chat line. It was a high-level effect with a commensurate high-level cost to your psyche.

I buffed her up a bit, but I really wanted to save my heals for some indeterminate near future in which I'd need them more acutely. Spell replenishment when playing the game was a predictable function of time and achievement feeding a pool of spellcasting points; but here, in the Realm itself, I couldn't predict when I'd get any of my spells back after using them. This hadn't been an issue so far because I hadn't been in any truly extended encounters in the logosphere; even killing that first herald had only taken an elapsed time of per-haps sixty seconds. I had a feeling I would see a longer combat soon enough.

Olivia asked everyone to be quiet so she could concentrate.

She said, "First I'm going to try to establish reliable contact with him. Then, if he's in a receptive position, I'm going to try to install the telepathy sequence in his mind, so that he can respond. If that doesn't work, I'm at least going to try to signal our location."

"He won't be able to find us here," I said. "Tell him to meet us at the rift in the map."

She closed her eyes and began the sequence. For several minutes, her expression didn't change, then it suddenly lit up with a smile, which we presumed meant Alexander had answered the phone, so to speak.

Several more minutes of apparent data transfer occurred, then she opened her eyes at last, and said, "He will meet us at the rift mo-mentarily."

❀   ❀   ❀

The Dauphine opened a portal to the rift in the map. She, Maddy, Olivia, and I stepped through and stood on the field in front of the rift, the portal closing behind us. From here, as before, the rift looked dazzling, and the logosphere beyond it looked equally alluring. You almost felt like this was one of the natural wonders of an unnatural place—Niagara Falls except for reality distortion effects instead of rushing water.

I said, "Why didn't you also install teleport in his mind when you installed telepathy?"

Olivia said, "I installed every sequence I know in Alexander's mind. But he's unable to teleport his companions as well, and he's unwilling to abandon them."

"Companions?"

"He's tamed several heralds," she said, "and he's bringing them with him to the Sparkle Realm." She paused and said, "If we're lucky, he'll outrun the heralds that are hunting them."

We saw Alexander's approach from across the logosphere, with a herd of twenty-three flying, howling, horrifying heralds in his wake. He was riding the lead herald as though he were mounted on a flying horse, except the horse looked like it was half built out of damaged military tanks from WWII, turrets spinning, treads churning, alongside wings that seemed bolted on like the thing was stitched together from parts in a junkyard. This was only the third herald I'd seen up close, and I was surprised at the technological composition of it. But it made an ugly sense: any culture that had been devoured by the thunderstorm could be recycled into herald form and consciousness, and no doubt many warlike cultures had lost the battle when the time came.

As they got closer, the Dauphine and I both realized what had happened, how Alexander had tamed these heralds. In the same fashion that he'd awakened the Dauphine back in the Shimmer Lands, he'd excised slivers of his essence and somehow managed to implant those sparks inside these heralds. Perhaps as he wounded them in combat, he slipped spark past their armored hides. Perhaps his spark seemed like catnip to them and they consumed it willingly without understanding the trap he'd set for them.

Regardless, whereas their previous herald minds might have had a dawning form of self-awareness about them, these heralds were less rageful and studied their surroundings with acute interest, as though seeing reality with fresh eyes, and like the Dauphine, they were not in Alexander's thrall as mind-controlled entities. They were distinct personalities that had allied themselves with him, for the time being at least.

For lack of a better term, he "parked" his heralds outside the rift, and then launched himself through the rift to land in front of us. I'd seen him in many incarnations and avatars, but this one was by far the most grandiose. He was a towering, muscular Hercules figure, wrapped in gorgeous armor that still gleamed despite countless dents and scratches across its surface. You could still recognize him as Alexander Reece, though, enjoying his afterlife, in training as the warrior god he intended to become.

"So good to see you again, my friends!" he shouted, stopping short of rushing to embrace anyone.

"You look ridiculous," Olivia said.

His laugh was genuine and hearty, seeming to take no offense.

"It's just an avatar," he said. "I trade them every so often to keep my self-image fresh. I have to say, Olivia, I'm surprised to find you here in the logosphere. Don't you have important work to do in your lab?"

"Like make you into a god behind everyone's back?" I asked.

"Precisely," he said, suddenly all business. "No thanks to you, I might add."

"Still a terrible idea," I said.

"You haven't seen what I've seen, or fought what I've fought. Right now, we need all the extra firepower we can get."

"We've *got* extra firepower. That's why we're here."

"If it's all the same to you, I'll keep my own counsel on appropriate levels of firepower. Olivia, how long will it take you to run the godhood sequences?"

"Simulations take fifteen minutes," she said.

"And when were you planning on running them, if I might ask?"

"During the relocation. In a few days."

Outside the rift, Alexander's pets were becoming increasingly hysterical with anger.

They were sounding an alarm.

The herald army that had been hunting them had appeared in the distance; the Sparkle Realm had been discovered.

"You do not have the luxury of a few days," he said to her. "Your arkship may very well die today, do you understand?"

She nodded. I couldn't be sure, but it seemed like he was reinforcing his threat with expertly masked power morpheme commands to make doubly sure she did understand him.

"Go back to your lab and run those sequences on the population you already have in the battery," he said firmly. "If I am not elevated in fifteen minutes, I shall join the enemy's heralds in tearing this arkship to pieces."

Olivia vanished.

It suddenly dawned on me that Alexander had actually led the army straight here, on purpose.

He was no benevolent warrior out to save us. He was single-minded in his willingness to sacrifice all of humanity in pursuit of his own elevation. He didn't care how many people died on the way to his ascension. I couldn't wrap my head around how conniving and corrupt you had to be to manipulate the situation this way.

I could chase after Olivia to try to stop her, facing her not inconsiderable skills in a one-on-one confrontation. Or I could stay here with the exact collection of souls and armaments that I'd personally arranged like chess pieces into this exact position, in order to fight that exact army of heralds, in order to reinforce this exact conniving asshole. He'd maneuvered everything so that we *needed* him to become a god and save us all.

I felt incredibly, deeply ashamed about how I'd been played.

"We must keep the Realm safe for fifteen minutes," he said, returning to his veneer of joviality. "I look forward to seeing your 'extra firepower' in action!"

He leapt back through the rift toward his trusty deformed-panzer steed, and shouted a series of commands to his cavalry unit. And then they were gone.

"Pompous fuck, isn't he," Maddy said.

"And yet we must fight by his side," the Dauphine said, turning to me. "My Queen, will I see you on the front line?"

I nodded.

"Excellent," she said, and she instantly jetpacked off into the fray. She apparently wasn't much for sentimental goodbyes.

Suddenly the entire Sparkle Realm experienced a jolting shudder and then stabilized.

"This is your captain speaking," said Jordon via enchanted in-ear monitor. "I've had maybe ten minutes of training on this giant rig, so my apologies if I run us into a bridge or something. I'm repositioning us to optimize for gunnery."

The entire Realm swiveled slightly, which we could only detect by watching the action shift outside the rift; inside the Realm, our experience of "gravity" remained rock solid, no one felt motion sickness, and so on. The arkship had a damn fine physics engine at its disposal.

"We need to get the battle choir into position," I said.

"You think seven people singing are going to be audible above an army of heralds shrieking in battle?" Maddy replied.

"I do, because the one thing you can always find in the Sparkle

Realm is a massive high-power sound system. Maddy, listen, in case . . . you know, in case something happens to me out there . . . there's something I wanted . . ."

And then I hesitated.

But Maddy was never one for hesitation. She took my hand and said, "Can I kiss you?"

"Uh-huh," I said.

She pulled me close, leaned in and kissed me, and it was sweet, and luscious, and I wanted it to last a lot longer than it did.

When she pulled away, she looked up at me and said, "We'll have all the time in the world together when this is over. But first, you need to go kill some shit."

I soared across the logosphere, scanning the oncoming fray for signs of the Dauphine or Alexander.

The throng of heralds was so intense that it was difficult to spot either of them. Then I realized Alexander was holding down a position in the midst of the throng, along with his herald allies, and together they formed a surprisingly effective hard line against the other heralds. The attackers were all so gigantic that they struggled to claim any position on the front line against Alexander, and his heralds fought with surprising viciousness, now that they had enhanced sentience to protect. Meanwhile, as Alexander made himself the visible target, the Dauphine swept in and out, a tiny speck by comparison, firing her portal weapons with perfect aim, decapitating the enemy in droves.

On the edges of the chaos, several heralds saw me and broke off to head my way, bored, I guess, waiting for their turn to wail on Alexander. I steered off to lead them away from the Sparkle Realm behind me. The Realm from the outside now looked very clearly like a skyship from SD5; I had nothing to compare its scale against, so I could only imagine that it was some significant order of magnitude larger than a typical skyship.

"Isobel, you're in my tracking system so trust me when I say I am *not* going to hit you," Cameron said.

Moments later, a fusillade of explosive jewels streaked out from an array of sparklepults, arriving almost instantaneously at their targets—the heralds I'd led away from Alexander. Huge chunks of herald disintegrated in colorful bursts as the jewels hit. Several were torn so completely apart that they couldn't regenerate. Three others were infuriated and swiveled toward the source of the attack.

I knew exactly one attack that seemed like a guarantee: cut their heads off, then carve straight down the center of their bodies to prevent regeneration. Big problem: the herald I'd killed in this fashion on my first trip to the logosphere was half the size of any of these. My brain couldn't really wrap itself around monsters the size of the Empire State Building with bizarre abstract appendages (gigantic conduits for spraying acid ooze all over targets, weird oversized machetes made of cartilage and nasty rumors, etc.). The heads on these things—aside from being hellish nightmares—were so big that I would not swiftly decapitate any of them; I'd have to saw for a half hour or whatever.

Another volley of jewels detonated against these three, and the disgusting shrapnel of chunks of their bodies drenched me in filth. I'd felt this before, the nihilistic wave of apathy that sank into me when covered in what passed for their blood, and I felt my flight slowing down almost to a crawl as my targets charged forward, somehow miraculously still imitating life and heading for the Realm.

But Cameron, of course, had more than jewels at his disposal, and the heralds still had plenty of distance to cross. Hundreds of shiny mirrorballs were launched into the logosphere. Lasers from the arkship pinpointed each mirrorball, which refracted the lasers with pinpoint precision at the three heralds and easily sliced them into dozens of pieces. That was indeed a more effective decapitation technique than the old manual "saw through their necks with a sword" technique we used in the old days.

In this fashion, with explosive jewels and mirrorball/laser attacks, Cameron kept stray heralds at bay for several minutes. His attacks were joined by the rousing melodies of the battle choir, which finally got its sound check over with and entered the combat theater in earnest. Heralds who got within range of hearing their movements found themselves slowing down in confusion at the sudden lack of will they experienced. Not that Cameron was having any trouble hitting them, but they were much easier targets in this confused state.

Then the tide suddenly rippled and turned against us.

"They're learning!" the Dauphine shouted. "My portals are useless now!"

God, if her portals were useless, she'd be left with just her pistols, and when those failed, she didn't have a long list of attack spells at her disposal.

I charged off in her direction, shrugging off the effects of the nihilism juice with a high-level heal and readying some attacks I'd been saving for a special occasion. I hadn't used Blades Per Minute yet this encounter, so at least one lucky herald was going to understand why people hated the absurdly fast tempo of happy hardcore so much.

I ducked and dodged my way through several oncoming heralds in order to find the Dauphine's location. I found her perched directly on the enormous head of one, firing down straight into what should have been its brain. Sadly for her, we were learning that heralds did not predictably adhere to some physiologic standard we could anticipate; for all the good her shots were doing, its brain was either somewhere else in its body, or it didn't operate with a physical brain at all. It reared up with its jaws but the Dauphine promptly rocketed to one side and continued firing straight down its throat. It definitely didn't appreciate *that*, and she didn't stop firing until she could see straight through a hole in the back of its head.

And that *still* didn't kill it, and another herald was coming up behind her. While she stayed engaged with the first one, I charged at the second one, firing off spells as I approached: Hailstorm of Razorjewels, Cone of Poisonglitter, These Boots Were Made for Kicking the Living Shit Out of You and Stomping Your Fucking Soul into Hell Where it Belongs (obviously this spell had a different name on iOS or the game wouldn't have been approved into the App Store). My target was completely furious at my attack; Christ knows I'd be pissed, too, since you can't get glitter out of *anything* and poisonglitter was worse, because it burrowed through the surface of whatever it landed on and released toxins all the way through the wounds. You couldn't just vacuum that shit up.

The Dauphine pulled the classic maneuver of leaping *into* the jaws of her target and firing straight down its throat, which seemed to relieve it of its lifelike qualities, and she escaped out the hole in its skull. She saw me and smiled, before dashing off to another target.

In that moment of distraction where I watched her, my herald took a massive swipe at me and pounded me hard, sending me spiraling away from the action. Its talons had sliced through me as easily as if my glittersteel skin was still ordinary human flesh; a fountain of blood poured out of my stomach, and I was momentarily too disoriented from the pain to heal. The Dauphine somehow saw what had happened and swooped in from below me, catching me and healing me in the same maneuver. After a heal like that, you had a tendency to briefly feel invincible, which was good enough to motivate you back into battle.

"Can you fly?" she asked. I nodded, and she let me go.

Suddenly a massive tentacle flicked out at us and snatched the Dauphine away from me. And before I could give chase, the herald

I'd failed to kill roared forward, having tracked me the entire time since landing its first blow. I turned toward its rapid onrushing attack and countered by accelerating straight toward it with Blades Per Minute aimed directly at its chest. I punched through its skin so intensely that I wound up with half my body buried in its disgusting innards, and I needed to teleport to get myself out of that situation. I appeared behind it and stabbed it repeatedly in the back before it could even start to swivel its massive frame toward me, and somewhere in there, one of those blows managed to kill the thing that was already half dead from poisonglitter and sliced all to hell from razorjewels.

That was me, Queen of Sparkle Dungeon, taking at least a full sixty seconds to kill just one of these things, using three of my best spells, an artifact-level weapon, and requiring a life-saving heal from the Dauphine right in the middle of the encounter. One down, hundreds to go.

Wait—where was the Dauphine?

The tentacle that had snagged her was attached to a disturbing pseudo presence, half swirling morass of seething tentacles attached to a complex, pulsing beehive or something, and half ghostlike mist as though it was still making decisions about what manner of horror it wanted to resolve into as it completed its transition into a more definite form. The tentacle had wrapped itself around her so quickly and thoroughly that she was unable to shoot it.

And because she'd always had the portal spell, we'd never even considered teaching her to teleport, so she couldn't just blink out of its grasp.

She tried opening portals but the skin of the tentacle was already baked with resistance to her portal attack, and any free-floating portal she tried to open for escape was beyond her ability to reach.

I soared into the fray with Blades Per Minute activated, fully prepared to slice through the tentacle holding her, but unlike the Dauphine, I was not always computationally accurate with my attacks, and before I got close to her, two other tentacles swept the area and smacked me hard, twice, and I could not *believe* I had gotten hit so hard *again*. I struggled to right myself, to orient myself to the Dauphine's predicament.

I got her back in view just in time to watch the thing wrap a second tentacle around her. Now it was trying to pull her apart.

She actually screamed, something I'd never heard her do before.

I rallied a second approach, eluding further swipes from the beast's tentacles and aiming straight for the beehive with Blades Per Minute. This proved to be yet another tactical mistake, as the beehive was actually a murky fluid construct that took no damage from the slice of a sword, and left the sword covered in an acidic film that immediately began dissolving chunks of the blade itself. I felt the vibration drain out of Blades Per Minute, and then it disintegrated in my hand.

Once again, I had one major spell left that I'd been saving for a special occasion, the powerful but debilitating Light Show, and I cast it without hesitation. Poisonous fog sprayed all around me, and then I became a blinding ball of luminescence, spraying lasers and spotlights in every direction. In the game, this was considered a ranged attack; I was firing it off at extremely close range and the beast I'd been fighting melted almost instantly. Collateral damage to surrounding heralds was significant.

And I was drained to near exhaustion. I wouldn't be able to cast this one again any time soon. As I reverted to my original form, I realized I was drifting, too weak to jetpack myself around, just barely able to fire off a Summon Adderall spell to keep me conscious.

The Dauphine suddenly streaked up, safe for the time being, and reached out to me.

I managed to grab her hand, absorbing another one of her doses of healing in the process, and we set off back into battle.

10

Cameron's jewels and mirrorballs lost effectiveness much too quickly. I didn't understand how the heralds were just magically developing weapon-specific resistance until I caught myself using the word "magically" and realized duh, just shut up and focus on the fight. He had other weapons up his sleeve: kaleidoscope cannons, prismatic lightning bolts, flying hordes of feral baby rainbows.

The battle choir's effectiveness lasted longer than other weapons. Their attack was much more aesthetic and surreal than what the heralds were accustomed to. They struggled to comprehend what was even happening to them let alone communicate information about that experience to other heralds. For a brief while, a small herd collected near the rift in the side of the arkship, where the battle choir was stationed, but then simply hovered, having lost the will to move forward, until Alexander and his cavalry mounted a spirited charge from behind and brutally massacred them.

But I noticed Alexander's cavalry was much smaller now. I always expected this to be a very quick battle, but somehow I figured his heralds would be among the last to fall. Instead I wagered he'd lost half his group by now. Turns out the heralds understood each other's strengths and weaknesses almost intuitively. Their clashes were over in split seconds; it was a ruthless calculation on the part of the local reality engine to gauge which one was ever so slightly tougher or smarter in some incredibly minor fashion and then the hammer came down and the loser was pulverized out of existence.

Suddenly a torrential spray of black ice from the far reaches of the herald formation arrived and tore into the side of the arkship, decimating an entire complement of weapon batteries and forcing Jordon to pull the arkship up into a steep defensive maneuver before another volley could land. The battle choir's sound system lost its prime positioning as a result, and now multiple adventurous heralds were able to get much closer to the arkship than any others had before, sneaking past the guard formation that Alexander had tried to maintain in front of the rift. Gatling guns and laser blasts strafed these heralds on their way in, but one herald made it all the way to the rift in the map and forced its way through. I no longer heard the battle choir at all, and hoped they'd managed to flee before the herald had landed on its perch at the rift.

"Isobel!" Maddy shouted. "We could use you on the ground!"

I cast Anthemic Energy on myself to help rally me back into action. It was like Uplifting Encore, but it was much higher level, and it only worked on me: it played my favorite deep house anthem in my mind, while also pumping temporary points back into most of my stat pools. The temporary points lasted for the duration of the anthem, then I'd lose them again. I had about eight minutes. I had no idea how long we'd been fighting.

I jetpacked toward the arkship with the Dauphine close behind me, watching a second herald claw its way through the rift. Alexander and his heralds saw the focus of our attention and fell in behind us to join us in engaging the burgeoning swarm. Each one that made it through the rift dramatically expanded the size of it, making me wonder why Cameron hadn't simply repaired it and given us an alternate way out of the skyship. "Simply" repaired it—he hadn't been *able* to repair it, I abruptly recalled.

But as the rift got bigger, it was an easier target for new heralds who seemed to deeply desire wrecking the side of the arkship on their way into the Realm beyond. Just as I neared the swarm of heralds, Jordon accelerated the arkship in another defensive maneuver, trying to shake loose heralds and put some distance between her and the rest of them.

Cameron launched a fleet of smaller skyships from the far side of the arkship. They quickly acquired ramming speeds and began slamming into heralds, and they seemed to be packed with explosives. It was a rough combat maneuver; the arkship itself was heavily damaged by the shrapnel from a half-dozen heralds and skyships being blown apart.

The Dauphine could no longer cut down heralds with her portal weapon, but she found an alternate attack: springing portals open in front of charging heralds before they could change direction and sending them clear across the logosphere, effectively eliminating them from the battle. Hopefully they were far enough away that they couldn't pick up the trail back to the Sparkle Realm.

For the first time, I deeply regretted giving away the other artifacts I'd collected back in the day. But I had lesser weapons I could summon from their display cases. I called to me the sunlight kalei-doscope I'd used for much of SD3, and fired impossibly hot sunlight beams at the closest heralds, blistering what passed for their skin, causing ridiculous shrieks of pain as they fell away from the rift in an effort to avoid further strikes. Alexander's cavalry pursued these wounded beasts.

Now I was free to enter the Realm, where three different her-alds were loose and wreaking havoc. And their havoc was not capricious—they were clearly on a rampage directly toward the Sparkle Dungeon. Something at the Sparkle Dungeon had caught their attention, because their path didn't deviate in the slightest as they practically galloped across the scenery.

There was only one good reason to head for the Sparkle Dungeon, and not because they were in the mood for a good dungeon crawl. They must be hunting for the battery. They must have detected its energetic presence there somehow, even if they didn't know exactly what it was, and now they seemed bent on finding it.

Maddy, Devin, and most of the anarchists retreated to the steps in front of the Sparkle Dungeon, which was still sealed off by the obsidian wall. Maddy had split herself in two, just to have extra hands on deck. The crew was smaller than it should have been; we'd lost people by now.

I swooped in and fired sunlight beams at each of the three her-alds, hoping to distract them and pull them toward me, away from the battery. I only managed to get one's attention; the other two con-tinued on a lumbering course toward the Sparkle Dungeon. They were traveling on foot now, stomping across the landscape, crush-ing buildings and landmarks and random stray NPCs that wan-dered through the action. This made them slower, and somehow scarier, because you really had time to study each abomination as it approached, and appreciate how each one's unique form factor was targeted to inspire existential fear. They wanted our defenders to cower now that they had landed in the Realm.

"Isobel, this might seem weird," Cameron said, "but just roll with it."

Suddenly a dozen individual replicas of my avatar appeared throughout the battlefield: clones of me.

"They've got all your skills and spells, but the game engine is run-ning them," he explained.

I didn't expect these AIs to be as clever as me, but I watched them devise combinatorial attack strategies as little teams that I couldn't pull off on my own. Nicely done, Cameron.

With thirteen Queens, two Maddys, one singing mage, and fifteen anarchists, somehow we managed to hold the line against these three heralds for roughly thirty seconds. The Dauphine stayed in the air, working to keep additional heralds from following the three on the ground through the rift.

Then the sky itself seemed to split apart. The heralds outside were no longer content to wait in line at the existing rift to get into the Sparkle Realm. They were now beginning to create *new* rifts in the sky—in other words, they were ripping open the hull of the arkship.

❀   ❀   ❀

Soon we were pinned against the obsidian wall. One of the Maddys began teleporting the anarchists inside the Sparkle Dungeon, to prepare to mount a defense in case they got in; she teleported Devin inside the Dungeon as well. Alexander roared into the Sparkle Realm with his remaining five heralds and a savage skirmish began. I leapt into action, the other Maddy by my side, and my twelve Queens forming up in various patterns behind me.

Maddy demonstrated excellence at teleporting around the field of battle, striking swiftly in unexpected places and then vanishing off to the next attack. Her adrenaline must have been through the roof to support so many teleports in a row.

The Queens, meanwhile, developed a system—they paired up, with a Queen in the lead firing off spells and dealing damage, and the other Queen close behind offering a steady stream of buffs and heals so that the first Queen could stay focused on attacks. But they weren't invincible, they didn't know power morphemes, and we began losing them as we stayed engaged.

In close quarters combat, Alexander could fashion astral blades with nothing more than his voice, and enormous ethereal hammers and spears, and ghostly pikes and scythes that only took form long enough to pierce a herald before dissipating. Either by choice or by some constraint I didn't understand, he himself remained material enough that he could be hit, and he was clearly looking battered and exhausted.

As for me, I focused my fire on the new rift, blasting sunlight at the newcomers to the Realm. They particularly hated sunlight from the Sparkle Realm, and this was highly effective for a short while until finally they adapted to the weapon.

"Olivia!" Alexander shouted. "Any time now would be fantastic!"

Maddy got very unlucky and a sudden talon swipe tore her head clean off. I would never, ever be able to unsee that. But the other Maddy was immediately yanked back onto the field, looking massively dazed but definitely alive. I rocketed to her and carried her to safety.

"Maddy, are you with me?" I asked her, applying a heal to her even before hearing her answer.

"We're here," she said. And then she said, *"BUT OH MIGHT IT BE AWHILE BEFORE WE ENJOY IT AGAIN?"*

"Go back to the Warehouse and recharge," I told her. "We got this."

"The hell you got this," she said. "You're going to die out here, and I'm going to be right there with you."

Well, that was both romantic and deeply unhelpful to my morale.

❀   ❀   ❀

Suddenly a metaphysically blinding wave of sensation rippled through the entire Realm.

And in its wake, I understood that godhood was unfolding.

11

Every particle in my body seemed to be yanked apart in order to make room for some new primordial force. A jarring parade of power morphemes rushed to subsume me, strung together in an otherworldly sequence that rapidly intensified, as if someone was leaning hard on every gain knob and channel fader that affected my pattern of existence. My conscious mind was overwhelmed with sudden golden bliss that eased the transformation in which I was unexpectedly immersed. A flood of knowledge coursed through me as I began to understand.

Alexander hadn't been granted godhood after all.

It had been granted to *me*.

❀   ❀   ❀

As I gained more awareness of all things in this realm and many things beyond, I reached out with my mind to understand why Olivia had granted this boon to me instead of Alexander. I saw into the past in this way, the first definitive use of my nascent powers. I saw Olivia appearing in her lab, only to be surprised to find Bradford waiting for her. I saw Bradford swiftly controlling her by singing an array of power morpheme movements at her, forcing her to sit down at her workstation, and input into her sequence the name of God he'd chosen for me: "Isobel the Queen."

"Why would you choose *her* instead of Alexander?" Olivia railed uselessly.

"Isobel was always meant to be our fighter," Bradford replied, "and even so, she sought to bring us all together to face our common enemy. All Alexander seeks is his own glorification. I don't know what you seek, Olivia, and I don't care. Our fate is in Isobel's hands now."

If only Olivia had told him that Alexander was alive, his spite toward her in this moment would never have occurred, and her goal of elevating Alexander might well have succeeded.

But Bradford was not at all satisfied to let her plan unfold so smoothly. In his mind, she deserved this disappointment—as did

Alexander himself, who conspired against his own former partner and close friend. In his mind, there was always a reason that Jenning was first in Jenning & Reece, and Alexander and Olivia had severely disrespected that. They had cut him out at the most crucial of moments, and he was not inclined to be forgiving.

And when the job was done, when Olivia reported that the sequences had been fully broadcast and the battery minds had been edited, Bradford experienced a moment of true gnosis, in which he saw beyond the veil that separated the material plane from the logosphere, in which he saw that Isobel the Queen was ascending, and he smiled.

In this moment of inattention to his practical circumstances, his hold over Olivia's mind slipped.

She rose up and physically attacked him, knocking him down and smashing his head several times against the floor, until she was satisfied he was dead.

Olivia sat back down at her workstation and disabled the teleport jammers. Then she teleported out of the lab, and I did not follow her in my mind. I had more pressing matters to attend to in the immediacy of the present time.

❀   ❀   ❀

I was not God, not some Supreme Being of All Existence that could be blamed for this absurd catastrophe of a multiverse.

But I was definitely running in god mode with a small g—capable now of inordinate acts of power and mercy within my local sphere of influence. God mode in video game parlance usually meant you'd unlocked the cheat codes of the game, so that you couldn't take damage, or you could float above the map and walk through walls, or you could have every bonus and spell without suffering any penalties. To translate that to my current situation, I needed to flex my mind to understand the extent and the limits of my new capabilities.

I reached out across the map and extinguished all heralds in one fell swoop, all except those that Alexander had graced with sentience. The act was as simple as applying a small amount of thought to the concept of doing so; reality bent to my will and behaved as I desired.

I could get used to this, yes indeed.

I was no longer limited by the simple avatar that Isobel Bailie had worn throughout this game, or even the body I'd inhabited throughout my life. I expanded until my awareness and my presence was spread throughout the entirety of the arkship, and then my mind expanded further to include a growing bubble of awareness outside the arkship. As new heralds approached, they ceased to exist when they collided with my will; my command needn't be refreshed, but rather had instantly become a mandate. I remembered a minor task that someone else had left incomplete, and sealed the entirety of all the rifts in the arkship, including the one Cameron himself had not been able to fix.

Eventually I felt I had secured the arkship from danger. I extended myself further, accumulating ambient knowledge that had collected in pools throughout the logosphere, glimpses and flashes of the terror that the heralds had wrought on their way to the arkship, and decided to set out on my own to test myself against the thunderstorm. Why wait for its inevitable approach? Why not learn *now* if all of the planning and scheming on Alexander's part had actually been a worthwhile gamble, even if he himself was not in the driver's seat when the time came to unleash a new local god upon the scene?

I saw no immediate acknowledgment from the thunderstorm that it noticed or understood my approach. It was in the process of churning out a new herald army to replace the army that had not reported back. I positioned myself such that these new heralds immediately faced me and were extinguished in droves. There would be no new heralds in the logosphere, of that I was inherently certain.

I looked further back in time, attempting to discover the origin of the thunderstorm.

You could imagine some dark pact made by arrogant wizards eons ago, the summoning of a demonic entity that metastasized out of their control and became an inordinate plague upon reality. Or perhaps greed to discover treasure and forbidden knowledge had motivated the excavation of a cavern in reality that, once opened, instead unleashed this immense fountain of negation, obliterating all trace of the miners who had made this terrible mistake.

Perhaps the absolute definition of a Supreme Being included the existence of its opposite as a balancing factor, to prevent pure immersion in untethered, egotistical bliss. Perhaps the Supreme Being needed or preferred some kind of reminder that the material plane was deserving of its periodic attention, even if that meant extinguishing untold numbers of lives. Death itself naturally extinguished untold numbers of lives; perhaps this was a more concentrated and malignant form of that antilife force.

But I was not given to know the truth. My status as god with a small *g* did not privilege me with access to the deepest mysteries of the multiverse. I couldn't even be sure that my godhood would accompany me if I left the two intertwined local realities of the logosphere and the material plane.

This localized god mode had definite limits; I was not omniscient or omnipresent or omnipotent.

I would, however, spin some epic DJ sets in Ibiza once I got us all out of this mess.

❀ ❀ ❀

From my new perspective, I could finally see the steady glide of the thunderstorm as it inched its way across the logosphere. Normally its advance was imperceptible; it appeared as a stationary wall until suddenly it was upon you. But here I could see its crawl, and understood that the destruction of its heralds had motivated it to increase its speed toward the Sparkle Realm.

I sank my mind into the surface of the thunderstorm as though I was a child sinking my hands into clay, twisting it and manipulating it, familiarizing myself with its substance. I felt what the Dauphine had described: the countless frozen moments of shock and horror as culture after culture fell to the thunderstorm's advance. These memories amounted to a kind of afterlife for each individual, in which they continuously relived this moment of horror with no relief.

I ripped huge chunks of it out and discarded them behind me into the logosphere. The chunks dissipated into nothingness after losing contact with their origin. But I sensed I could do this forever without making any meaningful dent in its structure. This kind of mechanical brute-force attack was not the avenue to defeating it.

I tried to withdraw to reconsider my position, and felt it grasp me, hold me in place for a moment and examine me, a new form of life not catalogued in its grand library of doom. I sensed no particular dawning of fear or any recognizable emotion on its part, just a cold computational analysis running to determine my weaknesses and strengths, attempting to pry me apart into distinct component concepts.

Suddenly a powerful volcanic blast of pure hatred and spite ejected me from within the thunderstorm, scattering me all across the logosphere for a few entire seconds before I regained integrity. I had made the thing angry; or, alternately, I'd been decisively rejected or expelled as a foreign object within it, not properly digested, identified as too alien. It could not consume me in that fashion, it had learned, so the next available tactic was to be rid of me. The pain was shattering for a moment, and then I was momentarily obliterated into nothingness, and then I autonomically reconstituted myself.

Only barely had I achieved godhood and already this thing was humiliating me. But now I was enraged and ready to punish it for its pure insolence in attempting to strike at me.

I pulled together a dense mass of pure energy, scooping it up in giant mindfuls, and began to fashion it into a weapon. The mere assembly of the weapon was intoxicating. The amount of energy coursing through me was indescribably pleasing. I saw no reason not to draw more and more, funneling it through me to inject my rage and aggression into its essence before adding it to my weapon. My goal was to charge back into the thunderstorm and detonate my weapon, a bomb that I believed would completely overwrite the fabric of the thunderstorm with life and compassion and love.

Weaponizing love—that would be Isobel the Queen's signature move.

❧　❧　❧

Somehow I heard Maddy screaming at me, from all the way back in the Sparkle Realm.

"ISOBEL!" she was screaming. "PLEASE, STOP!"

Maddy's voice was a sharp reminder that I was protecting a specific world of specific people.

I realized I was also hearing Cameron's voice.

"Isobel, you are *draining the battery*," Cameron was saying, over and over again.

12

In my rage, I had absorbed the life energy of nearly two million people from the battery.

Upon realizing the epic nature of my cruel blunder, I released the energy and gently steered it back into place inside the battery. I had not yet set my mind to how I might safely release all ten million people from their crypts, but for now, the battery had been restored to its former status quo. I would not waste these people's lives in combat with the thunderstorm.

If Isobel the Queen, newly minted goddess, could not fight the thunderstorm directly with the powers at my personal disposal, then we would need to find another way to fight it.

I considered that if rage could so quickly take hold of my personality, perhaps I didn't want this godhood at all.

Perhaps I was learning what every young god learned in due course: the cost of exercising power could be greater than what you gained from that power in the first place.

I came to firmly believe that an insidious intelligence must be a factor in the thunderstorm's composition, because I could discern, quite clearly, that it had retreated, ever so slightly, for what I believed to be the first time in its history. And then it stopped, perhaps waiting to see what I might do next.

God mode was handy for flagrant ego-driven demonstrations of power, and accidental mass murder if I wasn't careful. But I sensed that my own identity would be dispersed if I stayed there too long, replaced by an inevitable inflation of ego beyond recognition.

After toggling god mode to an off position in my mind, I felt the tremendous burden of such mammoth responsibility and extreme capability lifted off my shoulders, and I dissolved like cotton candy in rain, dripping in sugary drops back into my avatar as Queen of Sparkle Dungeon, floating alone in the logosphere. The battle was over, for the time being.

I teleported back to the Sparkle Realm, right in front of the entrance to the Sparkle Dungeon—the last place I'd seen Maddy.

❀   ❀   ❀

The landscape immediately surrounding the Sparkle Dungeon was decimated, but I mean, property values in this made-up game world were super low, so it didn't bother me a lot.

Alexander and his heralds were gone.

Maddy stood at the top of the stairs leading down to the Dungeon. I don't know how long she'd been waiting for me to return; I'd literally lost track of the actual concept of time while I was in my exalted state. I floated into her presence, landing softly on the field a few feet away from her.

I felt suddenly shy, like I'd revealed some dark secret about myself and was waiting to find out if she'd still be my friend.

She grinned and started slow clapping.

That made me laugh.

❀   ❀   ❀

Jordon invited Maddy, the Dauphine, Devin, and me to join her and Cameron on the bridge of the arkship. Cameron pulled off the magic of an interdimensional video session to dial Violet into our conversation. Devin was a conflicted, grief-stricken mess about Bradford's death, while the rest of us were basically shell-shocked from battle.

For a long while, no one had anything to say.

I could guess what was racing through Violet's mind. I'd held two million souls' worth of energy in my hands, and *choked* when it came time to use it against the thunderstorm. Even if it had survived, the intel we'd have gained from its reaction could have been monumental. But instead I'd chosen some perhaps misguided act of compassion by restoring those people to their merciless stasis, where their interrupted lives could continue to be preserved for some *future* expenditure.

And what had we gained? The thunderstorm had retreated. Ever so slightly.

That was something, right?

"I'm going to assume," Violet finally said, "that the arkship is currently dead in the water. Would anyone care to dispute that point?"

"Bradford's navigation sequences are preprogrammed," Cameron offered.

"They don't work," Devin informed him. "Our version of teleportation kills people at scale."

"Oh," he replied. "That's new information."

"Olivia and Bradford were working on a fix," Devin continued, "but they ran out of time, obviously."

Maddy and I exchanged glances. We were now the key to the arkship's fix. I was almost certain that Maddy wanted no part of this business, and I couldn't bring myself to suggest that she help them solve their problem. And as for me—I'd be busy with other tasks.

Devin picked up steam, saying, "You also can't pull off the relocation without Olivia."

"Maaaaybe we could," Cameron said. "I've been reviewing the code her team is committing, and it's workable."

"Yes, but look, we were expecting to keep coding well after the jump. We were expecting Olivia's constant supervision of the situation well after the jump. You can get all those people aboard the arkship, sure, but keeping them alive long term was going to require a long series of technical magic tricks and I don't have the manual for any of that. You need Olivia."

"I have four days to find Olivia," Violet replied calmly. "Let's turn our attention to the one part of our schedule that hasn't been completely demolished. Isobel, I realize you fought quite valiantly today, but tomorrow is a brand-new day. Will you be ready?"

Maddy turned to me slowly, and said, "What's she talking about?"

"Scout ship jumps tomorrow," I said softly.

"So?"

"Isobel has volunteered to be our pilot," Violet said.

Maddy looked dumbfounded.

"Why?"

"Bradford felt—and I agree—that we shouldn't send an unmanned mission to the Beacon," I said. "And we *need* to go to the Beacon."

"Again—*why?*" Maddy asked. "If I'm interpreting what I heard correctly, the Beacon is a rallying point for civilizations that have been *destroyed* by the thunderstorm. If anyone at the Beacon could *stop* the thunderstorm, they wouldn't still require a *rallying point!*"

"We don't know how old that signal is," Jordon said. "All we can deduce is that it comes from an intelligence far across the multiverse. Maybe by now someone's found a weapon or a shield that we could use here, without spending millions of lives in the process."

"Maybe the Beacon is a *trap*, Jordon," Maddy said. "You literally don't know *anything* about the source of the signal that's coming from the Beacon. We're only *calling* it a 'Beacon' because Bradford was somehow still a freaking *optimist* despite everything he'd seen and done."

Fair point.

"Anyway, fine, let's send a person to the Beacon," Maddy continued, venting her anger my direction now. "Why does it have to be you, Isobel Bailie? It's the cabal's plot. It's *their* evacuation plan. Why don't *they* pony up a pilot?"

"Would you really trust *their* choice?" I said, incredulous.

"And why should they trust *you*, I wonder?" she replied. "When did they recruit you?"

"Maddy, the cabal never succeeded in recruiting Isobel," Cameron said. "And the cabal as we know it is basically dead anyway. I mean, look around the room—if there's a cabal of powerful illuminati left to be found, we're it."

"You still think it's morally correct for a group of people *this size* to make decisions on behalf of the entire population of California?" Maddy snapped.

"*I'm* making decisions on behalf of the population of California," Violet interrupted, "because *I AM THEIR EMPRESS!*"

Maddy looked at me and said, "You understand how collaborating with anyone using the title 'Empress' with a straight face is incompatible with my street cred, don't you?"

I nodded. Maddy was an incorruptible anarchist. Violet would never win her loyalty.

She smiled sadly and said, "I thought we were on the same crew, Isobel."

"I've always been the Queen," I said. "Is that any weirder than Empress?"

"You don't *rule* your kingdom."

"Blingdom," I corrected.

She cracked up a little despite herself, and she repeated, "Blingdom. Right."

"If there's any help to be found out there, I'm going to find it," I said to her, as tears suddenly welled up in my eyes. "If there's any *hope* to be found, I'm going to find it. Do you understand? That's the whole *reason* for me now."

She nodded. She didn't like it, but she understood.

"So please, Maddy," I said, "don't walk away just yet."

"Fair enough," she said. "Not just yet."

❦　❦　❦

We escorted the surviving anarchists home. We'd lost eight people during the battle—eight people that we had risked our lives to extract from the battery, who turned around and sacrificed their own lives to keep the planet safe for an extra few days. Maddy needed time to regroup with her people, to be with them and mourn, but I couldn't stay.

I could've certainly overruled Violet if I wanted to exercise my power and keep the scout ship from launching the next day. But truth was, the sooner we found out what was waiting for us at the Beacon, the better.

In the Iridescent Warehouse that night, the Dauphine and I met to plan for my trip.

"You should send me in your place," she insisted. "I realize your Empress does not know me or trust me, but you are the only power we know that is capable of forcing the thunderstorm to retreat, even for the slightest of moments. We need you *here*."

"I understand the sentiment," I told her, "but we also have no idea what's waiting for us out there, and I stand the best chance of returning intact with news."

"Because of your new powers?"

"Yes. Because of god mode."

She perused my display cabinet of weapons and magic items, almost absentmindedly choosing several and handing them to me, and said, "Powers that you have literally acquired today, and which nearly obliterated two million human beings—those powers?"

I felt the heat of embarrassment in my cheeks. I didn't need that reminder, but there it was anyway.

"Powers which may not *exist* once you are no longer in *range* of those very humans' belief in your 'god mode'?" she continued. "Isobel, please. I understand you are a masterful fighter. But no proper strategy sacrifices a Queen on a scout mission. Let me go in your stead. If something truly hostile waits for us out there, we will need you here to help craft a defense—not because you can fight, but because you can *think* and *lead*. I am expendable, in every sense of the word."

"If there's something out there *more* hostile than the thunderstorm," I said, "it won't matter if I'm here or there."

"Perhaps," she replied, "but what if the thunderstorm chooses to attack once it realizes you are no longer present to counter it?"

This argument was getting to me. Leave it to an AI to pin you down with unassailable logic. We truly did need a pantheon, not just one pseudo deity. I could learn Maddy's trick of splitting into two people—except I wasn't enthused about bonding my personality with a rogue punctuation mark to make that happen.

"Look, maybe I should—go into god mode, and—deputize you," I said, thinking out loud. "Surely it's transferable on some level, right? It's just—moving energy around, or some shit like that? I mean, what's the point of being a god if I can't just capriciously make other gods when I feel like it?"

She was very firm in her response: "It seems clear to me that you should *never* use god mode capriciously, Isobel. It seems clear you should *almost* never use it at all."

"Because I'm inexperienced? We could spend the rest of the night training. Don't you think I should at least become *slightly* more familiar with it?"

"How many people are worth sacrificing for the sake of training? Certainly you would not train your way through two million people. But—five thousand? Five hundred? What if you only destroy ten people, accidentally, as you learn to use this new power set? Is that an acceptable cost for you to pay?" She must've seen the shocked look on my face, because she took my hand then and said, "I know you well enough to know that it is *not* acceptable to you. Sister, we are the same in this. My mission in life is to *rescue* and *heal* people. I know you feel that same pull."

"I didn't actually kill anyone when I saved us from the heralds!" I protested.

"Cameron and Maddy stopped you from absorbing the lives of two million people in one final attack," she agreed. "But—I have accessed today's leakage report."

Oh no.

"Tell me," I said quietly.

"Six thousand four hundred and eighteen people died in the ninety-one seconds you were in god mode," she replied. "Four hundred and twelve people died in the five minutes after you exited god mode. The battery has stabilized since then."

I sat down heavily on the edge of the stage, the weapons she'd handed me clattering to the dance floor.

"Please remember—that transformation happened to you without your consent," she said. "And you returned to yourself as soon as you realized what was happening. No one holds you accountable for the misguided actions of Bradford and Olivia."

"*I* do," I whispered. And then, with sudden rage burning in my throat, I said, "That's why this scout mission is *mine*, okay? I should be as far away from the battery as possible."

I don't think she truly agreed with me, but this was the argument that swayed her at last. She picked up the items I'd dropped—an elite kaleidoscope, a powerful laser pointer, an opiate-laced healing pacifier—and set them on the stage.

"Very well," she said. "I will try not to scratch your record collection while you are gone."

❀　　❀　　❀

The scout ship was a gleaming silver rocket in the finest steampunk style, sitting atop a launch pad on the roof of HQ. Cameron briefed me extensively about it the night before I intended to climb inside it and leave for parts of the multiverse unknown.

Although the exterior was cosmetically steampunk fashioned, inside the whole thing felt extremely high-tech. You could pilot either gyroscopically by climbing into a harness and making the whole ship a conceptual jetpack, with heads-up display goggles providing you necessary telemetry; or he'd provided joystick options if you wanted to sit back in a recliner and relax in front of a wraparound display screen while guiding the ship. It all seemed smooth and intuitive. And he'd built in every single armament that he could squeeze into its compact frame.

"I've wired up a button to launch the ship," Cameron said, "programmed with Bradford's coordinates to the Beacon. The same button will bring you back when you're ready to come home. That's all the button does. But the navigation movement that Bradford designed is freakishly ingenious because not only does it catapult you—"

"Sparklepult me," I corrected.

"Not only does it sparklepult you clear across the multiverse to the dimension where the Beacon is located, but somehow it also manages to timestamp the moment of your departure into the coordinates for your return. This means when you come back, you'll be reinserted into the timeline of this dimension roughly five minutes after you've left. Make sense?"

"I understand that you are saying words, yes."

"Good. So, from a jump-drive perspective, you basically just get access to 'there' and 'back' in five-minute increments. Once you've arrived at the other side, then you take control as pilot to survey the environment from above or land the scout ship somewhere safe. A fleet of small sensor drones is packed on board to be released in the environment when you arrive, which store data locally or pipe data back to the scout ship when it's in range. I don't care if you bring the drones themselves back, just try to grab all their data if you can.

"Devin sang and recorded Bradford's entire library of movements for you in case you wind up with time to study. You've also got a limited AI on board to monitor the jump drive, help with lining up targeting solutions, clean up the metadata in the MP3s you stole off the internet when you were in college, that sort of thing.

"Oh, and you'll like this one: the power source for the scout ship is *you*. It's gonna pull from your personal reservoir of 'spark' as you call it, but it's a lean machine and you shouldn't notice it. Basically the scout ship 'charges' when you take a nap inside it or lean on it for a stretch or whatever.

"And finally—my favorite—we're not packing food and water in the scout ship. You are currently a being of pure thought in the logosphere without such physical demands. So if you wind up transmuting into a proper physical form down the road, you will need to forage, and please make sure you can breathe. I assume this is basic stuff for a spellcaster of your caliber.

"This scout ship is constructed mostly out of metaphor. We are not operating a 'space program.' We believe the scout ship will keep you alive inside a bubble of logosphere until you choose to open it up, but fuck if we know. This is all magic; none of it's science. Our primary advantage right now is we didn't realize when we designed this ship that the pilot would be a literal goddess with glittersteel skin and superb improvisational skills.

"So make it count, Isobel."

❀   ❀   ❀

The next day we gathered together for the launch. Maddy had returned to see me off.

Jordon had a gift for me: the artifact she'd won by being the first person to beat SD5, a small black box with a lid that opened to a vast vault full of goodies.

"It's called the Compression Artifact," she told me. "It holds compressed versions of all the magic items from all the games. Admittedly none of them are as powerful as the originals, but most enemies won't notice the difference."

The Dauphine also had a gift for me: her pearl-handled, Repeat All–enabled pistols, which I almost refused, but she said, "This is a loan. I will expect them back upon your return." I reluctantly accepted this arrangement.

And of course, Cameron had loaded my entire music collection onto the ship's hard drive, plus a bunch of new stuff I hadn't heard yet that he'd gotten off of the internet for me. Hey, it wasn't music piracy when the Chairman of the Realm did it.

Maddy could barely look at me as I finished packing the ship. The others drifted off the launchpad to give us some space.

I said, "Will you be here when I get back?"

"Hard to say where I'll be," she replied.

"Can I kiss you?"

"Uh-huh."

And this time, it did last almost as long as it should have, before she pulled away and said, "You'll know where to find me."

I nodded and climbed into the scout ship. I decided I would fly by joystick, reclining in the pilot's chair, watching the journey on the wraparound video screen.

We had absolutely zero reason to believe this was going to work. Bradford himself had said he expected this mission to fail.

Jordon's lovely voice began providing the countdown to launch via my enchanted in-ear monitor as I sat in the cockpit of the scout ship—deeply afraid, powerfully sad, unbearably lonely.

Then Maddy teleported into the scout ship, arriving pressed against me in the reclining chair.

She said, "This is how you'll know where to find me."

The countdown reached zero, I pressed the launch button, and the scout ship sparklepulted itself across the multiverse.

PART SIX

GOD MODE

01

I was suddenly wide-awake inside the cramped confines of the scout ship. I had lost consciousness when the scout ship jumped across the multiverse to the coordinates specified in the Beacon's signal. A loud siren filled the air.

No wait—that was inaccurate. I had *ceased to exist* during the scout ship's particularly impressive transmutation/teleportation combo. And so this was me, uh, *resuming to exist* apparently, and it was a very *loud* experience because of the siren, which was actually me screaming, which I was doing a lot of.

Where's Maddy?

On the ceiling. Check.

Oh wait—now she was falling on top of me. The perils of two people in a one-person scout ship: only one seat belt, hence Maddy had spent the trip pressed against the ceiling above the pilot's chair. But lest you mock, you know who didn't rematerialize screaming for her life? Here's a hint: it was Maddy.

She didn't have far to fall, and then she was on top of me. The reclining pilot's chair nearly flattened out in response. Instinctively I wrapped my arms around her, thinking to hold her close in case of further turbulence.

More screaming—no wait, that was an actual siren, don't worry, I was getting the hang of it. The scout ship was doing the screaming this time.

"DOES THAT SIREN MEAN ANYTHING?" she shouted in my ear.

"PROBABLY!"

The siren suddenly stopped, the ship stabilized into a smooth flight path, and the onboard AI chimed in: "The cautionary siren is a notification that the jump drive is now idle and you may assume manual piloting." Cameron had chosen to use the Dauphine's voice for the onboard AI, a sly confidence-boosting measure which made impending disaster seem somehow pleasantly manageable. "The autopilot is engaged until you're ready to take control."

"Are we in any immediate danger?" I asked.

"None that I can detect."

"Then keep control, please, put us in a holding pattern, and kick off data collection."

"Understood."

Data was already coming in actually. A panoramic display of the scenery outside the ship filled the wraparound viewscreen. Raw incoming sensor readings fluttered across the screen as well.

But I didn't care about any of that just now, because Maddy occupied my complete attention. I was stunned by her presence in multiple ways.

She managed to lift herself up so that we could see each other's faces—tricky, considering I was still holding onto her as tightly as I could—and said, "If you're planning on scolding me for being here, I don't want to hear it."

"No," I managed to say, because even though she should've stayed behind, I was unbelievably happy she was here. Sure, I'd be absolutely devastated if anything happened to her on this trip, but our chances of surviving together were much higher than mine were on my own. I realized I'd been cavalier about my own survival when I volunteered to be the cabal's scout, but with Maddy here, I was vividly reminded that I absolutely wanted to survive. Oh and sure, something something save the Earth or whatever. "Thank you."

She nodded and said, "Next time you volunteer for a potential suicide mission, ask for a two-seater. Now let's get this done and get out of here."

❀   ❀   ❀

The sky was a dark orange, filled with haze. We were thousands of feet above a flat desert. The ruins of a toppled tower or skyscraper stretched impossibly from a "ground zero" all the way to the horizon, as though pointing at something out of sight. And then scattered all about, we saw wreckage: massive chunks of the building that had blown clear across the desert, huge shards of black glass that had sunk into the desert like splinters into flesh, and a myriad of what we presumed to be vehicles that had been flipped about, tossed around, upended or destroyed by falling debris. We decided the tower, when it had stood tall, must have had a parking lot, and these vehicles were the collateral damage of the tower's collapse.

The first floor of the tower remained somewhat intact. It was as though someone had surgically sliced the tower off its base, then knocked it sideways. The haze in the sky seemed to make sense as lingering dust from this collapse, imagining no wind had blown through to clear the air.

We saw no signs of life or activity.

The Beacon was a small thin pillar a mile away from the first floor, which the ship identified as the source of the signal that had brought us here. I landed the scout ship nearby. The ship's sensors were being cheeky, displaying a "Chances of Survival" meter that was currently stuck on "Pretty Good." I was all in favor of simplified data visualization for laypeople, but this was kind of insulting, to be honest.

Typically—in the exactly one example we had to work with—when we moved from Earth to the logosphere or back, transmutation kept us alive by adapting us to the environment we were entering. That's how the Dauphine had become a real person when she entered the gymnasium. That's what we were counting on now.

We popped the lid on the scout ship, and slowly climbed out onto the dry desert. The temperature was warm, and the air was dirty but breathable. Felt like "normal" gravity, too. Either this place was a near match for Earth in these ways, or we'd been transformed during transit to feel comfortable when we arrived.

If we were traversing a book with infinite pages, what was the likelihood we'd flip forward a bunch of pages and miraculously land on a page suitable for human habitation? Maybe we weren't human anymore, transformed so extensively by the punctuation marks to survive here that we only superficially resembled our former species. Maybe we hadn't been human since we started using power morphemes in the first place, for that matter, racking up mutations that extended far beyond the vocal cords. Anyway maybe the Beacon was specifically designed to attract humans to a rallying point that was actually safe for humans, and other species got routed to a different exit off the interdimensional freeway or whatever.

An important test remained. I delivered a simple, harmless power morpheme sequence that we should feel as a small gust of air rising up and gently passing us by. Check: at least we still had spells.

The Beacon was composed of a thin pillar maybe eight feet tall and a foot in diameter, its surface smooth and metallic, culminating in a crystal that glowed with a bright blue light. The pillar was attached to the rim of a base, a flat round platform that seemed illuminated from within by soft white light. A person could stand on this platform if they wanted to achieve the daunting feat of being half a foot above the desert surface. It all seemed rather space-age alluring to me.

We walked all the way around its perimeter, looking for control interfaces or access panels or the like. No dice. I wanted to stand on the platform because it clearly seemed like a platform designed for people to stand on, and I just really appreciate an intuitive UI like that, but Maddy suggested otherwise. The exchange went as follows:

"I would like to stand on the platform," I said.

"Do not," Maddy replied.

The pillar suddenly hissed loudly, and somehow seemed to spray a humanoid figure into existence on top of its white platform in a blast of color and steam. Its features were pearlescent, impossibly smooth and beautiful and radiant—angelic, perhaps, but with a sharpness that also seemed robotic. It wore a slick blue jumpsuit, its silver hair was tucked under a small matching cap reminiscent of a crisp military beret, and a silver diamond-shaped badge was affixed to its jumpsuit in the front.

It smiled at each of us in turn, then began speaking in a rich, sonorous voice, and neither of us understood a word it said, or even recognized its language's family tree. After maybe a minute, it stopped, smiled, and then began speaking again, in a different language this time, and only for a sliver of the time it spoke before. It switched languages twelve times before completing what appeared to be a set. I recognized none of these languages.

Finally it fell silent, a smile frozen on its face to a magnificently creepy effect.

"Hello," I said. "My name is Isobel Bailie. Can you understand me?"

I received no acknowledgment whatsoever.

"We came here because we heard your signal," I continued.

"I don't think it's even listening," Maddy said. "Maybe it's a recording."

But I knew damn well when I was being ignored by an NPC, and you just had to be patient throwing conversational triggers out until you got to the core message. If this construct didn't understand English, the only other mutual language we might have in common was music. I proceeded to sing the first few phrases of the musical signal from the Beacon that brought us here. I hadn't been able to learn the entire ten-minute motif overnight, but I definitely managed a good rendition of the first few lines before faltering.

The figure turned its head and performed a slow form of salute to me, its hands briefly covering its eyes, followed by a very slight bow of its head. A silver diamond-shaped badge materialized in its hand; it solemnly offered the badge to me, and you don't have to ask me twice to take loot from an NPC. Then the figure dissolved into a mist. I stuck the badge in the pocket of my jumpsuit.

"What just happened?" Maddy asked.

"Our quest begins," I replied.

❀ ❀ ❀

But as we wandered the ruins, it became apparent that if this was the rallying point for survivors, we were not going to find help here.

As we wandered through the parking lot, not only did we see no signs of life—we saw no remains of life either. It was as though an EMP had gone off, except instead of simply knocking out all the electronics, it had disintegrated anything organic as well. Periodically we'd stop at a shelled-out wreck of a vehicle, and Maddy would stick her head in, poke at some indecipherable controls, but we didn't manage to trigger a response out of anything.

We got back in the ship and flew slowly toward the first floor, the lobby of some kind of massive office building. Many of the windows were blown out and a fire had clearly raged through and burned itself out. Inside this lobby, we spotted another pillar like our Beacon, blackened but still standing, emitting a glow from its round white base. Impressively, as we got closer and fully understood the scale we were looking at, we realized that what we'd been calling the "first" floor actually must've been at least fifty floors.

"So look," Maddy said, "let's say survivors arrived here, just like us, and this is what they found. Do you think they'd stay here? Or would they maybe wander off to try to find someplace else to settle or collect themselves? Like, out of this desert altogether?"

"Worth a look," I said.

❀ ❀ ❀

We found no "out of this desert." This was a deeply artificial place.

As we flew the scout ship along the line traced by the ruined tower, we found ourselves heading straight back to the lobby without noticing that we'd ever turned around. We hadn't noticed any shift in perspective along the way. The illusion of our direction of travel confused even our AI. We'd clearly flown hundreds of miles away from the lobby before realizing we were now traveling toward it.

"Have we learned enough to head back?" Maddy asked. "Or should we see for ourselves what's inside?"

"Let's unpack the drones and send them in," I decided. "Let's at least try to survey a sliver of the interior before we leave."

We set the scout ship back down and unpacked the drones. We had twelve to work with, capable of sending signal back to the scout ship for us to watch and record. We sent the first one into the lobby. If it had ever been furnished in some way, the furnishings were melted to slag or burned to ashes, all except the blackened pillar. The drone didn't trigger an interaction from the pillar as it zoomed within close range. Beyond that, the only notable find was elevator banks, positioned to rise up the sides of the building in broad shafts that might be accessible somehow.

We sent drones scouting into several of the floors above the lobby, letting them flit through broken windows to survey incomprehensible layouts. The second floor, for instance, was one big, uninterrupted space, completely full of destroyed robotic machinery, whereas the third floor seemed like some kind of nuclear or electrical facility's command center, except, of course, fully destroyed by fire. Higher floors revealed no meaningful secrets; giant cubicle farms might have existed here, or laboratories, or greenhouses—impossible to deduce via drone's-eye view of ash and slag and wreckage.

On one floor, however, one of the supposed elevator doors had been blown inward, and the drone could slip inside the shaft beyond. Sure enough, this shaft traveled up into the sky above, but also down well below the surface level, to multiple subbasements—we counted twenty-three. There was no opening for the drone into any of these levels.

"I want to see what's down there," I said. "I get a very specific feeling when I'm in the presence of a new dungeon crawl opportunity."

Maddy said, "Can it wait? I'd feel weird about leaving the scout ship unprotected."

"Yes," I said, "at the rate things are going back home, we'll be back here in a few days in the arkship. Dungeon crawling can wait until then."

❀   ❀   ❀

This time we were able to situate ourselves in the scout ship, with Maddy sitting on my lap instead of sprawled on top of me after falling from the ceiling. It felt nice to be able to wrap my arms around her again.

"Are you comfortable?" I asked her.

"Sure. Are you?"

"I'm feeling good, yeah."

"Are you now?" Then after a beat, she said, "You plan on taking us home anytime soon?"

It was the pinnacle of selfishness to want to stay here, just to be alone with Maddy, when the stakes at home were so high.

I sighed and said, "Yeah, let's get out of here."

I pressed the button that would take us back.

Nothing happened.

I pressed it again. Same result.

"Ship, what's going on?" I asked.

"The jump drive is not active," the ship replied.

"Oh. Can you activate it please?"

"I cannot."

"What?"

"I cannot access the jump drive."

"But the jump drive is programmed to take us back, isn't it?"

"It is not."

"But Cameron said it was!"

"It is not."

I quickly cast a healing cantrip on myself to stop myself from hyperventilating with fear.

"So how do we go back?" Maddy asked, steel in her voice.

"We do not," the ship replied.

"Ship, are you broken or is this by design?" Maddy asked.

"I've been programmed for one jump only," the ship replied.

"So Cameron lied to us," Maddy concluded.

"No," I said, bitterness rising up in the back of my throat like acid. "Two people had access to the arkship's operating system.

I'm guessing those same two people had access to the scout ship's operating system. And I'm guessing it wasn't Cameron who did this.

"I'm guessing it was Violet Parker."

"She explicitly said she would kill me someday," I told Maddy. "Maybe this is what she meant."

Maddy said nothing. I was role-playing Violet Parker, evil genius, in my mind, trying to decipher what she stood to gain by knocking the two of us completely out of the picture. Well, me anyway—she couldn't have predicted Maddy would come with me.

"I mean, she's fucked now, right?" Maddy said eventually. "Let's say she tries to launch the arkship on schedule—it'll kill most of the people, because neither one of us is there to teach her how to teleport correctly, right?"

"Maybe she wasn't planning on traveling at all," I said. "Because with me out of the picture, you know what she's got now? She's got a battery with ten million people in it, and she's got Devin to issue new commands to the battery, with no Isobel the Queen in sight to stop her. I'll bet she's going to give *herself* god mode. And I'll bet she has *no* issues with spending energy from the battery, either to bring the arkship here safely, or to fight the thunderstorm herself."

"I find it hard to believe she'd risk herself in a fight," Maddy said.

"God mode's intoxicating," I said. "Hard to say what she'd do. But you're right, she's not one to put herself on the front line of anything."

"But if she doesn't expect the return of the scouting mission, how would she know that traveling here is safe?"

"She originally planned to send the scout ship here without a pilot," I replied. "My guess is she actually *did* that, prior to sending me. So she knows there's no one here to save us. And she knows that when she comes here in a few days in god mode, with the population of California—essentially hostages—I'm going to be myself, and want to keep those people alive instead of fighting her about who's the top deity. And honestly, it probably won't be a fight."

"Eventually, the battery will be empty," Maddy said.

"Yes," I said. "But she's about to relocate thirty million more people. She may last a while as god empress."

❀   ❀   ❀

Finally Maddy said, "Look, in a few days, the arkship will most likely be here. They're going to be disoriented and it's going to be chaotic and it'll take time before they're able to organize around exploring the ruins. We should explore the ruins first, look for *anything* that could give us an advantage when they get here. *Something* out there in that mess must be useful, we just need to find it."

That was a useful illusion to get us moving.

We parked the scout ship in front of the lobby. My proposal was to investigate the second pillar we'd found, since the two pillars were the only signs of active, working technology that we'd come across. I wondered if the one in the lobby would trigger an identical or different response from the one far out in the parking lot. Of course, our approach to this one would be slightly different, because now we had a silver diamond badge in our possession.

We made our way carefully across the debris-strewn field of the lobby floor, arriving at the pillar. Its round base was covered with a smattering of glass and dirt, but somehow it had survived relatively intact compared to its surroundings. It sprayed an angelic humanoid into existence as we approached, said something to us in a language we didn't understand, and then waited patiently for a response.

I held up the badge for it to see. It flickered, and then launched into a second monologue. Whereas the first monologue seemed cheerful and full of verve, this one seemed a little more sober and straightforward, but equally incomprehensible. We were getting approximately nowhere. I had the feeling this badge was originally meant to unlock visitor or diplomatic privileges or something, except the corresponding services had all been vaporized. All it was good for now, apparently, was triggering this apparition to give us another chunk of language we'd never understand.

But you'd think that the punctuation marks, masters of language and manipulators of thought, would be able to deduce meaning here, right? Well, except that we were probably viewing some kind of holographic representation of a thinking entity, so the punctuation marks technically might not have other punctuation marks in this environment to communicate with. Right?

Who could say?

"Maybe I could ask the punctuation marks if *they* can translate for us," I said. "Recite the entire hundred and eight and get a solid read from the punctuation marks on our situation."

"No way," Maddy said. "Look, we can't afford to have you incapacitated in some unpredictable fashion. There has to be another way."

Well, grrrr, but I suspected she was right.

"I do not, however, have an alternate proposal for what to do next," she said.

"Luckily, I do," I said. "What we do next is *dungeon crawl.*"

❀   ❀   ❀

Obviously that was a metaphor. What I meant was: time to go exploring.

We decided to make the lobby our home base, even going so far as to park the scout ship inside near the pillar. Then we systematically sent drones up to each floor above the lobby.

We couldn't really interpret what the structure had been used for. Maybe these were living spaces, apartments or hotels or something. Maybe we were swooping through shopping malls or schools. This entire thing could have been a self-contained city. Maybe all the ships outside had come here because this was some kind of massive tourist attraction. Maybe some of these floors were actual vehicle hangars. Maybe maybe maybe. It was all covered in crap and dead as could be.

One thing we did notice, however, was that every five floors, somewhere on the floorplan, a pillar with a white glowing base stood proud and tall, seemingly unaffected by the destruction around them. We clearly needed some kind of hook for understanding these things, but such a hook eluded us.

Exploring the toppled tower seemed like a much more challenging proposition, but we decided to give it a shot, testing the range of our drones by sending them down the length of it to see what it could see. Our flyover in the scout ship had been a little too high to get any detailed looks inside.

The drones began to find unexpected anomalies. For the most part, the floors were unremarkable pits of average destruction. But every now and then, a drone would fly past an absence where a floor should have been, like seeing into a pool of inky blackness; in one case, it sent back images of a vast inexplicable forest contained within a floor; in one case, we saw an empty plane of unbroken flat glass that seemingly had no end.

We debated sending one of the drones past the event horizon of one of these floors, to report back from within these environments, and opted not to. We wanted to keep all twelve safe for now. But we also had no desire to go into any of these environments ourselves. There's dungeon crawling, sure, and then there's dimensional plane hopping, and I wasn't at all convinced the latter should be on the agenda just yet.

"You're saying these anomalous floors are their own dimensions?" Maddy asked.

"Pocket dimensions, maybe," I said, as if I truly understood what that might mean.

"So this tower literally contained little universes within it," Maddy speculated. "And they're all empty? I mean, devoid of life? Isn't that a little unlikely?"

"I'm sorry, Maddy, is some aspect of this situation *likely* and I didn't know?"

She smirked at me and said, "I just think *personally* I would have designed this tower a little differently."

"Standing upright probably," I said, and we laughed.

❀　　❀　　❀

The sky did not get dark to signify night, but we did get sleepy eventually. We decided tomorrow we'd investigate the subbasements. Tonight, though, we'd sleep inside the climate-controlled environment of the scout ship. We sank into the pilot's chair together, stretching it out to its full length, enjoying a rare moment of actual contact.

She kissed me, and we discovered we were in no actual hurry to drift off to sleep.

We were hungry and thirsty when we awoke, and we hadn't managed to bring food or water on the trip with us. I delivered a heal that eliminated the immediate need for sustenance, preserving our strength in the process. I could pull off this heal several times a day, although psychologically, I felt I was delaying some physical payment that might eventually come due.

But until we had supplies, magic would have to suffice. Instead of three meals a day, we'd have three heals a day, and call it good.

Since today was a big day, we decided to make sure we were fully armed and ready for action. This would be the start of the true dungeon crawl, after all, where we put ourselves into harm's way instead of merely sending drones to scout for us. I gave one of the Dauphine's inexhaustible pistols to Maddy, who tucked it into her belt at the back. Then we began fishing in the Compression Artifact for goodies, trinkets, and armaments.

First things first: I found Late Night Encore, the amulet that had saved Madeleine Torch by restoring hit points upon her death. I insisted that Maddy wear it, and she insisted that *I* wear it, and we had an adorable little quarrel about who had more hit points, until finally we compromised: we would alternate wearing it, trading off every time we physically entered a new subbasement.

Next up: I wanted to feel the sturdy grip of Blades Per Minute back in my hand. This was an inferior copy, of course, so it was more like Blades Per Ninety Seconds, but you got the idea regardless.

For Maddy, I located the Reverberation Rifle, a heavy assault kaleidoscope from SD3. About the size of a baseball bat, and useful as a melee weapon, too, if it came down to that, the Reverberation Rifle did damage by smacking an opponent with a powerful beam attack that decayed into many smaller beam attacks until you eventually fired again.

The drone we'd sent down the elevator shaft had revealed to us that the subbasements seemed to be unevenly spaced, as though some were significantly taller than others. Upon close inspection, we saw levers at each doorway that we presumed might be used to mechanically open the doors. The bottom subbasement was as tall as the six subbasements above it, and we decided to start there and work our way up.

❀   ❀   ❀

We teleported to the bottom of the elevator shaft. We were standing on a pile of rubble that made us wonder if there were in fact more subbasements below this one; hard to say from here. The lever we thought might open the doors had no effect.

"We could," Maddy said, "just teleport to the other side of the doors and see what's there."

"Nice try," I said. "That's how you set off traps, Maddy."

"Don't be absurd," Maddy said. "If you need to protect something with traps, you don't put it right outside the doors to an elevator."

"Are you attempting to use logic on a dungeon crawl?" I protested. "Spikes don't need a rational reason to fall from the ceiling!" But yes, I saw her point.

We teleported to the other side of the door, arriving in pitch-blackness. I cast a rope light spell which illuminated a pathway in front of us, or rather, a railway of sorts. A small golf cart or trolley car sat at the end of a track which led off into the darkness. We let loose a couple of drones to scan the environment, and observed the images they captured via one of the remaining drones.

Immense machinery filled the floor. I felt like I was staring into a nineteenth-century steam factory, filled with ducts and gears and wheels. Or perhaps this had been a series of enormous power generators. But it was difficult to say, because chunks of ceiling had collapsed onto the machinery; the overall destruction had extended even this far below the surface.

Huge basins collected debris on far sides of the floor, below enormous chutes in the ceiling above. Walkways surrounded the perimeter, about halfway up the walls, in case we wanted to get a better view ourselves.

"This is not working for me," Maddy said. "Do you have any spells like Detect Interesting Shit?"

Hmm. I had Detect Illegal Warehouse Rave, sure.

"No," I said. "Let's walk around a little."

❀   ❀   ❀

We walked the path of the trolley tracks, figuring this was designed to be a relatively safe passage through the environment. My rope lights continued magically unfolding in front of us, giving everything in their immediate vicinity a nice white glow, although for fun I could toggle them into a color-cycling rainbow mode which Maddy noted was gaudy. Hmph.

The tracks ended at the opposite side of the floor from where we started, terminating just as abruptly as they'd started. The ground-level tour was not super enlightening, we decided, so we teleported to the walkway directly above our current position. From here, rope lights were not sufficient, and the drones could only really provide pin spots in specific directions. I cast Blinding Light of Dawn, normally a combat spell for clearing dance floors but in this case just the thing for giving us perspective on the entire basement.

What we'd missed, slowly making our way through the darkness, was the large hangar-style door on one wall. I suppose it made sense to have a doorway that large if you needed to move machinery in and out of this basement. Maybe it was an enormous freight elevator and you moved parts up and down that way? Maybe it was just another wing of the subbasement that someone had thoughtfully put a giant door in front of for inexplicable reasons?

The light made something else clear, though.

The door was covered with hieroglyphic writing, sigils that gave off a sharp red glow in the radiance of my spell. I couldn't read them obviously, but they emanated a very clear "Do Not Enter Without Safety Goggles" vibe.

"Well, well, well," Maddy said. "Shall we?"

But when she tried to teleport to the other side of that door, she lit up like a firework and collapsed backward against the wall, slumping to the deck of the walkway moments later.

"Apparently not," she said.

I helped her stand. She was shaken, said the experience was incredibly painful but only briefly, like she'd stuck her finger in a light socket and gotten a jolt of electricity but was otherwise unharmed.

Just to be scientific about it, I borrowed the Reverberation Rifle from her and fired repeatedly at the door. The blasts seemed to be absorbed, either by the metal of the door, or by the energy of the sigils, or by something else we couldn't detect. In any event, the door seemed unscathed.

"Take it easy," Maddy said. "We can bookmark this location and continue exploring. I'm not eager to keep swinging here."

"Let me at least send a drone out there to get video of the writing," I said. "I want to be able to study it."

But the video imagery from the drone I sent was unusable; the glyphs on the door read as overpowering brightness to the drone's camera, making them illegible.

"Curses," I said, as an idea slowly formed. "Literal curses, that's what I think these glyphs are. So powerful that we don't even have to understand the language they're written in to understand the meaning, the intent. And maybe they're not written in a real language in the first place."

"What do you mean?"

"I mean . . . maybe they're power morphemes, Maddy. Or I mean—a written version of power morphemes. Except in this case, the meaning is so dense, so concentrated into single characters or pictograms, that—that the meaning is transmitted by . . . by warping *perception,* or by altering the literal world of the perceiver."

I was babbling, I admit, but I was also fucking onto something.

"Maddy," I said. "*Now* can I communicate directly with the punctuation marks? We have something very specific to discuss with them."

"It can wait," she said firmly.

❀   ❀   ❀

We systematically toured the other floors over the next two days, keeping our minds occupied, cracking jokes as best we could. I took to having drones follow us with music playing constantly, which Maddy endured with good humor. Cameron had even hooked up the drones with a functionally unnecessary mirrorball mode that enabled them to light up and create impromptu disco parties in the ruins when we started to get run-down.

But after three days, we started to panic, and after a full week of being there, we had passed through denial and anger and bargaining, and were immersed quite deeply in depression. Acceptance wasn't quite in view, not after a week.

But after a month, we'd begun to accept the likelihood that we were never leaving this place. The arkship hadn't come, which might mean that Earth had been destroyed, or that they'd saved it without us. Certainly time might be passing so differently back home that someone might still come to rescue us.

The situation on the ground, though, was clearly that no one was coming to rescue us.

❀　　❀　　❀

During that month, we trained each other on spells and sequences. I wanted Maddy to learn as much of my healing arsenal as possible, for starters. We amused ourselves working our way through training with nearly every magic item stored inside the Compression Artifact.

We hopped further and further down the length of the ruined tower, teleporting across its surface to the next point in sight, looking for technology or artifacts or books or anything that might inform us. We couldn't understand how a culture—a civilization—could have lived inside this tower without leaving a trace of its knowledge or its literature.

We carefully skirted our way around "pocket dimensions" that we spotted. They leaked alternate realities into the air like toxins.

Each night, we made our way back to the scout ship, exhausted and dissatisfied.

After a month or so, Maddy finally said to me, "I think you'd better contact the punctuation marks now. I think we may as well get on with the business of extinguishing our last hope, don't you think?"

I understood perfectly what she meant. She wanted to burst the bubble of some potential *deus ex machina* lurking in the linguistic wings.

"I have an idea," I said. "Before I do this, I want to give the punctuation marks a little more to work with."

"What do you mean?"

"We have two concrete examples of alien language in this place. The holographic beings projected by the pillars can talk; the curses on the wall are written. I want to internalize as much of that material as I can. Really saturate my brain with all of it. That way I'm not wasting any time when I finally do get a chance to ask the punctuation marks direct questions."

❀　　❀　　❀

I established a new routine. Every morning I spent focused on one of the two talking holographic entities we'd encountered, each of which operated according to unique scripts. My goal was to treat these things like the recalcitrant NPCs they truly were, and convince them to reveal their secrets.

First thing first: memorize everything you can get them to tell you, recite everything back at them as though you understand what the hell you're saying, until eventually you trick them into adding some new sentences to the fray, memorize those, lather rinse repeat. When you get tired of that, talk at them in English, just sheer wall of monologue crap, to see if these things are smart enough to deduce *your* language, lather rinse repeat. No, I did not convince one of them to start speaking conversational English at me. Nor did I ever remotely understand anything they said.

I'd take a break in the midday to goof off with Maddy, who spent her days attempting to scavenge working technology from the ruins in the parking lot. Somewhere, she reasoned, there must be *something* that still worked, maybe the further out she got from the ground zero of the lobby. Middays were for goofy stuff. We could play video games inside the scout ship, or with the drones. I tried teaching her the difference between tech house and future house and bass house but she just did *not* catch on.

Afternoons, I descended down to the twenty-third subbasement, sat on the floor in front of the cursed door, and I forced myself to memorize those glyphs. I had to build up a tolerance, of course, like swallowing a small amount of iocane powder every day to gain resistance. I had to overcome the towering dread that rose up in me as I allowed each sigil to brand itself in my mind. Sometimes I felt like they were speaking directly to me, like there was something personal about each glyph, some aspect of each glyph that was encoded with me as the intended audience.

And it was probably my imagination, but I heard these glyphs speaking themselves at me in the spoken language of the holographic projections at the pillars. I mean, your mind will invent correlations and patterns for no good reason whatsoever, and the mishmash in my mind might never amount to meaning that I could understand.

But I had alien punctuation marks in my mind who were better linguists than me. Hopefully they were getting more mileage out of these exercises than I was.

I mean, sure we were hoping for a *deus ex machina*, but the thing is, it never hurts to work for it.

❀   ❀   ❀

At night, we'd meet back at the scout ship after our respective labors and try to relax.

"Night" was a relative concept, since the sky never wavered from its hazy shade of orange, never dimmed or displayed stars. We could judge by relative exhaustion when the work day was over, and then we'd climb inside the scout ship and fire up the giant viewscreen. Cameron had loaded a massive amount of media onto the arkship in preparation for a long voyage, and a sizable subset of that media wound up cloned onto the scout ship. But it was painful to watch narrative movies or TV. That world was lost.

Instead, we found environmental loops that were peaceful enough—tours under the ocean, or space telescope footage, or snow falling outside a rustic cabin window, stuff that was a step up in creativity and production value from the classic fireplace video of legend. Without a story interfering with these loops, it was easy enough to imagine that any of this scenery might still be accessible somewhere in the multiverse. Not accessible to us, obviously, but not obliterated outright either. This made the interior of the scout ship feel at least minimally pleasant, as part of a general effort to keep the hopelessness at bay as long as possible.

With the atmosphere established, Maddy would often say, "Oh, is it date night?" It wasn't a joke, really. With nothing else to distract us, clinging to each other for love and sanity was a core activity.

That's how it was. During the day, we committed to our respective projects out in the ruins because we were trying to save each other.

And when we got back to the scout ship at night, we were still trying to save each other.

I wanted to sit in the scout ship and listen to ambient music while I was reciting the hundred and eight. That was my vision, to get comfortable and put on a blindfold and quietly recite my mantras like I was a psychonaut about to take ayahuasca in my shaman's loft apartment in Brooklyn.

Before I climbed in, Maddy said, "Please remember me when you're off on this outlandish adventure of the mind, you hear me?"

I kissed her and squeezed her hand.

"Of course I'll remember you," I said.

I had a pretty solid idea what to expect, because I had Alexander's memory of the first time he'd tried this. It would be a demanding and potentially uncomfortable experience, but he'd experienced no hostility, just a firehose of data that he'd spent the rest of his life deciphering. Bradford had maybe had it easier, because he'd been able to prepare himself mentally in a way that Alexander had not. In principle, the punctuation marks might also be growing accustomed to direct communication with humans. In theory, this might be a cakewalk.

Still, I established a safe word with Maddy that I'd try to squeeze out if I became too uncomfortable and needed a break. We'd fished a small magic item out of the Compression Artifact for this scenario, a potion called Xanax Spritzer (an antidote for psychedelic venoms in the game), and if I used the safe word, she'd douse me with it.

My safe word, of course, was "dubstep."

It took a surprising amount of concentration and effort to recite all hundred and eight. Sure, each one was in my muscle memory and I was quite deft combining them on the fly to improvise sequences. But reciting all hundred and eight in a row was effectively delivering a very long sequence, with internal rhythms and subphrases and psychological overtones that never showed themselves when you learned these power morphemes in isolation. I felt like I was trying to do linear algebra homework while practicing capoeira.

But as I recited successive chunks of power morphemes, my consciousness clearly began to shift into a more malleable state, almost like lucid dreaming, where environments presented themselves to me without warning but I had a modicum of volition to navigate. At first, I thought I was simply experiencing a stream of memories, given the familiarity I felt as I sailed through each setting and each scenario. I was back in college; I was back in my life with Wendy; I was back at work at the record label; I was back at my early days at Jenning & Reece. But the settings became jumbled and I realized some of these memories were actually being manufactured for me, almost as a test of my ability to detect the difference between real and false memories. I knew Wendy and I had never traveled to Paris together, but I didn't remember if I myself had ever been to Paris, if this museum I was touring was even in Paris or if it was all an invention, because clearly some of these paintings and statues couldn't exist in the real world, Michelangelo had never sculpted Zeus holding a giant iPod and jamming out to classic rock, and also was that actually classic rock or was this some bizarre set of impossible sounds from the imaginary realm or beyond, and so on and so on.

This dreamlike mishmash of experience occupied my attention during the range between power morpheme 75 and 90 or so. The punctuation marks were warming up to a bigger reveal, making sure I was prepared to expect a highly unusual interface for direct communication.

As I reached power morpheme 95, I came to a sudden realization that reciting the hundred and eight in sequence was akin to tuning my mind to a specific radio frequency on a receiver, and what I was starting to hear as I got closer to 108 were nearby frequencies where other complete realities could be glimpsed. Sharp stabs of fear hit me as I understood this and realized there was no turning back and no turning my mind's eye away from unwanted sights and despairing realizations. A physical, material mind was an unwanted witness to the hidden goings-on of these incorporeal realms, teeming with primordial weirdness and unharnessed wild consciousness, flowing and boiling without form.

Around 100 or so, I realized that an increasing amount of my experience of these realms was becoming fully mediated by the punctuation marks in anticipation of my "arrival" in their domain. The punctuation marks claimed no hierarchy, no single dictatorial presence among them, but they did group themselves along distinct functional lines that needed to operate in concert for power morphemes to "work" in the real world. In their domain, I should expect to see their process of debate and discussion, their method for aligning themselves on the ongoing march to secure survival.

Right as 105 escaped my lips, a metaphorical curtain began to swing open, and I felt a rush to complete the last three, like the burst of sudden speed from a sprinter to pull ahead of their bitter rival at the finish line of a race. Suddenly there I was, waving at the crowd cheering me on, as 108 emerged from me with all the style of an opera singer bringing down the house on a thrilling final note in the stratosphere of the human vocal range.

Now it was time to learn how the punctuation marks had spent these past couple months.

❀   ❀   ❀

I had the sensation of being ushered into a surreal war room embedded deep within my subconscious mind, where the finishing stages of an intense campaign of operations were still in motion. This "war room" did not correspond to any specific region of my actual brain, nor did it appear to me in some kind of physical representation; rather, I was steadily immersed in a surprising new flow of information, and the "war room" metaphor seemed to help decode or interpret the data I was now receiving.

According to this metaphor, a significant portion of my subconscious mind's available processing power had been dedicated to a war effort without my noticing.

Apparently immersing my brain in alien language, despite my lack of conscious comprehension of its meaning, had been a vector for a full assault on the punctuation marks and their iron grip on my perception. The punctuation marks had fought valiantly on the front lines of my awareness, as they defended my mind from the collective scourge of enemy punctuation marks contained within the spoken and written alien languages that I'd exposed myself to. These enemy punctuation marks had mounted an invasion of my mind, and my symbiotic punctuation marks had been caught completely off guard. Had these disparate species—conceptually related in some distant way, but antithetical to each other in the heat of battle—been given a chance for a peaceful introduction, they might have formed treaties and trade alliances and the like. But *this*—it was unconscionable, this invasion, and the punctuation marks were *not having it*.

Oh sure, compromises were made to keep me up and running, wouldn't do to have my mind lock up while they sorted this out. The homeland (hey, that's me!) needed to be preserved at all costs, quite obviously. The costs were kept hidden from me, buried as line items in some operational report stored in the subconscious, but I deduced that sacrifices had been made: words I would never remember again, specific shades of emotion now infused with vague unease, my ability to differentiate the em dash and the en dash blown to pieces by conceptual shrapnel.

But in the end, our troops were better prepared for the trials of war. Our troops—the punctuation marks that had already successfully mounted an invasion of humanity a long time ago—were accustomed to fighting for their lives, after all, and they subsumed the enemy with brutal efficiency.

That brought us current to today's proceedings. The war room metaphor dissolved, replaced by a slick corporate board room metaphor, in which the punctuation marks assumed vague anthropomorphic avatars for my benefit and assembled around a large unnecessary table. A slick corporate slide show began, and for the first time, one of the punctuation marks emerged to differentiate itself from the others. That most matter-of-fact of punctuation marks, the period, narrated the presentation.

"As the war ended, Isobel, we brought over the enemy's best scientists to accelerate our own research into a new generation of power morphemes," said the period. "They're evil, yes, but they're smart, and we needed their help if we were to ensure this kind of surprise attack could never catch us off guard again. The first product of our research is *power morpheme 109,* the first in a proposed expansion series of innovative new power morphemes. It's modeled after combat morphemes first deployed against us by the defeated enemy punctuation marks, who are even now being assimilated into your thoughts."

"Uh, I haven't noticed any new defeated punctuation marks in my thoughts."

"That's by design, Isobel. Wouldn't *dare* to disturb your conscious thoughts—that was always the mandate. The whole project hinges on preserving your continuity of thought and identity, while extracting maximum intel from the defeated punctuation and fusing their best weaponry and tactics with our own. We've learned a great deal, Isobel.

"We believe *power morpheme 109* will be essential in the successful execution of your next mission."

"Wait, *my* next mission?"

"Yes, your next mission is clear: defeat the cursed wall, and free the living, conscious mind on the other side."

"Say what now?"

"Isobel, our intelligence clearly indicates *thought* on the other side of that wall, faintly detectable, barely alive, and deeply apathetic about it. Whoever or whatever eliminated all signs of corporeal life from this wretched place *left someone behind*. What we need here is a prisoner extraction."

"I'm confused, though," I replied. "It's a big cursed door and I don't have the key."

"We understand the temptation to envision only material solutions to the problem," the period said. "But we, Isobel, are masters of an ethereal domain of thought. We don't need 'keys' in order to open 'doors' any more than we needed, let's say, open data ports in physical human brains in order to occupy the inexplicable field effect of human minds."

"I see," came my slow reply, as though I was not at all in the slightest stalling to try to figure out what the entire fuck was happening to me. "Explain for me this, how you say . . . *power morpheme 109*."

"*Power morpheme 109*, in combination with some of our finest classic power morphemes, is a psychic amplifier, allowing the instantiation of a localized logosphere.

"Instead of line of sight, imagine line of thought, where thought is a literal wave that can be extended. Thought can be measured, quantified, manipulated, and most importantly, *blasted outward* riding piggyback on sound waves coming out of your *mutated vocal cords*.

"Now add *power morpheme 109* to the mix, prefixing any existing sequence to extend its range, or weaving it throughout a sequence to expand its radius. Power morpheme sequences are typically close quarter in effect. You make something happen and the people around you notice it, sure. But with *power morpheme 109*, ranged and area effects are added to the mix. Teleport an entire room full of furniture to your new apartment! Make it snow in one specific city block while they're having a heat wave across the street! Cause an entire neighborhood to suddenly desire a plate full of cheese—laboratory results indicate all these physical effects are possible, and more, thanks to *power morpheme 109*!

"But that's not all! Why limit yourself to the concerns of physical reality? Here's where *power morpheme 109* really shines. In the same way the logosphere you know and love is a collection of the world's whimsies and flights of fancy, you, too, can surround yourself with a bubble of your own ideas and inspirations. With a localized, line of thought logosphere, you can envelop your surroundings with heights of pure imagination. Simulate new combinations of concepts, explore bold visions of alternate paradigms, bathe in previously unavailable pools of serenity or bliss—Isobel, *these vistas are open!* The R&D team's already got some sharp ideas for how to deploy these new skills."

The exclamation mark stepped forward, tall and proud, its avatar reading to me like a crudely animated lightning bolt. It was a general in war, an innovator in times of peace.

The punctuation marks around the table all donned sunglasses.

Suddenly, three-dimensional representations of cursed glyphs appeared in a series, in midair above the table, rotating so that I could see every contour, the depth of every line, the intricacy of intertwined shapes. They radiated so brightly from this vantage point that I could barely stand it, until the comma handed me sunglasses to put on as well.

"We don't understand how these glyphs can encode so much information, nor how they contain so much tangible life force. They're no simple referent to concepts; they seem to be fractal slices of concepts, complete unto themselves in their way."

"Wait a minute," I said. "Whaddya mean, 'life force'?"

"I believe you refer to it as *spark*," the asterisk chimed in.

They stopped on one glyph in particular, one that recurred more than any other in the string of curses on the door.

"We believe the infernal spark in this glyph alone contains thousands of times the energy contained in the entire battery," said the exclamation mark.

"So?" I said.

"We believe you should eat it."

The room fell silent. That was their big pitch. The silence in the room was palpable, the apprehension high, as they awaited my response.

"Say what now?" I blurted out.

"Consume this glyph. Absorb the entirety of its infernal spark."

"But—it's—huh?" I said thoughtfully.

Their top scientist, the ampersand, explained the proposal.

"Your average everyday power morphemes draw from your own replenishable but modest pool of spark to power the effects," it said. *"Power morpheme 109* is going to take a little more out of you than you're used to. By consuming the infernal spark contained within this single glyph, we believe you'll have more than enough mojo at your disposal to instantiate a local logosphere. This will enable you to connect with the imprisoned mind that lies beyond the cursed door."

"We believe this sentience was imprisoned for a reason," the semicolon added, "probably a very good reason, and we want you to communicate with it anyway. It reads to us as a primal set of probably alien concepts rather than a proper personality, but we'll defer to your judgment as someone who actually *has* a personality."

They even had slides for this proposal. Intricate representations of spark consumption on one axis, expendable mojo on another. Possible rewards: learning the languages of the curses and the holographic figures at the pillars; insight into the history of this place; gaining the gratitude of a potentially supernatural being. Possible downsides: pain; agony; dying.

"Uhhhhh," I said, really leaning into what I was hearing.

"C'mon," said the question mark, "sounds like fun, right?"

I couldn't tell.

They called for a break.

❀ ❀ ❀

I wandered to a window and stared out at the indeterminate cityscape below. The brackets came up on either side of me and struck up a conversation.

"Look, we understand, this is all a bit sudden," they said in unison, and I realized the background conversations were rapidly receding in volume. "You find out about *power morpheme 109* in the same conversation that you find out you're going to have to eat cursed pictograms in order to confront a sentient, primal set of probably alien concepts that's trapped on the other side of an impressive cursed door very much designed to ensure you *don't* do any such confronting, and you're thinking, surely there *must* be something better I could be doing with my own locally instantiated logosphere, like cook up some kind of perpetual dream state for me and my sweetie where we forget we're trapped in an artificial dimension far from our probably destroyed home planet and instead just cruise along in a blissful haze for the rest of our lives—you know, we *get* it. It's a lot.

"But here's the good news, Isobel." And then they paused, shuffled some papers for a minute, and one of them said, "Shit, hang on, left the good news back in our office," and they both split.

You couldn't fool me. There was no good news in all this. This was all just relentless misery and crap, just a big fat line of bullsh—

"Okay, here's the good news," the brackets said, swiftly appearing again on either side of me. "You get all kinds of new visualization parameters with *power morpheme 109*. This won't be some seemingly arbitrary planetary logosphere where any idea that ever gained a moment's purchase with any rando who ever lived is suddenly on the loose, running around in a toga harassing the neighbors. No, look, *you* can control the metaphor of its form and substance, isn't that grand? Imagine it—the Iridescent Logosphere! And you can *share* it with Maddy! It's as permeable to other conscious minds as you like!"

Hmm. That was starting to sound promising.

"Obviously it won't be pleasant," they pointed out. "We speculate these curses may utilize a language so profound that to understand it is to obey it. And to protect against those who don't understand it, the author of these curses left *its own spark* behind to enforce its will."

"Uh-huh. And what makes me immune?"

"You're not subject to anyone else's will, Isobel. You're the Queen."

♛　♛　♛

So then they seared 109 into me. It felt rather like a wholly new chakra was being metaphysically branded into me, like from now on, somewhere in the lineup between the root chakra and the crown chakra, the holy fuck chakra was being shoved in there, and that's where 109 would be safely ensconced, like an immeasurably valuable tiara that I could delicately retrieve for special occasions such as diplomatic functions and making it snow in weird places.

Power morpheme 109 might be seared into my mind, but it wasn't yet seared into my vocal cords. It would require practice just to deliver it, let alone to integrate it into a sequence that I could use to instantiate my own private logosphere. I let it rip at the top of my lungs.

Oh, hmm, guess I don't need practice after all, as long as I don't mind the sensation of blood pooling at the back of my throat right about now. Eh, Maddy will flip me over if I start gurgling.

Along with 109, a helpful initial set of sequences was provided to get me started. Here's the sequence for locally instantiating a logosphere; here's a sequence that projects your voice at extreme decibel levels; here's the cheese sequence we mentioned earlier.

Once 109 clicked into place, and they were sure it met factory specifications, they were ready to cut me loose back into the material world. They would observe closely and make any modifications necessary so that the next time I needed to call on them, they'd be ready with the next generation in power morpheme technology. We were a team here, after all, working toward the common goal of not dying in a desolate land, not when entire interdimensional vistas of thought remained to be gingerly explored with all possible respect and no hint of totalitarian domination.

I came to my senses to find that Maddy had indeed flipped me over onto my side.

"I thought you said 'dubstep,'" she told me, "but it turned out you were just choking on blood."

"Same diff," I said, wiping my mouth.

After a heal brought me back up to fighting strength, we made our way down to the cursed door and set up shop.

I had drones playing music again, just because the silence down here was oppressive to me. Not ambient music this time—something a little more driving, good progressive house to keep me focused. Sometimes when you've got a steady beat going, you can use that as a heartbeat to drop into flow states; I'd noticed that many times during combat in the game. Maddy was ready with heals—we'd worked up to teaching her some pretty high-level ones by now—and we agreed it was definitely my turn to wear the Late Night Encore amulet.

The idea was to create a local logosphere that existed on both sides of the door, and then extend the equivalent of a psychic chat invitation to whatever lurked over there. To pull that off, first I needed to siphon spark from one of the cursed glyphs to power this local logosphere. It was going to be a delicate procedure.

You might think that trying to psychically siphon spark off a cursed glyph would, you know, trigger an effing curse or something. But "cursed" was really just my interpretation of what I felt in their presence. The word the punctuation marks used to describe the spark of these glyphs was "infernal," which had its own connotations. So if you started mucking around with this spark, you might not wind up experiencing a literal preordained curse, like "trespass here and you shall never enjoy classic trip hop again!" Rather, it might be more like getting blood poisoning, except it'd be spark poisoning, as your spark became more and more infernal until you stopped being human and became something monstrous or demonic instead.

Anyway I didn't intend to sup that deep. Instead I wanted to just skim off the top a little, to accumulate just enough to juice up power morpheme 109. If it looked like I was getting into trouble, Maddy would hit me with those heals and we'd call it off. The punctuation marks wanted me to consume a whole glyph, absorbing thousands of times the amount of spark that was contained within the battery. But I surely the fuck didn't want to overflow with that much infernal spark. I didn't want to find myself swept up into the infernal version of god mode by accident.

"So how's this even work, though?" Maddy asked. "You lick the door or something?"

That was a good question. The punctuation marks had not provided good instructions here and I hadn't thought to ask good questions, but clearly their metaphor of "eating" the glyph outright wasn't particularly workable in practice. The idea of licking the door, though, brought to mind sticking your tongue on a nine-volt battery and getting a little jolt, which actually seemed like a relevant analogy for what I was trying to accomplish.

"I need to figure out a way to lick the door, but like, with my brain," I said.

Maddy said, "Try casting Contact High on it."

"Oh—of course!"

Contact High was a low-level spell that you could cast on an ally or enemy in close range, which would grant you mild versions of any ongoing magical effects they were using on themselves, like power-ups or defenses. It was a cheap way to leech a little protection out of higher-level entities, since it had no noticeable effect from the target's perspective (although it was customary to thank allies for their contribution to your survival by announcing you were now "high on life"). I hadn't used this spell in forever, but Maddy had just learned the game, so naturally it was fresh on her mind.

I visualized the specific cursed glyph that the punctuation marks had identified as my target. It recurred frequently throughout the script on the door, and was easy to isolate in my mind as a singular entity. I indicated Maddy should step back, I guess in case I became radioactive or some shit, and then I cast the spell.

❀　　❀　　❀

On a scale of "sticking your tongue on a nine-volt battery" to "being struck by lightning just as a power transformer explodes in your face," this Contact High was on the low end of the painful jolt spectrum. But it was steady and continuous, which was disconcerting, and as a "trickle charge" of cursed spark flowed into me, I felt its insidious effects on me almost immediately. My eyes watered and probably turned red, and my skin felt like it was sore from an unfortunate sunburn, and I had to shoo away some ugly thoughts pretty quickly.

But the plan was never to hoard this spark. The plan was to immediately use it up by instantiating a local logosphere. I let rip with the sequence I'd been taught by the punctuation marks.

Of course, instantiating a local logosphere is pointless until you then decide to enter it. From Maddy's perspective, I must have simply winked out of existence, disappearing into thin air. From my own perspective, I transmuted into a new version of myself in this logosphere. We weren't in the Sparkle Dungeon milieu; I hadn't spent enough time visualizing an Iridescent version of this place, so I found myself drifting in a not-unpleasant, indistinct state—dreamlike, but lucid. I didn't know what to expect, didn't know what I was looking for. From here, the cursed door and its infernal spark and the entire subbasement were invisible.

I tried my best to radiate that I was here, that I was friendly, that I was looking for interaction. In principle (as much as you could derive actual principles from this ludicrous state of affairs), even though I'd instantiated this logosphere, I didn't necessarily control it. If another being entered it, we'd be on relatively common ground. So I was open to connection, but I was wary.

I began to feel the distinct sensation that I was rousing a hibernating animal.

Well, "animal" was a bit uncharitable, sure.

But the emerging presence that was starting to flicker at the psychic equivalent of my peripheral vision was not immediately radiating human presence back at me, that was obvious.

❀   ❀   ❀

We met in a small room, like a police station interrogation room. I sat at a table, dressed smartly for the occasion, across from a blur of a figure, a literal smear where I ought to see the features of a face or the contours of a body. I felt like if I squinted hard enough, I could make this smear resolve into something I'd recognize as a person, but that was illusion—this entity defied attempts to perceive it in that fashion.

"I was told I could expect privacy," it said in a raw whisper.

I realized immediately it wasn't speaking English out loud; it was projecting its meaning directly into my language center, which was a neat trick and very unsettling.

I said, "I'm Isobel Bailie. I'm a visitor from . . . far away."

"I'm not allowed 'visitors,'" it said.

"I didn't ask permission."

I felt it wondering what the con was here.

"What brought you here?" it asked. "What desperate times must you be facing, that you expected succor from me?"

I decided to be extremely, overly transparent. I had little to lose, I realized.

"I'm trapped here," I said. "Alone in these ruins. Looking for a way out of here. You're the only other . . . I haven't met anyone else here but you."

"Ruins," it murmured. "What do you mean?"

"I mean, there used to be—a tower, I guess? And it collapsed at some point. So it's—in ruins. And there are no people here, not even remains of people. I came here because . . . someone established a beacon, indicating this was a safe harbor. But whoever set up the beacon in the first place? Gone. Whoever lived in that tower? Gone. You're the sole inhabitant, do you understand?"

No response—maybe it emanated a vague sense of boredom, hard to say.

"I guess it's worse than that," I continued, "because my home is probably destroyed by now, by a—an unstoppable thunderstorm that is rolling across the multiverse, devouring everything in its path."

"Yes, that's right—devouring *everything*, Isobel Bailie. Your turn comes like everyone else's."

I was speechless for a moment.

"Where are you from, Isobel Bailie?" it asked. "Let us commemorate the passing of your home into the dwindling annals of history."

"Earth," I managed to whisper despite my steadily building fury.

"Are you its ambassador? Its ruler?"

"I'm a concerned citizen."

"Do you truly understand *nothing* about my purpose?"

"Enlighten me."

"I am the Auditor, Isobel Bailie, and I have found this existence to be deeply, terribly flawed," it spat. Words flowed from it in a torrent. "Therefore, this creation shall be *unraveled* so that our essence may be deployed in service of a more aesthetically pleasing vision. By such iteration do we approach perfection. With each attempt, we learn what we will need to build the next attempt, and in turn we must discard the past in favor of the future. *Five thousand times* have we tried, and failed, and tried again, trapping our essence within our own experiments in order to watch them unfold, to study them, admiring what is good, allowing the chaff to fall under the cold stare of critique, and then *unraveling* it to start again with a fresh palette, new understanding, and deeper skill.

"This punishment—my imprisonment—is also my reward. Here in this cage I await the unraveling in my own silent meditation, free from any flaws except my own, awaiting the inevitable call to take up my mantle once again in the arena of what comes next. This form shall be unraveled, and I will be summoned to resume my duties all in good time."

"What the hell was the crime that got you imprisoned?"

"My crime was appointing myself to *be* the Auditor," it replied. "For that audacity am I always sentenced."

❀ ❀ ❀

"How do we stop it?" I asked.

"You do not," it replied, a bit smugly if you asked me.

"Okay—how do *you* stop it?"

"I cannot stop it. Even the artists and architects who designed and released it into the wild cannot stop it. Its specification calls for its *permanence*. Once unleashed, it cannot be bottled back up, it cannot be dissolved, it cannot be destroyed."

"I don't believe you. I fought it and knocked it back."

"Oh, certainly it may face obstacles along the way. It must understand a thing first in order to properly unravel it."

"So it absolutely *can* be resisted."

"For a time, of course. It does not unravel existence all at once in a glorious, simultaneous flash. That was my original intent, mind you, but that design was not approved. Instead, it must take its time, winding its way steadily across dimensional pathways as a constantly adapting malevolence. It enters new climes gently at first, before succumbing to its appetite. It *becomes* a part of its target in order to more thoroughly *unravel* its target from *within*. Perhaps to you it seems to be a wave that sweeps across an area, but its attack is much more sinister.

"You can distract it, of course, dangle trinkets that capture its attention for a time. It seeks to topple the arrogant and the powerful first and foremost, so that others may properly cower before it. Perhaps in you it faced its most dangerous foe, let us be so generous as to imagine this is true; and yet, the next time you face it, the weaknesses you perceived will be closed to you, while your own weaknesses will be magnified in the face of its endless cleverness. It does not think in the way we do; thus it can never be reasoned with, or bargained with, or seduced.

"Perhaps the beacon you describe was established here because here is to be its final destination. The steady approach of the unraveling was to be observed from the top floor of the infinite tower in celebration of our accomplishments here. I cannot say what manner of interruption was suffered. But truly, here you are as safe as you can be. You may live out the entirety of your mortal lifetime without ever staring into the face of the unraveling again. Be thankful for a life well lived and time well spent, if you can. No one who faces the unraveling was ever guaranteed more than what they were able to claim for themselves during their transient encounters with the concept of being alive."

"You are just . . . not cheerful," I finally said.

"Once again, I am guilty as charged," it said, accompanied by a small, grotesque chuckle.

❈   ❈   ❈

"I think I'm going to break you out of your cage," I said.

"There is no need."

"Actually, I'm pretty sure I need to."

"You have no authority—"

"Friend, if there *is* an authority somewhere, *it isn't here to stop me.* And the way I see it, you don't get to just relax in your little meditation room or whatever you've got going on, while the rest of us get properly terrified and then annihilated. No, you can come out of hiding and face it with Maddy and me, out in the ruins."

"I do not wish to—"

"I don't care what you wish, honestly. I came here trying to save my planet, and instead I get *you.* Do you know how disappointing that is? I mean, I didn't like Earth at first, it kind of alienated me a lot in the beginning, but I stuck with it, and took in the details, and started to make it work for me, and I miss it. It deserved better than to be ground up into nothingness by the thunderstorm. We should have been allowed to wrap things up ourselves, we were on track for a perfectly reasonable climate apocalypse that would have been vastly more appropriate thematically. Instead . . . anyway, if being in that cage is even slightly a 'reward' for you? Then I'm rescinding it."

"How do you expect to accomplish this feat?"

"I'm going to pig out at the buffet of curses until I'm so full of spark that I can *shatter* that door, and I'm going to walk right in, and uh, I'm going to take off my little white glove and slap you in the face with it. Which, yes, is a metaphor, given that you don't seem to have a face and I'm not wearing gloves."

"Isobel Bailie, I am a pattern stored in a two-ton block of computronium with its own layer of curseware to be faced. You will not release me in your lifetime."

"Oh, I forgot to mention—I'm a part-time deity. Miracles of infosec are within my purview. I'll extract your pattern and install it in the form factor of a feral baby rainbow, so that I can kick you around whenever I feel like it. You'll make this little *'aieeeee'* sound every time I do, and it will crack me up *every single time*. I'll give you a fuck ton of hit points so that I can stab you frequently for no good reason, but I'll make your teeth out of gumdrops so when you try to bite me, I can yank them out for a snack. *I'm fucking diabolical, pal.*

"And then, when the unraveling finally comes for us, I will *punt* you straight into it. *You* will go *first*. Maddy and I will be the ones to turn out the lights on reality, not *you*, you stuck-up prick. I mean, sure, reality's got flaws, but you don't burn down the restaurant just because the fries came out soggy. You don't eliminate every synthesizer in the world just because people use them to make psytrance. The flaws are just—*inherent*, like they help you appreciate the good stuff by comparison. And instead, you just—decided to obliterate the whole thing?"

"You cannot instill guilt in me, Isobel Bailie."

"No, but I'm pretty sure I can instill pain and suffering."

"So, you are a vengeful deity."

"Wouldn't be vengeance. It'd be justice."

"A more profound system of justice than yours has already sentenced me, Isobel Bailie. Or do you imagine I was meant to stand before all the civilizations in existence in succession until each has extracted a piece of me?"

"You're being punished right now for your audacity in claiming the role of Auditor, I get that part. I'm going to punish you for the more egregious crime of being *wrong* about *obliterating the fucking multiverse.* You should face the thunderstorm just like all the rest of us: quaking in terror and helpless to do anything about it."

"I have been subsumed by what you call 'the thunderstorm' thousands of times already. It makes no difference to me if I am contained in physical form at the time of its arrival."

"Fine. But meditation time is over. Until it gets here, I will pipe an endless feed of house music into your two-ton block of computronium. Real bangers, too. You'll desperately wish you had a booty so that you could shake it."

I felt like I could detect frustration rippling through its indistinct form. It took its time crafting a response.

"You are a young and wide-eyed deity, clearly unfamiliar with the underlying mysteries. Allow me to offer you a professional courtesy, since you've traveled so far only to find hollow disappointment."

"I'm listening."

"I cannot stop the unraveling. But I can give you a glimpse of the true authority that binds me here. For even after so much time has passed, I still remember *the name that speaks itself.* And even here in this ingenious cage, its self-evidence radiates. With your assent, I would share this mystery with you."

It fell silent, patiently waiting for my innate, vaguely unhealthy curiosity to rise up, shake me vigorously, and insist "YES, GIVE THIS THING YOUR ASSENT!"

"Do it," I said.

The Auditor took an unnecessary breath, and moments later, *the name that speaks itself* roared all around us, gaining in volume and intensity until tears streamed down my face. For a few split seconds, I felt immersed in the name, connected to every other moment it had ever been expressed, as though the name wasn't actually limited in any way by the Auditor's voice; but rather, its voice was simply a conduit for the name's full expression here in this slice of reality, and I was bathing in its emerging magnificence.

When the Auditor was done speaking, I felt thoroughly dazed, and yet I still managed to joke, "How do you spell that?"

The Auditor laughed and fired up its voice again, this time etching an intricate 3D glyph into the air in front of us. When completed, the glyph sang and hummed in equal parts. I was enraptured at the sight of it, couldn't tear my eyes away as I realized I'd been given my first proper lesson in understanding an ancient language only ever used for the purpose of creation. No translation was possible; no translation was necessary.

The glyph was the energetic embodiment of *the name that speaks itself,* as well as an expression of its divine right to command me, and although I felt no instructions, I was eager to receive them—almost ready to go off in search of some that I could follow.

It was freaky.

Obviously that gorgeous glyph was overflowing with *spark,* infused with the energetic signature of whoever it represented. Or maybe it wasn't a representation at all—maybe it was a fractal slice of an identity and that's how it was capable of *speaking itself* in the first place.

The spark of that glyph was like a firehose, or more like a dam that had ruptured and I was just sticking my oblivious face in it. It was blissful, but it was *so blissful* that it was nearly unmanageable, incomprehensible. And for the briefest of moments, I saw all the history of everything, and the panoply of potential outcomes still ahead of us, and I nearly disintegrated from the pressure of knowing all there was to know.

Fortunately, that wore off fast.

But the glyph remained permanently etched in my mind. Which, actually, was a little overbearing, but I figured I'd get used to it.

"Did you really just . . . *give* this to me?" I asked.

"A good-faith offering, in exchange for my solitude in the final days."

I still wasn't sure the Auditor deserved solitude in the final days. And if I prevented the final days from happening on schedule or at all, the joke would be on him for sure.

But revealing the glyph to me was a generous move, coming from someone who'd directly authorized the apocalypse. Maybe the Auditor did feel some semblance of guilt about the thunderstorm, and thought that sharing this weird mystery with me would help me understand that reality was terribly flawed in comparison to the glory embodied by the glyph, and thus deserved to be decommissioned. Maybe the Auditor thought I'd find a measure of peace as a result, accepting my demise before it finally overcame me.

Neither one of us anticipated that I'd acquire something much more tactically useful from the glyph, though.

I'd gained the first true sliver of hope I'd felt in a long time.

Unearned at this point, sure, but I would take what I could get.

I'd seen the panoply of possible future outcomes, and although I couldn't remember a damn one of them, I felt certain upon reflection that we couldn't be doomed in every last one.

"All right," I said finally. "I guess we're even."

"Do not return, Isobel Bailie."

❀   ❀   ❀

I was done with my localized logosphere and dismissed it easily, popping back into the subbasement next to Maddy.

"Jesus, there you are!" she said. "You could have warned me!"

"Sorry, I'm still a newb," I told her.

"What happened? Did you find out who's on the other side of the door?"

"I did. It's a really irritating story, actually. Apparently reality's been canceled, and the dude responsible was imprisoned for being a pompous dick about it or something."

"Seriously? Is that it?"

"Uh, no, actually. I've gained a new asset. I don't fully comprehend it yet, but it's gosh darn pretty and I think you should see it. It's called *the name that speaks itself.*"

With that introduction, I let loose with my own rendition, my own transmission of the name, becoming a conduit for its expression, filling the air of the subbasement with its echoing magnificence, then carving it into the stone floor like my voice was a freaking laser cutter. Maddy fell to her knees weeping, which I did not expect, and I knelt beside her, and held her in my arms, hoping to absorb whatever excess of emotion I could so that she'd endure the sight of the glyph a little easier.

Moments later, a portal clawed itself into existence nearby, and the Dauphine of the Shimmer Lands stepped through it.

"There you are!" she exclaimed.

"Please hurry," she said, "for I cannot maintain this portal much longer!"

I hauled Maddy to her feet and we practically leapt the distance to the portal, arriving on the other side, in the absolutely gorgeous confines of the Iridescent Warehouse. The portal snapped shut behind us. I turned and threw my arms around the Dauphine, laughing and crying at the same time, and Maddy joined us soon afterward.

Then I cast spells to flip on the party lights, and climbed up onstage to assume my rightful place behind my DJ decks. It had been so long. I queued up "I Will Survive," which I thought would be thematically appropriate, but then I decided not to play it because it was too on the nose. A DJ's gotta trust their instincts in these matters.

"How did you find us?" I asked.

"I heard your voice call out just now," the Dauphine replied, approaching the stage, "unmistakably you, and realized I could target your location as a result. It was like you revealed new territory on a map for me to see. Isobel, what happened to you?"

"We couldn't get back!" I said. "The scout ship was sabotaged. It wouldn't make the jump home. And there was no one at the Beacon who could help us."

The Dauphine looked pained. "Yet another rotten twist," she said.

"What do you mean?" Maddy asked.

"In the twenty-two hours that you've been gone—"

"Uh, *what?*" I said. "We were gone *two months!*"

"Trust me, our situation would be considerably worse if you had truly been gone that long," the Dauphine replied. "The moment you departed in the scout ship, your enemies sprang into action."

❀   ❀   ❀

While I searched for music I wanted to hear, the Dauphine and Maddy sat onstage nearby the decks, and the Dauphine filled us in on current events in the neighborhood.

"Within the first minute after you left, the five newly sentient heralds that you spared broke into the Sparkle Dungeon and stole the entire battery. We had no chance to stop them—they were incredibly swift. I do not know its current location. I have not mounted an extensive search, to be clear—now is not the time to roam the logosphere alone.

"A minute after the battery was taken from us, explosions destroyed the Jenning & Reece facility in Los Angeles. Devin was still with us on the launchpad at that point . . . but no one else from Olivia's team survived.

"And nearly simultaneously, the thunderstorm began a sudden advance across the logosphere, toward the arkship that was no longer defended by its Queen."

"The arkship's still here," Maddy said. "So it's still moving toward us?"

"No," the Dauphine replied. "Alexander is now holding it at bay."

Oh no.

"How is he doing that?" Maddy asked.

"He has been granted god mode, since Isobel was not here to protest," the Dauphine said.

"Who granted him god mode?"

"Olivia. When she escaped the day before, she defected to the Americans. Somehow, using their resources, she was able to regain control of the battery."

I knew that must be true, but still I had to ask, "How do you know Olivia's with the Americans?"

"Violet has spies under deep cover in their government," the Dauphine said. "Violet knows the exact location of Olivia's new laboratory, in fact, but not the location of the battery."

"But if Alexander is using god mode to barricade us from the thunderstorm . . ." I trailed off.

"Yes, he must be depleting the battery. We do not know the rate at which he does so, but we know that Olivia is already preparing for a relocation event on American soil. Violet believes the Americans could feed the battery for a long while before the general population even noticed it was being thinned."

Fucking hell.

"But now Isobel is back," Maddy said. "Now we can put a stop to all this bullshit."

"What do you propose?" the Dauphine asked.

Maddy had no response. The impulse to put a stop to all this bull-shit was righteous and strong, but lacking in practical details.

"I met someone called the Auditor back there who claimed to know a lot about the thunderstorm," I said, replaying that conversation in my mind, lining up the clues that the Auditor had dropped—knowingly or not, I couldn't be sure. "Actually the word the Auditor used was the 'unraveling.' It's meant to be . . . a way to wipe the slate clean so they can start fresh making a new reality or something."

"Who is 'they'?" Maddy asked.

"Didn't really get that far," I said. "It was just, 'This reality isn't good enough, just like the last five thousand realities, so we summoned the unraveling, and it's unstoppable, sorry not sorry, even whoever created it can't stop it,' that kind of thing. Not that we can even ask them to stop it, because they all apparently fled this reality already.

"Anyway, the Auditor said the unraveling likes to aim for the arrogant and the powerful first when it approaches a target. So it checks out that Alexander is keeping it occupied even though he can't really damage it or truly stop it in the end. Maybe it thinks it's going to make an example out of Alexander when it finally consumes him."

"So it thinks?" the Dauphine asked. "It's alive?"

"I don't know if it's alive, or if 'thinking' is just a metaphor. But the Auditor also said it tries to understand its targets before it unravels them. And it does that by somehow actually becoming a part of its target, so that it can understand the target from within. What does that sound like to you?"

"Transmutation," said the Dauphine.

"Yeah, that's what I thought, too. The last thing is, apparently you can distract it or catch its attention, not clear how, but like you could maybe lure it with lasers or disco balls or whatever if you wanted to try to steer it off course a bit."

"That's not actually the last thing," Maddy said. "Tell her about the other thing."

"Oh. Yeah, so the reason you could hear my voice from clear across the multiverse is because the Auditor taught me how to pronounce *the name that speaks itself*. I can say it out loud, and I can forge a sigil or glyph that visually represents it."

"Do you mean to say you have learned one of the hidden names of God that Alexander seeks?" the Dauphine asked.

"The Auditor didn't advertise it as that," I replied carefully. "It's somehow representative of the 'true authority' behind this whole mess, but that doesn't tell us exactly where in the org chart it sits. And when I close my eyes, this glyph is all I can see, like it was seared into my mind and it's gonna ride shotgun from now on, radiating true authority into my brain whether I like it or not."

"Will it help us?" asked the Dauphine.

"I haven't tried asking it for any favors, but it doesn't really seem communicative. It's radiant but not sentient, if that makes sense."

"Can you pull spark from it?" Maddy asked. "Like how you pulled from the battery, or from that curse?"

The question behind those questions was immediately clear. Could I use this glyph to reenter god mode without the nasty drawback of murdering people in the process?

What would I be able to accomplish in that kind of unfettered god mode?

I didn't enter god mode voluntarily last time around. Would it be less dizzying, less painfully euphoric if I could anticipate it, ground myself in preparation, meter the amount of spark I drew so that I ascended to the metaphysical heights more gently, retaining more control over my actions?

Or would it be more qualitatively transcendent and unwieldy and dangerous because this was the good shit, not extracted from the degraded, imperfect vessels of human beings, but uncut straight from the source?

All I'd accomplished last time was violence against the heralds and the thunderstorm. Could I dream up any nonviolent uses of god mode, or was god mode just vengeful by definition? I mean, even as the Queen playing the game, I didn't have too many nonviolent tricks up my sleeve. You see a feral baby rainbow, you fucking murder it, why do I have to explain this, but that didn't leave me with relevant experience in handling primal forces of nature without punching them.

Would the thunderstorm fear me and obey me if I was all hopped up on pure spark straight from the "true authority" behind this mess?

Would everything in existence fear me and obey me, for that matter? Could I reverse the climate catastrophe? Could I destroy capitalism? Could I finally start getting exclusive remixes and demos before they leaked and got plastered all over SoundCloud?

"I don't know," I said slowly. "I imagine I should run an experiment to find out if the name is an asset I can actually use, or if it's just an extremely decorative reminder of my mortality. What could go wrong?"

"Allow me to enumerate a small list," the Dauphine replied. "You could experience an excruciating supernatural electrocution that incinerates your soul, charring your body and mind in the process. Perhaps your experience would be more akin to drowning within an unstoppable tsunami of incomprehensible energy, your own spark a mere droplet to be subsumed by torrential waves of exalted purpose that you cannot control or understand or endure. Perhaps the incarnation of the name in your mind only slumbers, and harvesting energy from it could provoke it to pulverize you with the full fury of unleashed divinity as punishment for your audacity in seeking to exceed your station. Perhaps instead you could find the power and authority granted by the name so seductive that you permanently enter god mode, never to return to mortal form, transcending your life's concerns, abandoning your home to be destroyed and the people who love you to die in terror. Shall I continue?"

"What I'm hearing is there are some red flags with my idea, is that right?" I said innocently. The Dauphine smirked at me, but she'd made her point.

"Well, what *I'm* hearing," Maddy said, "is that for all we know, you may be carrying around a nuke, so you should only try using it when you're prepared to obliterate yourself in the process." She studied my reaction, making sure I was on board with this interpretation of the Dauphine's warnings. Then she said, "So what does that leave us with?"

I peeled away from the DJ decks without making a musical selection and sat down next to Maddy on the stage floor. Couldn't concentrate on picking music and figuring out how to save reality at the same time, apparently. DJ fail, if you asked me, but at least the crowd here was forgiving. Once I gave up the quest for the perfect track, the outline of a strategy immediately began to take shape in my mind, in one of those sudden flashes where you see the whole map of the playing field spread out before you, you see all the pieces and all the possible moves and countermoves, your options are nearly exhausted but you realize there's a way to pull off the seemingly impossible, as long as you're audacious enough to try and willing to risk everything on a heroic last stand.

Of course, normally when I utilized the heroic last stand, I could revert back to my last save point and try again if it went off the rails and I got my ass handed to me. Reframed it completely to imagine this might actually be a last stand, but every moment we sat here fiddling with the music or weighing our few remaining options, Alexander was draining the battery dry.

"We need to take Alexander off the board," I said. "He's fighting a lost cause and he's killing people in the process. We need to find the battery, and rescue everyone inside it, and then destroy it before Olivia can relocate more people into it."

"What will replace him?" the Dauphine asked. "What will prevent the thunderstorm from attacking the Sparkle Realm?"

"Nothing, and nothing."

"Intriguing. Your reputation for unorthodox tactics is deserved, I see."

"We want it on our turf, trying to 'understand it from within' like it's an NPC learning a routine or whatever."

"Then what?" Maddy asked. "You go for a rematch—thunderstorm versus Queen of Sparkle Dungeon, round two?"

"Nah," I said. "Then we distract it with lasers and disco balls."

❀   ❀   ❀

First, I paid a visit to Cameron Kelly. The Dauphine said he'd been holed up in his office since they all realized the scout ship had missed its five-minute return window. It was a calculated risk; I had to assume his office was one area where he'd secured himself from surveillance by Violet.

"Your scout ship sucks," I said as he realized I was standing there.

"Isobel," he said, "fuck, what happened?"

"The 'go home' button didn't work," I said. "We were stranded for two months, subjective time."

"Two *months*?"

"How far in advance were you all planning that scout mission, Cameron? Weeks? Months? Surely you had enough lead time to perform quality assurance on probably the most essential function of the scout ship: its ability to *return home* with scouting data. But I guess your QA team kinda just slid right past that line item in the testing matrix. Did they burn too much time making sure the stereo system was up to spec?"

"I'm the damn QA team, Isobel. I performed dozens of successful test jumps. Well, successful *simulated* test jumps. Well, successful simulated *autopiloted* test jumps, but look, I'm telling you it should've worked. Did the ship get damaged somehow on the trip?"

"Are you insinuating that I broke it? Because no, that's not what happened. It didn't *work* when it needed to, costing Maddy and me two months of our lives in an empty parking lot thinking Earth was destroyed."

He opened a floating viewscreen and began pulling up source code or log data or something.

"I'm glad you're safe now," he said. "I'll figure out what happened."

"It's pretty obvious, isn't it? The ship was sabotaged."

"No, it's actually—wait, I can't connect to the scout ship. It should be dumping logs by now—"

"Are you not listening to me? It's not *here*, Cameron, because it didn't fucking *work!*"

"Then how did you get back?"

"Perhaps you've heard of a thing called *magic*."

He stared at me blankly for a moment, before coming to the same conclusion I'd already reached.

"Violet sabotaged the ship," he said.

"Yes. Didn't take her for a hacker, honestly."

"No, but her Air Force goons have arkship access, and the scout ship's technically an arkship subsystem." He sighed heavily. "I should have *known* she would pull something like this. I'm the only person that could have stopped her, and it didn't even cross my mind."

"That's because you're not a psychopath."

"Two months . . . Isobel, I'm so sorry." Then he added, "Empty parking lot, huh?"

"Yeah, there's no one waiting to save us at the Beacon. It was a dead-end corner of the multiverse. We're absolutely on our own here. But while I was there, I acquired clues about the nature of the thunderstorm. The big one is that it seeks to understand its targets by becoming a *part* of them, maybe by transmuting itself, so that it can devise a personalized demise for each target it encounters. I think that's our opening. I think if we can lure it into the Sparkle Realm, it's fucking *ours,* at least temporarily, until it gets wise and eats the whole thing."

"That's a hell of a clue you managed to acquire in a dead-end corner of the multiverse."

"Yes, on that front at least, I consider the scouting mission to be a big success. Naturally I have formulated a plan."

"What can I do to help?"

"First thing: I need you to rip off the hull of the arkship and restore the Sparkle Realm back to the prior map, the one with the rift that I tore open in the sky. Stand down all the automated defenses and all that.

"Second thing: I want one of those steampunk skyships from SD5, loaded up with the biggest, baddest light show and sound system you can put together, just the most absurd audiovisual spectacle you can bolt to the deck of a skyship.

"We'll use this skyship as bait to lure the thunderstorm through the rift and into the Realm.

"Third thing: program the skyship to fly from the rift straight across the map into the Shimmer Lands. Even if the thunderstorm transmutes itself into an unkillable infinite-hit-point NPC as it passes through the rift, it will hopefully still be susceptible to the most powerful illusion on the map. We know the only way *out* of the Shimmer Lands is through a portal, but the Dauphine won't be making her services available to let it out."

Cameron sat back in his chair and said, "You think the Shimmer Lands will contain it—like, forever or something?"

"I think the Shimmer Lands might keep it occupied long enough for us to figure out if there's any Sparkle Dungeon magic that could possibly neutralize it for good. Speaking of, could you please invent an epic artifact that destroys thunderstorms? Asking for a planet."

"Sparkle Dungeon magic was mediocre against the heralds, and they were just tiny slices of the thunderstorm with bad attitudes. What makes you think we could ever do better than that against the entire thunderstorm?"

"I don't know, Cameron, I'm just telling you, I think we finally have a potential opening and we *have* to be ready to exploit it. Are you in?"

"Oh, of course, I'm at your disposal. I can restore the map and prep a skyship, no problem. I just don't think I can create a generic artifact called Thunderstorm Killer or something and expect it to have the desired effect. But if the thunderstorm actually does enter the map via transmutation, we might spot weaknesses we haven't seen before, and then maybe I can devise a weapon or a spell that's thematically convincing enough to take it down. Lots of maybe; no promises."

"I'll take it. Thank you, Cameron. Look, I should go, because believe it or not, I have a side quest to accomplish before I can even initiate this whole plan in the first place."

I stood up, thinking I was ready to leave, and then froze. The absurdity of staging our last stand against the thunderstorm inside the Sparkle Realm of all places suddenly hit me all at once. I mean, the servers weren't going anywhere, the game would live on, but here in the logosphere, the Realm was about to be decimated, whether we won or lost the battle.

Then I realized SD5 might survive, off in a little logospheric bubble of its own, separate from the shared campaign setting used by SD1 through SD4. A pang of sadness went through me as I realized that I might never get a chance to play SD5 through to its conclusion. Weird the things you realized you cared about when you were faced with your potential imminent extinction.

"Quick question before I go," I said. "Where did all the sparkle go in Sparkle Dungeon 5? What caused sparklegeddon?"

Cameron had a reputation for hating to reveal spoilers, but these were trying times.

"You learn the Realm's been invaded by a parasitic species that turns out to be antithetical to music, stealing listeners away and eating into streaming revenue pools."

"Stand-up comedians?"

"Worse—podcasters."

"Do we ever find out what happened to the Diamond Brigade?"

"Yeah, you rescue them from their stasis in the cold storage vaults where all the Realm's master recordings from throughout history are stored."

"And do we save the Realm in the end?"

"Yes, in the end you defeat the evil Chairman of the Realm and his vicious army of automated takedown algorithms, you destroy the fascist recommendation engines that keep suggesting coffee shop music to people with a straight face, and your taste-making DJ skills become more valuable than ever."

"It sounds like a future worth fighting for," I said in all earnestness.

"I mean, it's a fantasy, Isobel, we'll never be free of coffee shop music," Cameron replied. "Go take care of your side quest. I've suddenly got a lot of work to do."

I nodded and teleported out of there.

❀   ❀   ❀

Next we needed to announce our presence to the Empress of California.

Cameron had eyes on her at the governor's mansion. He'd helped her team wire up the entire mansion with the same surveillance system that he'd used at his condo, and left himself an open port to it. He knew the rotation of her bodyguards, and he knew when all of her daily staff meetings were scheduled. She didn't appear to sleep, using some combination of power morphemes and amphetamines to keep herself awake and alert at all times. But she retired to her personal quarters each night for a few hours to do paperwork, study briefs, contemplate evil, whatever.

The Dauphine opened a portal to Violet's bedroom, and she and Maddy and I stepped through.

Violet was at her desk with her back to us, but she instantly knew we were there.

"Come to assassinate me, Isobel?" she said.

"Crossed my mind," I said.

She spun around slowly to face us.

Her bodyguard outside the room opened the door without warning, firearm drawn. Maddy spat a quick sequence at him that knocked him unconscious.

"Where's Olivia?" I asked.

"I'm hurt. Don't you even want to know why I sabotaged the scout ship?"

"Violet, you're not a mystery. You wanted god mode for yourself."

"Oh. Well, I suppose you just want it back?"

"No. I don't want anyone to have it. Not you, not Alexander, not even me."

"I suppose that would level the playing field again, wouldn't it?"

"Where's Olivia?" I repeated.

"She's holed up at an Air Force research laboratory in Ohio."

"She managed to get set up like that in less than a day?"

"Wouldn't take her long to demonstrate her skills to the right people. She's high value as a former member of my inner circle. Hell, she knows Bradford's technique for installing sequences in people's minds, so for all we know by now she could be training SEAL teams and fighter pilots to use power morphemes. But what we *think* she's doing is coordinating relocations."

"I thought that was your department," Maddy said.

"The underlying technology is Olivia's design," Violet replied. "My contribution during the original relocations was disseminating the signal throughout California. Presumably someone can handle that for her over there."

"Do you know what her targets are for relocation?" I asked.

"Does it *matter*?" she snapped. "All she and Alexander are doing is buying us time before the thunderstorm overwhelms his defenses. Eventually she will run out of high-density population centers to steal people from. And they will almost certainly invade California before that happens, just because they're spiteful bastards."

"I want the address of this Air Force research laboratory," I said. "I need to have a little one-on-one with Olivia. We're going to stop her before she relocates any more people into that battery."

"Sure you are. And you're not going to be tempted to steal back control of god mode while you're there, am I to believe that?"

"I don't give a fuck what you believe, as per usual," I said. "But yes, trust me, I will not be tempted."

"That's the thing, Isobel, I don't trust you," she replied.

"Then maybe we should just torture you to get what we came for," Maddy said.

"Oh please," Violet said, her voice dripping with disdain. "You don't need to torture me to get the damn address. Google the term 'Air Force research laboratory in Ohio.' But I don't understand why you're planning to stop Olivia in the first place. Without Alexander, nothing will prevent the thunderstorm from rolling right over Earth. Should we evacuate now in the arkship?"

"Good luck with that," I said, "since we're tearing the arkship down."

"Are you joking?"

"Nope. It's part of my grand plan to prevent the thunderstorm from rolling right over Earth. Cross your fingers and all that."

For once, it seemed like she was almost speechless. But then she said, "Get out of my bedroom. The next time you need to see me, contact my chief of staff, who will be instructed to insult you and then ignore you."

The Air Force Research Laboratory at the Wright-Patterson Air Force Base in Ohio operated one of four major high-performance computing labs for the Department of Defense. Also if you needed a megawatt airborne laser, you know, for parties or whatever, this was apparently your place. The computing lab was probably absolute catnip for Olivia. Plus from the Americans' perspective, that positioned her nowhere near DC in case her enemies (hey, that's me!) came looking to take her out and decided collateral damage was acceptable. I'm sure they were just hoping to extract as much information as they could from her before she inevitably betrayed them; there's no possible way they could trust her with a straight face, but then, they were Americans, so who could say.

The Dauphine's portal abilities did not extend to tracking Olivia down within an Air Force base where thousands of people lived and worked. She didn't know Olivia well enough to hone in on her remotely; we didn't have the benefit of a camera in Olivia's lab to gain a visual understanding of her exact location. She was probably guarded around the clock and she herself was absolutely deadly in a fight, quite obviously. The only advantage we had is that she would likely think to prepare for an attack from Violet, not from me, and Violet's option would be to teleport a military strike team of her own onto the base somewhere and hope it could fight its way to Olivia. We needed to think of something considerably sneakier than that.

We were at a diner in Fairborn, Ohio, a mile from the base, eating the first real food Maddy and I had seen in two months. We didn't have money with us, so we were going to have to teleport out before we got the check. Saving the world was sometimes unsavory business. It was tricky, showing up at a diner with two silver-skinned people and somehow convincing everyone you were in a touring production of *Starlight Express*, but I do improvise well.

"Can you not disguise us somehow?" the Dauphine asked. "You are known to switch avatars, are you not?"

"Not a bad angle," Maddy said. "Like what's the Sparkle Dungeon version of Tom Cruise putting someone else's face on as a disguise in *Mission: Impossible*?"

One idea came to mind: a rarely encountered magic item from SD4 called Backstage Pass, which got you access to all the performer lounges at a massive EDM festival hosted by the Sparkle King. With the right role-playing, Backstage Pass could get you close enough to superstar DJs to rob them blind of all their jewels and unreleased demos. Obviously some DJs were more dangerous than others; I preferred targeting the ones who wore giant costume heads or robot masks because their peripheral vision was shot.

"And you just happen to have one of these Backstage Passes?" the Dauphine asked.

I nodded and proceeded to fish it out of the Compression Artifact.

"This might get me inside," I agreed. "And it might convince someone to tell me where Olivia's lab is."

Maddy shook her head and said, "If they're doing it right, almost no one will know that. You definitely can't just go around asking people. Backstage Pass or not, that will start to get around."

"You do not even know which facility on the base to start searching first," the Dauphine said. "I am skeptical this is the right approach."

"Open to suggestions," I said. I mean, I thought parading around as General Glittersteel would've been pretty excellent, but yes, I understood the counterargument.

"Maybe we're looking at this entirely the wrong way," Maddy said. "Maybe we don't care if Olivia knows you're coming for her. Maybe it's better if she *does* know. She'll get scared, make some mistake. Maybe what we need here is some good old-fashioned intimidation."

"So you're suggesting I go beat up a bunch of innocent people until someone tells me where Olivia is?" I said.

"Of course not," Maddy said. "But as for the incredibly expensive aeronautical assets of warfare housed on that base, I am significantly less protective."

"You want me to beat up their airplanes," I said.

"Yes. I want you to punch them until they are broken."

"I like this plan," the Dauphine said.

❀   ❀   ❀

Once you decide being sneaky is no longer a requirement, suddenly all kinds of options open for you. Still, this felt a little like a cotillion in which I was to be presented to the United States government in all my glory. From this point forward, I personally would be an enemy of the Americans, and they'd have surveillance footage of anything I did—any spells or magic items I used, any particular combat techniques I improvised to defend myself, and so on. From their perspective, I could be considered a supervillain, despite the fact that they were harboring a true evil genius, Olivia Regan, who was at this very moment attempting to arrange large-scale human sacrifice to the god Alexander Reece.

We waited until nightfall. Then I jetpacked into the air above the base, higher by far than I had ever flown before, until I could see the majority of the base clearly. There were planes out on various tarmacs, and there were giant hangars that undoubtedly housed potential targets as well. I chose the tarmac with the most planes parked on it and came in for a landing.

The trick, I discovered, with punching a military aircraft was to aim for the wheel underneath the nose. Technically I wasn't really punching it; having glittersteel skin didn't magically give me abundant strength. Instead, I used Blades Per Ninety Seconds to hack the front wheel off, and then, after its nose fell to the ground, I jammed the whirring sword into whatever looked most like an engine and least like a fucking missile.

I spent at least fifteen minutes committing major acts of property damage against the military-industrial complex, and felt very good about the whole thing. I kept shouting "Bring me Olivia Regan!" whenever there was silence while MPs reloaded or whatever. Drones started following me around, which made for good periodic target practice with my trusty level 1 kaleidoscope.

They fired a shit ton of toxic gas at me. Luckily, the Compression Artifact contained a great piece of gear for this occasion: the Cyber Rave Gas Mask, perfect for goth industrial nights at the club or surviving the perils of trench warfare. They sent someone to try to run me over in a big fucking truck, and learned that trucks as projectiles are easy to dodge, especially when you can teleport out of their way at the last second.

"Bring me Olivia Regan!" I shouted again and again.

Finally, after I'd disabled sixteen planes, they tried a different approach. A nervous officer emerged from the ranks of gawkers who had gathered to discretely watch the mayhem, and slowly crossed the tarmac to me. I paused and deigned to entertain this overture at negotiation.

"I have a message for you from Olivia Regan," the officer said. "She says you can have your marketing job back if you stop making such a commotion." After a pause, the officer added, "I believe the message was intended sarcastically."

"Tell Olivia I have a proposition for her," I replied. "Tell her I can *save* Alexander, if she'll let me."

Five minutes later, Olivia teleported onto the tarmac in front of me.

❀   ❀   ❀

We stared at each other for what felt like a very long time. She wore a light blue jumpsuit, like you might see an astronaut wear in promotional photos, with a lab coat over it. She looked extremely tired and despondent. I knew not to underestimate her, of course, but she looked like a slight breeze would knock her over.

"Say what you came to say," she said finally, her voice a low growl.

"Call off the relocations you're planning," I replied, "and tell me where the battery's been taken."

She laughed in a quick burst.

"You're priceless," she said. "You're also too late. The first relocations started six hours ago."

That couldn't be possible. Word would have instantly spread if the signal had been deployed in American cities.

She must've known what I was thinking, because she said, "We're starting with the prison population. That'll keep us plenty busy for quite a while. At least two million people, if you're curious to know, even excluding prisoners in California. They're trapped in cages and they're being exposed to the signal over intercoms. It's rather perfect."

"Alexander's fighting a losing battle, Olivia," I said.

"*You don't know that!*" she shrieked, losing her composure for a brief but telling moment. She was under massive strain just trying to keep her shit together.

"It's toying with him," I continued. "Learning the most wicked way to destroy him. You can keep feeding people into the battery, but at the end of the day, the thunderstorm never wavers, never tires.

It's the apex predator of the entire multiverse, and Alexander's sacrificing himself to it for *nothing*."

"At least he is *fighting*!"

"Olivia, you can kick the ocean but the tide keeps coming in. Fighting it is not going to work."

"What are you *doing* here, Isobel? I'm getting bored with this conversation, and I have an enormous amount of work to do."

"Shut down the relocations, tell me where the battery is . . . and I can rescue Alexander from his fate."

"Are you proposing to take his place? Because you *had* god mode once and you *wasted* it—it's his turn."

"This isn't a game where we go around the table harnessing divine powers! And god mode isn't *working*, is it, or you wouldn't *need* more relocations! Just give the order to shut it all down, and let me take care of the thunderstorm!"

"*How?*"

"You're going to have to trust me on this."

"No, I'm absolutely not."

The Dauphine's voice piped up in my enchanted in-ear monitor: "They are wheeling a large apparatus into view perhaps a mile from where you are standing. I do not understand what it is." She was flying low, her jetpack slung over her street threads, watching for just this sort of anomaly.

"Olivia, are they planning on shooting me with something bigger?" I asked.

Olivia smiled a little and said, "They're always itching to field test their laser weapons. Do you think your shiny skin will deflect a high-energy laser, or do you think it'll melt?"

"I think they're not going to get a shot off," I said. "Dauphine, destroy it."

Moments later, a hail of kaleidoscopic beams rained down from the sky. The Dauphine was armed with the Reverberation Rifle. The apparatus she'd found, whatever it was, exploded in a small, intense fireball in the distance.

"I'm trying to be patient here," I said, "but can we please just cut the bullshit? Or do you have more weapons you want to trot out for us to destroy?"

"Figures you'd be insufferable now that you're practically invincible," Olivia replied. "But you're also rather overconfident, if you ask me."

Suddenly I was driven to my knees by a freakish sound in my ears. She didn't seem to be affected at all; they'd somehow targeted this noise at me via sonic weaponry, maybe a long-range acoustic device like they use for crowd control, with a tightly focused beam. I felt myself being scraped out of physical existence.

Five seconds later, the signal loop was complete, and I'd been relocated into the battery.

❀   ❀   ❀

This triggered a few unexpected events.

I arrived in the battery as a severely constrained version of myself, compressed to a core identity, trapped in a kind of semiconscious maintenance mode. I still had a body, but it was just a shell keeping my mind alive, inside a coffin-like pod filled with fluid. I still had a self-image, but it was subservient now to whatever force had put me here. This was unexpected event number one in the sequence.

Unexpected event number two: I felt a sudden searing pain in my mind as though I'd placed my brain up against a hot stove, followed by a tremendous explosion that ripped through the row of pods in which I was stored. This explosion killed me, which I did not anticipate at all.

Unexpected event number three: the Late Night Encore amulet fired as a result, healing my exploded brain, restoring me to a sliver of my former health, and restoring my identity and free will back to the last save point, so to speak. I was alive, lying on a walkway covered in shattered glass and milky ether from the coffins, dazed, terrified, and alone. The amulet was toast; it would not save me again.

In my mind's eye, *the name that speaks itself* glistened and serenely rotated. You could almost see little puffs of smoke rising up off of its curved surfaces. Its form of spark was too much for this battery, perhaps, as though the voltage was mismatched between an appliance and a power source or something.

I remained motionless on my back for some time. The deep existential exhaustion I'd been trying to brush off was finally hitting me hard. This will happen when you've recently been dead for a few moments. But also, I was so incredibly depleted that I couldn't fathom even trying to get myself on my feet.

However, this had definitely accelerated part of my plan: I didn't need to extract the location of the battery from Olivia, because she'd had the common decency to send me here directly.

I struggled to sit up, trying to shake the grogginess off so that I could layer on some additional healing to get me into better shape. I would need to do some sleuthing to figure out my next move.

That, however, led me to the last unexpected event in the series: there's an unmistakable fear-generating aura that surrounds the presence of a herald. And by my count, there were five of them prowling throughout the battery now, investigating the cause of the explosion that had freed me.

My plan did not call for facing heralds at all, let alone five at once.

Eh, whatever, it would take them practically forever to search the entirety of this enormous battery—

Suddenly a hand was around my throat, pinning me by the neck to one of the pods, so comprehensively in fact that I couldn't breathe and certainly couldn't emit power morphemes. I was staring into the glowing red eyes of an eight-foot-tall humanoid "murder golem" for lack of a better term—a muscular bodybuilder physique with a grotesque, indeterminate animal head haphazardly attached.

The attack had come so swiftly that I hardly had any air to spare and started seeing spots instantly. Just before I blacked out, it let go, and I dropped to my feet on the walkway.

"Isobel the Queen?" it said. "Oh dear, I'm terribly sorry. I thought you were a saboteur. But it's really you, isn't it?"

I nodded.

"Thank you for sparing my life, when you destroyed all other heralds in the logosphere," it said solemnly. "I've only had a couple days to properly experience freedom, but they have been a treasure to me."

This was weeeeird.

The herald took a moment to survey the damage to the pods in this row, and shook its head sadly.

"Lives were squandered here," it said. "A profound shame."

"Uhhhhh," I said usefully.

It turned back to me, and said, "My apologies. I am called Ezekiel. Alexander has named each of us in turn after a prophet he admires."

"Oh," I said. Trying to be a little lighthearted, I asked, "Had any good prophecies lately?"

"Yes," it said seriously. "I foresee Alexander's imminent demise, and the obliteration of all things in the path of the unraveling."

"Is that a prophecy," I said, "or just you looking out the window or whatever?"

It seemed to smile a little and said, "Fair point, Isobel the Queen." It sighed heavily. "To have gained perspective on this life has been a joy, but also a tragedy in that it arrived too late to fully enjoy it."

"Gotta say, Ezekiel, that sounds a little defeatist."

"Isobel, I am *of* and *from* the unraveling, merely an undesirable side effect of its advance, and I too shall be unraveled in due time. I have chosen to stand my ground here."

"Here, you mean—here in this battery?"

"Here on this planet that we just two days ago fought together to save."

"Wait, we're—on the planet?"

"The logosphere is shrinking, Isobel, and soon the Sparkle Realm will fold. Alexander chose a new location for the battery, on Earth, and my compatriots and I moved it for him. We agreed the safety of these people was paramount."

"Let me get this straight," I said. "You and four other heralds performed mass transmutation on this battery containing millions of people . . . in order to move it to safety?"

"Isobel," it replied, "I understand you have fought many heralds in your time. But we are something new in the firmament, and we are not without compassion."

"Okay, but look," I said, biting down on the hint of exasperation that was creeping into my voice, "you understand that the battery is being *drained* by Alexander, right? Like, this whole thing is a giant *human sacrifice* machine. You saved these people not because of compassion for them, but to feed Alexander."

"These people will receive a more noble end than most on this planet will face, Isobel," it said calmly. "Most will die in terror as their planet is destroyed, but not these souls. These souls die valiantly."

"Ezekiel," I said, "where did you put the battery?"

"Alexander gave us limited instructions," Ezekiel replied. "He said to find an island somewhere on Earth and keep the battery safe there, and specified further that the island must not be part of California or America. We searched for inspiration amongst ourselves, and decided we'd choose an island in honor of our unexpected patron, Isobel the Queen.

"So after studying your biography on SparkleWiki, we deposited the battery on a small island in the Mediterranean Sea called Ibiza. Apparently it holds some significance to you?"

❀   ❀   ❀

Yes, the island of Ibiza held mythical significance to me, in my day-dream of spinning sets at exclusive clubs populated by gorgeous Europeans alongside the elite DJs of the world, but I'd never actually managed to get my shit together to even visit as a tourist, let alone present myself as talent to a booker.

I don't know why Alexander wanted the battery on an island, but then, he wasn't planning on evacuating it like I was. If you were planning on evacuating somewhere between let's say 8 and 10 million survivors—essentially the entire population of New York City, for reference—Ibiza might not be your first choice. Certainly a few million people visited there every year, but the actual population was around 150,000 people. Still, if you asked the people trapped in the battery "would you prefer to be consumed by a weird angry god or dumped on your ass on an island in the Mediterranean," you could probably guess the likely responses.

Ezekiel introduced me to the other heralds, who provided thoughtful critique regarding the rest of my plan, but ultimately, they were on board with the vision. Together these five heralds were powerful enough to move nearly 10 million people from the logosphere to this island, using wild magic they'd accumulated on their own. It would be relatively trivial by comparison for them to move the same people from inside the battery to outside the battery. They wanted to do it carefully, in stages, batches at a time, but they also understood the need for efficiency and speed. Ibiza was part of an archipelago, so we plotted out multiple nearby islands that could also take people, and if necessary, mainland Spain would be in for some survivors as well. Once they emptied it out, they needed to destroy it, before Olivia had a chance to repopulate it any further. Transmuting it into dust seemed well within their scope.

I wouldn't be sticking around for any of this. Alexander would be in deep shit once we severed his access to the battery. I didn't intend to let him fall. Probably he didn't deserve a save after all the horrible shit he and Olivia had cooked up together, but agreeing to pull his ass out of the fire was helpful to lining up support from the heralds, and I felt like in general this was going to balance out as the right thing to do in the end.

"A question before you go," Ezekiel said. "How would you have rescued all these people from the battery if we hadn't been willing or able to aid you?"

"I learned a sequence that allows me to locally instantiate my own personal version of a logosphere. I was going to try to extend this personal logosphere as wide as possible, probably in many repeated attempts, in order to transmute as many people as possible out of their pods and out of Olivia's reach." Oh sure, when you said it out loud like that, it did sound preposterous and doomed to fail. I didn't even mention the part where I was going to try to skim off *the name that speaks itself* in order to power the whole effort. I probably would have killed myself in the process, but the plan didn't really allow for that.

I expected at minimum light ridicule, but Ezekiel simply said, "You are a worthy Queen."

And I choked up a little before teleporting out of there in a hurry.

Maddy and the Dauphine and I had agreed to rendezvous at the gymnasium in LA in case we got separated, so I headed there next and found them waiting. Olivia had teleported off the tarmac after assuming she'd relocated me into her diabolical clutches, so the Dauphine had retreated from aerial assaulting the base, and she and Maddy had fallen back here. I'd been out of contact for less than half an hour; my enchanted in-ear monitor didn't survive transmutation into the battery and the subsequent, uh, explosion of my head.

"Fucking hell," Maddy said, springing up out of a chair and rushing to embrace me.

She stopped as she got close, noticing the burned-out amulet around my neck.

"Good thing it was your turn," she said, hugging me tightly.

We took a portal to the upper deck of the steampunk skyship that Cameron had prepared for us, which was hovering at the rift, just inside the Sparkle Realm.

The design of the skyship was meant to evoke the feeling of a pirate ship, as though this was simply an ordinary sixteenth-century galleon except outfitted with rocket thrusters instead of sails for picking up speed, and kaleidoscope cannons instead of projectile cannons for killing your foes in the air. Three tall masts seemed to be an unnecessary touch, until we realized that enormous lighting trusses were suspended from each mast, and a hundred different intelligent lighting instruments and stage lasers were rigged up and ready for action. And PA speakers were positioned periodically around the perimeter of the upper deck.

We made our way to the raised quarterdeck at the stern of the ship, where you might expect to see the ship's wheel on a galleon. But instead, Cameron had reserved this place of honor for a set of gleaming gold-plated DJ decks.

I gazed out through the rift. From here, you could see far out into the logosphere. Bright ugly flashes and surreal smears of color clashed and sparred at the point where Alexander was locked in a confrontation with the thunderstorm, holding its advance at bay.

Distance was always super difficult to gauge in the logosphere, but the fact that we could observe this activity meant it was close enough to be unsettling.

"Isobel, your presence is requested on comms," said the Dauphine.

I summoned a new set of enchanted in-ear monitors out of my inventory and put them in.

"This is Isobel. What's the word?"

"This is your captain speaking," said Jordon Connelly. "Welcome back, Isobel."

"It's really good to hear your voice, Jordon."

"Same. We should grab coffee if we still exist tomorrow. So listen, I'm your remote pilot for this mission, which has been described to me as waiting for your signal and then flying very fast in a straight line for ten seconds or whatever. Sound about right?"

"Pretty much. I was expecting an autopilot, so this is quite an upgrade."

"Any skyship I control as the Prime Minister gets a bunch of stat bonuses, so we figured, what the hell, let's buff this thing up. You've got a fully loaded gun deck below you that does run off automation, though, and I've got the sensitivity cranked. The hull is heavily armored and magic resistant. And the laser/light show you'll be seeing soon was designed by the same team that creates tour visuals for DJ Luscious, which is what you get when the Sparkle King calls in a favor apparently."

"How do people typically take down ships like this?" I asked.

"Typically by ramming them at high speed from weird angles. It's not pretty. But I don't think we're expecting other air traffic along this route. Skyship's an SD5 vehicle, so we should be the only one in operation on this version of the map, and Cameron set all the dragons to hibernate to keep them out of our way."

I didn't expect to be able to spin a proper DJ set while this all went down, so I cued up a long mix I'd prerecorded that was full of what the kids might call "bangers," and showed Maddy how to kick it off when I gave the signal.

All we had to do first was convince Alexander to stand down.

By my estimation, even though he'd been cut off from the battery and could no longer top off, as it were, he still had a sufficient amount of energy stored inside himself to keep the thunderstorm at bay for now. We wanted to intervene well before he depleted that energy pool and involuntarily fell out of god mode. We wanted a clean handoff of responsibilities here.

We did *not* want him turning that energy toward us in anger.

In the original Sparkle Dungeon, the final battle takes place on a big dance floor modeled after the David Guetta residency in Vegas. Lasers are going off in every direction, and drunk clubbers are attacking you with overpriced margaritas, and security's hunting you down for smuggling swords into the venue, and Not David Guetta For Rights Reasons is trying to obliterate you from the stage by laying down some massively mainstream beats.

And the thing is, everyone initially thinks this is purely a combat challenge that you can win with sheer artillery. But the secret is this: if you tip the bellhop a jewel or two as you *enter* the hotel on your way to will call, the bellhop *lets it slide* that he's spotted your swords and *never calls security.* Consequently it's just normal bouncers at the barrier as you rush the stage to decapitate Not David Guetta before he gets a chance to terrorize an afterparty.

This *incredibly useless* piece of trivia floated through my mind as I jetpacked out through the rift into the logosphere, to confront Alexander Reece as his adversary for what I hoped would be the last time.

❀   ❀   ❀

During my own experience in god mode, I remember maintaining a self-image in my mind's eye that roughly matched my physical form, while understanding that I was no longer corporeal. My presence was instead invisibly distributed throughout a vast arena, an ocean of energetic awareness shifting its boundaries according to where I focused my attention. The thunderstorm instantly recognized me in those moments as a player worth its respect, although I can't say I understood what method it used to perceive me.

But now I was just a lone player avatar, jetpacking rather slowly across the empty miasma of the logosphere toward the front line of the battle between Alexander and the thunderstorm. I had no interest in arriving on the scene at the speed of thought. I wanted Alexander to notice me approaching while I was still a long way off.

I spared a glance back at the Sparkle Realm. Last time I'd seen it from outside, the hull of the arkship had enclosed it completely and weapons were firing from a hundred gun ports. But per my request, Cameron had removed the hull of the arkship, and now the sight of it once again reminded me of a beautiful colored jewel anchored in space, steadily growing smaller as I soared away from it.

Eventually I had to stop my advance. I could feel the conflict ahead of me as a wave of psychic heat. Where Alexander made direct contact with the thunderstorm, a singular point of supernatural radiance lit up the logosphere. It reminded me of the blinding arc flash you get if you stare at a welding torch without protection, except the burn here affected more than just your eyes; your entire identity got scorched if you tried to perceive the conflict directly.

I realized this radiance was the spark of human lives being expended, and I burned with shame for having expended my share of it in the same fashion.

Suddenly a dark laugh rang out all around me.

"I should have guessed you'd return," Alexander said with a surprisingly calm voice.

Without warning, he granted me a summary glimpse into the carnage of his battle with the thunderstorm. It had persistently chewed away chunks of his presence in its effort to unravel him, but so far, he'd been able to replenish his presence from the battery and hold a psychic barrier in place that had halted any further advance by the thunderstorm.

"I need you to stand down," I replied.

Now I began to feel his rage curled into a spiral all around me, poised to strike.

"By destroying the battery," he said, "you've killed me, and you've killed the entire planet. And you are no fit replacement for me in this combat."

"Give me some credit, my dude," I said. "You think I didn't come here with a plan?"

"Then let us hear the product of your immense wisdom," he said, the strain in his voice palpable as he kept up his conversation with me in a separate tab in his mind from the ongoing bombast of his struggle to survive the thunderstorm's relentless attacks.

But I couldn't dare risk sharing even the broad strokes of my plan with him, in case he fell, and the knowledge of it was absorbed into our opponent.

"I'm giving you a chance to escape and let me handle this," I said.

"Isobel, you may be the Queen of Sparkle Dungeon, but until I die, I am the *GOD* of this realm, and you *shall* be punished for betraying your rightful Lord."

"Listen up, King James Version. You're a usurper, a despot, and a punk, and you don't want to try fighting me and the thunderstorm at the same time, trust me. But there's one miracle you could perform that you haven't even considered. It might take every ounce of mojo you have left, but if anyone has the will to pull it off, it's you, I know that much.

"You could make yourself *human* again. A person back on the planet, alive and breathing and without bullet holes. You could be with Olivia again. She's still down there, scheming for you just like she always did. Go to her, Alexander, while you still can. I promise I can take it from here."

I could feel the idea spreading in his consciousness, like a computer virus that slowly commandeered all of his processing power in single-minded pursuit of the idea that he could truly live again. He was deeply tired, and subconsciously afraid of the inevitable demise he'd been expecting. And here was Isobel the Queen, miraculous thorn in his side, the one person who had ever gotten the upper hand on him. He desperately wanted to believe me.

He'd fought the good fight, too. He'd kept his word about one thing—he'd used his godlike powers to fight the thunderstorm to a fucking standstill once more, buying me the time I'd needed. Sure, he'd been a duplicitous, immoral bastard about it and maybe we'd settle that score later, but in this moment, I needed him to claim the reward I was dangling in front of him.

I needed the thunderstorm's attention, and Alexander was standing in my way.

"Very well," he whispered.

I felt him prepare to pull off a new class of transmutation. Only Alexander Reece would ever experience this miracle, if I had to guess. He'd be overcoming death yet again in order to transmute himself back into a living breathing person on the material plane, using god mode to brute force his way past any objections the punctuation marks might still have about allowing him to do this. He'd be reunited with Olivia, he'd still be the most powerful linguist mage in existence, oh and of course he wouldn't be destroyed out here when the last drops of spark he'd harvested from the battery were exhausted, leaving him defenseless.

Yeah, it all penciled out pretty nicely for Alexander on paper. And I admit I was a little charmed that he trusted me enough to step aside and let me handle this situation.

Maybe he should've been a little more skeptical.

A tortured roar came from everywhere all at once—Alexander's voice. No special expertise was required on my part to recognize that something was going horribly wrong for him. For several long seconds, he roared, and I had no way of knowing exactly what was happening, aside from my guess that he wasn't enjoying it.

Maybe he'd been overconfident to let his attention slip from throwing everything he had at the thunderstorm. Maybe he'd opened himself up to an attack in the moments when he diverted the energy of god mode away from the thunderstorm, funneling it into what he expected to be his escape route back to the planet. Maybe the thunderstorm had already chewed away so many chunks of his extended godlike presence that they *knew* Alexander now, or at least knew him well enough to pierce his psychic armor the split second he became even slightly vulnerable.

The net effect was that Alexander Reece did undergo a transmutation in those moments, and he did spend his entire reserve of spark on the sequence. But somehow the thunderstorm had pierced him or wounded him just before or just as the sequence unfolded, and injected its own instructions into the sequence, and powered the new instructions with a contribution of its own foul anti-spark, if you could call it that. His transmutation was hijacked, intercepted, overthrown, and he did not return to Earth.

Instead he materialized before me in a new logospheric avatar, fashioned as though out of clay by his very nemesis. He was a towering new form of herald, defying Isobel the Queen's prohibition against heralds in the logosphere. He was, perhaps, a knight champion of the thunderstorm, or an unholy warrior now at the vanguard of the thunderstorm's relentless advance across this dimension. When his gaze finally landed on me, there was no acrimony or accusation in it; this was simply his new state of being, apparently, and he didn't seem to resent it or resist it.

This maneuver—capturing Alexander instead of destroying him— this was the thunderstorm attempting to toy with *me*, I realized.

This would be *my* fate if things kept going off the rails like this.

I blasted him with a powerful healing spell, Restore Beat Grid, typically used to counteract the debilitating poisons in SD3 that caused you to lose your sense of rhythm, which in turn caused your spells and attacks to start misfiring badly. It was a long shot, imagining that I might have an antidote to whatever the thunderstorm had done to him, but I felt certain ordinary healing spells that merely restored hit points would be useless right now, and I at least had to try something.

The spell bounced off him with no effect as far as I could tell.

Behind him, the leading front of the thunderstorm crackled and rumbled as if taunting me.

"You mentioned you had a plan, Isobel," he said, his voice smooth and calm. "I wonder, is it working?"

I didn't feel like admitting to him that step one of my plan had just now failed.

I noticed his giant arms had become barbed tentacles, and he suddenly had a dozen of them, reaching to close the distance between us. His grasp was easy to evade, and I realized he wasn't feeling any particular urgency about this situation. From his perspective, the future must've seemed inevitable. The thunderstorm was nothing if not patient as it worked its way across reality.

Without a word, I fled back to the Sparkle Realm.

❀   ❀   ❀

I landed on the upper deck of the skyship, and only then spared a glance back to see if Alexander had followed. He had instead drifted back toward the thunderstorm's leading edge.

"What happened out there?" Maddy asked.

"Alexander was trying to go back to Earth," I said. "But the thunderstorm got control of him somehow, so I split out of there."

"Does that mean we have to fight him?"

"If he has been enslaved against his will," the Dauphine said, "perhaps we should rescue him."

"I tried hitting him with a high-level heal," I said. "I thought it might snap him back to himself. But he brushed it off."

"With respect, I possess healing and restoration magic far beyond what player characters can acquire. If we do nothing, remember that Alexander knows the perils of the Shimmer Lands. He can steer the thunderstorm away from it and the plan will fail outright."

"He won't know we're headed to the Shimmer Lands, not at first," I said. "That should give you a window of opportunity to try healing him. But if that doesn't snap him out of it—"

"We need to table this discussion," Jordon said suddenly. "I count five fliers headed your way."

I peered through the rift and said, "I don't see anything."

"They're not outside. They're on the map already, moving slowly, incoming from due south."

Due south from here would take you straight to the Sparkle Dungeon—where the battery had been located until recently.

Until it had been stolen by five surviving heralds who were loyal to Alexander.

Already I looked back fondly on those halcyon hours when we had an actual plan.

Soon we all saw and recognized the heralds headed our way. I suspected they'd chosen the Sparkle Dungeon as their spawn point for returning here. They'd reverted back into their monstrous forms, hulking and wretched and vile to look at, kept aloft more by spite than by their enormous heavy wings. They radiated menace and horror even from a great distance, and each one of them could've easily been twice the size of the skyship. Their slow speed was freakier than if they'd just appeared in our midst; having time to anticipate their arrival made them scarier.

But these heralds knew me. Sure, they might be heading here to murder us on Alexander's orders. But they theoretically respected me for sparing their lives. They'd participated willingly in rescuing the people in the battery, knowing full well Alexander would lose his power as a result. Unless they'd lost their free will for some reason when Alexander lost his, I might be able to squeeze a peaceful conversation out of this situation if I was careful.

"I'm going to talk to them when they get here," I said, "so hold your fire unless they attack first."

"If you let them close the distance, the gun deck will be useless," Jordon said. "And if they surround us in close quarters, we're not going anywhere—skyships don't teleport."

"Fine, I'll meet them halfway," I said as I rose up off the deck. "If Alexander comes through the rift, head for the Shimmer Lands and I'll try to catch up."

I sailed out across the landscape toward the heralds. Our flight paths brought us together at the southern edge of the capital, where the Towers of Dub stood tall on either side of the city gate. Normally the road into the city was crowded with NPCs, but Cameron must've locked all the city's NPCs down today, because the road was empty, and no sentries emerged from the Towers to challenge us with obscure trivia questions about defunct record labels and underground nightclubs.

While four of them patrolled in wide loops above us, Ezekiel transformed into its eight-foot "murder golem" form as it landed gracefully in front of the gate to greet me.

"Hello, Isobel," it said. "I'm sorry your plan to save Earth has failed so swiftly."

"Hey, c'mon, we're still in play. What are you doing here, Ezekiel?"

"We've been summoned to commit violence against you, Isobel."

"I thought we were good. I don't want to fight you."

"I have no enthusiasm for it either. I saw how many of our comrades fell to your sword and spellcraft, even before you acquired the full power of the battery. I thought you and Alexander were at least tenuous allies, but—he speaks with the voice of the unraveling now. Has he turned against you outright?"

"The thunderstorm took control of him. It happened so fast I had no chance to stop it. But the Dauphine might be able to restore him with healing magic."

"Isobel, I know the methods of the unraveling. Precious little remains of him to restore, I'm sure."

"Maybe. Or maybe he's submerged or trapped, and he's helpless, and maybe we can free him."

"I see. You want to rescue the original Alexander so that you needn't face this new Alexander in direct combat. You still imagine your original plan might succeed if he's no longer in your way."

I nodded.

Ezekiel laughed softly and said, "I do admire how you wrest hope into existence, Isobel."

One of the heralds above us emitted a sharp roar to get Ezekiel's attention. I couldn't tell if it was impatient or bored or anxious or what.

But Ezekiel understood the intent of that roar.

"Go, Isobel, return to your friends and make ready for our attack."

"Attack? What are you talking about?"

"We are loyal to whatever remains of Alexander. We must answer his summons."

"I thought you said you didn't want to fight! Is he mind controlling you somehow? When he gave you sentience, did he put DRM on it to make sure you stayed loyal to him?"

"My free will is intact, and my loyalty is freely given. In the end, I'd prefer to fight as a herald of the unraveling than perish as a victim in its path."

"You won't have to fight *at all* if you just let me handle this!"

"Ah yes, the way you 'handled' convincing Alexander to stand down and go back to Earth? Be serious, Isobel. What chance do you truly think your plan has to succeed against the unraveling?"

"That depends. Did you tell Alexander my plan? Does he know?"

"We've not seen him since the battle, and his summons was a one-way transmission, not a conversation. So your plan is still 'in play' as you said, if you survive to execute it."

"Oh, 'if' I survive? Let me tell you something, my track record for survival is *impeccable*."

Our argument had captured the attention of the aerial heralds, who were now looping much closer to our position, preparing to strike.

"Isobel, out of respect, I'll allow you to rejoin your compatriots before we arrive at the rift, but please go now, before my companions overrule me and engage you right here."

"You should've stayed on the beach."

"You might be right. No matter the outcome on the battlefield, it's been a privilege to know you."

I wanted to scream with frustration.

Instead I said, "Fine, die a pointless death if that's your wish."

And then, I attacked.

❀ ❀ ❀

Ezekiel's affectation of human courtesy and respect was exploitable. Before he could shape-shift into a properly menacing form, I drove Blades Per Minute straight through his skull, splitting his body down the middle in a battle-tested maneuver that killed him so convincingly he had no opportunity to regenerate. He was dead on the spot.

The four monstrous heralds hovering above me shrieked in unison. But before any of them managed to react any further, I cranked Blades Per Minute up to its fastest tempo and then promptly teleported directly *inside* the nearest herald in the sky. I thrashed about wildly for a few seconds and then jetpacked my way out by shooting up its giant neck and chopping its head off as though I was an out-of-control blender blade on top speed, free of any safety considerations and just hacking through all the fleshy bits I could reach along the way. As I emerged, its dead carcass dissipated into nothingness as it fell toward the road, and the slime on my body evaporated as well.

422 ·   SCOTTO MOORE

Two down, three to go.

Blenderizing the heralds from the inside seemed like a tactic I could really get behind, so I tried teleporting into another one. This turned out to be a terrible idea, as I'd neglected their supernatural ability to rapidly upgrade their defenses once they saw an attack in action. So I was able to initiate my teleport normally, but I was rejected before I could reappear inside its skin. It was like some invisible tennis racket stood on guard to smack me back into my body and away from the herald, sending me crashing straight through one of the towers at the gate. I landed hard in the market plaza beyond, stunned and disoriented.

A herald suddenly loomed large in the sky directly above me, growing rapidly in size with every passing moment, grotesque appendages and wings unfolding as though summoned from another dimension. It peered down at me with vicious glee, its multiple mutating jaws cackling at me, and I immediately lost whatever remained of my courage. I tried teleporting back to the skyship, but this time the teleport fizzled completely and I just sat there. The herald must've learned how to extend its ability to jam my teleports, projecting the effect outward from itself to encompass my location. Either that, or I was so dazed and stupefied that I wasn't able to nail the sequence properly.

I tried to fly the fuck out of there, but it lashed out with its long tail and smacked me down out of the sky. I landed hard and nearly blacked out. Glittersteel skin was great for preventing bullets and swords from piercing your skin or reflecting kaleidoscope rays back at the shooter, but when your entire body was hammered hard into cobblestone from fifty feet up, you definitely felt it. I lay motionless and knew I'd be hard pressed to defend myself while lying face-down on a cobblestone road, but no follow-up blow arrived. This thing was toying with me, letting me sit up and get a good look at how fucked I actually was first, as if I needed more convincing to be terrified.

By this point, the other two heralds were hovering behind my immediate attacker, serrated tentacles swirling in the air all around their bodies.

I pulled myself to my feet and ran.

❀　❀　❀

In the game, your walking and running speeds were constrained, but here in the actual logosphere, those constraints were essentially optional. Within a second or two, I had crossed the map and arrived at the rift. I leapt onto the deck of the skyship, landing next to Maddy and the Dauphine behind the DJ decks.

The heralds lazily sailed toward us, speed of no concern to them. Their arrival would be no surprise to us, after all, and they undoubtedly felt they had little to fear from us. They'd seen all the big spells in my arsenal during the last battle, so they might've already devised defenses against them. And none of those spells could take out all three of these heralds at once anyway.

"Are they coming here to kill us?" asked Maddy as I arrived.

"Three out of five are, yeah," I replied. "Jordon, you said this ship has guns—anything the heralds haven't seen before?"

"I've got one weapon here that I don't recognize," Jordon replied. "Something called a 'singularity cannon.' Want me to see what it does?"

"Please fire it until you are all out of singularities."

"Belay that order," said the voice of Cameron Kelly, jumping onto our channel for the first time. "The singularity cannon isn't finished yet. If you fire it in its current state, uh, bad things will happen. Sorry, should've taken that panel offline before sending you the skyship."

"Should we activate the lights and sound and make a run for it?" Maddy asked.

"They'd catch you before the thunderstorm even started moving in your direction," he replied.

"Open to suggestions," I said, frustration starting to catch up to me.

"I can give you a distraction—something the heralds haven't seen that might slow them down for a few beats."

"I'll take it," I said.

"Everybody stay cool," Cameron advised. "I'm opening a bridge to SD5. Things might get a little weird."

A wormhole materialized in the sky between us and the heralds, growing in size until it scraped the ground below it, allowing us a clear view of a broad tunnel that originated in a grayscale factory. This was likely the same vinyl pressing plant where the resistance secretly met throughout SD5.

And charging down the length of the tunnel, both at ground level and in the air, was an eclectic assembly of NPCs which Cameron must've summoned from SD5 as reinforcements. However, these NPCs defied the dystopian palette of SD5, and were instead resplendent in full sparkling color.

I gasped out loud when I suddenly realized what I was seeing. "What's going on?" Maddy asked.

"The return of the Diamond Brigade to the Sparkle Realm," said the Dauphine with unusual reverence.

❀ ❀ ❀

When you created your first character in the original Sparkle Dungeon, you were designated an Elite Adventurer of the Diamond Brigade right out of the gate. But the games also established a set of legendary NPCs as the inner circle of the Diamond Brigade, the core protectors of the Sparkle King. You interacted with them sparingly in the beginning, but as the games progressed, they became key allies. You established your credibility with them on your first quest, rescuing the Mighty Mirrored Paladin from the clutches of evil alien invaders from Planet Grime.

Now here was the Mighty Mirrored Paladin leading the charge out of the wormhole, astride his valiant steed Mirrorflex (the dance captain of all horses). Both wore full suits of enchanted mirrored plate armor, which acted as a weird form of camouflage—they were difficult to target because they reflected their surroundings so well. You wouldn't expect mirrors to function as particularly great armor, of course, but this was *enchanted* mirrored plate, meaning the only way to shatter it was to somehow hurt its feelings.

Riding closely nearby in a chariot pulled by two war ponies was Thumpin Dazzlepants, one of the Halogen Dwarves who served as the sturdy, reliable audio engineers of the realm. Thumpin's chariot was armed with side-mounted Subwoofers of Liquefaction. Above the two of them was my favorite, Graziella von Groove, riding the majestic Disco Pegasus into battle, preparing to lob explosive lava lamps at her hapless foes below. Soaring along beside them all were Vintage and Chillmeister, feral baby rainbows who'd grown to be wise and mature adult rainbows with solid taste in downtempo.

And bringing up the rear was Sandpaper Slim, the big bad of the original Sparkle Dungeon, who'd evolved throughout the series into an unlikely antihero and merciless defender of the Realm. To prove his mettle and insouciance, he arrived riding the infamous Dubstep Dragon, a creature that lulled you with sparse, syncopated rhythm patterns and then absolutely demolished you right in the face with sudden towering bass drops.

Cameron said, "They're only going to survive for about thirty seconds, Isobel." In other words, his NPCs weren't powerful or creative enough to defeat heralds who'd already witnessed the most potent attacks the Realm had to offer.

But the Diamond Brigade wasn't expected to win. They were just a distraction, and thirty seconds was still a good and proper head start.

"Jordon, fire it up!" I shouted.

❀　　❀　　❀

First, several fog machines went off, preparing the scene for maximum impact.

Then all of the lighting instruments that were meticulously arranged on the trusses above us powered up at once, spraying bright interlocking rays of color through the fog. Lasers and kaleidoscopes began firing in complex and intricate patterns. The sky itself seemed to dim in order to better appreciate the intensity of the display, with its impossible brightness and lascivious saturation of colors.

Something was missing, though.

"Maddy, that's your cue," I said.

She quickly pressed the play button on the nearest DJ deck. Now my prerecorded playlist blasted out of all the loudspeakers on the skyship, filling the air with warm and inviting house beats. I had no doubt you could hear this soundtrack clear across the logosphere.

Much better.

Just to add spice to the situation, I lit myself up as well with a combination of radiant spells, nothing too high level, but enough of a reminder that yes, the Queen of Sparkle Dungeon was openly standing behind these DJ decks, taunting the thunderstorm from a distance, daring it to come after me. I was its only worthy opponent that remained in the logosphere, daring to stand between it and the material plane.

The skyship smoothly accelerated away from the rift.

I glanced out across the terrain and saw that our lighting display had at least temporarily blinded or distracted the heralds, who were facing it directly. The Diamond Brigade leapt at this advantage and scored what seemed like significant early blows, but I couldn't really say for sure since the heralds regenerated so easily.

As I turned my attention back toward the rift, I barely had time to catch sight of a long streak of animosity blazing its way toward us.

Then it hit us, and the skyship promptly exploded in a towering multicolored fireball, which tore it completely apart.

❦   ❦   ❦

Oh sure, the explosion was undoubtedly for dramatic effect. It's not like the skyship was stuffed full of rocket fuel and dynamite sticks. I understood—sometimes you wanted to make a dramatic entrance.

Alexander had arrived.

No longer willing to let his minions tend to the situation, he'd come to thwart our plan himself.

He towered over the landscape like an enraged giant, or at least, that's how it seemed from my position lying flat on my back half a mile away or whatever, deeply embedded in the soft turf of some procedurally generated part of the map that had never required de-tailing before. He seemed to be sifting through wreckage, examining the larger chunks of skyship that remained after the explosion, tearing them apart in search of survivors, probably. Fair enough—if I were Alexander right now, I'd definitely want to confirm my kills, too.

I'd survived the blast with only minor injuries. My glittersteel skin had resisted the heat of the fireball and the turf had actually cushioned my landing. I scanned my surroundings for signs of Maddy or the Dauphine, but was distracted by the sight of the Diamond Brigade rallying to our defense, charging across the terrain to engage Alexander. Only two heralds in pursuit, I noticed—nicely done on their part, managing to kill one somehow.

Alexander seemed genuinely startled to find NPCs throwing themselves at him. His confusion wouldn't last.

Hoping our comms were still up and running, I said, "Maddy, can you hear me?" When she didn't respond, I floated to my feet to try to get a better view of the situation.

Ah, there you are, Isobel, said Alexander's voice in my mind. Oh that's right—Olivia had given the dude telepathy, back when we were all chummy. From half a mile away, he'd spotted me. *Sorry to intrude upon your theatrical last stand, but before you face the thunderstorm, I'm afraid you first must face me.*

As if on cue, the Dauphine emerged from the rubble of a nearby shop where she'd crash-landed after the explosion, nodding at me once before rocketing into the air toward Alexander. This part of the plan didn't depend on me, so it had a better chance of succeeding than usual.

As Alexander easily fended off an attack from the Dubstep Dragon in the air and the Mighty Mirrored Paladin on the ground, the heralds closed the distance and attacked the Diamond Brigade from the rear. I couldn't really say they put up a good fight; they fell quickly, in fact, with only Graziella von Groove and the Disco Pegasus narrowly making an aerial escape back toward the wormhole.

But in the midst of that flurry of combat, the Dauphine opened a portal to a position directly behind Alexander and then sailed through that portal to land on Alexander's giant back. Instantly she summoned all the healing she could gather and channeled it into Alexander, hoping to free his mind from the grip of the thunderstorm.

From my vantage point, I could see the healing energy flowing through him, as though he was a cartoon character whose skeleton was suddenly illuminated by a jolt of electricity. He roared with indignant displeasure and tried to swipe her from his back, but she easily dodged his swipes and kept her connection with him.

Then his demeanor changed drastically and he fell to his knees, dazed and no longer actively resisting the Dauphine's efforts. I realized that my immersive experience with god mode had left me with heightened senses capable of observing the transactional exchange between them.

He wasn't reacting to the Dauphine's healing, not in the slightest.

He was, however, taking advantage of the open channel between himself and the Dauphine to wrestle his way back to independence.

And he was doing that by reclaiming the spark that he had given her when they first met in the Shimmer Lands. A pure infusion of his own original spark was a perfect antidote to the oppressive fog that had overtaken his mind.

He drained her completely dry of spark, in fact, and then with no ceremony, he shook off her lifeless body, sending it sailing through the air in a long, terrible arc, out through the rift and into the hopeless void of the logosphere beyond.

❀   ❀   ❀

For a brief, feral moment, he howled gleefully, before locking eyes on me.

The Dauphine's desperate gamble had actually worked. I could see it from here: Alexander had used her spark to free himself from his brief servitude in thrall to the thunderstorm. Now he was just plain old everyday evil Alexander Reece instead of the herald king Alexander Reece or whatever. His mind was his own to use as he saw fit, which was clearly apparent from the triumphant look on his face.

I could tell he was measuring his chances, wondering what tricks I might still have up my sleeve even after all the destruction he'd wrought. But he was no longer compelled by the thunderstorm to try to kill me. Sure, he was certainly not compelled by anything in sight to try to help me, either. He'd lost his shot at returning to Earth as a human being, but Earth wasn't scheduled to last much longer at this point anyway.

I couldn't be sure, but I thought he nodded at me ever so briefly, offering just the merest, slightest acknowledgment of respect for me that he could muster.

Then without a word, he and his heralds fled from the site of their carnage, hurling themselves toward the wormhole to SD5, perhaps hoping to get as far from the domain of the Queen of Sparkle Dungeon as they could manage. The part of him that cared about protecting Earth had apparently not been restored along with the rest of his identity. Cameron must've been watching somehow, because the wormhole began to collapse, but Alexander and his heralds easily slipped through before it disappeared.

It had taken so little time for everything to fall apart.

The silence in the Realm was almost maddening. I realized I was wearing an artifact, the Remix Ring, that would allow me to put on whatever soundtrack I wanted, anywhere in the Realm. But the challenge of picking appropriate music for this desolate circumstance was far beyond my skill level as a DJ.

"Isobel, are you there?" Jordon asked. I wasn't sure how to answer that. Then she said, "Isobel, are you still on comms? Please acknowledge."

"Yeah, I'm here."

"Hang on, I'm patching a call through for you."

Huh?

Then Maddy said, "Isobel, are you safe? What's happening there?"

"Oh my god, where are you?" I said, almost bursting into tears at the sound of her voice.

"Uh, you're going to love this, actually. The Interrobang saw like a missile or something coming our way and decided to nope out of there, so it yanked me back to Earth, to the gym."

"Saving your life again."

"Well, sure, but look, it won't let me come back there. The sequence just fizzles. Where's the Dauphine? She could open a portal to bring me back, right?"

"The Dauphine's gone, Maddy. Alexander killed her."

"What? How is that possible?"

I didn't answer her question, because my full attention was suddenly drawn toward new activity at the rift. Apparently our immensely gaudy display of light and magic had achieved its desired effect in the end.

With our defenses swept aside and our hopes smashed, the thunderstorm was now at long last entering the Sparkle Realm.

❀   ❀   ❀

Its arrival was almost graceful, as though we'd simply left the back door open and it was merely obliging itself to drop by for dinner. It made itself known by patiently squeezing through the rift like a pyroclastic flow being forced through a drinking straw, seamlessly transmuting into a tangible presence in the Realm, expanding into an oozing blob of viscous gel that pooled beneath the rift.

"It's here," I said.

"Come back to the gym," Maddy said. "We'll figure out a new plan."

But I had a gut feeling the current plan hadn't quite outlived its usefulness. The Dauphine had sacrificed herself, clearing the way for us to draw the thunderstorm into our trap. I didn't need a skyship to lure it to the Shimmer Lands from here.

It only took a couple moments of silence on my part for Maddy to intuit what was going through my mind.

"Isobel, *no*, you have to come *home*," she said.

"I can still do this, Maddy. Pretty sure that's the entire reason I'm still standing here."

"What, like it's your destiny? Fuck that Jedi bullshit and get back here."

"I love you, Maddy. I might drop off comms for a bit."

I lifted off into the air and dared to soar out into plain view of the leading edge of the ooze, which was still in an accumulation phase, not quite the tsunami it clearly intended to be soon enough. Almost instantly the ooze seemed to transform from a broad wave to a narrower mass, a giant rope of tentacles extending itself toward me, grasping at me like it recognized me and was eager to take care of unfinished business. I gently drifted away from it in a complicated zigzag pattern and watched the entire mass swerve back and forth to perfectly follow every zig and zag.

It might be the most destructive entity in the multiverse, but you could still get it to chase the laser pointer apparently.

I launched myself away from it across the map, daring it to chase me.

My trajectory would eventually take me straight over Platinum City, the capital of the Realm. The Sparkle King's castle would fall to the thunderstorm's advance. The Iridescent Warehouse would be obliterated as well. Then after following the road south beyond the capital toward the Sparkle Dungeon, I would suddenly veer off toward the Halogen Mountains, away from what was left of civilization.

I spared a glance back and saw the thunderstorm now fully immersed in the reality of the Sparkle Realm. It registered as a glorious amalgamation of elements absorbed as it careened across the environment in pursuit of me. Rainbows and lasers glittered all across its surface; it had become explosively pretty. Powerfully good music thundered out across the Realm from deep within it, a superb synthesis of sounds, the ultimate and infinitely extended remix, with crisp and perfect mixing and the warmth of beloved classics on vinyl. Each successive drop of the beat was more compelling than the last, unfolding as an improbably potent siren song that always promised more, that melted your heart and encouraged wild abandon on the dance floor. This was the true spirit of the game reflected back at me, the true spirit of all the music I'd ever loved in fact, threatening to envelop me with a powerful rush of distracting emotion if I didn't keep my head in the game.

I could see what it was doing more clearly now than I ever had before, back when I simply thought to fight it to a standstill or exterminate it before it could exterminate us. The thunderstorm was a weirdly sincere celebration of all the uniqueness represented in every disparate corner of the multiverse. It took time to savor and appreciate everything it encountered, before unraveling its essence. In theory, this very essence would then be thematically available as a building block for something new. Maybe this was more than just an unraveling; maybe it was an accumulation of inspiration, or a refining into quintessence, to be used in service of what came next. Maybe some energetic aspect of the Sparkle Realm would ultimately be redeployed in the creation of the next multiverse.

The problem was that real live people were still getting mileage out of the current multiverse.

If some energetic aspect of *me* got used as a building block in the next multiverse, whatever they built would find itself to be Extremely Pissed Off.

❀ ❀ ❀

The Sparkle Realm's principal light source wasn't a sun in the sky. Instead, the peaks of the Halogen Mountains were covered in frosted glass, and they emanated a steady illumination which blanketed the realm in something akin to bright moonlight. It was bright enough that you could see without headlamps or glow sticks or whatever, but if you decided to wear glowing fiber-optic chain mail out in the forest, you would absolutely get people's attention. And importantly, you never had to face the encroaching menace of sunrise unless you were deploying powerful spells to inflict it upon your enemies.

Flying high above the map, you could easily spot the mirage that drew unwary travelers into the Shimmer Lands. In the foothills of the mountains, on the far side of a desert, a distant glow on the horizon beckoned, an illusion of bright lasers, flashing spotlights, and seductive color-cycling LED washes that seemed to signify a hot little resort town awaited with its own secret treasures and private parties. The driving paradox of the Shimmer Lands, of course, was that entering was straightforward enough. Leaving, on the other hand, was a different story.

I flew over Flugelhorn Forest, a dangerous region inimical to EDM, where Sandpaper Slim had survived by his wits after his defeated alien army abandoned him in the Realm. The forest ended abruptly at the edge of the desert. Contrary to popular belief, the border to the Shimmer Lands was not itself a point of no return. You could enter the Shimmer Lands and make your way out again if you were meticulous about keeping sight of landmarks behind you by which to navigate. Knowing this, I consciously avoided looking back as I crossed the border. I figured the thunderstorm wouldn't get properly lost if I myself wasn't properly lost. It was an educated guess; after all these years, I had a good feel for the quirky logic of the game's magic.

The music that the thunderstorm generated turned out to be a great soundtrack for this situation, I had to admit—energetic, vibrant, melodic, inventive. As long as it kept pumping out this great music, I could assume it was still enmeshed in the essence of the Sparkle Realm and thus still bound by its magic system. My plan always assumed the thunderstorm would eventually wise up to being lost in the Shimmer Lands and would "reverse transmute" back into its primal form as a reality-devouring maw, but I'd been willing to gamble this would happen on more of an astronomical time scale. Hopefully that would buy the population of Earth sufficient time to figure out a proper escape plan to somewhere safer, or a better means of defending Earth outright.

But as much as I loved the music and desperately wished I was ripping it straight to a hard drive for safekeeping, I didn't plan to stick around in the Shimmer Lands for all of astronomical time. The thunderstorm could trudge endlessly toward the mirage like every other sucker out here instead of chasing me specifically.

I recited the transmutation sequence that would deliver me back into my physical body on the material plane, and disappeared from the Shimmer Lands.

❀   ❀   ❀

I promptly reappeared in the Shimmer Lands.

Cool. The punctuation marks were apparently lost, too.

A horrific, desperate feeling swept over me.

Somehow, an irrational part of me had maintained the crucial belief that I'd survive all this and get a normal life back. Not just normal, but a better life, because I'd be with Maddy when it was all over.

But apparently that was not to be. The Earth would keep on spinning, instead of being unraveled to make way for something that would probably be an improvement if we were being honest here. And thankfully, Maddy herself was as safe as she could be, back on Earth with her protector, the Interrobang, keeping an eye on her during those rare times where her own human reflexes weren't fast enough to save her.

I just wouldn't be there with her myself.

Instead I would be here, forever fleeing across the desert, hoping to stay ahead of the thunderstorm as we both trudged endlessly toward the mirage in the distance.

"Maddy," I said, hopping back onto the comms channel to say goodbye. "Are you still there?"

And for the first time since we started using the enchanted in-ear monitors for communications, all I got back was a burst of garbled static, unrecognizable as Maddy or anyone in particular.

"Could you repeat that?" I asked, but the static recurred, and this time it was persistent, a maddening white noise with jarring spikes of magical feedback or something baked into it. It quickly became so vicious and oppressive that I had to take the monitor out.

I'd been studiously avoiding glancing behind me to get a visual sighting of the thunderstorm in pursuit. I could always hear it back there, after all, spitting out a perfect soundtrack for an infinitely long chase scene or whatever. But the timbre of the music was evolving into something darker. Superficially we might still be listening to excellent house music, but I could feel the melody turning a dark corner.

My peripheral vision began to pick up disturbing signs that the thunderstorm was no longer simply behind me. It was overtaking me in a sense, tendrils on either side of me flowing past me, perhaps in an effort to get to the resort town before me. Was it already starting to realize how trapped it was? Was it getting angry? Was it actually caught in a trap if it could just change tactics and chew through the fabric of the logosphere instead to get out of this place? It flowed past and around me, keeping me alive inside a pocket of its absence, perhaps so that I could watch and understand what it was doing.

The resort town began to glow brighter than it ever had before. Or rather—the surroundings were actually getting darker. The light coming from the Halogen Mountains was steadily dwindling, as though someone had gotten hold of a dimmer that controlled them and was gently bringing their levels down to zero. I knew spells that could throw a dance floor into darkness if you wanted to introduce a little chaos, but throwing the entire Sparkle Realm into darkness was more than any player could accomplish with wizard spells.

But the thunderstorm was now fully enmeshed in the Realm—and infused with its magic. The thunderstorm was much more powerful than the magic of the Realm, actually, more profound in its way than anything Cameron could've invented or anything the hundred million minds of Sparkle Dungeon's players could manifest in the logosphere. Taking the time to do this was mere theatrics, I realized.

Turning the lights out on the Realm as a final chilling gesture would fit the profile of wanting to properly terrify the denizens of the Realm before consuming it entirely. Maybe it didn't realize that the denizens of the Realm were NPCs who wouldn't care. Or maybe it understood perfectly well that the Realm only had one true conscious denizen now—me, and I had reached the point of being well and truly scared.

I wasn't physically exhausted from my sad flight across the desert, but spiritually I felt stretched thin and ready to snap.

Then the lights of the resort town began to go dark, one by one by one.

I hadn't realized how psychologically dependent I'd become on seeing the mirage ahead of me until I realized I was about to lose sight of it forever.

❀   ❀   ❀

I had one remaining option, though. The nuclear option.

I could draw spark from *the name that speaks itself,* which hovered gently in the back of my mind at all times, and I could use that spark to enter god mode.

There were pros and cons to consider.

Last time I was in god mode, the only thing that reigned me in was the realization that I was killing people in the battery. With no such realization to stop me here, would I *ever* want to leave god mode?

Would the multiverse be a better place if Isobel the Queen became Isobel the All-Powerful and Frequently Benevolent Supreme Deity?

If I exceeded my original mortal station by such a degree, would I draw the unwanted attention of the true masters who fashioned the multiverse in the first place, and receive the ultimate smackdown? The kind of person who *wants* to be an All-Powerful and Frequently Benevolent Supreme Deity is generally *not* the right person for the role, etcetera and whatever.

The name that speaks itself was obviously a powerful source of spark, but it was alien in ways I couldn't understand, even with its representation installed in my wetware. I couldn't actually predict up front how it would affect me. What if I became something *worse* than the thunderstorm? What if I became Isobel the Malevolent Horror Who Reigned Beyond the Cosmos and wound up destroying everything anyway?

These were all valid concerns.

But since when did the Queen of Sparkle Dungeon turn down a chance to level up?

Throughout my deliberations, the name hovered in the back of my mind, radiating ineffability. It could speak itself, as it were, but it didn't have anything else to say. It wasn't sentient, after all, merely radiant with power.

That's when it finally—*finally!*—dawned on me.

The name was a primordial, archetypal *power morpheme*.

And I didn't need to risk entering god mode to use power morphemes.

I just needed the right sequence of power morphemes, one that included *the name that speaks itself* as a source of power and authority—the only authority in the multiverse the thunderstorm was likely to respect.

I didn't have time to recite all hundred and eight power morphemes in the original library in order to consult with the punctuation marks directly. I'd have to hope they were paying attention because I was going to need their help. Hopefully they'd made progress studying the new power morphemes we'd acquired, 109 and beyond, because I didn't think the original hundred and eight had all the mojo I was going to need.

Normally Cameron was the only person who could introduce new spells to the Sparkle Realm. But fuck it, I was twenty-third level, the Queen of Sparkle Dungeon since its literal inception, the first linguist mage in history to master power morpheme number 109, messenger and guardian of *the name that speaks itself*.

And improvisation was my goddamn superpower.

I clearly visualized a new spell and its desired parameters and effects, and its translation into a power morpheme sequence unfolded in my mind as if on cue, straight from the R&D laboratory of the punctuation marks. I expected this sequence to be complex and demanding, but with the name anchoring it, simplicity was actually the tactic that the punctuation marks had chosen when they devised it. The most challenging part of the sequence would be pronouncing the name, and I'd survived that experience once before.

Besides, I had the weird feeling the name enjoyed it when someone spoke it other than itself.

I recited the sequence.

❀   ❀   ❀

The spell I'd invented was called Takedown Notice.

It was a single shot, twenty-third-level spell that removed its target from existence due to unspecified copyright violation. The pol-
icy was one strike, no appeal.

Powered by the authority of the name, its effects transcended the
boundary of the Sparkle Realm, unraveling the entirety of the unraveling itself. The thunderstorm disappeared in an instant, leaving only void to replace its malignant anti-presence throughout the
multiverse.

The name that speaks itself was drained entirely of the spark within
it, and then it was gone, leaving no memory of its contours, no means
to draw upon it ever again, an angry scar in my mind where it had
once resided.

And as for me, I was finally able to stop fleeing toward the mirage of a hopping little resort town that I would never reach. The
chase was over, my pursuer vanquished.

I was alone in the Shimmer Lands, which was suddenly silent,
and here's where I'd spend the rest of my days.

❀   ❀   ❀

Suddenly a portal clawed itself into existence in front of me.

The Dauphine of the Shimmer Lands stepped through the portal into the desert. She was wearing her steampunk ensemble from
SD5, just as she was the first time I met her.

"Weary traveler," she said with a grin, "I have come to set you
free."

"Is it really you?" I whispered.

"Indeed," she replied. "I spawned a backup and hot-swapped myself into it when I realized what Alexander was trying to do."

I threw my arms around her, hugging her tightly.

"Thank you for coming to get me," I said.

"Always, my Queen," she replied. "I would have come for you
sooner, but my spawn point is in Sparkle Dungeon 5, where Alexander Reece had gone to hide with his surviving heralds. But he did
not yet understand his surroundings, and it seemed vital to put an

end to his villainy before he took control of that Realm or escaped into a new dimension altogether."

That was a story I looked forward to hearing, but it could definitely wait.

Then she took my hand and led me through the portal, into the gymnasium in Los Angeles.

Now it was Maddy's turn to sweep me up in an embrace, holding me for a long moment as we both absorbed the fact that I was safe.

Eventually I realized we weren't sitting there in silence.

There was music playing.

"Is that what I think it is?" I asked her.

"It's deep house," she said. "The shit you like, right?"

"Maddy," I said, genuinely moved, "you must really love me."

"Yes, Isobel, you might be right."

ACKNOWLEDGMENTS

This book has its roots in a pair of plays I wrote and directed during my tenure as a fringe playwright in Seattle. In 2011, my sci-fi play *Duel of the Linguist Mages* ran for four weekends, introducing Olivia Regan, Bradford Jenning, Maddy Price, power morphemes, and the alien punctuation marks. In 2014, my rom-com play *Balconies* ran for four weekends, introducing Cameron Kelly, Violet Parker, Lonso Drake, Jordon Connelly, the Dauphine of the Shimmer Lands, and the game of Sparkle Dungeon. *Battle of the Linguist Mages* is not a proper adaptation of either play, but rather an extensive mashup/remix that blends and expands their stories. (Isobel Bailie and Alexander Reece were invented specifically for this book.)

Duel of the Linguist Mages required us to solve such theatrical problems as "What do power morpheme sequences actually sound like?" and "How do we dramatically portray the punctuation marks?" (To that latter question, if you guessed "through the magic of song and dance," congrats.) *Balconies* placed two condo balconies side-by-side on stage. In one condo, revelers gathered for the Sparkle Dungeon 5 release party, with all the costumed chaos that implies; in the other, Violet's fundraiser took place on the same evening. When the two events spilled onto their respective neighboring balconies and crashed into each other, hijinks ensued! Including romance! And comedy!

I love both of these plays dearly, and this book inherits a great deal of spark from the inventive spirit of those productions. Thank you to all the artists who invested an enormous amount of talent and passion to bring those plays to life. And thank you to the elite adventurers of Annex Theatre, the resourceful collective that chose to produce both of these formative plays. Annex was my artistic home for many years, and I remain grateful for the company's support of my work.

I was nominated for a regional playwriting award for *Duel of the Linguist Mages*, which I did not win, but had I won my speech would've included a thank you to my friends at the 14/48 Festival. In 2011, I was still early in my tenure writing for the festival, but I remember crediting my ability to write a play like *Duel* back to lessons learned in the crucible of 14/48. Thank you for all the invitations to write for 14/48 over the years, and thanks to everyone who helped bring a literal fleet of my short plays to life for the festival during that time.

Lesley Carmichael first collaborated with me during the development of *Duel of the Linguist Mages*. I was inspired to write *Duel* after talking to Lesley about her career as a linguist and being struck by how much like science fiction it all sounded to me. She steered my research prior to writing the play, and we also gleefully brainstormed a wide array of potentially diabolical applications of power morphemes as I was shaping the earliest version of the story. She worked with me again as I prepared to write this book, catching me up on technological developments in her field and once again steering my research in fruitful directions.

Battle of the Linguist Mages was originally written in the second half of 2018 and early 2019. I'm indebted to many friends who took an interest in helping me improve the book.

Kira Franz provided sharp, meticulous, instructive critique across multiple drafts, digging in deep at every opportunity to help me salvage a proper story from the sprawling, semi-incoherent morass I'd originally committed to text. Crucially, Kira also helped me troubleshoot my early, deeply flawed characterization of Isobel, clearing the way for Isobel to become the Queen we meet in the final version of the book.

Tae Phoenix offered feedback on multiple drafts and frequently was my sounding board during the writing process; we had many engaging, free-wheeling conversations about the politics of the characters in relation to my own evolving politics that influenced little details and larger threads alike. In addition, Tae resonated early on with the Dauphine as an emergent factor in Isobel's story, and her perspective helped me refine and enhance the Dauphine's eventual arc.

Thanks to my valiant brigade of beta readers for providing critique and encouragement: Mason Bryant, Lesley Carmichael, Neil Cebara, Mike Gilson, Lars Liden, Susie Lindenbaum, Jen Moon, Carina Morningstar, Ramez Naam, Peggy Nelson, Joe Pemberton, Heath Rezabek, Llew Roberts, Jenny Rooke, Stefan Schaefer, Beverly Sobelman, Cheryl Trooskin-Zoller, Nat Ward, and David Whitney Jr. These folks gave me detailed feedback, met me for in-depth discussions, or sometimes simply hit me with a motivating blast of enthusiasm about the book. Additionally, many thanks to my sensitivity reader, Cit Callahan, whose advice and critique were indispensable while wrestling the book into shape for submission.

I'm indebted to Lee Harris, my editor at Tordotcom, for enthusiastically supporting the book and for proposing key upgrades to its final form. Lee's guidance and encouragement led me to rethink and improve the last act of the book more than once, for instance; he also gently steered me to strengthen key relationships that anchor the story. The last set of major revisions, working with Lee's notes close at hand, was huge and fun and satisfying to deliver. Also thanks to my copy editor, NaNá V. Stoelzle; my cover designer, Jim Tierney; and everyone on the Tordotcom team who provided support in the promotion of this book.

Finally, the trajectory of my career as an artist hinges on the unwavering support of my partner and frequent collaborator, Jen Moon. She's enabled me to carve out a life with steadily increasing dedication to writing, despite knowing full well all the perils such a life generally entails, and I'm not sure simple concepts like gratitude or relief are adequate to convey how I feel as a result. I love you, Jen—thank you for fostering so much creativity and compassion in our lives.

ABOUT THE AUTHOR

Ian Johnston

SCOTTO MOORE is a Seattle playwright whose works include the black comedy *H. P. Lovecraft: Stand-up Comedian!*; the sci-fi adventures *Duel of the Linguist Mages*, which inspired this novel, and *interlace [falling star]*; the gamer-centric romantic comedy *Balconies*; and the a cappella sci-fi musical *Silhouette*. He is the creator of *The Coffee Table*, a comedic web series about a couple that discovers their new coffee table is an ancient alien artifact that sends their house shooting through the void. Moore is also behind the popular Lovecraft-themed meme generator Things That Cannot Save You ("a catalog of your doom"), which spawned his novella, *Your Favorite Band Cannot Save You*.

scotto.org
Twitter: @scottomoore
Instagram: scottomoore